The Lost Magic

THE NETWORK SERIES
BOOK FIVE

KATIE CROSS

KCW

Contents

To my sisterwife.
It will never be as easy without you.

List Of Gods And Goddesses

THE GODS

Ventis, god of wind

Ignis, god of fire

Tontes, god of thunder

Gelas, god of ice

THE GODDESSES

Deasylva, goddess of the forest

Prana, goddess of the sea

Sarena, goddess of the desert

Selsay, goddess of the mountains

Chapter One

The crunch of splintering wood broke the air like a strike to my eardrums. A pained cry followed a second later. I winced, unable to help myself, as a nearby Guardian recruit dropped to one knee.

Ouch.

My grandfather, Marten, sighed happily next to me.

"There's nothing like blood and swords in the morning," he murmured. "I love working with the new recruits."

My lips twitched with a hidden smile. "There shouldn't be blood," I drawled. "At least, not after our second class. Those are wooden swords."

"Ah, but then it's no fun."

He clapped a hand on my shoulder and turned his gaze to peer at the top of the Wall. A group of broad-shouldered witches stood there, silhouetted by the rising sun. Cool air filled the lower bailey below them, where the new recruits trained at my command.

"Enjoy such bloodshed on my behalf," Marten said. "I must check on the delegation from the Eastern Network. They are supposed to arrive at any moment."

"Good luck."

He slipped away. Two other Guardian recruits attempted to parry in the lower bailey nearby. They caught my eye with their lazy stance.

"Straighten your hips!" I called. "You're turned too far to the side. You need to face your opponent with your *hips*. Not just your chest."

The recruit on the left—not all that much younger than my twenty-one years—looked down to his hips. The recruit on the right took his opportunity and slashed, slamming the edge of his wooden sword into the shoulder of the inattentive Guardian. He howled. His sword clattered to the ground, and he dropped with it.

I sighed.

Recruits were so dramatic.

Around me, other Guardian recruits worked in ten small circles where they parried, lunged, and attacked each other. The basic sword movements we'd practiced yesterday played out now, but with more bruises and less certainty. As Sword Trainer of New Recruits, I assigned them small group work to provide confidence before they had to perform in front of each other. So far, this rag-tag group had failed even the most basic sword movements.

Three years had passed since the War of the Networks had ended. The bloodthirsty desperation that the Guardians from those days fought with had faded. The recruits that came through my classes now had already started to forget the havoc of war. Thankfully, peace had a way of calming fear.

I grabbed the uninjured arm of the fallen Guardian and hauled him to his feet. The boy had startling dark eyes and shaggy hair. How could someone only a few years younger than me look *so* young?

"You'll recover this time because it's just a practice," I said firmly, "but you would have died the moment you gave up your sword in a battle. Pick it up. Swallow the pain. Try again."

His head dipped in a quick nod.

"Yes, Miss Monroe."

The sounds of sword practice continued. My naked feet were almost silent on the flagstones as I circled each pair and watched. A few showed promise. Most were already fatigued after a grueling day of sword work with me yesterday. While I slipped around the bailey with a watchful eye, sunlight glowed from behind Letum Wood. The magical forest cast long, dark shadows over the lower bailey. My heart stirred at the thought of the trees, and I heard a quiet, distant singsong.

You belong to us.

The peal of a single, dainty bell rang through the air. I glanced back to the top of the Wall, where Marten now stood. Guardians lined the outer Wall in polished half-armor that winked in the rising sun. They stood in lines twice as thick as usual in anticipation of the Eastern Network's arrival. High Priest Niko Aldana and his cohort would be the last Network leadership delegation to arrive for the two-week annual Celebration.

Papa initiated the yearly event at the end of the war three years ago.

To bring us together, he said. *To maintain peace through mutual understanding and cooperation. Not more isolationism. Now, we communicate.*

Every midsummer, each of the five Networks in Alkarra gathered their High Priestesses, High Priests, and Ambassadors in a collection of Esbats—or political meetings—meant to draw the Networks together. The Esbats allowed each Network to create lasting peace, communication, and avoid the toll of war.

As with all political machinations, drama abounded. Punctuating the Esbat schedule were dances, luncheons, lavish dinners, several elegant balls, and other opportunities to mingle with the cultures, languages, context, and food of each Network. After a hundred years of isolation, no amount of time across borders felt like enough. These social delights became breeding grounds for the gossip that raged through each Celebration.

Now, Papa, the High Priest of the Central Network, stood in the middle of the outer Bailey Wall. He leaned forward, palms planted on the waist-high stone wall. His gaze was directed toward the road that led to the castle from neighboring Chatham City. Most witches wouldn't see past his easygoing manner, but I could feel his tension.

Two male witches flanked him. Baxter, Papa's Assistant, on his left. A witch a few years older than me, bright-eyed, and quick to smile. And Marten, the Ambassador of the Central Network, on his right. Next to Marten stood Scarlett, the High Priestess, appointed after Stella died in the War of the Networks three years ago.

The exact same formation had been in that spot when the Northern Network arrived two days ago. Only that time I hid, like a coward. My heart clenched as I remembered catching a glimpse of my former sweetheart, Merrick, as he stood next to the Northern Network High Priestess, Geralyn. He'd been stony-faced and quiet, but his gaze had roved around. He'd looked for me, subtly, but he hadn't found me.

Because Merrick hadn't been mine for almost three years.

A voice rippled across the lower bailey to snag my attention. Heartbroken thoughts of Merrick shoved aside easily enough these days. I'd certainly had practice.

"Miss Monroe!"

I hustled through the half-heartedly fighting bodies and toward the call. Curious eyes followed me. This group of recruits had only worked with me a few days, so they still watched me out of the corners of their eyes. My movement distracted them now. One bonked another on the head with his wooden sword. Another struck empty air as I passed him.

All of the recruits were annoyingly curious at first. Not just because I was the only female teacher in the Guardian ranks, but because of my reputation after the War of the Networks. My former teacher, Mabel, had kidnapped me and whisked me to the West in an attempt to destroy the Central Network. Not only had Papa managed to spring me free from her clutches, but I'd helped Papa defeat her in the final battle against dark Almorran magic.

Now, the recruits watched me with curious uncertainty. Eventually, they will learn I was just another teacher. Their advocate. In some ways, their friend. The weird looks would stop when they forgot to be intimidated by a years-old reputation. Their admiration turned to a son-like loyalty by the time they graduated into the next level of sword work with Marten.

Just as I approached another pair of frustrated recruits, the sound of a horn rippled from the closest turret. The recruits snapped to attention. I swung toward Papa and held my breath. Several recruits whipped around in the middle of an attack sequence, their backs and arms absorbing blows.

A distinct, answering bugle from farther away came next.

"Great," I muttered.

Niko, High Priest to the Eastern Network had finally arrived. Now the Celebration would officially begin.

And so would Network-wide tension.

A recruit turned to me, clearly confused by the sudden onset of somber air on the castle. For the last two years, the Celebration had been an exciting event. A pall had already fallen over this year, however, with Niko's continued attempts to circumvent Papa's efforts to protect the Southern Network.

"Will High Priest Aldana challenge your father?" the gangly-armed boy asked.

"He will."

"Won't win," he immediately said, with a fierce confidence

I'd seen in other recruits that idolized Papa. "Niko will die if he tries."

A stone sank into my stomach. The truth wasn't that easy, or that simple. In politics, it never was.

"Maybe," I murmured.

My thoughts ran to the unstable Council attempting to rule without Papa, and then to the Southern Network. They had lost their ability to do magic in the war and struggled to remain safe in a world of witches now. The security issues in the South couldn't be ignored, but Niko had been trying. This Celebration was Papa's chance to dissolve those problems once and for all.

"Form ranks," I called, but more quietly this time. The stillness that had fallen over the bailey sent a shiver through me. Once the recruits stood in two lopsided rectangles, I waved an arm. "Put your swords away and return to your rooms until you're called for. In the meantime, run fifty drills with your training sword. Tomorrow, we'll be chopping wood for the kitchen and running for an hour, so come prepared."

With a chorus of groans, the recruits shuffled to obey. They moved just fast enough that I couldn't snap at them for taking their time, but slow enough to delay their departure because they wanted to see what would happen when the East arrived.

Would Niko and Papa snarl like hissing cats?

Would the Eastern Network be as pompous as most believed them to be and insult Central Network hospitality?

Unlikely on both counts, but curious all the same. Within moments, the bailey cleared of all sounds, swords, and bodies. The moment the last recruit slipped back into the Wall where they lived, I issued a transportation spell.

As High Priest, it was Papa's job to entertain other Network leadership and further diplomacy.

Not mine.

Chapter Two

That evening, the forest unfurled around me.

Lungs burning, legs flying, I soared down a verdant foot trail through lush undergrowth. Only a few steps away, a stream fifteen paces across cut through the rich earth. I leapt into the air and used a quick transportation spell. It skipped me over the muddy stream in a breath, and I landed without breaking stride on the other side. In the distance, the chatter of the trees filled my head with gentle words.

She has returned.

You belong to us.

You care for us.

We are yours.

Heady with the euphoria of freedom, I sped past low bracken and leapt over a root as tall as my knees. Bushes bent out of my way. Leaves skittered through the air, brushing past my cheek as the trees whispered their usual refrain.

She always comes back.

Letum Wood surrounded me with mossy trunks. Too far overhead to see clearly, leaves as large as my body blocked the sunlight. They hung off branches thicker than houses that extended into never-ending lengths. Only a magical forest could support trees of this size. Undoubtedly, Letum Wood existed *because* of magic. Or did the magic exist because of the forest?

Whether the magical system created Letum Wood or gave it life, I had no idea.

The heat of midsummer felt damp and heavy in the air. Sweat collected over my spine and trickled down my back, soaking my linen dress. A spell, one I'd used countless times, bunched my skirt around my mid-thighs in a scandalous show that would have drawn several outraged gasps. I'd ditched my sandals to run barefoot after this morning's training class. The start of the Celebration gave me an unusual afternoon off. Naturally, I filled it with my forest.

My heart hammered in my chest, and my mind picked up a familiar refrain. *I'm sorry,* it beat with each step, as if the ghosts of all those I'd lost still chased me. *I'm sorry it was you. I'm sorry Mabel orchestrated such evil and I survived. I'm sorry.*

I'm sorry.

I'm sorry.

Behind me, the stalwart, sentinel trees of Letum Wood soared overhead. Here, the forest was younger and not so imposing. Age and weight and magic didn't burden the air here. In the depths of the wood, the trees grew taller than Chatham Castle and wider than several turrets put together.

After I left the recruits, the trees led me to a new growth of strickenine moss I had to neutralize, in addition to a jammed stream that used to feed new saplings. Uplifted by all the running, I returned to my cottage in the woods.

Hints of Isadora lingered in the old cottage that I'd inherited shortly after the war settled down. The floor creaked, but the windows streamed sunlight. A wide hearth allowed bright, warm fires. This part of Letum Wood had more space between trees, so occasional beams of sunlight warmed my porch. Footpaths led from my front and back door to all different places.

Letum Wood surrounded me on every side, but no danger found me here. I suspected that Isadora had some form of protective incantations on the house that still survived.

When I stepped inside, the fire had died. I didn't bother stoking it with a spell when my stomach grumbled. I settled on a quick, cool bath and a change of clothes. A few biscuits and salad greens remained from last night, so I washed them down with goat milk, then slipped into my favorite summer dress. Leda hated the slit in the bottom that went just above my knee.

A pang for my old sword Viveet hit my chest when I passed various weaponry that dotted the wall, right next to a poorly embroidered sign that said *The Wits*. In place of my sword, I'd attempted all manner of weapons. Cudgels, bows, axes, anything I could get my hands on. Mama's house sword was too light, clumsy, and unbalanced. Papa's and Marten's swords were too heavy.

Nothing felt as good as Viveet. Merrick and I had attempted to find Viveet's forger, Andrei the swordmaker in the South, to have her fixed. He had disappeared during the war, and no one knew where to find him. After two weeks, we gave up. Viveet lay buried beneath my favorite tree, near the roots.

"You know," drawled an unexpected voice. "I really hate what you've done with the place."

A lithe figure filled my doorway. Wild brown curls framed a dusky face and eyes the color of mint. Baxter, Papa's Assistant.

I scoffed. "You have no great decorating ability yourself."

Baxter twirled a finger. "Reeves could change this place, you know. Maybe the teacups will stop disappearing if he had a hand in things. I think they don't like your style."

I laughed.

Teacups filled a ledge above the fireplace, placed there by Isadora, and left to collect dust after her death. Every now and then, a teacup would just . . . disappear, like little pieces of the Watcher disappearing with time. Ten remained, their delicate flowers and leaves hand-painted. Some of them had a more masculine feel. Bolder strokes. Firmer colors. Not for the first time, I wondered about Isadora's past. Did she have a husband? She died at over 120 years old, so if she had, she'd long outlasted him.

"Reeves would have a heart attack the moment he stepped inside this place," I said, then narrowed my gaze. "What disaster drove you to escape here again? Did the fairies return? I told you—"

"Not the fairies."

He flopped onto my bed with a yawn that nearly popped his jaw out of its socket. He slung an arm onto his forehead. Baxter randomly showing up at my cottage wasn't that unusual. He escaped castle life more often than he lived it.

"Aren't you supposed to be orchestrating things at the castle?" I asked. "The East has arrived, and Niko Aldana doesn't take kindly to poor social etiquette."

"The initial dinner is underway. It buys me an hour reprieve."

"Ah. The puzzle solves itself. You came here because everyone is trying to find you, you need a break, and no one hides from society better than me."

He pointed to me, eyes already closed. "Precisely. Your cottage is remote, calm, and protected by magic."

Despite his casual pose, he was pristinely put together. His freshly laundered shirt was pressed into crisp lines. A hint of stubble on his jaw and dull leather breeches that looked like new. Only his sandals, which I'd convinced him to try a year ago, appeared less-than-perfect.

His pulled-togetherness belied the exhaustion in his eyes. With the arrival of the final delegation came a massive amount of coordination and responsibility. As Papa's Assistant, he bore a heavy weight.

"Also wanted to confirm the events you'll be attending," he

murmured, a low drawl of sleepiness to his voice. "The Central Network Dinner in two evenings, of course. I'm rather proud of the Central Network covens that will be represented through a parade of food. Particularly because none of the food here makes any sense at all. Figs in bread? Anyway, you'll also attend the ball. Your dance with Derek last year is still talked about now. Several delegations have mentioned looking forward to seeing another one."

A grimace rose to my face. Despite a good experience at the Celebration ball the last two years in a row, I still dreaded the thought of another ball. I managed to make my voice not sound strangled when I said, "I'll be there."

"Good," he mumbled, and then yawned again. "Oh, and Scarlett wants to know if you'll be attending the opera review. With all the delegations milling around and calm, operatic music in the background, she's hopeful Derek will speak with the North about a training swap. You could form your Sisterhood, they could learn from our Brotherhood."

At the word *Sisterhood,* my spine immediately tensed. "I'll follow up with her on that," I said, then quickly added, "I tried to practice with the axe you found near the Southern Network border."

"And?"

I shrugged and lifted the axe off the wall. Leather straps bound the head to the handle, locked in and tightened by spells. The pristine, sharp edge gleamed. Only craftsmen from the tribes in the South could work such skilled magic. They used to, at least. Now that all the witches in the Southern Network had lost their ability to do magic, that axe would be worth more currency than I'd know what to do with.

"Too unbalanced?" he asked.

"Not sure why I don't like it." I shrugged. "Just . . . wasn't right."

Baxter contemplated that, climbed to his knees, set the axe

on the wall, and flopped onto his stomach. He rarely used magic for simple things, such as replacing a weapon on the wall, like the rest of us.

His sooty lashes closed as he stacked his head on his arms. "You'll find the right one," he said.

I scoffed. "When I'm eighty, at this rate."

"And too grumpy to recognize it. What about something that you could throw?"

"What could I throw that would incapacitate like a sword?"

"Besides your attitude?"

I sent a burst of air his way that stirred his curls. "You have no room to talk about attitude."

"Son of a god," he murmured with a jaunty grin, his favorite joke whenever he was unnaturally good at something. His eyes closed again. While I split a strip of leather to re-lace one of my sandals, his breathing evened into a quiet sleep.

A small scroll appeared in front of me and whisked thoughts of the upcoming ball away. The crimson string that tied it closed told me immediately who had sent it. I plucked it from the air and rolled it open.

Bianca,

I would like to meet with you tomorrow evening after the initial Esbat, if possible. My office at 9:00 pm should suffice.
Also, you and I have discussed the possibility that you could give Leda a nudge if I didn't hear from her. I haven't heard from her. I would like a final answer. If the option of you speaking to her on my behalf is on the table, I'd be most grateful for your help.

Yours,
Scarlett

"Leda," I murmured under my breath. "You silly witch."

With a shake of my head, I sent the message into the fire. Baxter slept on with a peaceful expression. My magic carpet, or Volare, waited in a circular case that I flung onto my back. I tugged my dress sleeve back over a thin, short sword I kept on my forearm and ran a comb through my tangled black hair, which fell to my shoulder blades. I used a spell to put it into a braid that ran down either side of my head, then coiled in a bun at my neck.

Then I transported away, Leda heavy on my mind.

* * *

The Great Library of Burke was a massive building made of wood and stone. It loomed several stories high and extended seemingly without end into Letum Wood, where it had resided in the centuries of its existence. Despite being a library, no one knew when or where it began.

Eternal hallways drifted into the shadows of the forest and disappeared into the trees. It grew year by year as it collected more literature, articles, and other items of cultural significance. Most of it was, at any given time, closed off to witches. But the librarians would open several wings in rotating shifts, revealing areas that no one in memory had seen. Now that borders were open after almost a hundred years of isolation, literature poured in from all over Alkarra. Expansion had been continuous.

Librarians with impressive magical power wandered the halls. The lesser-regarded Underlibrarians followed them, all of their magic maintaining the books, shelving, and general air of pompous intelligence. To maintain order and prevent theft, the Head Librarian of hundreds of years ago had designated a transportation room and blocked transportation within any other area. It kept the vast place as still as a tomb.

A hush fell on the world when I entered the library through

glass double doors. Swirls of stained glass decorated the entrance in an image of Letum Wood. Panes of cerulean blue topped it. Beneath, swirls of emerald gave way to umber tree trunks.

Several witches milled inside, under the smell of ink and decaying scrolls. A female witch with silky black hair sat at a sprawling reception desk made of twigs and leaves. Birds fluttered in and out, building nests. She beamed when I walked up in the ropey sandals I'd bought from her family in the West.

"Merry meet, Sanako."

"Merry meet, Bianca." Sanako tucked a monocle away, into a pocket of her dress. "How is your part of Letum Wood?"

"Quiet. Yours?"

She brightened. "Normal." Her eyes sparkled when she leaned forward and whispered, "I believe I may have met a goddess the other day. It's hard to tell, but I have my suspicions." She waved a hand around my face. "You can see it in their eyes. Queer."

"Really?"

Her eager nod amused me, but I schooled it. Sanako collected history with serious intent. No one *but* Sanako thought about the goddess paradigm anymore, which earned her an official and coveted Librarian badge. While Underlibrarians like Leda scrounged for any notice or praise from their Librarian overlords, Sanako breezed her way right to the title of the Librarian Expert on Historical Folk Tales in the Division of Goddess and God History.

Something that had sent Leda into an annoyed smolder for weeks.

"Where did you meet a goddess?" I asked.

Sanako pointed out the doors. "On the water in the West. Where else?"

"And which goddess is water again?"

"Prana is the *sea* goddess." Her sharp reprimand sounded like every other Librarian here. Did they train them to admonish patrons with the same tone? If so, they succeeded. "If we don't remember both gods and goddesses, one day we'll feel their wrath. It behooves all of us to invest education in their ways and their preferred appreciation for all they've given. For Prana, it's blatant and pointed adoration."

I matched her sober tone with great effort. "Of course, Sanako. Thank you for your reminder. Is Leda in her usual office?"

She nodded. "Waiting for you, I believe."

"Thank you. Merry part."

Sanako waved and pulled her monocle back out to study a book sprawled open in front of her. A bird twittered by and landed on her shoulder. Several other patrons approached with questions about lost scrolls in the Ancient Scrolls and Grimoires of the Kukkan Time division. I left with a wave, but she'd already turned her attention.

Stacks of books, hallways, offices, and more passed as I headed toward the west wing of the library. A few months after the War of the Networks, Leda had left her job as Scarlett's Assistant. She'd hidden away at home with her siblings for weeks to try to recover from everything that had happened. A month passed before she couldn't handle her family and their chaos anymore and desperately applied to the Great Library of Burke for a position.

They gave her the groveling position as assistant to a group of ten Underlibrarians—the very bottom of the Great Burke job ladder. She'd been working her way through the library hierarchy ever since. She currently resided as Underlibrarian in her course to achieve the supposed greatness of a titled Librarian . . . preferably in the Languages Division.

I navigated to a small closet with a book-sized window that overlooked the forest. It had been given to her as an afterthought, and only after she'd promised to improve it and make it more functional. Inside was barely enough space to turn around in.

Tentatively, I knocked.

One annoyed huff later, the door creaked open and a pair of differently-colored eyes peered out. On seeing me, Leda straightened. The last few months after gaining Underlibrarian, she had become even more insufferable. Happy in her own way, but occasionally oppressive to those of us less intelligent than her.

"Merry meet, Bianca," she said, then turned back around to face her desk. The door would only open a pace or two when she sat in her chair, so I leaned against the doorframe outside.

The closet was utilitarian at best. A candle sputtered near her elbow as the only light, except the window. She hadn't decorated the closet at all, but she did make it functional. An inkpot holder had been nailed to the wall over her desk because there wasn't sufficient space for one. She'd attempted something similar with a candle holder, but it had fallen and nearly caught her hair on fire. Several new shelves had been repurposed from broken boards cast on the ground. Books and scrolls filled them, organized by size and color.

"Merry meet," I drawled. "Can you take a break for our weekly dinner?"

Her gaze dropped to my bare legs with a reproving eye-roll. Instead of lowering all the way to the floor, my summer skirt tapered up to my knees in the front, then dropped in the back to hover just above the ground. It left my knees and ankles bare and was, in her terms, *a ghastly representation of women these days.* Leda could always brighten my day with her unflappable annoyance.

"Don't you have any other dress?" she muttered.

"Several, but my other dress doesn't make you as angry as this one, so it's not as fun."

"Why you feel joy from irritating me," she growled, "I will never understand. I'm just about finished here."

Scrolls bearing ancient languages littered a desk which was little more than a single board nailed to the wall. Her legs barely fit when she tucked them underneath, which forced her to sit at an uncomfortable angle. I gazed at the scrolls with a nauseous feeling. Leda had always found refuge in closets, which made sense with as many siblings as she had. But it was her willingness to *stay* in closed spaces for so long that always amazed me.

When she finished packing the scrolls into a neat line organized by length and width, closed the book she made notations in, and capped her inkwell with a lid, she stood. A cleaning incantation took care of the ink stains on her fingers while she slipped out, perfectly presentable. Her white-blonde hair was pulled back in a tasteful bun that looked exactly like every other Underlibrarian.

Maybe they trained for those as well.

"So," I said as we walked down the hall together. "How has your project on ancient languages been going?"

"Thrilling," she cried. "There's something so fascinating about diving into history through language. The Declan language, for example, is one of the most developed languages of which we have notation. If I keep studying it, and that old man in the Language Division finally joins his family in the lands and lives beyond, I could be promoted to Librarian over the *Declan* Language Division within the next . . . five years!"

Forced brightness filled her tone. Under it, she sounded dreadful.

"Sounds . . . very exciting," I managed to choke out. "I know some Declan words, and their spells are . . . interesting."

Leda said nothing, rolled her eyes again, and huffed impatiently. "They're more than *interesting*, but I wouldn't expect a witch like you to understand."

Her words *a witch like you* rang through my head with a suppressed chuckle. Leda's exasperation toward me always held an affectionate note, although she sometimes buried it very deeply.

We turned a corner, then pushed outside into a circular garden open to the forest. Other offices stacked four stories high peered down on us. Letum Wood created a ceiling of thick branches and boughs overhead, but the library's walls protected this garden from errant creatures. Leda liked her outdoors with a side dish of heavy magical protection and control.

She set the pail of food she'd brought with her on a stone table, and I slid into the bench across from her. The Volare remained on my back. Even though I'd already eaten a little, I still felt famished after an afternoon of running. As usual, she brought enough for both of us. Apparently, her time after work was hard to fill, since she did her favorite pastime—reading—as a job. She'd taken up baking as a new hobby.

An oblong-shaped cold pie, filled with an assortment of greens and what must have been minced lamb, filled the inside. I tore off a bite and savored each morsel.

"Delicious, Leda. As usual."

"Thank you."

A few moments of quiet passed before I dared break it. "So . . . have you responded to Miss Scarlett's request?"

Leda stiffened like a board. Her nostrils flared, but she maintained a calm mien with her usual dignity.

"As I said last week," she said carefully, "I will not be responding. I am not interested in working at the castle again or with . . . I will not be working for Scarlett."

"She needs you, Leda. Her team is still untrained and young and not ready for the political realm. She fired two of them, and I think she has *one* Assistant now. It's been terrible for her since you left. She's never been able to replace you. Besides, Assistant to the High Priestess is far above an Underlibrarian here. It's one of the highest positions in the Network."

And you've already given it up, I thought, but knew better than to voice it.

Leda's nostrils flared. "I'm well aware, thank you."

Until now, I hadn't pressed her on Scarlett's offer to be her Assistant. I figured Leda would fight it for a week and then give in—because when had a second chance like this *ever* presented itself? Never. Not in a political structure at Scarlett's level, anyway. But no, Leda had dug her metaphorical heels in yet again.

"Why not?" I asked, my tone laced with exasperation.

Her light eyes flickered to mine, then back to her pie. For the first time in awhile, she appeared discomfited. Leda had gained absolute control over her life in the last three years. She lived the exact same routine, which allowed her to forget our deceased friend Camille and her lost brother. In fact, she hadn't set foot in the castle since the dissolution of the Almorran magic that almost destroyed all of Alkarra.

"You know why," she muttered. "I won't go back there after ... after ..."

"The battle?"

"Yes. It was hard enough those first few months." She shivered. "To return?"

"Camille doesn't haunt Chatham Castle, Leda. I'm sure she's moved onto better things in the afterlife than following you around."

She cut me a sharp glare. She hated it when I said Camille's name. Her head tilted back a little, just enough to be haughty, with her pert nose in the air.

"That's not why."

"Liar."

The back of her neck flushed red, but she'd perfected her placid expression. Leda and I had held onto each other in the grief that followed the fracturing of Almorran magic. Only lately had the ever-changing circumstances of a post-war climate started to fade. Papa had brought consistency back, and that bred life instead of desperation. Living through war was brutal. Recovering from war was heart wrenching.

"I don't want to be at the castle, Bianca. You know that. This isn't a topic that's up for discussion."

"I think you're making a mistake."

In an unusual move for both of us, I reached across the table and put a hand over hers. Leda tolerated touch from her mother and no one else. She sucked in a sharp breath, but didn't pull back.

"Camille isn't coming back, Leda, and you are destined for great things. Your talent and magic are wasted in this library, and you know it. You can't hide forever."

Her stormy eyes gazed at me through almost translucent lashes. "And how is your own self-loathing around failing our friends during the war?" she asked lightly, but her tone had a hint of vindictiveness in it.

The knife twisted a little in my heart, and I grimaced. A flicker of regret appeared in her gaze, but it quickly faded. She didn't take it back, and I didn't expect her to. Fully-fledged adult Leda had become more ruthless than ever. Or perhaps this was just Leda fighting an equally ruthless world.

She peered past me, jaw tense. "I'm sorry," she managed. "That was low. I just . . . I don't want to think about Camille or my brother. I don't want the memories associated with . . . with that place."

She shuddered again.

"But you're wasting your life and your talent here."

"Says you," she shot back. "I'll have you know I've implemented several routines and practices that have drastically improved turnaround time for patron consumption of ancient scrolls."

I faked a gag.

"You," she muttered darkly, "will never grow up."

I sighed. "I don't mean to open old wounds. I just . . . the Network needs you. And Camille would be livid if she knew that you avoided the future you once wanted very much just because of her memory."

"That's not the only reason."

"Then what is the other one?"

Her face dropped into a pretty scowl, but it didn't have a lot of heart. She picked at her pie while I waited for her response.

"Nevermind," she finally muttered. "I don't want to talk about it."

We both ate. Eventually, her expression cleared. I decided to let her ignore my question when she changed the subject.

"The Head Librarian, Abena, was invited as a political honor to the dinner tonight, and the initial Esbat tomorrow."

"Oh?"

I tried to infuse surprise, but I couldn't muster much. Leda's tone had turned searching, and that meant trouble.

She had a dainty bite of pie crust.

"Abena was as excited as I've ever seen her. Of course, she's not the only witch eager to hear what is discussed during the initial Esbat." A low drawl colored her tone, and I knew exactly what it meant.

I matched it. "Of course she's not."

My gaze dared her to ask the question that burned under her words. We met in a glare-for-glare battle until she gave up with a sigh.

"Please, Bianca," she murmured. "Tell me you aren't going to sneak into an Esbat of that size? It's . . . unprecedented. Your father will be in the history books for defeating and destroying Almorran magic, but also for successfully holding the Celebration and post-war peace for several years in a row after a hundred years of mutual isolationism. Arguably, the last three years of peace are a direct result of the Celebration. If he pulls off a solution to the Southern Network issue this year, he's all but cemented as the greatest High Priest to ever rule. To have *you* sneak in on it . . ."

She trailed away. I fought not to take offense. Then again, she had a point. I wasn't known for political correctness or alacrity.

"I'm meeting with Scarlett afterward. I don't have to spy. You could be part of the initial Esbat, you know, if you'd just take Scarlett's offer," I said because I couldn't help myself.

Her scowl deepened, but my distraction had a point. I pawed a lock of hair away from my face.

"I'm twenty-one years old now, Leda. I hardly need to creep around hidden passageways in the castle to hear a meeting."

Her gaze tapered to slashes. "You *aren't* going to 'hear a meeting.' You're going to spy."

To my relief, a watch in Leda's pocket gave out a strange *bleat* that announced the hour. She'd found an old grimoire with magic centered entirely around clockwork a few months ago. Her joy over magical alarms had been intense for days. She set her half-eaten pie back in her tin, and I finished the last bite of mine, finally satiated.

When Leda stood, her straw-and-green-colored eyes remained guarded, but not quite so heavily. "Thanks, Bianca. It's always good to see you."

"I'll be back in a week, as usual."

She nodded and brushed past me. "I will look forward to it."

Chapter Three

When I was a sixteen-year-old pupil of Mabel and desperate to save my own life, I snuck into Chatham Castle and attempted to find my way into a Central Network Esbat. Somehow, I managed to not be killed. The Esbat tonight wasn't much different.

Except . . . it was *very* different.

Over the course of the next two weeks, the real work of the Celebration would commence in these daily meetings. Each Esbat was a delegation of the leadership from each Network—High Priestess, High Priest, and Ambassador—with an occasional meeting here and there that invited other dignitaries, like Council Members, Librarians, or High Witches.

The same High Priestesses, High Priests, and Ambassadors would attend every Esbat. Each meeting would be at least eight hours long—though one had gone as many as sixteen hours last year—and each had a particular agenda.

The initial Esbat, which would occur in less than an hour, was the most important. Each Network would establish its priorities for political progress over the next two weeks. For the most part, agendas seemed clear, but Networks always surprised me.

Papa and Igor, the High Priest of the South, wanted to drum up more military support for the Southern Network. Now that all witches in the South had lost their magic, they had minimal protection against the rogue witches that used magic to transport in and harass, rape, and rob them blind. These problematic witches left behind only devastation.

Niko from the East had disputes with the North over fishing rights *and* with Papa's plan for all Networks to support the protection of the South. Geralyn from the North would likely make an announcement to re-establish borders, which would naturally segue into fishing rights. Then the North and the East would work out the details over the next several weeks or months.

If I requested an invitation to the initial Esbat, I'd only draw suspicion from the other Networks. For the last three years, I'd avoided being visible around political events, although I couldn't entirely avoid them. To request a spot at the initial Esbat would be . . . odd. Networks would wonder why I showed an interest.

So would Papa.

Scarlett's plan to push a Sisterhood of Protectors lay at the forefront of her own agenda. Papa had refused so far to bring it up with the issue of the Southern Network at the beating heart of Alkarran problems. She wanted me to lead the Sisterhood, but that was the last thing I'd do. I needed to attend the Esbat to hear firsthand what was discussed so I could be ready.

If Scarlett managed to get a word in, I wanted to see the reactions of those present. Hearing second-hand what she could say wouldn't cut it. What did they think? Would the other Networks be concerned? Monitoring their reactions would help me form my rebuttal when Scarlett confronted me later tonight, after the Esbat.

Getting *to* the Esbat would be easy.

Getting *inside* would be a different matter.

Papa had gone out of his way to inform me that all the hidden passages to the Esbat room would be patrolled by Guardians and Protectors. Those passages were my first instinct, but I automatically dismissed that option. Physical space was too limited, and first instincts were almost always too easy.

The second, most obvious course to get into the Esbat was transformation, but the magic alone made it rife with too many issues. Discoverability, for one. Protectors and Guardians would be feeling for every type of known transformative magic. They'd out any witch they found, and that was precisely what Leda had counseled me to avoid.

The third and most viable option?

Invisibility.

Maybe as obvious as the other two but packed with far more potential. With invisibility magic, simplicity meant success. My plan to attend the Esbat invisibly wouldn't be as straightforward as I might have wished, but the magic could be simple. The plan would be multifaceted and happen in distinct stages.

The average invisibility spell would be foolish here. Protectors would root me out and transport me away without a word. No doubt they were already in the Esbat room, concealed, which meant they could be anyone.

No, I had to be smarter than them, which wasn't easy.

The biggest concern was the implication and the embarrassment of being caught. If I were caught, the Central Network would look foolish, perhaps suspicious. Papa would seem out of control. The rest of the Networks would question why they were restricted in attendees, but we snuck witches in.

The tentative peace that had been floating around for three years was ready to break at any chance. Networks were still twitchy around each other. We'd grown up without exposure to other cultures, and Papa's attempts to braid us back together came with obvious discomforts. More precisely—some

Networks would take any opportunity to crush that peace and gain more land now that borders were open.

With mental gusto, I shoved those thoughts away.

The bustle and heat of the kitchens surrounded me as I snuck down the back stairwell and into the servants' quarters. Kitchen maids slept in small, stone rooms with little more than beds and boxes underneath to accommodate their clothes.

Celebration or not, Chatham Castle always bustled with life and noise and movement. Even at night, when the fire boys and cleaning crews swept through. To slide into the closet where the maids kept fresh uniforms, slip one under my arm, then disappear under an invisibility incantation was disturbingly easy.

Under Mildred's reign, and with the threat of Almorran magic on the horizon, the Central Network Esbat had been a far more secretive affair. Council Members entered through a place called the anteroom, a special entrance on the eastern wall of the castle. It required specific incantations to get in and protocols to prove yourself. Since Mabel's defeat and the destruction of Almorran magic, Papa had opened the Esbat and removed the layers of secrecy.

Hilarious, in hindsight, because Mildred had been protecting against an enemy that had already been *inside* the Esbat.

But she'd known that all along, too.

Twenty minutes later, I strolled down the hallway to the Esbat room, my hair transformed to dark blonde. It was cut to my shoulders and bounced with curls reminiscent of Camille. My eyes were a pale hazel, my nose a replica of Leda's, my teeth now slightly crooked in the front. Even my skin was several shades darker so that only my face shape remained vaguely the same. Tonight, gentle earrings sparkled in my earlobes. In my arms was a shiny silver tray filled with red wine in elegant flutes.

With a breath to gather my courage, I slipped past a group of witches and stepped into the Esbat room.

Smiling wide, I forced myself to play the part of a happy, trained servant. After ten minutes had passed, I'd refilled my tray twice. In that time, no one mentioned a maid using transformative magic, I relaxed a bit. No one pulled me aside. No one even seemed to be following me, which I may have just missed. They were all too busy talking, wrapped up in bits of gossip, the excitement of the Celebration, and glasses of unusually strong wine.

Speculation and gossip surrounded me, valuable enough to venture here just to listen in. Surely, I wasn't the only maid with a dual purpose. Undoubtedly, several maids were paid by other Networks to listen and report. Only a fool would talk about anything real before the Esbat started.

"Niko will accept Derek's offer of deeper Network ties for Southern protection," murmured one woman with the heavy accent of the Eastern Network that drew the *e* into a song. "How could he not?"

I breezed past, pretending not to hear.

"The Southern Network," tutted a droll voice from Newberry, a city north of here, "is a bloody mess. Not our problem to clean up, is it? They brought this on themselves by having Mikhail as a leader."

"I'm surprised their eyes didn't turn amber when they lost their magic," said the high-pitched tone of a woman in response. "Mortals had amber-colored eyes before they were banished from Alkarra thousands of years ago."

"But these are witches that lost their magic," chided another. "Entirely different from a mortal. The mortals wreaked havoc on magic. These were still witches."

"*Is* it different?" replied the woman archly.

"The magic didn't leave the witches entirely," said another voice, somewhat belligerently. "The young children born after the war have already shown magical ability. The witches that lost their magic because of Mikhail are not mortal. They're just . . . incompetent."

With ease, I slipped around the Esbat room itself, my gaze attentive to every detail. Stone walls in a broad setting. Thin windows reflected candlelight from tiny mirrors in a chandelier overhead. Maroon banners which dangled from the walls stirred in a loose breeze through the open windows. It alleviated the stuffiness of the gathering in the late summer days and made it easier to breathe.

In the middle of the room, a sprawling oak table held a ring of padded, velvet chairs. Other witches leaned against the wall here and there. The ceiling jutted two stories above. Bouncing, bright voices echoed around it. I surreptitiously handed a wine goblet to a passing diplomat—Southern, if the very short, squat stature meant anything—and conjured a few more. White wine, this time, for the more mellow crowd.

Marten stood on the other side of the room. The bouncing chandelier light flickered off his bald head as he spoke with Niko. Lines of stress decorated Niko's once-smooth skin and genial expression. Gravity filled his expression now, darkening his black hair and umber gaze.

Had Priscilla come with him? No lovely red hair appeared in the crowd around him. He must have left her in the East. Tension had been high between the Central Network and the Eastern Network for the last few months. Still, I doubted she would have chosen to stay there for the Celebration.

Thinking about it gave me a moment of pause.

Marten's gaze drew toward me, so I slipped behind some Western Network tribal leaders wearing ten necklaces of thick beads and turned my attention back to my plan.

Alkarra held countless magical systems. Some of them were known, and a handful of them used enough to be familiar to the majority of witches, but most magical systems were likely not yet discovered.

Magic stemmed from grimoires, or books of magic that contained incantations and rules for a particular set of magic. No one knew where the grimoires came from. Some witches claimed that grimoires came from goddesses, who spent most of their time creating magic systems. But no one believed that ridiculous idea. Others said the grimoires made themselves because the magic just existed.

The everyday magic used throughout Alkarra was regarded as the Muran magical system. *Comfortable magic*, Leda called it with a haughty sniff. *Magic used to make our lives better.* It was one of the first times in history that all Networks practiced the same basic magic so diffusely, though other systems were still active.

Familiarity with a magic system also allowed a witch to recognize or feel it in use. The more practiced in that magic, the more strongly it was felt. The Protectors and Guardians here would be feeling out magical use now, mostly from the Muran and Declan systems. Which meant *other* magical systems could be used without a high chance of detection. The more ancient and unknown, the better.

While dodging Marten's too-perceptive eye and attempting not to spill the wine, I scoured the edges of the room. Ideas flowed through me now that I stood here in the pre-ambiance of the Esbat.

Transformation into an animal wasn't entirely off my radar yet, but it would be too difficult to maintain the magic *and* pay attention, particularly in such a large room. I hadn't practiced maintaining an animalistic disguise for more than thirty minutes, except once in the West when captive by Mabel. That magic was too obvious anyway. Plus, the type of animal had to be taken into consideration. Worms were easy, but they couldn't hear. Spiders, moths, and all the obvious small ones had their own limitations. Household cats were ideal. Small. Lithe. Nimble. Great hearing, but too suspicious by half.

Before I could move on to a new thought, Papa entered the room with his booming voice. He drew half the witches' attention, which lowered conversation for a few moments before it resumed again. He worked his way into the room, clasping forearms with witches as he greeted each by name.

I ducked behind another diplomat—Marten had edged this way—and glanced overhead. Now *there* was something interesting.

Wooden beams crossed the ceiling as support rafters three paces wide and extended through the room. Most of the wood in the castle had been enchanted with architectural spells that gave them unusually long lives.

The Central Network was a wet climate in the summer, and wood tended to wear quickly. Those support beams would have magic to help them last for centuries on centuries. Unlikely the Guardians would be familiar with that magic, so it could act as a mask. Hyper-sensitive Guardians might think they detected magic on one of those rafters, but if the magic never moved or changed, they might attribute it to a prolonged-life spell.

Worth a shot.

Dust littered the tops of the rafters, which would be problematic if it were to fall on the table. It would need a little tidying session. My mind had mulled over the prospect for a moment too long. A body slipped up to my side and grabbed onto my wrist before I could glide away.

"Excellent wine tonight," Marten murmured.

I shot him a glare. There was no use pretending. He wouldn't have touched a servant, which meant he knew who I was and wanted to prevent my escape.

His lips twitched.

"And what is my infamous granddaughter planning?" he asked quietly.

It was a problematic, but not unexpected, obstacle that he

found me so quickly. Perhaps I hadn't mingled enough. Too much focus had given me away, I'd wager.

Still, he was distracted by the question, so I initiated a collecting spell toward the ceiling. With any luck, the dust would collect to the corner that I commanded it to and not draw attention.

"Would you like some wine, sir?" I drawled.

He smirked, but his tone lowered. "The High Priests and High Priestesses of all five Networks are here with their Ambassadors. They're each allowed one Assistant in the Esbat. You, my dear, are not one of those. Do I need to ask why you're here?"

"You could have let me attend as your Assistant," I murmured, smiling as I handed a wine glass to a witch wearing a pair of glasses without any lenses.

He laughed. He stood slightly behind me now and attempted to fix a pocket watch, no doubt to avoid drawing attention to me.

"For your sake," he murmured, "I hope you're leaving soon."

With a whisper, he was gone. He hadn't exactly given me permission to be here, but he hadn't blatantly banned me from the room, either. He could have outed me. He'd done so before.

It meant something that he didn't.

My attention drew away from the ceiling when a low murmur rippled through the room. Geralyn, the High Priestess of the Northern Network, stepped into the doorway with a warm smile.

Regina, a close-watching Master of the North, flanked her. My stomach tightened. Regina was in her late thirties and wildly skilled with magic. She trained me for a few lessons after the War of the Networks, when plans for a Sisterhood still had hope, and the former High Priestess of the North, Farah, was alive. Geralyn had taken over for Farah when she died after falling ill from a fever. The fracas that followed prevented me from returning to

Regina, whom most considered to be the Northern Network equivalent of Papa.

Then Merrick left on Geralyn's command, and I wanted nothing to do with the North.

Today, Regina wore half armor. The plates weren't as thick or expansive as the men's, and the leather was not quite so broad. It fit her strong, slight frame so well it must have been tailored by magic or a skilled craftsman. Her hair flowed into a knot at the back of her head. She was elegant, but fiery, with a firm expression and intense stare.

Our Protectors blended in, and no doubt a Master or two did the same now, but Geralyn must flaunt Regina for a reason. I couldn't help but wonder why.

While the crowd remained distracted and my tray empty, I slipped to the edge of the room and headed to the door. Papa called the crowd to attention, and as all their gazes turned to him, I ducked behind a cluster of tall-backed chairs. Then I sent the tray away with a spell and faded into nothing.

The magic I used to fade would be temporary. A quiet magical system, the Timan, taken from the Western Network seashore. It allowed me to be invisible as I sidled next to the wall, shucking the maid's outer layers to only the simple red dress underneath. The clothes spelled away. Then I used an incantation that made the tips of my fingers, my hands, and my toes sticky and I climbed the wall. Both spells were active as I peeled my fingers away to place them higher above me one space at a time. A faint, wet indentation of a sprawled hand remained behind, but it would dissipate.

Papa's voice rang over the crowd. "We have gathered this evening . . ."

He faded to the back of my mind when I arrived at the main support beam. I paused. No one looked up except for a thick-chested man with a bright purple kerchief around his neck. He stood on the other side of the room and frowned at my wall. A disguised Protector, likely. There was always something vaguely familiar about them. Like me, most didn't bother to change face shape or ear placement.

This one had a vague familiarity, but I didn't waste time trying to figure him out.

I stretched across the top of the support beam, wrapped my arms around it, and issued a different magic to keep me hidden. This one from the Southern Network and very obscure. It had taken several weeks to get the pronunciation right. If anyone from the South was familiar, it wouldn't matter. They couldn't detect magic anymore, which is just why I'd chosen it.

Then I waited.

The man across the way shifted, his gaze lifting along the wall beneath me slowly. No doubt he sensed a new magic, but it was unlikely he would be familiar enough with it to peg more than a vague uncertainty. The way his full lips puckered likely meant he wasn't sure what he felt. He didn't want to call unnecessary attention to something that might be a fluke.

Which is why I couldn't move *at all*.

Movement would draw his attention back and be less like a stagnant magic that he'd eventually ignore.

Up here, the air was even warmer. The collection spell had worked, forming a neat pile of dust in the far corner of the rafters. Sticky grime coated the top of this beam, and I almost sneezed into a collection of dusty bird poop just beneath my nose.

Lovely.

"To celebrate our third Celebration . . ." Papa continued, but I tuned him out. He'd keep the speech short. Papa hated political drivel, but it was a necessary means. Finally, he held up his glass and said, "To negotiation."

A murmur of assent followed. Seconds later, the room quieted while a witch in the corner chanted a lyrical blessing on the proceeding. When it was finished, everyone except for eleven witches slipped out.

Nine remained and stood around the table, facing each other. Most of them were High Priests, High Priestesses, and their Ambassadors, aside from Geralyn and Regina from the North, and Lana, the newly appointed High Priestess of the Western Network. Only a maid accompanied Lana.

Two Guardians positioned themselves at the doors as they started to close. I had little doubt a few Protectors sprinkled the room in various places, hidden under their own layers of obscure magic. The man on the other side of the room had disappeared. Baxter stood a few paces behind Papa's chair. His eyes flickered to the rafters momentarily, then away.

Could he . . . ?

No.

Impossible.

"Let us begin," Papa called and drew my thoughts back to the present.

The doors slammed shut.

* * *

"Let us start at the heart of this meeting," Papa said. "The establishment of individual agendas, starting with the Southern Network. A transcript of every Esbat will be provided at the end of each day."

A clutter of enchanted quills scratched away on parchments in the far corner of the room, noting each word spoken and who spoke it.

"Igor." Papa motioned to him. "You may begin."

The High Priest of the Southern Network tensed. He already sat straight-backed in his chair, expression slightly hostile and strained. Dark hair swept away from his face and onto his shoulders with streaks of gray in the front. A groomed beard, braided around a giant topaz gem, fell onto his chest. Pompous, as usual. A typical display for the South and their abundance of precious gems. I couldn't blame his wary gaze. His entire Network lost their magical ability, himself included. I could only shudder at the thought.

Lost magic.

What a terrifying life to lead.

Next to him, the Southern Network Ambassador, Alina, sat with her head held high and expression unbothered by the strange tone in the air. She didn't seem frightened in a crowd of powerful magic users even though she and Igor were like fat piglets in a den of forest lions. The almost-but-not-quite-mortals.

Undoubtedly, Alina's history as a shieldmaiden to the former High Priestess—arguably the most talented shield-maiden, according to rumors—gave her some physical advantage. That would do very little to protect her against spells, however. She gazed on the room through thin, assessing eyes. Her dark, silky hair fell all the way down her back.

Igor stood.

"As per the agreement in the post-var negotiations after the var of the Netvorks, ve have adequately prepared our Guardians to fight as best they can." His voice rippled through the almost-empty room now, belying their weakened state against magic users. "I have overseen the training of our Guards, and it has exceeded my expectations. For vhat ve can do against magic, they do vell. The charms that the Vestern Network has provided are helpful but do not prevent direct violence." His gaze flittered to Niko, then away. "And direct violence is our greatest problem."

The edges of the wooden beam dug into my thighs now. I carefully shifted. Lying on a board two stories high while unable to see my own body was tricky, at best. Treacherous, at worst. Everything had to go by feel, but any movement to feel intro-duced the potential to make a sound. So I gritted my teeth and endured the faint, metallic stench of bird poop in my nostrils and the digging pain of splinters in my thighs.

The pull of the magic felt steady, but not draining, so at least it didn't waver. I would only need to repeat the incantation every ten minutes to keep me hidden for now. The power of this magic was gentle, like a spring breeze, unnoticed until it was gone.

Igor sat. His establishment had been unnaturally short, but Igor had always been candid. A normal delegation leader presented for half an hour. His quick recitation established an odd dynamic for the meeting.

Papa waited for a beat, then motioned to Niko.

Handsome Niko, his thick black hair and brown eyes as captivating as ever. Leadership had placed worried lines around his face that hadn't been there before, and he seemed to have aged ten years in the last three. His slight Eastern Network accent filled the room with long *e*'s and crisp consonants, though his enigmatic personality hid his verbal tension.

"While the Eastern Network regrets the steps that the former High Priest of the Southern Network took to erase magic from the former witches in the South, we cannot—and we will not—support the safety of another Network. It is an impossible request. First on our agenda is this discussion, as well as fishing rights on our Northern borders."

He spoke clearly, firmly, and right at Papa with a challenging gleam in his gaze. Tension tripled through the room. Scarlett sat at Papa's side, her gaze direct and shoulders pulled back. Still, she seemed to contemplate this odd start more deeply than her expression revealed.

After a breathless moment, Niko sat back down with a hostile stare aimed at Igor and then Papa. Papa acknowledged Niko and his equally short presentation with a neutral nod.

Niko was in his early thirties and still a young leader. He'd taken the throne as the war began. With Papa's help, he'd navigated the poorly trained East Guards through the battles to relative success in many cases. Papa didn't agree with Niko's reasoning in most political things lately, but like all the Aldana High Priests before him, Niko trod his own paths.

Igor's nose twitched after Niko's direct rebuttal, but he revealed nothing. Unlike the former High Priest of the South, Mikhail, Igor wasn't as closed-minded of a leader. Mikhail had hated all *vomen,* me included. Igor had established Alina as his Ambassador almost immediately, introducing a woman and a clan witch into a leadership role.

Reputedly, she was also his lover, despite the fact that he had a harem of wives at home. Igor had inherited Mikhail's broad disaster and rallied better than many might have expected.

My gaze drifted to Geralyn, who watched the proceedings with detached interest. Only a fool would miss the calculation in her gaze. If the Northern Network taught their Masters with the Central Network Guardians and Protectors, training would go faster. We could enable more witches to protect the South until the new generation of magic users could rise and provide that protection for themselves. Beholden to our generosity, the Southern Network would guarantee peace with us.

But would Geralyn agree to merge our training?

Geralyn's agreement to train with the Central Network was the "in" Scarlett had been waiting for. It would provide her the chance to start the Sisterhood by allowing Regina or other Masters to help train me.

Or so Scarlett hoped.

Other problems awaited. Former slaves to Mabel, for one. They filled the Western Network and refused to return to the wilds of the South, which created an imbalance in jobs and tension across cultures. Now that borders had fallen, Lana, the ambitious High Priestess of the West, might be tempted to invade the South and increase her power. A mighty Western Network would spell disaster for all Networks.

With the Southern Network under our protection, the West wouldn't be able to take over entirely. Still, Papa sought to tie the second most powerful Network—the North—with us, the most powerful. Despite isolating themselves for years, they had more resources, a broad sweep of population across mountainous regions, and a mostly-stable leadership structure. Such an overarching plan would guarantee the safety of the South . . . for now.

If the North would give way.

Lana cited a long list of grievances to be repaid as her initial agenda. The tension in the room ratcheted higher at every point she named. Baxter's shoulders tightened imperceptibly when Papa stood after Lana took her seat, then spoke for the Central Network. Almost with a bored gaze, Baxter looked up my beam, then away.

I leaned back and a thread on my dress scraped against the wood. I wobbled for a moment. By sheer willpower, I didn't gasp, and the slight *scritch* of snapping fabric went largely unnoticed. Still, I held my breath and waited, heart racing.

No one called me out.

The Esbat progressed. When Igor brought up a grievance to Lana's agenda, I pressed my chin into the wood to wait it out. Time ticked slowly by. Agendas were finalized. Terms like *criminal negligence* and *border protection* and *magical suppression tactics* volleyed back and forth. My thighs and ribs ached. My empty stomach felt sick from lying on it.

Still, I didn't move.

A Guardian strolled through the room, but they were ignored. Their eyes flickered my way, but my magic hadn't changed, nor had my position.

Finally, I heard the words I'd been waiting for.

"Geralyn." Papa gestured to her. "I cede the floor to you."

Geralyn stood and her elegant magenta skirt rustled. She wore a pale teal turban that was more decorated than previous turbans. Glittering pearls of various sizes connected by ribbons of silk wrapped around it and the bright colors filled the room. Regina stood just behind her chair, but not so close that she had to step away when Geralyn pushed her chair back.

For several quiet moments, the air lay burdened with anticipation. Then Geralyn sent Papa a bright smile.

"The Northern Network wishes to return to our previous isolationist state. We are closing down all trade, negotiations, and delegations, effective within one year. This will be our last Celebration with the lower Networks."

Chapter Four

That evening, Scarlett waited for me by her bay window. Firelight brightened her pristine bun and rigid perfectionism. Her shoulders remained back, strong with a confidence I'd never seen falter. She certainly filled the role of High Priestess, even if some considered her too opinionated. The nickname of *Little Mildred* had swirled in Scarlett's wake for the last year or two.

A higher compliment, I couldn't imagine.

Her office windows were tall, gabled, and had thin metallic edging in between each pane. Each window spanned from her knee to several paces over her head. The tops were a warm crimson, lined with mauve, in a design that reminded me of unfurling flower petals. They overlooked a shared balcony that connected with several other Council Members' offices. One of them was open and a cool wind trickled by, soothing my heated cheeks.

After hours in that stuffy Esbat, I'd gladly take an arctic tundra right now. My legs and stomach still ached. Even my ribs hurt. The smell of dust resided in my nose. Geralyn's announcement had happened within the first hour, but I'd spent another two hours lying on that beam before I could exit.

Underneath my shock and disappointment lay a sense of relief. At least I hadn't been caught.

Outside, night had fallen. Stars winked over a dark sky, and a fire brightened Scarlett's room from a hearth on the left. Letum Wood had become little more than a thick band of darkness under half the sky. I could hear the faintest whisper of the trees calling for me. I wondered, not for the first time, how far away I'd have to be before the forest couldn't find me.

You belong to us.

Scarlett turned around, her brow lifted slightly. It was as good a welcome as I could expect. Scarlett had been the first teacher I met at Miss Mabel's School for Girls. She was also my toughest critic, and one of the women I looked to for advice, like an adopted mother.

How Leda ignored this second chance, I would never understand.

Scarlett motioned me closer with a wave of her hand, then peered out on the grounds again. Her dark hair had been pulled away from her face in her usual sharp bun. An expression of intensity followed her around, but she had a way of softening it. Now, she appraised me with that defined, still-lifted eyebrow.

"How are you?" she asked. "It's been a few weeks since we've spoken."

"I'm great."

A hint of a smile appeared on her face. "As ever. You have excelled since you started to train the recruits."

"The recruits keep me busy, and so does Letum Wood. We've left the war behind now. I'm happy about that and where I've landed."

She studied me for several long moments, and in that pause, I thought I saw a flicker of something undefinable. Regret, perhaps? Uncertainty. Scarlett wouldn't miss the implied statement I hadn't said. *I'm happy. Let's not change the status quo with a Sisterhood.*

Scarlett clasped her hands in front of her. "And what did you think of the Esbat?" she asked.

I feigned ignorance. "I'm sorry?"

"Sure," she murmured, "you don't know. You just happened to show up at my office when the Esbat ended, and without me informing you that I was ready."

Too late, I realized my mistake. I'd been so distracted by the fallout of the North's declaration, I hadn't been thinking clearly.

"See?" I muttered. "No way am I ready for a Sisterhood."

Scarlett smiled. "You preempt me, Bianca. But as long as you're talking about that, let's continue the discussion. You have always been loyal to the Network. Contentment aside, I think it will soon be time to act on the Sisterhood."

A pool of something cold slid through my veins.

"But the North just—"

"I know what Geralyn said, and I was not surprised."

"You weren't?"

"They are not the only route we could take, Bianca. One route, to be sure. But I have bigger ideas than mimicking what has already been done."

The protest died in my throat. She pressed her lips together and waited.

My thoughts bumbled around awkwardly. Before becoming High Priest, Papa had been the Head Protector in the Brotherhood of Protectors, an elite, selective regiment of up to fifteen specialized Guardians whose magic, secrecy, and sheer skill kept the Central Network safe. All of them were trained in deep magic, subterfuge, and disappearance.

After Almorran magic had been destroyed, Papa had briefly mentioned me starting a Sisterhood—a female version of the same job. But the bitter desperation of life after the war had settled in, and the idea had been forgotten in lieu of more immediate concerns.

Or maybe I'd gotten rid of the idea.

I'm sorry, came the refrain, unbidden. *I'm sorry I survived and you didn't. I'm sorry you died.*

"I haven't considered it since we last spoke a year ago," I said.

"I didn't ask if you had. I merely mentioned our time to act could be soon approaching. We face new problems, Bianca. New problems require new solutions."

Hesitation stalled my response. "But the North is backing out of the merged training. You can't justify a Sisterhood to the Council without them."

She peered peevishly at me, "Can't I?"

Irrational fear had me by the throat. *What* did I fear?

And why?

Scarlett frowned. "All that Geralyn knows is isolationist tendencies and hiding. With all the issues stemming from the South, the tension in the East, and Derek's demands for each Network's help, no doubt it seemed her safest bet."

"What about the South now?" I asked. "We can't support them on our own. Obviously, the East isn't likely to help."

"Each Network will have to gain control of their witches, for one, and stop them from bullying the vulnerable South."

"Easily said," I replied, grateful to be off the subject of the Sisterhood. "But not so easily done."

She agreed with a gentle dip of her head.

The Southern Network had no reputation for warmth or hospitality. Not even in these desperate circumstances. There was always a possibility that the Central Network could help the South for decades, only for them to turn on us later.

Would Papa take that risk? If he didn't help, that would doom the South to generations of fear, tyranny, and looting. Particularly if Niko didn't get control over his Network.

"Derek is in a tough position," Scarlett allowed carefully.

"Four of the ten Council Members think that our current leadership structure has contributed to our issues. They want to overturn the Highest Witch structure."

"Can they?"

"Only if they prove your father is incompetent as a leader, vote him out of power by a majority vote, and gain a Highest Witch in favor of such a thing. That Highest Witch would have to destroy the Esmelda scrolls that have guided our government and Highest Witch for centuries."

"That would require *you* to support such a thing, Scarlett. If they voted Papa out, you would become the Highest Witch."

"Unless they voted me out after proving my incompetence as well," she said mildly, but I sensed an undercurrent within. This was not news to her, and I suspected Scarlett and Papa had discussed it for some time. If a Council had enough support to get rid of Papa, they could also get rid of Scarlett.

I scowled.

"Four other Council Members support the Highest Witch structure and the remaining two are paralyzed somewhere in between. Right now, your father walks a careful line, because each side of Council Members is voting together and often freezing the vote into inaction. The Council only stalls measures not related to the Guardians, Protectors, or inter-Network relationships of course. Your father still controls those things, and the Council focuses on internal affairs. But still . . . it's a dangerous precedent. They only need to remove trust in your father, prove his incompetence, and he will be gone."

"He'll end up a puppet between them," I said bitterly.

"Your father is many things," she said coldly, "but he has never been a puppet."

"Then he's about to be if something doesn't happen. He needs to remove the Council Members that are plotting to overthrow the Highest Witch structure. It's that easy, Scarlett!"

"Only a tyrant removes those with ideas other than his own.

There's removal, and then there's silencing. As I said, your father walks a thin line."

I sighed and tilted my head back. She had a point. History was replete with Highest Witches who *silenced* their opposition —right into the tyranny of the Network. But there were Highest Witches like Mildred who walked the line with a firmer hand than others. Just thinking about all these angles tired me.

Leda loved this kind of thought process, not me.

Letum Wood called to me again, and I wanted to answer. My rattled emotions needed an escape, and the trails would be an ideal one. Running at night, however, was almost a death wish. Too many close calls littered my past. I'd have to wait until morning.

What I wanted most was to see Papa again, but he'd be waylaid for several more hours, then go straight to bed. The second Esbat and more socializing awaited tomorrow. My tired body still ached from hours on that beam. A quick, hot bath and a good rest would stave off the inevitable soreness.

"You're right," I murmured. "I'm sorry."

She sank into her own chair. An expansive desk separated us, but it was still not as large as the one that Mildred used. Mildred was my grandmother on my father's side, only I hadn't known it until after she died. Still, there were days when it gave me courage knowing her steel-laced blood ran within me.

"To my original point," Scarlett continued, "I anticipate that the troubles our Network could face after this Celebration may warrant a . . . change in tradition."

"By forming a Sisterhood?" My voice pitched high with confusion. "But . . . how? We've had peace. Sure, the Council is a bit hot right now, but you can help them see reason. Everything will be fine."

Scarlett folded her hands in front of her. "If you were Leda and tracked these things, I might trust your response as an opinion and not a denial, but I know you better than that. Tell yourself everything will be fine, Bianca, if you wish. But there is no evidence to prove it."

Heat crept through my face, but I pushed it back. *I might trust your response as an opinion and not a denial?*

Denial about what?

"Today's Esbat made it abundantly clear to me that our Network needs a new kind of help," she continued. "While things on the surface are cordial, there's fire building underneath. Niko is determined that the South will figure their own problems out, and Derek is just as determined that we help them. The West poses a stoic middle man, and the North acts friendly, but they wouldn't back up any Network but themselves. The tentative peace of the last three years has started to fracture. We'll soon fight a new war and need a new plan if things go the wrong way. If we want to stay ahead of the upcoming issues, we need to be ready."

"But—"

She held up a hand to stop my protest, somehow seeming to anticipate what I'd say. "I just want you to consider it, Bianca, so we can be prepared for the inevitable future. I am not asking for a vow. Besides, there was a time when the prospect thrilled you."

Yes, there had been a time when I felt excitement over the Sisterhood. I'd even trained with Regina. But then Merrick had left. Marten asked me to help him with a class of new recruits, and I hadn't stopped. My job gave me purpose. The recruits loved me. With them, I felt like I belonged. Like I *really* served and found my place in the Network. With time, peace had come.

"There's no other witch more qualified to start such a thing than you," she continued, pulling me from my spiraling thoughts. "Believe me. I've looked. I always come back to you, for obvious reasons."

I scoffed. "The Council would never approve of a female Protector. They'll try to prove that it's within their realm and stop it the moment you start."

Her gaze tapered into flinty sparks. "You let me worry about the Council."

"You don't think the Brotherhood can handle what's coming next?"

"Open your eyes a bit, Bianca. The Brotherhood have their place, there's no denying that. But they're too similar and too routine. There's room for expansion outside of the norm. At best, they're predictable. Merely do me the favor of reconsidering?"

"Sure," I said uneasily.

"You're impetuous, like your father, but you've come a long way since the hot-headed sixteen-year-old who showed up late to her first day of school. Let's stay on the path of open eyes and improvement, please? I appreciate your consideration."

Affection tugged at her voice despite the firmness, and I couldn't stop a smile. "Thanks. I'm a constant work in progress."

"As we all are. Now, I have notes to take and things to plan. I will see you at the Central Network dinner tomorrow night, then follow up with you on this regard after the Celebration. You are dismissed."

* * *

The *Chatham Chatterer* sprouted headlines like new seedlings the next day.

The North withdraws.

Fissures form between Networks.

War impending?

The second Esbat would be dedicated to deciding whether the North would earn a participative vote in the Celebration now, and require the North to set out a proposed schedule and tentative plan for withdrawal. In politics, nothing happened quickly. Celebration business would have to proceed as usual.

While Papa dealt with those heightened tensions, I transported to the East. In the meantime, Priscilla's absence from the Celebration had loomed heavily over my mind. Why hadn't she come? Was something wrong? Her only response to two letters had been, *Let's have lunch again.*

I'd eagerly accepted the offer. Escape to the East would give me a chance to mentally prepare for the Central Network dinner in the evening. The extravagant feast required me to smile, speak to witches I'd never talk to again, and try not to take my shoes off.

Waves crashed onto my toes while I gathered my wits after a long transport. The glittering sea stretched out to the end of the horizon, where sunlight glinted like discarded diamonds. Agitated waves, frothy as whipped egg whites, battled with distant ships. A band of humidity lay over the sea.

Priscilla stood on the sand nearby, ankles wet from the racing surf. She wore a cream-colored dress with emerald ribbons laced through the sleeves in a criss crossing pattern. The wind blew her long red hair off her face in whipping strands, like strings of firelight.

"Merry meet, Bianca!" she cried.

The Volare bobbed against my back as I grinned, waved, and headed through the sand. Despite her wide smile, I sensed tension beneath the jauntiness. She threw her arms around me.

"They're watching," she whispered. "Say nothing other than pleasantries until I say."

My stomach tied itself in knots as I returned her embrace. Who were *they*? Why was she being watched?

With her smile still firmly in place, she pulled away. Her hair bobbed around her jawline, frizzy in the humidity. Once-porcelain skin now had charming freckles that softened her expression. The wind flipped past us as she reached for a basket at her feet.

"I brought us a picnic." She gestured to the left, where dark, scraggly rocks formed a cave. "Let's go to the cove back there. It'll be more protected from the wind."

"Great! I'm starving."

"It's ragged today, isn't it?" she called over a gust. She turned around before I could respond.

My mind wandered as I stepped in her sandy, barefoot footprints. Years ago, Priscilla's skill with transformation led her here. Papa sent her to teach East Guards how to use transformation to defend themselves. Niko had fallen head-over-heels for her, so she stayed in the East after the war. For the last two years, she'd lived more as a mistress than a High Priestess.

We didn't speak until we entered the mouth of the little cove of rocks. The howling wind and crashing waves softened dramatically in the bowl-like structure. A blanket leapt out of the basket and spread itself on the ground ahead of us. Priscilla set the basket on top and lowered to her knees, then gestured to me to do the same. The blanket felt like coarse wool under my toes when I stepped onto it.

Her gaze lifted to mine, as serious as I'd ever seen it. "As long as you're touching this blanket, our words will be disguised. I'll explain everything, I just ask that you act casual. Smile, laugh— or pretend to. Give no one a reason to suspect what we're talking about." Her lime-colored eyes blinked at me as she widened her grin. "We're just two friends catching up."

A foreboding feeling crawled over me as I lowered myself down. I nodded and gave a returning smile, but I'd never been as good at this as Priscilla.

"Got it."

Food unpacked itself on the blanket. Thin crackers. Packets of seeds. A flat, round loaf of bread with cheese cut into triangles. Dried herring. All my appetite had fled in the face of her grave concern, but I pretended ravenous interest. Priscilla reached for a piece of bread littered with air pockets and set it on a porcelain plate.

"Thank you for your letters and for coming."

"I've been worried," I admitted, then grabbed the end of a baguette. "When you didn't show up at the Celebration . . ."

The warmth in her smile was genuine. "I couldn't reach out to you while Niko was here, but I figured you would write as soon as I didn't show up. I'm so grateful I was correct."

I made a show of dishing up cheese with a smile, as if she said something funny. My attempt to force a serious question felt slighted and unnatural.

"What's going on, Priscilla?"

She fidgeted with her piece of bread. "It's . . . it's Niko." A moment of uncertainty flitted through her eyes, then disappeared behind a forced smile. "He's . . . I don't know. Stressed, I suppose. Paranoid. I'm not sure which word applies more when they both apply so much."

Cheese crumbled into flakes in my fingertips as I broke it in half. I had a bite, letting the sharp texture melt on my tongue. It might as well have been sand for all I tasted, but it kept up our illusion.

"Paranoid about what?" I asked as I pushed a piece of hair over my shoulder.

She tugged a square, brown cracker out of a pile and studied it before setting it on her plate.

"Everything that has any possible ties to your father."

This wasn't startling news. After the war, Niko had been under enormous pressure. Even though his grandfather, Diego, had never seen such hardships, the witches in the East compared Niko to Diego constantly. Marten and I had a newsbook—the Eastern Network equivalent of our newsscroll—and we watched the headlines. Inheriting an impossible challenge had been hard on Niko.

Papa rose to a position of trust in our Network almost immediately, thanks to the years he spent as a Protector, and that only made Niko's position so much more desperate. He scrambled for approval against an aged Council and witches that still struggled to find their way. Consequently, Niko's resentment against Papa had been palpable for the last year. His hostility to Papa had affected our friendship. Sometimes, I missed him as a friend.

"How long has it been like this?" I asked.

"A few months at least. Just yesterday," Priscilla continued quietly, "I found out that Niko ordered all witches from the Central Network to be quietly gathered together. If they don't return to the Central Network under an escort, they're to be kept on an isolated island off the east bank until . . . I don't know when."

"Only Central Network witches?" I asked in a poor effort to hide a surge of shock. Such an action was nearly an act of war in the new post-war climate.

"Just them."

She laughed and looked out at the ocean, but there was no levity. Just a wild edge, close to hysteria. My eyes darted around. Who watched, and why? To keep up the charade, I attempted a smile, but I had a dark, sinking feeling in my stomach.

"Even you?"

A silver kettle manifested, then tipped toward a cup that appeared seconds before hot tea dropped into it. The tea steamed lightly. Priscilla accepted it, lost in thought as she sipped. Another cup floated to me. Tea cookies formed a petaled mosaic on a porcelain plate of the lightest pink. They were crumbly, delicate cookies made from the molasses that Eastern witches loved.

"Yes," she finally murmured. "Even me, to some extent. A . . . *friend* . . . told me about the underground Central Network witch edict. That's when Niko told me he didn't want me to attend the Celebration. Later that night, I also found out about a handful of women that Niko had ordered to follow me. They report back to him."

I couldn't help my gasp of outrage.

"You?"

She nodded.

"But why?"

"I believe that he's . . . he's started to think that I'm some sort of traitor. That the last three years has been nothing but an attempt for me to gain information for Derek, or something. He's suspicious of everything now."

"That's outrageous."

She smirked with genuine annoyance. "I think so too, but he doesn't."

"There must be something that has caused this."

She shrugged.

For several moments, we nibbled food, sipped tea, and sank into our thoughts. The implications of Niko rounding up Central Network witches and sending them out of his borders were a precursor to something ugly.

Did Papa know? Niko may have waited until now to execute such a command when Papa would be so distracted by the Celebration that it might go unnoticed. But had it? The Protectors provided subtle eyes and ears everywhere. More likely than not, Papa already knew.

Priscilla broke my thoughts apart with another comment. "He's put off our betrothal announcement again."

I scoffed. "For the tenth time, is it?"

Her shoulders arched back. She stretched two arms over her head in an easy, casual stretch. To keep up with the facade of a friendly lunch together, I reached for another wedge of cheese. Meanwhile, my mind spun.

"Do you still want to handfast him?" I asked. "Do we need to get you out of here while he's distracted and gone?"

Priscilla's eyes closed with a fleeting, pained expression.

"I'm not sure, to be honest."

Niko had quietly proposed to Priscilla two years ago. *We*

must wait before we announce it, he had said after she accepted, then told me later with a broken heart. *This will break hundreds of years of tradition. The time must be exactly right.*

No matter how much the Eastern Network witches loved her, she couldn't change the fact that she came from the Central Network. The Eastern Network High Priest, for several hundreds of years, had always taken their High Priestess from amongst the poorest of the Eastern Network witches, but Priscilla had been raised in a wealthy home. This tradition was an intentional mimicry meant to repeat a fantastic history of a High Priestess who had once risen from the dredges of society to create peace again. Such a tale actively worked against Priscilla, who was neither.

Didn't matter that Niko and the witches deeply loved her or that she'd forsaken everything—her family, her home Network, and her life—to live in his quarters of Magnolia castle for the last two years.

Niko had always loved her in a subdued, but fierce, way. They'd come together at a frightening time. He'd needed someone to give him hope, and she needed a new life away from her parents. Now, real life challenged and tested them. On some level, perhaps it found them—or him—wanting.

Is that what happened to me and Merrick? came the question.

I banished it.

In the end, I didn't know what to say. Grief brimmed Priscilla's eyes. Niko's actions must feel like a betrayal of the worst kind to her. She'd have to release more than the witch she loved to get out of this, but also the witches she served and her new, independent life away from selfish parents.

"I'm sorry, Priscilla."

She traced the edge of her teacup with the tip of her finger. A wisp of wind stirred her hair with a sigh.

"I'm beginning to see what you've told me for the last several months. Niko is never going to announce our betrothal. I've been holding onto a lie. We're not going to handfast. Maybe we never were, and *he's* the one using me as a spy. Now, our fate seems inevitable. I love him. I'm sure that I always will, but there was a limited time for my patience and it has passed. He's standing against all wisdom in his frustration with the Southern and Central Networks, and I don't know him anymore. It's time for me to leave while I still can. I'll . . . sneak away, I think. Get settled before he returns, maybe? Also, I'm pregnant."

A sip of tea nearly choked me. I sputtered and coughed for several moments before I found my breath again.

"What?"

Her expression didn't waver, but she'd lost any form of playfulness. When she looked at me, I saw only sadness. Turmoil.

"I haven't told him."

"Is *that* why you didn't attend the Celebration?" I cried.

"No." Her brow furrowed. "He wouldn't allow me to leave. I think he's worried I'll have too much opportunity to betray him. Not that I ever would, but I believe it's what's on his mind. The baby is why I desperately wanted you to come. I needed to tell someone. To tell a friend. To tell *you*."

Her eyes, so like the tempestuous ocean right then, slammed right into me. She reached across the blanket and gripped my wrist with a cold hand. The ferocity in her tight lips caught my breath.

"*You* who have always been able to take care of yourself and those you love. Who won't judge me when I leave Niko without telling him about the baby. You who . . . who understand how hard it is to be a woman. An outsider. A . . . witch whose life is at the whim of others. There is no one more fierce in her protection of her friends than you, and I need you, Bianca."

"Priscilla—"

"Listen, please? A child would break Niko. He's under pressure from the Council, from me, from Derek, from Igor. A child from *my* womb would force him to make a decision I don't want him to make."

My comprehension moved faster than my words, and it took me several seconds to articulate her supposition. "Would he harm you?"

"Or worse."

"You think he'd kill you?" I asked.

She chose her next words carefully. "I think he'd do whatever he had to do to preserve a very fragile Network. We cannot stop our witches from attacking and raiding the South because our Guardian force is drawn too thin. *That* is what Niko will never tell you. No matter what image Niko tries to give, the East hasn't recovered from the war. Witches are hungry. Fishing has been poor, which is why he's challenging fishing rights against the North. We are years behind the Central Network in terms of recovery. No matter how hard he tries, Niko is no Derek."

A thousand sorrows rushed through me. The Eastern Network and I had a tempestuous past filled with flaming arrows and a wily High Priestess who had wanted to murder me, among other things. But the witches were good and didn't deserve such trials.

Did anyone?

"The pregnancy is recent, I think," she continued, her voice like cracking glass now. "I will have the child in the late winter or early spring, so there is only a little time for me to decide whether I'll tell him or not."

"Will you tell your parents?"

"Eventually." Her hand dropped to her stomach but she kept her gaze on the ocean. Without looking, she grabbed some food from her plate and proceeded to tear it into pieces. "Once I've established my new life. For a few years, I want to disappear."

Shock still had me in a tight-fisted grip, but I worked out of it to comprehend that she needed a contingency plan. My protection wasn't as strong as she believed—plenty of others had died before I could save them. Mama. Grandmother. Camille. Their ghosts still called to me, and I tried to soothe them with my rhythmic, atoning chant. *I'm sorry. I'm sorry I survived and you didn't.*

Despite my inability to save her, I would willingly give her whatever protection she needed. Even if it was false. Her fingers felt like ice when I covered her hand with mine.

"You and your child always have me, Priscilla. Whatever I can do, I will."

Tears filled her eyes. She nodded, too overcome to speak at first. "Thank you," she finally whispered. "That is the greatest comfort right now."

"Do you need help getting away? We'll transport now to Letum Wood. You can disappear."

"No, there is one thing here I must do. One witch I need to say goodbye to. I can get away myself, I just needed a place to escape. And I will leave soon. I will come to your cottage, if that's all right? Maybe tomorrow evening? I'm not sure when it will be."

"Anytime."

"You—"

She paused, head canted to the side as she looked beyond me with a furrowed brow. I followed her gaze to the beach, where a rumpled something had appeared on the sand.

"Is that a witch?" she asked, straightening.

I stood. From here, the dark spot against the sand was little more than a lump. A hand appeared. A witch, for sure. They rolled onto their back and didn't move again. The water foamed around the body as the ocean rushed around it, then faded back.

"Looks like it."

"Impossible." She frowned. "This beach is protected. They would have to be from one of the Navy ships. But that is no uniform and stowaways are killed on sight."

She crossed the cave and headed onto the sand. The wind whipped past her. I followed, propelled by the shock in her voice, until we came up to the body. A dark skirt with slender legs appeared next. Definitely a witch. A young girl, with small shoulders and delicate ankles.

Priscilla stopped a few paces away, but I stepped up to the girl. Hair the color of autumn leaves—umber mixed with gentle hints of black and red—plastered her face. She had at least three different colors of hair faded together. Braids the size of my little finger extended from above both ears and back, where they gathered in a knot behind her head. Her single-layer dress, tattered and full of holes, reached to her knees where angry, crimson scars marred her legs. The dress was more of a robe, it appeared, with sheer sleeves from the shoulder to the wrist.

I pulled her free of the welling ocean water. She sputtered, but she didn't wake up. Once I dragged her out of the surf, I crouched at her side.

"Are you all right?"

The girl mumbled something incomprehensible, her voice low. Gently, I shook her shoulder.

"Merry meet?"

Nothing.

I gestured to the strange dress and asked Priscilla, "One of yours?"

Priscilla stepped closer. "Not from any known parts of the Eastern Network, I'd wager. Her hair looks like it has three different colors in it, and I don't recognize her or the outfit. Odd, isn't she?" Priscilla murmured. "She's almost familiar . . ."

Priscilla's thought trailed away, and my heart went with it, like the tide had taken it away. Familiar, yes. Darker skin aside, the girl looked so much like Camille it made my chest ache.

"Do you have an apothecary that could come here?" I asked. "She can't be more than ten. I think she might be—"

With a gasp, the girl's eyes burst open.

Water bubbled out of her lips as she coughed it free. Terror filled her eyes. Priscilla let out a little cry and leaped back. The girl reached up, grabbed the front of my dress, and said something I couldn't understand. Her words clattered together, unfamiliar and sharp. Then her eyes rolled back in her head and she slumped to the sand. Dread started welling at the bottom of my stomach, and then it burst inside me with a cry of alarm.

Her eyes were the color of pure gold.

Mortal eyes.

Chapter Five

"Bianca, no."

With a spell, I levitated the girl's body back to the cave and set her gently on the blanket. She lay there, pale and half-drowned. Priscilla stalked up next to me until we both stood once again on the rough fabric. Priscilla challenged me with a stern glare.

"This . . . *girl* . . cannot stay here. Bring her back to the beach and leave her."

My heart squeezed at the thought. Leave her on the beach? If this beach was truly protected, someone would have seen the girl arrive. Niko's cronies would likely be here any minute. They'd take her away and what? Torture her? Kill her? If he was already so paranoid, it would be nothing pleasant, that was for sure. My mind thought of Camille so many years ago when I'd first met her at Miss Mabel's. Bright, happy, carefree Camille.

So like this girl.

"No," I said firmly. "I will not leave her."

"She's a *mortal*," Priscilla hissed. Her eyes darted around, searching for witches that we'd never see. "This is . . . we cannot . . . I mean . . ."

"I won't abandon her."

Priscilla closed her eyes, jaw clenched. "This is a fluke. She can't be a mortal. They haven't been seen for thousands of years. Maybe she just has a different eye color."

"Her hair is three colors. That's odd, too."

She pinched the bridge of her nose between her fingers. "This isn't happening. Not now, of all times."

"Calm down, Priscilla. Just . . . let me think through this before we make any false assumptions."

"False assumptions?" Priscilla cried. "You saw her eyes!"

Despite my bravado, the word *mortal* struck a dark, terrified place deep inside me. It felt dirty and foreign. Mortals were long gone. Thousands of years gone. Banished. Dead, for all we knew, on some gods-forsaken place on the other side of the world. If history made one thing clear to all witches, it was one giant truth: Mortals changed witch magic.

They made our magic volatile and unpredictable. Some stories even said that mortals removed magic just when a witch stood in their presence. The fear of such an event, particularly in light of the Southern Network's great loss, felt bigger now. Even if such a rumor didn't make sense, it didn't matter. The fear seized me all the same.

"We don't know who or what she is for certain." My voice remained surprisingly calm despite my quivering heart. If this girl *was* a mortal, the implications were outstanding. Catastrophic at best.

Almost 2,000 years had passed since the mortals boarded countless ships and headed onto the waves, banished by the High Priestess Esmelda. They departed Alkarra with no plan to return and we had nothing to do with them. In that amount of time, not a single mortal had surfaced. None reported, anyway. They'd been all but forgotten. We erased them from history as the future unfurled, as if we were ashamed that mortals should be so much like us, but not quite enough.

Mortals, reputedly, differed from witches in only two ways: their absolute lack of magic and their eye color. Every mortal had the exact same eye color, an inherited legacy from tainted bloodlines.

Amber.

Liquid gold.

Honey.

My throat thickened at the thought. There was no mistaking her eye color, nor the panic in her expression before she collapsed. A parade of questions raced around my head. Who was she? Where did she come from? How did she get here? She couldn't have swum all that way.

Why was she here?

Priscilla paced back and forth on the blanket, muttering under her breath. Even if whoever it was that spied on her couldn't hear us, they'd see her agitation now. "This is a disaster," she muttered. "A total disaster. Niko has spies watching me all the time. They would have seen her as well. He's going to panic."

"They wouldn't have seen her eye color."

Priscilla paused to consider that while I studied the girl. She hadn't stirred since I brought her out of the waves. Would she even survive? Would she want to? The moment word spread that a mortal had appeared in the East, witches would be out for blood. This spindly, half-dead girl didn't stand a chance.

"Maybe she's from a tribe in the West." Priscilla's tone was as wild as ever now. "Her skin is that light brown color, like Baxter. Didn't he come from the West? Maybe she was on a boat for some reason and ended up here."

I cast her a long-suffering glance.

She scowled. "All right, it's not likely. The East hasn't allowed any other boats in our waters for the past year. The South?"

"No."

"But . . . no, you're right. Doesn't explain the eye color. Fine." Priscilla chewed on her nail and studied the girl the way one might a particularly large slug. "There has to be some explanation."

I leaned back on my heels. "The question is whether we'll find it out. She may die before we hear it."

The mortal girl's chest moved, but that was the only indication of life. There was still a chance she wouldn't make it after her time on the water. No boat or driftwood lingered on or near the shore in explanation, either. So how had she survived the ocean? I wracked my brain for a spell that might help this girl, but my thoughts remained stalled on the word *mortal.*

I didn't *feel* any different.

Just to test it, I stirred up some sand with a spell, then transported it to a different spot. Worked just fine.

So who was she? If she was mortal, were those just historical rumors about mortals' effect on magic?

Priscilla collapsed to her knees and pointedly looked away from the girl. "What am I going to tell Niko?" she asked in a stark voice.

"That you found a witch who needed help and . . ."

My thoughts trailed away with my voice.

And what?

What were we going to do now?

"Nothing," I finally said. "Because you'll be safe at my house before he returns."

Relief bloomed on her face like an unfurling flower. I couldn't blame Priscilla's wariness. Any amount of things may have changed for the mortals between the time when they had been banished and now. Maybe they had found magic. Maybe they were as powerful as witches. Maybe they were still just . . . mortal.

Or maybe they wanted Alkarra back.

"She is quite young," Priscilla said quietly. "What, ten? Eleven?"

"Not much older."

"I wonder who sent her here?"

"If anyone sent her at all. There's no way of knowing until she wakes up."

My mind filtered back to the unknown language she spoke with another feeling of dread. How would we speak with her if she were mortal? Another stretch of silence passed. Resolve filled Priscilla's face when she turned to me.

"Niko will kill her the moment he finds out," she said grimly. "The Eastern Council would too, just as yours might."

Papa wouldn't kill this girl for being a mortal, but the Council might. Even those undecided to either side of the split members would want to get rid of her once they got more information. It might be the only thing that united them, and a united Council that opposed Papa could still win if they had such a sweeping majority.

I frowned.

Whoever this girl was, she didn't deserve death. Not yet. For her to die now would be worse. We had to know why she was here and how she got here. What if more were coming?

"Would Niko give her a chance to explain herself?" I asked.

Priscilla thought about it, then said, "Yes, but it wouldn't be pleasant or even humane, I fear. Get her out of here, Bianca. I have no power to save her from Niko's wrath." Quietly she added, "I'm barely able to save myself."

The longer I stared at the girl, the less I could accept her demise. Her hair, dark as a chestnut layered with burgundy, was wound in wild curls like Camille's. The lines of her face were soft and a bit gaunt, as if she'd been hungry for too long. She had thick eyelashes and a youthful appearance. Whether it was the inherent danger the girl now faced, or the living memory of Camille bright in my mind, I wasn't sure.

The decision rushed out of me all at once.

"I'll take her."

Priscilla opened her mouth, then closed it again. Her relief was palpable. "What are you going to do with her?"

"Take her to my cottage. She'll be safe there. For now."

"But it's the Central Network dinner tonight."

"I'll miss it," I said.

"Then what?"

My stomach clenched at the thought of not showing up. Papa would be worried. My absence wouldn't go unnoticed, but no one would suspect that I'd stumbled onto a mortal girl and hidden her in the forest, would they?

"I don't know yet. Try to talk to her. Confirm our suspicion. This may be just a misunderstanding."

"Yes," Priscilla murmured. "That's a good plan. A much better plan."

"Can you handle escaping?" I asked as I tugged the girl into a sitting position.

Priscilla nodded. "Yes."

"Then good luck." My gaze dropped momentarily to her stomach, then back. "I'll see you tomorrow night. Let me know if you need anything else. I'm always here for you. Both of you."

* * *

My heart almost burst when the transportation spell to home ended.

Transporting long distances required more magic, skill, and energy. The ability to bring someone else that far was a gratifying skill to have, but inherently dangerous. Had I not been so caught up in the moment, I might have considered the lacking wisdom of taking an alleged mortal girl into a transportation spell, but Priscilla's panic had rubbed off on me.

As I lay in a heap of gasping breath on my floor, I realized just how stupid that had been. It may not have worked on a mortal. I could have killed her. Or her very presence could have made my magic unpredictable, as all mortals did to witches, and killed both of us mid-transport. Transportation had killed plenty of witches in the past.

The girl groaned in a reassuring sign of life as I dragged her to my hearth and commanded a fire spell. Exhausted from transporting, only a weak flame sprouted. Still, the darkening world now had a breath of light. I could build from that.

Outside, Letum Wood started the gradual fall into early shadows. The canopy was so thick that the sun slipped away sooner than outside the forest. My heart twirled when I remembered that the Central Network dinner would start soon.

"Jikes," I muttered and scratched a quick message to send to Baxter with a spell.

Can't make it. Everything is fine. Talk later.

B

The hastily folded paper made a *pop* when I transported it to him. I pitched more dry kindling onto the tepid flame. It blazed, illuminating the girl's face and chest. Water spread across the floor beneath her, but she didn't appear to be cold.

I collapsed to the floor until my heart slowed.

Slowly, the fire resurrected as I fed it more magic. Warmth filled the room again. I left the girl on the floor while I lit a candle with a simple spell, drew the curtains closed, and turned to face her.

Further study revealed a gentle, sloping nose, full face, twiggy body, and broad cheeks. For a mortal, she seemed innocuous enough, but she reminded me too much of Camille to be comfortable with her.

Now that I had her here, how was *I* going to talk to her? A mortal wouldn't speak our language. Before their banishment, mortals had spoken the Declan language. Could it still be in use? Perhaps this girl spoke a root of it. Enough that I'd have some familiarity, I hoped.

First, I needed to make sure she woke up. Her death would be the worst possible outcome. Not only would I have something to answer for, but there would also be remaining unknowns. Dangerous questions.

How had she made her way back to Alkarra?

Why had she come?

Were more on their way?

After I made sure she'd survive, I'd . . . well, I'd figure out the next step after she woke up. I knew enough Declan that I'd be able to get a sense of whether we spoke the same language.

Having a plan made me feel marginally better, but I still sent trepidatious looks her way. She seemed to be nothing more than a girl, and a young one at that. If I hadn't seen her eyes, I would have disregarded her. Yet, this girl held the potential for a thousand more deaths from war because of her not-so-innocent bloodline, which only made this situation all the more gut-wrenching.

A flicker of color caught my eye near her waist. Carefully, I leaned over her. Nestled in between the folds of her dress was a long chain. The metal was a dark, slate gray, nothing like the gold and silver mined in the South. The end of the chain was so long that, if she were to stand, it would reach past her waist.

The tips of my fingers ran down the cord until it stopped, pulled tautly. A hint of color peeked out from within her dress. With one careful glance at her still-sleeping face, I carefully tugged.

A gem plunked to the floor, the color of moving firelight. It was bigger than my fist, multi-faceted across the front and back, and visible all the way through. A strange, likely rare, mixed burnt orange and red color moved throughout. Unlike the gems of the South, this one glowed, as if it held light within. Tones of yellow mixed with the crimson overtone every few seconds, as if someone had stuffed a flame inside. Around it, the air felt charged, as if it brought something sinister with it.

Something . . . old.

Was it magical? If so, it wasn't magic I had encountered before. Mortals didn't have magical abilities like witches, but perhaps they'd harnessed it somehow. Whatever it was, I wanted nothing to do with such an eerie thing.

As I reached to tuck it back into her dress, my thumb swept the outer edge. A ripple of shock moved through my body like a bolt of lightning.

I gasped.

The gem threw me back, like someone had shoved me right in the stomach. My spine slammed into the wall. I dropped to the ground, the breath knocked out of me. Heat flared in my body, as if flames had entered my bloodstream. I let out a cry, but it was drowned in the sound of a crackling fire.

The heat slid through my bones and into the ground, consuming me. The earth trembled. Even the forest screamed, distant in my ears. Darkness bound my eyes, sat on my chest, then engulfed my soul with its bright, hot, mesmerizing flame.

Pinned to the ground now, I felt as if I'd been crushed by the weight of something massive.

Moments before darkness swallowed me, a whisper slipped through my mind. A crackling voice, like a curl of flame, followed.

You are not welcome here, witch.

* * *

When I woke up, a splitting headache threatened to cleave my brain in half.

Cohesive thought returned gradually to the pool of

charred darkness in my mind. My entire body ached all the way to my bones. My throat had become dry, leaving an ashy taste behind, as if I'd swallowed fire. My arms and legs felt stiff, like I'd been running for days. A pained groan reverberated through my ears, and I realized moments later that it was me.

What happened?

This wasn't the first time I'd awoken without recent memory. In training, Marten might deliver a blow that knocked me unconscious or I would accidentally transport right into a tree while running. One time I'd tripped over a root, hit a rock, and woken up hours later with saplings bent protectively over me.

Only this felt different.

Chilly air pressed on my skin. My body felt damp, as if I'd broken out in a cold sweat. I lay in absolute silence. Such quiet. Such . . . dullness. The dark ceiling of my cottage loomed overhead. Flickering light came from the hearth, but it gave off no warmth.

How many hours had passed?

With a moan, I sat up. My head banged in a painful, uneven staccato. Normally after I hurt myself, the trees went into a fit of concern. Tonight they were oddly quiet. A few blinks later, my eyes fell on a girl.

She blinked at me.

A mortal girl.

The last day came rushing back all at once. Priscilla. Mortal. Amulet.

Fire.

With a shout, I shot to my feet. My head banged into the edge of the table and I shouted again. Pain rippled through my sensitive skull and all the way into my teeth. I collapsed back to the floor and reached back to rub away the sore spot.

"The good gods," I muttered.

The girl remained frozen in place, eyes wide as saucers. With a growl, I sent a spell to build up the fire.

Nothing happened.

Impatient for warmth, I sent the spell again. The fire remained as still as before. The girl had clearly built it up herself, because more logs and twigs lay on it in a triangular pattern I would never use. My cottony mouth still tasted ash, but I ignored that for now. The fire spell was second nature. I hardly needed to even use the incantation anymore.

So why didn't it work?

I must have hit my head harder than I thought. After I forced my wild heart to calm, I tried the spell again.

Nothing happened.

My fingers trembled as I stared at the thumb that had touched the gem. Heat built inside it in an ebb and flow. The tip had a blush of red skin. A faint stripe of smoke drifted off, though no burns or blisters remained. Only a faint mark, like a brush of charcoal over the top of my skin. When I wiped at it, it remained.

My body felt different. Strangely empty. Like a void opened inside of me. As if something had been wrenched away, like my soul. Tendrils of my life taken violently away by that consuming fire.

No, not a void. The trees. That's what was missing. Where were their constant voices? They were never silent when I hurt myself. In fact, their childlike concern often annoyed me.

Panicked, I shoved off the ground and threw open the door. A dizzy whirl overcame my head and my legs gave out. I dropped to my knees, dug my fingers into the dirt, and waited to hear the welcoming song of the forest.

No calling voices.

No reassuring whispers.

"Where are you?" I shouted. My words slurred, blurred by a darkness creeping from the edge of my mind. Distant nighttime sounds filtered through my ears. The warm reassurance of my trees had disappeared.

Gone.

And so, I realized, was my magic.

With a cry, I spun around and crawled inside. My weakened body failed halfway across the floor. The girl pressed herself against the wall near the hearth, knobby knees pulled into her chest. She tracked my every movement with her wary eyes. The strange chain hung around her neck, but the gem was hidden.

The picture of her terrified expression swam before my eyes as I struggled to find my quill. A letter. I had to write something . . . had to . . .

Only a shell of my mind remained now. That remnant had only the power to comprehend that my greatest nightmare had just come to pass.

I had lost my magic.

Blackness threatened to sweep me back under. The mortal girl squeaked something. I turned my head to look at her, groggy with fear and fatigue. She clutched the gem in her hand and stared at it in wide-eyed horror, then looked at me. The mesmerizing, coal-like face of the amulet had turned black as pitch. A fissure shot through the middle of the gem, breaking it in half like cloven coal.

My mind swam, too burned to think.

"What have you done?" I whispered.

The darkness overcame me again.

Chapter Six

Hours later, morning hinted in between trees.

I stood at my window and stared out, willing the forest to speak to me. A word. A cry. A revolt. Anything. Nothing but the infernal silence filled my mind, insidious in its grasp. In its place came my darkest thoughts.

My magic is gone.

My magic is gone.

The mortal girl hadn't touched me while I had passed out a second time, from what I could surmise, but she had moved. A small sword was missing from my wall, and crumbs littered the ground in front of her. Although a supposed enemy of mine held one of my weapons, I felt nothing but numbness.

Most of the night had passed while I lay unconscious. I had awoken to feel only marginally less like death. The headache lessened its vise-like grip. My body ached, but it functioned. Now I could only comprehend the new, ugly reality.

My magic is gone.

The air felt different now. My body felt different. My mind felt different. Did the magic infuse us in ways we didn't know? I'd never been without it before, so it was impossible to be certain. Is this what witches in the Southern Network felt like three years ago when Mikhail broke the Mansfeld Pact and they lost their power?

Was there any *getting used* to a terror like this?

With a shake of my head, I pushed my focus onto the next step. If I wanted the magic back, I had to do something other than focus on the truth.

My mind was a bog as I paced. Shakiness worked out of my legs with the movement and I felt less caged. My thoughts stilled enough for control to squeak by. First, I had to find someone I trusted.

Then, I had to find my magic again.

Magic to keep me and the mortal girl safe while we unraveled this disaster. She'd brought that evil gem into my world, but I still couldn't fault her for it. I'd been the idiot that touched it. There was an inherent innocence in her expression that prevented my rage from forming fully on her, but I couldn't deny her guilt.

The girl watched, her face peaked, as minutes passed. Every now and then, her eyes darted over to the cupboard and back to me. Still hungry, I'd bet. There wasn't much to eat there. With a new recruit class, I ate at the castle.

Finally, I stopped pacing. Frightening her wouldn't change anything. Nor had the plan really changed.

I had to talk to her now more than ever.

When I stopped a few steps away, she flinched and leaned back. Her gaze met mine, and I saw a hint of defiance hidden in the depths of her stare. I crouched down, hands held in front of me. We stared at each other.

If the fear in her eyes meant anything, I probably looked wild.

The temptation to take her back to Priscilla overcame me, but it was another foolish thought. How would I do that? I couldn't transport. Regretting my impetuous decision wouldn't help the situation either. The decision had been made. The only path forward was one with me *and* the mortal girl.

Besides, she had to be as afraid as me.

I pressed a hand to my chest, where my heart beat like an intrepid thing, and said, "Bianca."

Her twisted expression softened. She mimicked my gesture and said, "Ava."

"Ava?"

She nodded.

I pointed to the chain. She reached for it, fingering it uncertainly. When I made a motion to tug it up, she obeyed. The long cord eventually gave way to the black amulet, which looked like a captured fire that had burned away. In the back of my mind came a *pop*, like heated sap in a piece of wood. Fire rushed through me again, and a darkness gave way in my mind, then faded with a livid hiss. I grimaced and backed away.

She closed her fingers over the amulet.

"What is it?" I asked.

Her head tilted to the side in silent question—she didn't understand me. Of course. A frisson of frustration moved through me. This wouldn't be simple and we didn't have time for language barriers! I needed to know what she'd brought into Letum Wood right now and whether or not I could get my magic back.

With a breath, I schooled my annoyance. First, I pointed to her eyes and then her whole body.

"Mortal," I said.

Her face scrunched. I searched for the word in Declan, not at all sure I had it right, and pointed to her again as I said, "Mordares."

Her expression darkened. She pointed to me with a scowl. "Wizales."

The Declan word for witch was *wichares*. Wizales could be a derivative of it, if it meant what I thought. Or it could be something else entirely. The terror in her tone told me more than the words. But this was a waste of time. I certainly wasn't the witch that could speak to her. In the space of a night, I'd stumbled on a mortal girl, brought her home, and then lost my magic.

Time for Marten.

But how to get to him?

Chatham Castle was at least a full days walk away through Letum Wood. Without magic, that kind of a trek was a death wish. Any village would be just as bad. They might recognize something different in me, and they'd see her golden eyes. Questions, then fear, would follow. They'd likely kill both of us before answers could be obtained.

Neither could I leave her here alone. What if someone stumbled by?

What if she left?

In a moment of inspiration, I reached for the Volare. The rug slipped out of its sheath and fell inert on the floor. The magic that imbued it seemed to be gone . . . but how could that be? The magic wasn't mine—it existed without me. Wasn't the magic in *me* gone? So was it just another rug now?

My heart crinkled, as if I'd lost an old friend. Maybe the Volare would go to another owner now. Unless they were bequeathed, the magical rugs chose their owners. I flexed my hands, agitated at the thought. The Volare was like my closest friend. Perhaps the fact that it *hadn't* disappeared meant something. Maybe I still had my magic. It could be paralyzed.

Ava stared at the Volare and then at me with unmasked curiosity. No doubt she wondered why I looked so broken-hearted over a rug.

The implications of the lost magic continued to unfold with frightening clarity. There was no way to send Papa or Marten a message. Shouting into the expanse of Letum Wood was wasted breath. No one lived here. No, there was only one thing left to do: Ava and I had to venture into Letum Wood and *find* help.

Why would a young girl like her come to the land of witches anyway? She may have just destroyed the rest of my life. Had something terrible driven her here with some sort of amulet?

Or was *she* that terrible something?

The frightened look in her eyes caused a memory to flash through my mind.

"Shield up," Papa called.

Defensive magic built in my hands and body like heat, even though I was only eight years old. Papa paced in front of me, analyzing the position my shield took. Too high, this time. Should have been a bit lower. I couldn't move it now, because uncertainty revealed a lack of confidence.

Papa crouched next to me, his expression serious, but sturdy.

"Even in a magical fight, your shield could save your life. You may have to fight witches far beyond your ability, B, if we are to save you before the Inheritance curse kills you. This isn't your fault, but it is your responsibility. I'm sorry you have to bear it."

With a blink, I jerked out of it.

Ava looked just like me at that age. Ferocious, mixed with determination and a healthy amount of fear. It was the look of a girl that fought for her own life. A girl that had no other path.

Still, she'd brought that evil upon me. Like it or not—and I definitely didn't—we were tied together now because I couldn't get my magic back without some answers. I didn't want to see her again, but I had to.

Once I stepped out that door, everything in my life would officially change. My magic might be gone, which meant there would be no living alone in Letum Wood, no running the trails by myself. Papa would lock me in the castle until after the Celebration, and maybe forever.

From this point on, I had to help this girl if I wanted to help myself. If both of us were to survive, we'd have to move forward together.

With a trembling hand, I reached for her.

Ava hesitated. She stared at my hand and then at me. Something must have convinced her I wouldn't harm her because she slowly set her hand in mine.

I tugged her to her feet and pointed outside.

"Foretaire."

Her expression darkened, but she swallowed hard and nodded. Unlikely that my word conveyed my meaning, but she seemed to understand grim resolve. Her clothes were wrinkled and appeared dry, but I pulled a cape off the wall and handed it to her anyway. Ava peered at it, then twirled the cape onto her shoulders with a nod. She seemed to understand fully when I strapped a knife to my arm, Mama's sword to my back, returned the Volare to its case, and tossed it over my left shoulder out of sheer habit.

I turned to face the forest with a hearty sense of terror. There was one place left to go within walking distance. Help awaited in the very wood that threatened us.

In all likelihood, we'd die before we arrived.

Chapter Seven

After the war, caring for Letum Wood had fallen to me. I'd ventured farther into its depths than most ever dreamed possible or even safe. Letum Wood made me uneasy, even when I had magic.

Now, it downright terrified me.

On my adventures, new creatures arose often enough to unnerve me. Mostly-harmless gnomes for one. They chattered from the ground, the trees, the vines. When they sensed an enemy through their exceptional hearing, they dispersed in thick swarms, armed with tiny knives and spears. Most of the time, they sent a spell of mustard-like gas that clung to clothes and hair for days. The noxious fumes turned most creatures away, but if that didn't work, they'd jump and fight together. Though rarely larger than my forearm, when they attacked en masse, they were a foe to be reckoned with.

The hideous, secretive beluas were the most annoying. Monstrous, eyeless creatures that lived in the trees and never touched the ground. Their mottled skin was a blue-gray, and their purple spit burned through rock. They kept the forest lions under control, though, and tended to stay out of my way. Like forest lions, I rarely saw them.

Trolls hunted every now and then from where they hid in the northern mountains, but I had only seen signs. Forest dragons, of course, were the most dangerous creatures in Letum Wood. My magical power drew them closer even as they hated me for it, but I wasn't sure what would happen now. Curious creatures, but they had never been fond of me.

It was the presence of the trees that usually negated most of these dangers. They whispered warning, comfort, direction. Guided me away from dangers that lurked unseen, like strickenine moss or open spots of the forest where magic didn't work or the occasional fairy pack with a particular vengeance against witches.

Now all of those dangers separated Ava and me from safety . . . and the trees were silent.

With any luck, they'd still be protective.

Ava trotted dutifully behind me, eyes darting here and there. Mama's old sword was too light to be as useful as Viveet, but it gave me comfort when I gripped it. A good parry by a thicker, firmer weapon would shatter it, but it would stop an oncoming attack. With the right use of force, it could harm someone before they harmed us.

Letum Wood without magic in me felt far darker, far more formidable. The presence of falling gnome chatter soothed me, however. In the silence, Letum Wood became nefarious. I steeled myself to keep moving.

Two hours later, I grabbed a leaf and twirled it by the stem in front of Ava's attentive gaze. Her breath came fast despite an easy pace, as if the forest burdened her.

"Leaf," I said.

I rubbed it between my fingers and handed it to Ava. She regarded the green triangle in her hand with a sober gaze then said, "Tapa."

"Tapa?"

"Tapa."

The Declan word for leaf was *stana*, but that could refer to a peppermint leaf for a potion I'd used in the past and not *all* leaves. *Tapa* could be a specific term or a broad one. Or she may not speak anything like Declan. The game filled the time, however, and kept her from wielding that little sword she'd taken from me. For now, I let her have it.

We might need it.

We continued through Letum Wood, using our language game to break the tension. A tribe of burrowing gnomes followed us as we slipped through their territory, shrill voices shouting incomprehensibly. I ignored them and followed a footpath likely made by mortegas: four-legged, quiet creatures with wide brown eyes and a narrow face that ate the grass and ran away at the smallest of sounds.

Every now and then, grubby burrowing gnome faces, thick with dirt, popped up from the underbrush. One scowled at me, the round face ringed with dirty white hair, then disappeared into a hole in the ground when I hissed at it.

Ava regarded them with amusement at first, then fear when one threw a rock at her face. It gave her a little gash and bruise on her cheekbone. She skittered closer to me with a cry, and I found my first laugh since this whole disaster started in the East.

Now, we kept walking.

Ten paces later, I stopped, though I wasn't sure why. When I held a finger to my lips, she pressed hers together. The forest lay silent. My stomach clenched. We were only minutes away from—

A burst of fire slammed into the tree just above me.

I yanked Ava to the ground as the heat burned through the outer layer of bark on the tree behind us. When shards of fire fell, I scrambled away. Ava followed. I braced for the keening noise of a pained tree, but no such sound followed.

Only a derisive, smoky snort.

I leapt back to my feet and glared at the unnecessarily injured tree.

"Seriously!" I whipped around to yell. "You used your secundum on *me*?"

A hulking, black-scaled forest dragon slithered into view, as if appearing from nothing. Just my luck, it was the crotchety red female. Her ebony scales dripped with crimson, like spikes of rain falling down her flanks. She had recent whelps that made her overly protective and hotter than usual. The moment I encountered her, I normally transported away.

Next to me, Ava let out a terrified cry.

Burning shards of bark fell from the tree and landed on the dirt, where old bracken smoldered in gentle coals. Forest dragons had a *secundum,* or second fire, that clung to things with tenacious fire and continued to burn for hours after being thrown. At my back, the tree smoldered.

The red unfurled above us, no doubt arrogantly attempting to assert dominance. Her wings spread wide, the sturdy membrane webbed with veins. Glints of fire-like crimson sparkled off her chest. Heat rolled through the forest as she drew herself to her full height, which felt hundreds of paces away.

Nicholas, my Dragonmaster friend, characterized the dragons with witches' height as a comparison. "Ten witches," he'd said of the red once, meaning the measurement from claw to the top of her head fully extended. "She's a little one."

That *little one* growled with teeth full of flames now, her eyes pointedly on Ava. I stepped in between them. He claimed they understood our language, even if they didn't speak.

"She's under my protection," I called.

The red snorted. A fireball slammed into a nearby tree next to us, but I forced myself not to flinch away. I couldn't help but agree with the dragon's derision. The red's gaze narrowed, darting from me to Ava, as if she sensed something amiss. My lacking magic, perhaps? Or something different about the mortal girl?

Two whelps tumbled out of the forest, larger than me by at least five witch heights, but still young. Their wings were just gaining thickness now. The webbing between bones must have been strong enough to support flight because the smaller glided down from a tree. The bigger of the two showed hints of bright yellow in its marbled scales.

The red lowered her head, the crimson-lined scales on her neck rippling. Her face hovered over the ground as she peered at me through slitted eyes.

"I know," I snapped. "Something is different. You probably can't feel my magic anymore. That's why I'm here. I need to see Nicholas and Michelle."

The red growled when Ava peered around my shoulder. The beast snapped, her pearly, hot teeth too close for my liking.

"Stop it!" I barked, as if I had the authority to command a forest dragon. Fear pushed me to action—even if it was scolding a dragonian creature. What was to stop the red from gobbling both of us up right now? Nothing. No one would ever know what happened. The thought sent my heart racing.

Unfortunately, the red was in no mood to deal with commands from a mere witch. Or former witch—perhaps I was mortal now, too. She screamed in a blast of scorching breath into the trees. Her tail cracked like a whip overhead. I ducked and yanked Ava to the ground with me just as the tail whistled by.

The red threw her head back and bellowed fire into the understory. Vines caught flame and burned. Smoke made the air hazy. Responding dragon cries echoed all around us. A second dragon dropped from the canopy and landed on all four legs ten paces away. Another, mauve in color, glided from the treetops. A hiss overhead came next, only paces away. Then another. The forest dragons bellowed flames in our direction, but the fire never quite reached us.

"Stop!" I cried, choking on the smoke.

Sweat popped out along my spine. When the red bounded toward us, her whelps out of sight, I shoved Ava behind me. We backed against a different tree. Ava shouted something that I couldn't understand and I snapped at her to be quiet.

My sword hissed as I unsheathed it. Seven forest dragons towered overhead, their angular faces and narrowed yellow eyes bright against the terrifying backdrop of Letum Wood.

Their tirade of fire calmed enough I could see them through the haze. Smoke filtered through their nostrils and mouth as they glowered at us. Fire heated the air into shimmering lines that made it hard to breathe. I tightened my grip on the sword while Ava scrambled to hide behind me.

"I may not be able to beat you," I muttered as I pointed my sword at the red, "but you better believe I'll die trying."

She snarled.

I braced myself.

A deep voice rippled through the air, sent with a spell to magnify the sound. "Back off, all of you!"

My legs trembled as a familiar body stumbled into sight and I almost collapsed in relief. Nicholas.

"Come on!" he shouted. "Back off. You know Bianca is with me!"

The red yowled like an annoyed pet but shuffled back a step. A reprieve from the oppressive heat followed as the mauve dragon faded into the trees. Moments later, all dragons indignantly slipped out of sight.

Nicholas spun in a circle, muttering. He had a wide body and broad shoulders. Michelle's delicious talent in the kitchen had thickened him up. His hair fell in front of his eyes as the dragons reluctantly belched smoke and finally disappeared entirely.

Nicholas turned to me.

"You all right, Bianca?"

Sweat stains ringed an old shirt that was torn on one shoulder. He impatiently shoved thick locks of hair out of his eyes.

"Fine."

Ava peeked out from behind my shoulder. Nicholas glanced quickly at her, then doubled back.

"The good gods," he whispered, going pale. "That's a—"

I held out a trembling hand. "I know what she is. Before I explain, promise me you're not going to hurt her, or I'm leaving right now."

It was an empty threat, because where would I go? He'd just saved us from death already. His gaze locked on Ava. Reluctantly, he looked back at me. Shock glazed his expression for several long moments.

"That girl is a mortal, Bianca!"

"Her name is Ava, and I think so, yes. But we don't know for sure."

"What's she doing here?" he yelled.

"There's . . . more to it than just her being a mortal. I'll explain everything, but not here. It's not safe."

He blinked several times. His gaze darted overhead. Sanna, the previous High Dragonmaster, had left him with an odd legacy. Historically, some Dragonmasters could communicate with all dragons through their minds, though others may not have been able to. Dragonian history was a messy thing and nothing seemed clear for more than a few decades at a time. While Nicholas wasn't a pure-blood Dragonmaster like Sanna, the ability to hear them in his mind had grown slowly with time.

Still, even *he* seemed disinclined to tempt their tempers today.

He hesitated, then nodded. "Fine." His expression didn't soften when he muttered, "Come on, then. Michelle will have lunch ready soon."

* * *

The squall of a baby crashed through the air when we arrived at Nicholas's house, formerly owned by the Dragonmaster Sanna, Isadora's twin sister.

Sanna's home had been a small place, but after Michelle and Nicholas returned from an expedition into Letum Wood to find the history of the Dragonmasters, Nicholas had expanded the home. A larger and more family-friendly house stood in its place. One of my best friends, Michelle, met me at the door.

Michelle graced me with a quiet smile that radiated fatigue. A baby wiggled in her arms, half asleep. Clutching her skirts was another young girl, not quite three, that gasped when she saw me. The little girl darted away from her Mama and tossed herself into my arms.

"Bee!" she cried. "Bee!"

Michelle's daughter, lovingly named Sanna, let out a happy screech, and she wrapped her arms around my neck.

"I'm sorry, Sanna. No sweets today."

Her bottom lip jutted out, but she laughed when I tickled her. The sound lightened my heavy heart. She kicked her chubby legs with a squawk of protest. I gently set her down to scamper into the house.

"What an unexpected surprise," Michelle said as she hiked the baby up on her shoulder and patted her back. An enormous belch bubbled out. The infant pressed her face to Michelle's shoulder and closed her eyes with a contented smack of her lips. Michelle's expression turned curious. "Who is your friend back there?"

Nicholas shot me a sharp glance that I ignored. "Her name is Ava. We won't stay. We can't. But I desperately need your help."

"What's wrong?"

I reached behind me and pulled Ava into view. Michelle regarded her curiously until her expression dropped. She clutched the baby.

"A mortal?" she whispered.

Ava shifted closer to me, gaze wary.

"I think so," I said. "In all likelihood . . . yes. But I can't confirm it. She doesn't speak any language that I've ever heard."

Nicholas and Michelle exchanged concerned glances.

"Can you send an urgent message to Marten?" I asked. "Tell him to come immediately, and we'll leave with him."

"Of course." Her brow furrowed. "But why can't you message him?"

This would be harder to say than I had expected.

"My uh . . . my magic is gone."

Michelle's mouth moved wordlessly, her face as white as a sheet. Nicholas advanced, meaty fists at his side.

"You didn't tell me that!" he cried. "Did she do this to you?"

I slid in front of Ava with a cold glare that stopped him in his tracks. I gripped the pommel of my sword, unsheathing it in his direction. "I did it to myself," I hissed. "So if there's violence you want to do, I suggest you bring it to me. I don't want to hurt you, Nicholas, but we both know I would if I had to."

The gleam of my sword aimed at his chest seemed to bring him back to his right mind. He backed away, more agitated than ever. I lowered the sword, but kept a tight grip and a wary eye on him.

"This is what mortals do!" he cried. "The legends are clear. Their presence messes with our magic. It changes things. Our magic is more dangerous, more volatile. Unpredictable! Sometimes it doesn't even work. We can't let her stay here. The dragons are ready to eat both of you. I can hear them. They're . . . livid. They say you can't stay, that you must never come back."

"I'm aware they hate me," I said wryly. "They always have."

"No, this is more than that. This is a step too far, Bianca," Nicholas muttered. "You've done many wild things before . . . but this?"

Despite the cutting tone, I understood his fear. Ava was so much more than just a little girl . . . she was the potential for an

Alkarra-wide catastrophe. Or the living realization of it. Without her, the amulet would have never come here and my magic would be in my body where it belonged.

Michelle reached out with a trembling hand and put it on Nicholas's back.

"Nicholas," she whispered with a slight tone of warning. He jerked away, hair standing on end after he ran a hand through it.

Michelle turned to me, close to weeping now. "What are you going to do with her, Bianca?"

"She's Papa's problem. I'm going to take her to him. I'm here to protect her until we can figure out why she's here and how I get my magic back. Without her, I have no hope. Please, send for Marten?"

Ava shifted as she ducked behind my back again.

Michelle's gaze narrowed. "She . . . she looks a bit like Camille, doesn't she? The freckles. The face. She . . ."

She sucked in a sharp breath, then straightened. Tears sparkled in her eyes.

"Of course," she said firmly. "We'll help you right away. Nicholas, go soothe the dragons, please. I won't have them tramping all over the forest and my garden." She gave Ava a wary, but surprisingly warm, smile. "Please, come inside while I send the message. You both must be thirsty."

Chapter Eight

"Well," Marten murmured wryly. "You've really outdone yourself this time, B."

He ignored my glare to study Ava with a perplexed expression. One hand rested on his chin, like she had posed a particularly complex math equation he couldn't figure out.

Even within Marten's protection and the stolid walls of Chatham Castle, I couldn't relax. I paced back and forth across his turret office while Ava shoved food into her mouth at Marten's desk. With the patience of a mother, he slowly gave her small chunks of bread, apples, and soft white cheese. She slurped hot bone broth and fresh water with a keen eye on him, but her expression had calmed.

The intensity of my fear faded in the comfort of Marten's office. Bookshelves filled with old grimoires, scrolls, and other knickknacks cluttered the space. As usual, a pot of tea stayed warm on his desk. The warmth curled in my belly when I sipped at it, an untold comfort. Even though the day grew warm, the snap of a small fire soothed me.

When he'd transported me here, the magic on my skin felt . .

. odd. Hot. The usual pressure had been magnified, even for so short of a distance. After attempting a few more spells to prove my theory, an empty feeling persisted in my chest. The void terrified me.

Marten set a small apple on Ava's plate and turned to me. "You did well, B. I'm thoroughly impressed that you survived hours in Letum Wood without any magic, and with a mortal. One that happens to carry a formerly powerful amulet of unknown magic. If there's anything dragons don't like these days, it's magical power they don't understand."

"Thanks?"

"But now," he murmured with a furrowed brow and a low tone, "we must figure out what to do with *both* of you."

Relieved to turn the problem to him, I rubbed my exhausted eyes. "Papa will protect her, I'm sure."

Marten said nothing.

The thought of telling Papa what happened sent a bolt of terror through me again. Papa's ferocious protection of me paralleled only my own intensity. He would not be happy with me for many, many reasons.

First, I missed the Central Network dinner, and surely that conjured questions he couldn't answer, which would have concerned him. Second, I'd taken a mortal into my care. A mortal I had no business taking responsibility for, but couldn't turn away. And finally, my magic was . . . gone? Tied up? Paralyzed?

Well, it wasn't working, and that was bad enough.

Marten broke the silence with a mild, "Ava?"

Ava paused with a piece of bread halfway to her mouth, looked at me, then back to him. Marten asked her name in Declan. Tentatively, she spoke back, but I didn't recognize the response. A silence hung in the air following her words.

"Well?" I asked.

He shook his head and sighed. "I didn't understand her, but

she has tones of the Declan language. Fascinating. Imagine going back in history. Could you speak our current language then? Of course not. There would be similarities, but the tone, accent, culture, even idiom and emphasis would make it hard to understand. I believe there are similar roots in these languages, but they're still different."

"That's not much help."

"None at all."

A knock came on the door and turned my stomach into knots. Ava tensed. I stood up to put my body between her and the door as it swung open. Papa strolled inside with an easy smile. He took me in in one quick glance and instantly frowned.

"B?"

Marten shut the door with a spell, then sent a silencing incantation after.

"What happened?" Papa demanded.

Tears blocked my reply at first. Until I saw him, I hadn't realized how frightened I'd been. How terrorizing and traumatizing this whole mess had become. Now that he stood in front of me with power, confidence, and strength, I wanted to melt into his arms. My vision went watery until I blinked the tears back.

Marten put a warm hand on my shoulder and opened his mouth to help me, but I held up a hand to stop him. This one needed to come from me.

"I've lost my magic," I whispered.

Papa's brow grew heavy with concern. He gave no other response except a nod to indicate I should continue.

I explained everything in detail, from the moment I left to meet with Priscilla to this very second. He remained unusually calm through the retelling, even with details of Niko's paranoia and a mention of the voice that had spoken to me when the amulet broke my magic. I had given Marten enough information to get the gist when I arrived, but now he knew it all.

Once I finished, I stepped aside to reveal Ava.

She remained small and quiet in the chair, as if she sensed Papa's importance. Her strange braids, variegated hair, and odd eyes. He stepped forward to peer at her. She tilted her chin, seemingly resisting the urge to cower. Through it all, she held onto the desk for dear life.

For a long time, Papa studied her.

Eventually, he blinked out of his thoughts. His breathing remained steady but deep. He turned to Marten, his expression strained.

"Marten, please return to the forest and give a blood vow of secrecy to Michelle and Nicholas regarding the mortal. Then, find this girl some fresh clothes and a hot bath. Take her to my apartments after all of that is done. We'll house her there."

"Consider it done."

"Thank you."

Papa turned to me with fury in his eyes. He grabbed my upper arm and pulled me closer with a firm grip.

"You are coming with me."

* * *

"Papa, I—"

"Not. A. Word," he ground out between clenched teeth. We stopped in the empty hallway just outside Marten's office. The tingle of a transportation spell began, but I called out.

"Please, don't!"

Nostrils flared, he strode down the hall with me at his side.

"Jikes, Papa, let me go," I hissed. "I'm twenty-one years old. Witches will suspect something is wrong. I will follow you to your apartment, I vow it."

He complied.

Quietly, we worked our way through the halls of the castle down less-used paths. Once inside his apartment, the butler Reeves appeared from the back room and bowed. His dark hair had turned to gray around his temples, with dusty tones feathering back over his ears. A droopy nose, droll mouth, and crisp black-and-crimson uniform completed his daily appearance.

"Reeves," Papa said, "please stay and hear what Bianca and I have to say. She's found herself in a very unfortunate situation that will require your help. After this, you will be sworn to secrecy with a blood vow."

Reeves tucked himself next to a wall and awaited, apparently unbothered by such a speech. I stood before the hearth and braced myself.

Papa whirled on me.

"A mortal?" he hissed. Rage filled his voice. "You brought a mortal into our Network when she had originated elsewhere, without consulting me, and then you touched an unknown amulet in the process? Bianca!"

"Papa, it was an accident. The amulet, I mean," I added. "I didn't mean to touch it."

"But you transported a mortal here on purpose?"

"She was going to be tortured or killed if I left her in the East."

And she looked like Camille, I thought of adding. *And I didn't save Camille, did I?* But I sent the thought away.

"You don't know that," he cried. "You made a daring decision on a vague assumption."

I rolled my eyes. "Papa. Come on. You know Niko wouldn't have given her the chance to explain herself. At least not with any humanity."

Papa paced long strides in front of me. "Your assumptions may get all of us killed, B."

"I didn't think that—"

"I know you didn't think!" he shouted. "The Central Network will now pay the price for you *not* thinking. Do you realize what you've done? You brought a mortal girl into the Network during the Celebration. When the leadership of every

Network has assembled to discuss peace in the same place. A Celebration that will make the history books because we are already on another downward path to war!"

"Yes," I snapped, enraged by his hot tone. "I believe I'm bearing that burden now, thank you."

Something in my response must have brought him back to himself. He stopped, grabbed my shoulders, and jerked me into his arms. His warm embrace swallowed me for a moment. Tears bubbled into my eyes again, but I forced them back.

"I'm sorry, Papa. Truly," I whispered into his shirt. "I was trying to save her. I was . . . she looked scared. She reminded me of Camille. It wasn't until later that her amulet took my magic."

He sighed and his shoulders slumped. He pressed a kiss to my hair and pulled away. For an eternal minute, he studied every part of my face before he seemed satisfied and let me go.

"Your magic is gone?" he asked quietly.

My stomach ached when I nodded. "Or doesn't work, I don't know which."

"How does it feel?"

"Like a piece of my soul is missing. Like I'm empty but don't know where to turn. It's . . . terrifying."

His hand lay heavy on my shoulder. "We'll get it back, B. We'll figure this out. It's unlikely that an amulet could have taken your ability to do magic entirely. Maybe the magic is paralyzed with a protective incantation to prevent the wrong person from using the amulet or something. Maybe, with time, your power will return."

The darkness in his tone told me what he didn't say. That, if an amulet worn by a mortal could take my magic, it could take the magic of any witch. We could all be reduced to mere mortals, just like the Southern Network.

That I truly *had* introduced a most frightening disaster to the Network.

Such thoughts had occurred to me during the trek through

Letum Wood, but I hadn't dwelt on them for long. There was *some* hope that this departure of magic was temporary, but something deep in my gut didn't believe it. This emptiness had become far too encompassing.

Until we spoke with Ava, all of this was conjecture.

"I'm sorry." He ran a hand through his hair. "I overreacted out of fear for you. I love you, B. I came on a bit strong back there."

"It's fine, Papa. I deserved it."

He sat on the edge of a divan, hands clasped into a fist near his mouth, and stared into a low fire. Reeves hadn't moved, but his expression had darkened. He may not say as much, but the old man held a deep affection for us. Although only minutes had passed since we left Marten's office, Papa's mind spit out plans anyway.

"You'll stay in my apartments. If you leave, a witch that's able to transport another witch must leave with you." He turned to glance over his shoulder. "Reeves, do you feel confident that you could transport away from here with Bianca if needed?"

"I do, Your Highness," Reeves said.

His voice was deep like a river and rolled like thunder. If he sang, he would be a beautifully melodic bass.

"Thank you." Papa gave me an assessing look. "Will you fight me on this, B?"

Wordless, I shook my head. The terror of Letum Wood replayed through my mind. Chatham Castle wasn't much safer than the forest. Not just politically, but physically. If the right witches knew that I'd lost my power? They'd seek to kill me. Papa had made plenty of enemies in all his years as a Protector, and now as High Priest. Staying in the castle wasn't ideal, but it was still safer than bumbling around alone and without magic in the woods.

Papa rubbed his hand along the back of his neck. "In the

meantime, I'll find a place where we can send Ava away until I figure out what to do with her."

"What?" I cried. "No! You can't send her away. She's the only answer to restoring my magic."

His tone dropped into a low drawl of warning. "Bianca—"

"Papa, she needs to stay with me so I can figure this out. She's not safe anywhere else. If she dies, my chances might die with her."

"And you'll be able to protect her, will you?" he snapped. "With all your magical abilities locked up?"

My mouth hung open, unable to respond at first. "Well, no. But Reeves can use magic, and I can fight."

Papa growled. "You want me to keep a mortal girl in the castle? If the Council found out, B, you and I would be finished in the Central Network. They'd accuse me of harboring a mortal and probably something ridiculous, like using her as a weapon against other Networks. No. She must get out of here before anyone else sees her. I walk a fine enough line as it is."

"We need to *help* her. If she could speak to us then we—"

"Michelle, Nicholas, Reeves, Marten, you, and I will be the only ones that know about her. That's it. Who in that group can navigate the nuances of an unknown magic while the Celebration is happening? None."

"Not Baxter?" I asked, astonished. "You aren't going to tell him?"

He hesitated, and in the long space between my question and his delay, I sensed something else.

Something big.

"Papa?"

"I'll deal with Baxter later," he muttered, and I couldn't imagine why he looked so frustrated after. "We'll need his help protecting you when you attend the ball in three nights."

"The ball?" I screeched. "What do you mean?"

"Your absence was noted and missed from the dinner last

night. We cannot avoid the ball without drawing suspicion and rumors, which is the last thing we need. Certainly not now."

"I'll be going to the ball without magic. Are you insane?"

"We don't know that," he said crisply. "Your powers may return by then. I'm sorry, Bianca. You must be there. As much as I hate to say it, there is an image we must maintain. Any crumbling now will . . . let's discuss this later."

A clock nearby let out a little chirp, indicating the hour. Papa shot to his feet.

"Have to go. Ava can stay here until I find her another place to go where the Council won't see her." He pointed to me. "Do not leave this apartment, Bianca. You and I are not finished here."

* * *

Ava's bright, golden eyes were wide as saucers when she shuffled into the apartment ahead of Marten.

Marten transported her right to the doorway in a quiet moment when no one would see them, then quickly closed the door behind him. Protective incantations prevented any witch from transporting directly inside Papa's apartment, which would help immensely in keeping us safe.

Reeves tutted over Ava now, grunting and frowning with unusual zeal. The moment she saw me, her shoulders slumped with relief. Unbidden, she darted to my side, as tall as my shoulder. For a girl that appeared to be ten or eleven, she wasn't overly tall. I gritted my teeth and wanted to push her away, but held off. If she felt safer with me, perhaps she'd cooperate more.

Marten regarded the two of us.

"Based on your expression," he said drily, "things with Derek weren't concluded to your satisfaction."

"No."

"I urge you to remember the tight spot your father is in. The

Council watches his every move. They have witches following him constantly, waiting for a mistake. I believe that some of them have created alliances with the East, and perhaps even the West, over your father's head. Something of the magnitude of a mortal . . ."

"The Council would vote to kill her, Marten, as soon as find a way to communicate with her. And then I'd never get my magic back."

"Is this just about your magic?" One of his eyebrows rose. "Or is there something else?"

A ball of emotion had lodged in my throat and tightened now at his question. The way he peered at me knowingly told me it was likely that he already knew the answer, but wanted me to say it anyway.

"No." I turned away. "It's not just about my magic."

It's about Camille, I thought. *And Mama and Stella and Isadora. Everyone we lost. Everyone I didn't save.*

"You are likely correct," Marten murmured. "The Council wouldn't work to save her. They'd get as much information as they could and then put her to death."

"There could be more, you know. Maybe she's a precursor. Maybe all mortals have amulets like that and we're in deep danger. Hiding her without attempting to communicate would only make that worse."

His dour expression suggested he'd already thought of that.

"Perhaps. And perhaps your father simply needs to put off tackling this problem for another time. Derek knows that she can't hide forever. But how can he help her without drawing suspicion at this exact moment?"

I sighed. Perhaps Letum Wood wasn't as frightening as the political ramifications of something like this. Marten was right. Papa just needed more time.

Ava pulled away from me to study Reeves, who collected a shiny silver tea set and began to lay it out. Amongst the teacups and cookies were a few small toys. A slate with chalk to draw. A doll. They seemed to have piqued Ava's interest, so I gave her a nudge in that direction. She hesitated. Reeves snapped two fingers, caught her gaze, and pointed to a chair.

She obeyed.

"I'm going to figure out how to talk to her, Marten, and get to the bottom of this. If Papa wants to hide her away, we'll do that too. Just not yet. Because I *will* get my magic back."

Marten gave me a blithe smile, drew in a shoulder-expanding breath, and said, "That is of no great surprise to anyone, B. Let me know how I can be of help."

With that, he gave Reeves a nod and stepped back into the hallway. A creeping suspicion told me Marten had assumed that's what I'd do all along. The tone I'd heard in his voice had been relief. Was it relief over my determination to figure this out? Or that I'd take on this seemingly impossible task?

His departure left my mind in a churning turmoil.

Despite the mess I needed to sort out in my head, the path remained clear: I had to speak to Ava. Through speaking to Ava, I'd figure out the why, how, when, and what of her being here. Then I'd solve my magical dilemma.

Didn't have to be difficult at all.

I spun on my heels and headed for the desk to write a note that Reeves would have to transport.

Fortunately, I knew the perfect witch for this very scenario.

Chapter Nine

A dreary rain pattered the windows that evening.

Rainwater splashed across Papa's stone balcony in broad puddles. The gloomy, verdant lines of Letum Wood shimmered through the darkening haze. Across the world lay a gray, foggy blanket. Reeves kept a fire in the hearth, staving off the cool air that seeped through the windowpanes. Doused torches smoked in the downpour, a depressing sight.

Behind me, Ava hummed quietly to herself while she braided her hair into a complicated knot of dozens of smaller braids. The effect was stunning. The changing tones of her hair shimmered in the firelight almost like the amulet. She sat on a plush chair near the fire, a book with painted pictures in her hands and a blanket over her legs.

Language barrier aside, I hadn't seen Reeves this happy in a while. He tutted, tucked, and pampered Ava, seemingly unbothered by her mortal status. A life to care for was a life to care for. For Reeves, that seemed to be enough. He kept her supplied with an endless array of food, alternating between clucking his displeasure when she ate too fast and crooning his approval when she ate everything.

For the tenth time, I reviewed a short note from Baxter that arrived minutes before.

B,

Missed you at the dinner. Everything all right? Your father is concerned, and so am I. He came back from a meeting with Marten surly as a bear.

—Bax

What could I say?

Papa's hesitation to tell Baxter replayed back through my mind. Why wouldn't he pull Baxter into this mess right away? Papa couldn't operate without Baxter's organizational mind to keep Papa's schedule, messages, and life together. Baxter knew more about Papa's life than anyone, even if he had no political power. Was Papa trying to protect him, perhaps? Or to think things through? Papa involved no one in any plan until he knew the clear path.

I sighed.

A longing for Letum Wood and its calming effects rippled through me. My physical tie to the forest felt like a two-headed monster: loving and welcoming on one side, treacherous and devious on the other. Danger had always lurked in the shadows, I just hadn't realized how much until I couldn't fight back.

Ava made a noise in her throat. She stared, wide-eyed, at a painting of a sea serpent, then quickly slammed it shut. Next to her, an open copy of the *Chatham Chatterer* lay on the table. A few headlines blinked here and there, but nothing outstanding. I ignored her strange, throaty sounds as she returned to the book, carefully skirting the page with the sea monster.

My gaze wandered. The apartment wasn't the same as when I moved out almost three years ago, and the evolution of changes had been interesting to watch through the years. Reeves had slowly replaced old furniture and updated art, even though Papa could care less about sculptures. The apartment felt new. Even my old bedroom, which Reeves had turned into a guest room, felt strange.

The girl-witch that had lived here before didn't exist anymore.

Did we always become someone new? Was life a constant state of shedding one persona to slide into the next, and they all built on each other? As if life was the sum of all the parts of itself.

One great, collective whole.

So, what did it mean that my magic had been taken away? Would all the other parts of me collapse together into a totally different witch?

A knock on the door interrupted my sleepy thoughts. I startled out of my deepening spiral to find Reeves already at the door. He pulled it open, comprehended whoever stood there, then opened it wider within moments. I straightened away from the window as a shockingly familiar head of white-blonde hair appeared.

Leda gave me her most imperious look as she entered, swamping the room with her presence. A well-kept, but also well-worn, bag hung at her side.

"Bianca."

I rushed to her side and threw my arms around her in a crushing embrace. "Thank you," I said against her shoulder. "Thank you for coming so quickly."

Her haughtiness receded slightly. Her expression was pale beneath a thick coating of annoyance. Whether it was the circumstances that brought her back to the castle or just being *here* that bothered her, I couldn't tell.

She scalded me with a glare. "What have you done now? Your letter was annoyingly vague and very dire."

With a sweep of my arm, I motioned her to the divan closest to the fire. "Have a seat. We have some catching up to do and almost no time to do it. We need to get started before Papa returns."

Twenty minutes later after I'd recounted the whole story, while leaving out the details of Priscilla's pregnancy and Niko's derangement, Leda's rigid spine had tensed so much I thought she'd snap.

With disbelief, she turned to me.

"You have single-handedly managed to bring a mortal girl into the Central Network during one of the biggest political meetings of our generation, then simultaneously lost your magic. Not only did you somehow survive Letum Wood without magic, but you have also now asked me here to figure out an ancient language from a young girl, and against your father's wishes?"

Her scathing look seemed to frighten Ava, who shrank back against the couch. Leda ignored her.

"It's not *against* Papa's wishes," I said diplomatically. "He doesn't know we're doing it. He might agree, but we can't take the chance that he won't. So we just have to do it."

Leda growled like a hissing cat, her back arched as if she were about to strike with pretty claws.

"Now I will have to be under a blood oath of secrecy," her arms lifted to the side in a gesture toward Ava, "to rescue a mortal girl that may be here to kill us all!"

"You can see it that way," I said carefully, "or you can see it as an opportunity to rescue your Network."

"Bianca!"

Her reprimand cut deep, but I couldn't pull back now. "Leda, I need you. The Network needs you. Papa wants to stuff Ava away somewhere else in the hope that the Council doesn't find out until later, but we don't have time for that. What if Ava is one of many mortals? What if more mortals are coming? How do I get my magic back? We have to know *now*. Papa doesn't have time for it. Not with the Council so hostile to him and all the Networks here. But *we* can do something. It starts with getting through to Ava. If we can talk to her, we can figure this out."

She stood up, arms folded across her middle, and stared at the fire. For several long moments, I hardly dared to breathe. The strain around her eyes told me just how difficult coming back to the castle, and all the ghosts of the witches we'd lost, had been.

An angry Leda was a Leda that cared.

"And thank you for coming," I said more soberly. "I know how much this cost you. I appreciate you being a good friend."

Her insufferable glare lessened just a smidge when she turned back around. "Trust *you* to get into this predicament."

My lips twitched with a half smile.

Leda sighed heavily. "I can't promise anything. Language is fickle and constantly changing. I have books at the library that may help us but . . . that doesn't mean we'll get anywhere."

"So you'll try it?"

She eyed me, then Ava. For a long moment, she just stared at her. Then she nodded and a hidden sigh lived in her eyes. "I'll try. It's quite lucky that you happen to be best friends with the foremost expert on ancient languages in the division on the Mortal Wars."

My grin stretched wide. "Very lucky."

This time, she did smile a little. Then it faltered and concern replaced it. "Are you all right?" she asked softly. "To lose your magic . . ."

Beneath her near-constant vexation with me beat the heart of my truest friend. My wild nature leaned on her logical one more often than not. In the moments when Leda did conjure compassion, however, it levied a powerful effect on me. I swallowed hard.

"I'm surviving."

"How does it feel to have your magic removed?"

"Like . . . a vital part of me was taken away. I feel empty."

"Well, I am sorry it happened." Her lips pinched together in a move so much like Scarlett that I wondered if the two of them *should* work together again. "I'm sure that you'll be able to figure it out. You've always been insufferable when you had a goal in mind."

"Thanks."

A moment lingered before she quietly said, "My Foresight curse is fading, you know?"

"What?"

She fiddled with the edge of her bag. "There are some indications in obscure texts that the Foresight curse, if cast before puberty, can decrease in strength over time. Something with changes in the female body after a certain age, usually seventeen." She waved a hand. "Doesn't matter. The point is that the curse is . . . a ghost in me now."

Startled by this revelation, I blinked several times. How had she not mentioned *this* before? The Foresight curse had been a shadow over Leda's whole life. Given to her as a baby from a stranger in retribution for something her father had done, it had changed her very eye color. Altered the way she interacted with the world, even her response to crowded places.

Like a Watcher, it gave her glimpses of the future, but hers were far more unstable. Quick flashes, like a memory, she once said. It often imposed itself on her, giving her no choice. Watchers were more powerful and relied on actual magic they could control and trust. Leda's had been, truly, just a curse. A hindrance and an annoyance.

To hear that it had been fading felt like part of Leda had left also. A part that, perhaps, she didn't mind releasing.

"Why didn't you say anything?" I asked. "That's . . . kind of a big thing."

She smiled blandly, but a flicker of something appeared in the recesses of her eyes. Maybe she *wasn't* liking the withdrawal of it. The less Leda spoke about something, the more it bothered her.

Her head tipped back. "I told you that in some effort to prove that I know what it's like when magic leaves you, even if the circumstances are vastly different. You are not entirely alone. I'll be back in an hour."

* * *

Leda returned exactly one hour later.

Ava watched her unload ten books onto the table. Ava shifted to the edge of her chair, hands braced on the armrests, until I stepped next to her. When I put a reassuring hand on her shoulder, Ava relaxed. I pointed to Leda and said, "Leda."

Leda's blessedly neutral expression allowed ample time for Ava to process. They sat several paces apart, squared to each other. Ava fiddled with the amulet chain and assessed Leda.

Finally, Ava put a hand to her chest.

"Ava."

Leda kept a studious eye on Ava for several long moments. Then she flipped open the top book, gazed through a few pages, and spoke in a different language for a sentence or two.

Ava stared at her mutely.

Leda set the top book aside, perched carefully on the table. She gently opened the second book, frowned, then said something to Ava again. This time, her words sounded rougher, more throaty. She glanced up.

Ava blinked, clearly confused.

Leda set that book aside.

This went on several more times. While Leda spat out dialects of ancient languages as if it were second nature to her—apparently, it was—I marveled at the capacity of her mind and at

Ava's complete blankness to all of it. Slowly, one book at a time, my hope started to flicker.

After nine books, with one book left, Leda held up the final book. It was so small and had so few pages that it could have been a scroll. Instead of Ava, she looked at me.

"This is a book I found last year in a far recess of the library. It had Declan-esque wording in it, so I wanted to pursue it further. I studied it for a week or so, tried to cross-reference with other existing books, but found little. My suspicions say it's a dialect of Declan spoken mostly in mortal collections, but I could never confirm because of the lack of historical detail. Witches don't want to remember the mortals and what they've done, which makes us historically blind. Idiotic, if you ask me, but that's a discussion for another day. Then I forgot about it until today."

"Are there enough words in there for you to speak?"

She lifted one eyebrow.

"Let's hope; because it's the last dialect of which we're aware."

Cautiously, Leda said a few words. They weren't strung together in a clear sentence the way the others had been, and her confidence wasn't as bold. It seemed more like a tentative question than a statement.

Ava brightened. Quick as a bird, she chattered something back. Her lips moved so quickly, I caught little more than consonants. This time, Leda blinked. Her nostrils flared as she looked at me and said, "I have no idea what she just said, but it had familiar sounds."

"Try again!"

With a flick of her wrist, Leda unfurled the pamphlet. The pages were thin and jagged at the ends, almost like oiled parchment. The ink had faded out in some areas, and the handwriting had an older, flowing style that made it nearly impossible to make any sense of. Leda skimmed it with ease. The tip of her finger hovered over the page as she'd say something, look to Ava, and wait for a response. Ava's responses were quick as lightning. She leaned forward in her chair, hands gripping the edge.

"Is it—"

Leda held out a hand in my direction in a command to be quiet, keeping her whole focus on Ava. When Leda pointed to a window and said a word, Ava repeated it back, but slightly different. I backed away and paced near the fire.

Leda held out a hand, two other books appeared. She turned to me, her expression grim, lips pressed. She looked exhausted, although she'd been here less than an hour. When she rose to her feet, Ava scrambled after her, as if desperate to keep Leda close.

Leda pressed the fragile book into my hands.

"She's speaking a different dialect of Declan," she stated. "The Mortal version, if you want to have something to call it, although there's little solid historical basis on whether the mortals actually spoke their own version. Suppositions arise when you consider—"

"Leda," I growled in warning.

She cut me a glare. "Fine. I'll figure out the scholarly implications later. To your end, it means there will be things in her language that we can't figure out for a while because we don't have a lot of original literature," she said shortly.

"But eventually?"

Leda cast Ava an uncertain glance. "The roots of many words are somewhat the same," she murmured, deep lines in between her nearly transparent eyebrows, "but the words themselves are different. The endings, mostly. It's enough that I can figure out some communication for now, at least until we can find the rhythm of it. At the very least, we can figure out some basic vocabulary and build from there."

"It's something."

Leda turned to me with a troubled expression. "Yes, it is *something*, but to really understand this language will take time.

I can't just conjure an understanding like this out of a single conversation. The complexity of verb conjugation and tenses and—"

I held up a hand.

"Please, just tell me what you can do and on what timeline?"

Leda sighed. "Considering that she's a mortal, we'll need confidence and precision before we know whether we understand her clearly or not. I'd say that with daily work and the foundation of the Declan language that I already have, Ava and I could be mostly conversant within four weeks. But that still isn't a *detailed* conversant."

My heart dropped into my stomach. Four *weeks*? She'd be dead by then if anyone found out about her. Papa's scorn at my bravado replayed back through my head. *And you'll be able to protect her, will you?*

No. Not against Networks and Councils. That was Papa's job and he was too busy for it.

Leda gathered the books in her arms, although she left the pamphlet for me. "I have to work tonight," she said. "I'll try to request some leave, but I can't promise anything. If Derek removes her before I return, I assume you'll go with her. Tell Reeves to let me know where to find you. Merry part, Bianca. I hope to see you soon."

Just like that, she left. The light in Ava's eyes bled to disappointment, and I couldn't blame the uneasy fear that seemed to follow.

I felt the same thing myself.

Chapter Ten

The flutter of paper over my head woke me up the following morning.

I opened my eyes to find a letter shaped like a butterfly hovering over my face. Gentle puffs of air fanned my cheeks from inked parchment. Words lay visible through the delicate wings, which were as thin as early shadows. I blinked away sleep, startled by the light smell of char in my nostrils.

Priscilla.

Gently, I reached up and plucked it from the air. My eyes felt bleary and hot from a sleepless night filled with dreams of fire. I yawned as I tapped the paper wings twice so that they unfolded in my palm.

Priscilla's handwriting filled the inside.

Bianca,

I have arrived at your cottage safely and, I believe, unde-tected. I transported several places in Letum Wood, and moved around enough, I doubt anyone followed. The castle lay quiet when I left, and it would be at least twelve hours

*before anyone would discover my departure. Niko has no
idea, I believe.*
*Considering how you and I parted last time, I'm
concerned. There is no sign of you having been here. Are
things well? Are you all right with your new friend?*
*Thank you again for everything. I will go to see Michelle
soon. Let me know how I can assist you while you're
helping your Papa with the Celebration. I anticipate your
return home. It's . . . very quiet here.*
Please destroy this, just to be safe.

Yours,
Priscilla

A thousand questions streamed through my sleepy head.
How did she feel after leaving the East? Was it hard to untangle
herself from Magnolia castle without suspicion? Unlikely, with
Niko gone. The staff tended to love her. But still . . . her life had
been decidedly more complicated the past several weeks. I hoped
it hadn't been too difficult.

Relief that she was somewhere safe overpowered my questions. I blinked out of sleep, read the letter one more time, then
tossed it into the fire. The edges curled in the flame, burning to
ash in red lines of fire before collapsing all at once in a flash of
heat.

Dawn hinted on the horizon, leaving a burgeoning
world below. With my head tangled in thoughts of Niko,
Priscilla, and the Declan language, I wouldn't be able to
relax back to sleep anytime soon. Instead, I pulled on my
day dress, ran a comb through my hair, and headed for the
door. A flash of movement caught my eye at the window. I
glanced through the thick glass panes to see someone
walking across the rolling, grassy hillside that separated the
forest from the castle. The manicured gardens of Chatham

Castle, known for their creative beauty, shimmered through the fog.

My heart hiccuped. I'd know that graceful figure anywhere.

Merrick.

Although it had been two years since I'd seen him as anything more than a vague figure on the Wall to avoid, those broad shoulders and that sandy hair were still as familiar as anything I'd ever known. His hair was longer, pulled in a queue out of his face. I couldn't see details, but I could picture flushed red cheeks and a bright, white-toothed smile. The same smile that would appear seconds before he captured me in a soul-shaking kiss.

My thoughts dissolved all at once. I could only stare as he strode across the rolling green hills of the Chatham gardens below. Mist collected over the ground, swirling in his wake. He moved like an otherworldly god, and flashes of memory exploded in my head like bright candles.

Running.

His lips on mine.

The smell of the forest on his skin.

With a sharp breath, I turned away from the window and banished those thoughts. *No,* I thought. *Go away.*

My heart pooled in my belly and flopped around like a useless thing. Merrick. Merrick, who had to leave. Merrick, who had broken my heart.

Merrick, who . . . came back?

He came for the Celebration, of course, to help protect Geralyn. Why hadn't I thought of his return? It was inevitable. Although I didn't want the questions, they accosted me anyway. Why was he in Letum Wood? Was he looking for me? Did he go for a run for the sake of remembering our life together again?

With Merrick and the sorrow of losing him fresh on my mind, I missed my trees with a keen pang of sorrow. They had always comforted my troubled heart whenever it remembered him.

Reluctant but unable to stop myself, I looked back. Merrick had disappeared. Only the quiet grounds lay in the morning dew, as if waiting for me to join them.

* * *

Out in the main apartment and far away from thoughts of Merrick, Papa waited. He stood near the curved bay windows that overlooked the same stretch of grounds I'd been staring at from my room. The growing light from outside gave him a quiet, ethereal glow.

"You're up early, Papa."

He spun to look at me. A smile crossed his face, tinged with warmth. I joined him at his side to peer out. When he spoke, his voice had a gentle burr.

"Morning, B. Why are you awake so early?"

"Couldn't sleep."

He grunted.

I lifted my brow. "And you?"

"It's not that early. I have to be up before the sun most of the time, now. Today, however, I'm meeting with Baxter and Marten to prep for the Southern Network breakfast this morning, before the Esbat begins. Just wanted to take a few minutes to think before I head to my office."

"Your office?" My brow rose. "The three of you normally meet here and have breakfast together, don't you?"

His lips pressed into a firm line. "I know."

Marten already knew about Ava, but Baxter didn't, which could mean that Papa didn't want Baxter and Ava to run into each other. Why that would be the case, I couldn't even fathom.

"Why?"

"I don't want Baxter here."

"Are you hiding Ava from Baxter?" I asked, incredulous at the thought. Baxter had become Papa's most trusted Assistant. He managed almost Papa's entire life. For Papa to actively hide Ava from him specifically was . . . shocking.

"For now," he murmured.

Astonishment colored my tone. "But . . . why?"

Papa paused, then said, "Let's just say that he and I need to clear a few things up before he gets to know everything. Now is not the time to have that conversation with him. I plan to do it after the Celebration when both of us don't have so much to do. Keep Ava to yourself for now, please? *I* will be the one that informs him when he needs to know. Got it?"

"Sure."

I didn't articulate all of my questions yet, mostly because I didn't want to push Papa into irritation. Any frustration on his part would only push him further away from keeping Ava here with me. At any moment, he could take her away, and how would I recover my magic with her somewhere else?

Considerations aside, a comfortable silence grew between us. It's what I'd always loved best about Papa. Our easy camaraderie extended to the quiet times as well. Behind us, on the table, lay a spread of Papa's favorite breakfast. A sizzling slab of ham. A hardboiled egg. Fresh milk to wash it down, all with a thick, hearty roll made of sprouted grains. He hadn't touched it, despite usually waking up ravenous.

"I can't stop thinking about Marie," he said quietly.

Mama's name fell gently off his lips. My breath caught. It had been so long since either of us had mentioned her. We didn't avoid speaking about her, but she had been gone for so many years now that bringing her up no longer felt natural. I cleared the sudden cobwebs out of my throat.

"Why?" I asked.

He half smiled, but it had ghosts in it. "I don't know."

"Do you miss her?"

"Forever. Always."

"Oh."

He shook his head. "It's more than that. I just . . . I keep asking myself if this is all there is?"

"To life?"

"To everything." He lifted his hands, as if to gesture around us. "To . . . us being here. To being High Priest. To . . . whatever this life is. Without Marie at my side, it's . . . not what I wanted. I never thought *this* would happen, of all the things I pictured for the three of us."

"Becoming the High Priest, you mean?"

He shrugged. His gaze had turned cloudy, as if frustrated, although his voice maintained an even edge.

"Perhaps. I'm not sure what I mean. I just know that I've felt robbed ever since I lost your mother. And sometimes, on quiet mornings like this, it . . . it just seems bigger."

"She loved mornings," I murmured.

He smiled. "Yes, she did. Mornings, tea, and quiet."

"I miss Mama, too."

"I know you do." He turned to me, one eyebrow lifted. "Do you think about her much?"

"At least every day."

"Me too. What do you think she's doing right now?"

I laughed. "Assuming the afterlife is real? Planting something with grandmother. The two of them were insufferable in the garden together."

He grinned. "Just like her daughter."

I punched him in the arm and he laughed. Light lined the sound, which reassured me that all the gathering pressure I'd seen in his eyes yesterday hadn't driven too deep yet.

"Speak for yourself," I muttered.

He chucked me softly in the shoulder. "I love you, B. And I'm sorry about what's happened. We'll figure this out."

The feeling in the air quickly sobered. "I had Leda come and meet Ava last night. I think there's a good chance she'll be able to speak with Ava soon. There are hints of familiarity in Ava's words that align with the Declan language."

His brow hung low over his eyes with his thoughts. "Huh."

"Please, Papa. Let Ava stay here. I'll take responsibility for her. She might be the only way we can get my magic to work again and possibly prevent something worse from happening to Alkarra. What if more are on the way?"

A heavy sigh dropped his shoulders. "I thought about it all night, and while I don't like the idea of keeping a mortal here, I like the idea of you being somewhere else even less. Magic or not, I have no doubt you'd find Ava wherever I put her. So yes, I will let her stay. For now," he tacked on.

Relief made me weak.

"Thank you, Papa."

He cut me a sharp glance. "Nothing dangerous, B. Nothing at all. She is here to learn how to communicate with us, and then I will take it from there *after* the Celebration. Our focus has to be meticulous. We'll give my attention to Ava when we're through the Celebration. All right?"

"I understand."

"You are not to ask her questions about the magic or where she lives or anything until I am in the room. Understood?"

I nodded. Of course, it would lay out differently from that . . . but let him feel in control here.

"Sounds fine," I choked out.

The amused twinkle in his eye told me he didn't buy it at all, but he let it go for now. He clapped a hand on my shoulder and stepped back.

"I need to clear up a few things with Baxter. Stay in the apartment as much as you can. If you have to leave, go with Reeves or someone that can get you out of a bad situation. Marten and I will figure out how to get you to the ball tomorrow night. Your absence again will only draw suspicion."

"Jikes," I muttered. "I totally forgot about the ball."

He flashed me a pearly smile. "I didn't. I'll figure something out so that you stay safe. Don't get too bored in here, and *don't* go into Letum Wood."

"Fine. I promise."

He clasped me in a quick hug, kissed the top of my head, and shoved me toward the breakfast table. While he walked toward the door, a leather belt with hidden daggers and a sundry of other weapons zipped across the room and into his waiting hand. He paused at the door and spun around as he tightened it around his waist.

"Merrick asked about you yesterday," he said. He studied me with a too-acute gaze. I tried to pretend as if I didn't care. When Merrick had left the Central Network under Geralyn's express command, there had been a sense of relief in Papa.

"Oh?"

"Told him you were doing great." His expression darkened, then cleared. "I'll have Baxter follow up on the ball, all right? Have a good day, B."

He opened the door and disappeared into the hallway.

Chapter Eleven

After Papa left, I sat at the breakfast table and dully comprehended my day. What would I do with my time? My mind drifted to my magic. More than a full day had passed since I touched the amulet, and I still felt the withdrawal of magic like a physical pang. The hollowness stretched through my body like a cavern. No amount of thought or wishing would fill it back up. Beneath it murmured a low, quiet roar of emptiness.

I frowned at a plate of fried eggs while Reeves puttered around the table, fussing with my half-filled teacup. He cast surreptitious glances over to Ava's door, which remained closed and lifeless inside.

"Good sleep, Reeves?" I asked.

He nodded.

While I poked at a piece of bread, Reeves strode down the hall. He returned with the same crisp, even staccato of shoes on stone.

"Ava is gone."

His calm declaration startled me like exploding sap. I leapt out of my chair and screeched, "What?"

"Her room is empty. The bed is unmade. She is not in her room or your room. I have not seen her this morning."

Panic coursed through me. That meant she must be somewhere in or near the castle, which was the *worst* possible place for her to be alone right now. The delegations would be in the hallways after the Southern Network breakfast and on their way to the Esbat room any minute now.

"Where could she have gone?" I asked as I stalked to the wall where my sword hung. "What time did you get up?"

"I'm not certain where she went, and I woke up two hours ago."

Halfway to the door, I forced myself to slow down and think. Without magic to keep me invisible, or safe, any mistake could result in death for me or Ava. I had no magic, and she was visibly mortal.

"I'm going to look for her," I called over my shoulder. "I'll be back. Stay here in case she returns."

"But—"

Before he could protest, I rushed into the hallway.

Once there, I paused again. Now what? It could take a full day to scan every room and hallway. For all I knew, she roamed the cobblestone streets of Chatham City by now.

With a muttered curse word, I followed a hunch to the left. It led away from the main body of the castle and toward the gardens. She wouldn't know that, but because the outside wall of the castle was in that direction, she might instinctively go that way.

My heart slammed in my chest as I hurried down a turret stairwell, smiling at a gaggle of maids as they passed. They sang a chorus of, "Merry meet!", their arms full of brooms. Buckets flew behind them.

A tug of envy pulled at me. They didn't even know how good they had it with their easy magic.

Sheer uncertainty kept me from asking if they'd seen a girl

like Ava. No need to draw more attention to her. At the very least, they didn't mention anything different about me, which meant something.

I hoped.

The maids disappeared behind me as I continued down the stairs and outside. A search of the nearest gardens came up empty. Guardians called to me, and I waved but hustled away before we could speak. The main floor revealed no Ava. Not in the kitchens, the laundry, or anywhere that servants mostly congregated.

I paused in a stairwell to gather my thoughts and catalog the places she could hide. Or her reasons for leaving. What was her motivation? Had someone taken her? Leda rarely woke up this early unless compelled, and she would have left a note. Reeves would have known the signs of a struggle in her room, and I doubted Ava would go with any witch without a protest.

After an hour of fruitless searching, I stopped in a hall with a defeated sigh. Best that I check to see if she'd returned before I started to search more private, secluded areas. Those halls would make it more likely that I could run into a high-ranking member of another Network, and the last witch I wanted to talk to was any of them.

Reluctantly, I headed back to the apartment. Paranoia ran high as I attempted to avoid all workers, waved every now and then, but otherwise acted like I had my total focus on something else. I avoided the halls that led to the Esbat and the visiting guest rooms and wound my way back through the castle.

Just as I turned a corner, I skidded to a stop. A body materialized out of nowhere, knocking into me. A pair of hands caught me just before I tumbled to the ground.

"Oh! Forgive me, Miss Bianca."

When I recovered myself, Niko's dark, wide eyes met mine. He appeared as startled as me, but it faded quickly. The pressure of his fingers around my arms disappeared as his hand dropped.

"The fault is mine," I said with a forced smile. "Perhaps I shouldn't always be in such a hurry."

Niko tilted his head to the side, gaze tapered as he took me in. His hair was slicked back and shiny this morning. With a freshly-shaved face, strong jaw, and patrician features like his grandfather, he cut an impressive political figure. Standing before Niko Aldana without magic felt like walking into a room naked. How did the Southern Network delegation stand in front of witches every day?

Too late, I realized I'd been staring at him for an awkward amount of time. Something like concern appeared in his features.

"Are you . . . well?" he asked.

Panic filled me like cold snakes in my belly. Could he sense my missing magic? Was there something visibly different about me without it? Neither Papa, Marten, nor Leda had insinuated there was. Before I could summon up the brainpower to reply, he shook his head.

"I'm sorry. You are lovely, as always. Forgive me if that was rude."

His observation had an echo of concern, but more of surprise. Surely, something *seemed* different about me, but maybe he couldn't articulate what he sensed. In that case, I could slip out of here.

"Rough night," I said with a wan smile. "Just a little tired."

He ran a hand over his eyes. "I understand. These political meetings can be very intense."

"You're not sleeping well?" I asked, eager to turn the focus away from me. "Is there something we can do to make you more comfortable?"

Niko gave a stiff smile. "Tracking hounds, perhaps?"

The wry joke sent me into a confused cloud of thought after I huffed off a laugh. Tracking hounds? Niko's tight lips held all the warmth of a glacier now.

"You were with Priscilla two days ago, correct?" he asked. A hint of something lingered in the words.

"Yes. We had lunch together."

"Have you seen her since?"

"No."

He assessed me yet again, as if he thought I might be lying. After what felt like too long for propriety's sake, he sighed.

"She has gone missing."

"Is she in trouble?"

"I can only assume so, because I cannot find her."

"Allow me to help? I can transport over there and—"

He held up a hand to stop me. "My witches will have it under control soon. I came this way with the hopes to ask if you'd seen her. She mentioned an appointment to have lunch with you the other day."

There was something odd about *this* Niko. When we first met years ago, he had been amiable. Fun, even if it was subdued. I'd considered him a good friend through the trying war days when we shared misery and relief in the same breath. But that had been Niko, grandson of the High Priest.

This was Niko, the High Priest.

"I'm sorry, Niko," I said and managed to mean it. "But I haven't seen her since our lunch. I want to help the effort to find her. What are you doing? What can I do?"

Niko's gaze tapered, as if he puzzled through something. "Yes," he murmured, then shifted. "It's an interesting situation. Because a third body was reported at your lunch. A potential stowaway, perhaps? Escaped from a ship and found their way to land, was what I heard."

The word *body* set me on edge. What a weird word to use, and I couldn't shake the feeling that it was intentional. He certainly hadn't said *witch*. I filed away the fact that he didn't attempt to hide the fact he'd been spying on us.

"Stowaway?" I repeated.

"It's a crime in the East, you know." He shrugged with a too-charming smile that looked more dangerous than trustworthy now. Any trace of amiability had disappeared in a flash. "Witches from the South stow onto our fishing vessels and try to work in our Network. They take our resources and then demand our protection. It's not very fair, is it? We've had to crack down. Mercy is . . . well, let's say that mercy *and* justice must live together."

"I see."

"Do you?" he asked. An expression of false delight came to his face. Underneath it lay a current of challenge that set my heart racing. "Do you really *see* what I mean?"

Rankled by his condescending tone, I gave him an equally bright, equally razor-sharp smile. There had been no outlet for my budding frustration, and a confrontation with Niko about Priscilla's desperate circumstances was the perfect chance to release my rage.

"I do see. I see that stowaways must be a real pull on your society. Same as the criminals from the East that use magic to pillage the South and send them into such dire circumstances in the first place." I leaned closer, my smile feral. "But that's not what I mean. I *see* that you're having Priscilla watched and now you're concerned that she's gone. How—to use your word for it —interesting. Why would a High Priest need to have his *betrothed* watched? Or can you even call her that if you're unwilling to announce it publicly?"

His nostrils flared. I paused, brow raised, and waited for him to reply. His shoulder twitched when he said, "My beloved is always well protected."

"Who?" I feigned surprise. "Oh, forgive me. You said your *beloved* and I thought you said your *betrothed*, but neither can be true if we're speaking about Priscilla."

Niko's lips tightened. With a politically composed response, he said, "She is so well protected, in fact, that stirring rumors about a suspicious person on our shore have caught my attention. Of course, I would allow no harm to come to Priscilla. She is being watched for her protection."

"Or your paranoia."

He studied me, as if curious about something. "How much do you know, Bianca Monroe?" he murmured.

The hair on the back of my neck stood on end. Yet again, he didn't say *mortal* or *witch*, but there was some hidden allusion to it there. No, he was playing a game here, but I didn't know what. Nor why.

What did *he* know?

Had Priscilla told him about the mortal girl? Impossible, because her letter reported that he hadn't known she left, and I doubted she would have sent a letter.

"I can't imagine why a single stowaway would be of concern," I said, "since your Network clearly deals with this every day."

Niko folded his hands behind his back, pulling his slender shoulders into a wider position.

"Of course you don't. How could you? The Central Network has no idea what we've been suffering the last several years. It has been focused on its own interest and *mission of peace*." Scorn resided in the words. "Rest assured, my witches are exploring exactly what happened on the beach that day. We will know who that person was. Because it wasn't so much the stowaway that got my attention." His gaze tapered. "It's the fact that *you* left with them. Now why would you leave with a stowaway a few days ago and today act as if you hadn't? Quite . . . interesting."

His expression remained lazy, as if we spoke about our next tea. Under it lay an edge of promise. My heart did a double *whomp* in my chest as I stood there, utterly unable to respond.

He had me locked into position now because I hadn't anticipated a confrontation so direct. I'd put myself in a corner, just as he said.

I clamped my lips together.

"Nothing goes unnoticed in my Network, Bianca Monroe," he added quietly. "Absolutely nothing."

I couldn't help myself.

"Except for the whereabouts of your betrothed, of course."

"Merry part." He gave a tense bow. "I expect to speak with you again very soon."

Once he left the way he came, I let out a long breath. My mind felt like scattered leaves in the wind. Before I could process all that Niko had just revealed—or was *challenged* the better word?—Reeves cleared his voice behind me.

"The lost item has been found. I beg you to return and see if it remains to your satisfaction."

With relief, I turned around to face him.

"Thank you, Reeves. Let's return together."

* * *

"Food."

"*Dainta.*"

"Water."

"*Omo.*"

Ava sat next to me on the couch a few hours later, a curious expression on her face. Not long after I'd left, Reeves reported that a gentle knock came on the door. He had opened it and admitted her back inside. She had smiled, stridden to the breakfast table, and begun to quietly eat.

She hadn't even flinched at my concern when I stormed back into the apartment behind Reeves. She just listened unknowingly to my tirade, fiddled with the dark amulet, and managed to look somewhat contrite.

But not really.

Not for the first time, I questioned her motive. Why was she here? What did she seek? Was it courage or young stupidity that sent her into the world of witches unprotected? How could I tell her that sneaking around only made it *more* likely the Council would have her killed?

Papa wouldn't be able to protect her if she wandered around so recklessly.

Now, she regarded a book sprawled across our lap. Reeves had thoughtfully found several scrolls and books used in young schools that Ava and I had sorted through most of the morning.

While we pointed to pictures and swapped words, I mentally flailed. Thoughts of Niko, lost magic, and mortal girls swirled in my head. It seemed unlikely that Ava was the only mortal still alive. So where were they? Were we in danger?

Could my magic be restored?

With a shake of my head, I admonished the spiral of thoughts with one final hope: Papa would figure it out once he had the mental space to do so. Yes, of course he would. He'd do what was necessary to get my magic back and protect the Network.

We just had to communicate with Ava first.

The sound of a knock rippled through the room. I peered over the top of the book as Reeves answered the door. A moment passed before he pulled it wide open. Several bags entered in advance of a flustered witch with a dark cape pulled far over their face. Flyaway hair and arms full of books emerged from the cape as soon as the witch advanced into the room.

A familiar voice chirped, "Satchels in the hall if you please, Reeves."

All of it—except the books—landed on the floor with a thud seconds later. I blinked, then straightened as Leda haughtily shook the cape off her head and peered our way. Ava followed my gaze with a murmured question that I didn't understand. Leda's eyes were bloodshot now, rimmed with fatigue.

"Everything all right?" I asked, setting the book aside.

Leda propped her hands on her hips. "I've quit the library."

"What?" I screeched.

"I couldn't get any time away to help you speak with Ava," she continued primly, brushing her hair out of her face and onto her shoulders. "Frankly, everything at the library pales in comparison to what you're now dealing with, Bianca, and I'm loath to let you keep mucking things up on your own."

Dire circumstances forced me to let that comment pass.

"But why?"

She pointed at me, ignoring my question. "Let it be known that this resignation from the Great Library of Burke does not mean I'm accepting Scarlett's offer. Far from it. The last thing I want to do is to work with that—" She forced out a sharp exhalation. "I'm here to crack this language with Ava. It will give me a better shot at the position of Librarian over the Declan and Mortal Wars Language division than what I have been doing, as ridiculous as that sounds. I strongly believe they'll take me back, should I wish to go, after I have solved this little . . . issue."

Ava made a sound at the back of her throat as I stood there, attempting to take all of this in. An underlying sense of panic seemed to roll through everything Leda said, but her calm mien meant she hadn't given into it yet. Clearly, she still processed what was, for her, a very quick decision. She usually mulled things over for ages before she took action.

"I trust there's a room here in which I can stay?" she asked.

"Of course. I . . . thank you, Leda."

Reeves shuffled closer, arms full of satchels, a basket of scrolls, another of ink bottles, and quill feathers tied together with twine. He set the baskets next to her, then reached for the heaviest satchels and began to carry them down the hallway.

Leda watched which room he turned into, then squared herself to me again.

"You're a mess, Bianca. Can't do magic. Stuck with a mortal girl that all Networks will want to kill as soon as they find her. Your father is on the verge of a total dissolution of peace and another potential war. The only way to fix your significant problem is to speak with Ava, so I'm here to do that—and to figure out what that atrocious amulet *is*—by breaking the language barrier. The only way to fix your father's problem is for you to be present as he works through the political sludge. I can also help you suss out the political ramifications of what you're about to do."

Leda always put my mind in a whirl, and this moment was no exception. I blinked several times as my brain caught up with hers.

"What *am* I about to do?" I asked.

Her eye roll would have knocked glasses off the top of her head if any had been perched there.

"The ball? Did you forget that that is tomorrow evening?"

I groaned. "No, but I wish I had. Papa reminded me about it this morning. Do we have to talk about it?"

"You already missed the Central Network dinner, and the *Chatham Chatterer* poured out rumors about your whereabouts for hours. To miss the ball would be catastrophic for your father. As we've already discussed, he is—"

"It's a ball." I cried. "The first time I went to a ball, Mabel tried to kill both of us. Only you and Mildred kept me alive."

Leda pinched the bridge of her nose between her thumb and forefinger and said in a long-suffering tone, "I'm very aware of that memory. Thank you. You will go to the ball because it will allow your father's opposition on the Council to see you together. To see that *both* of you are committed to the Network, and you are by your father's side. For obvious reasons, namely the fact that both of you were instrumental in saving Alkarra from Almorran magic, the Network sees you and Derek as a single unit. They love or hate you both. You must be strong *together*."

"Fine," I muttered.

I suppressed another groan. Papa had already made it clear he expected me to attend, lacking magic notwithstanding. But I hadn't understood why he pushed it when I didn't have magic. Did he have a plan for me *not* getting killed while there? Or inadvertently revealing the fact that I was practically a mortal myself?

Leda softened just enough for me to see the humanity in her glare. "Do you want to save Ava and get your magic back?"

"More than anything."

"Do you want the Central Network to be safe from another inter-Network war?"

"Of course."

"Then, you'll trust Ava to me and turn your attention to what you can do. You'll go to that ball tomorrow night and you'll do what your father can't."

She paused for dramatic effect, and again I wondered when she'd be convinced that being High Priestess was her future.

"Which is?" I drawled.

"You're going to dance with the Southern Network High Priest, Igor."

"What?"

Warmed up now, she propped one hand on her hip and nodded. "You're going to find a way to slide *mortals* into the conversation, then figure out if he knows anything about Ava. Cracking Ava's language is going to take time, time we may not have. You can get more information about the mortal situation while we wait."

"You're kidding."

"I'm not.

Leda's plan slid into my mind like a puzzle that finally came together. My lips rounded in an O as comprehension dawned.

"You want me to find out if other mortals are hiding in the Southern Network."

She spread two hands. "Where else would they be?"

The implications shuddered through my mind quickly afterward. If Ava wasn't the only one here, then *any* mortal could be in the Southern Network without drawing suspicion—amber eyes aside. If mortals were present in Alkarra and had somehow harnessed magic, which the amulet posed an arguable position for, we could be in *big* trouble.

Leda's assumption was a wild shot, of course. Ava may be the only mortal here. She may not even *be* a mortal, which was an option I didn't really consider because Ava had demonstrated no magic. Leda might even be assigning me this ridiculous task to keep me busy and out of her hair while she dealt with Ava.

But Leda was also somewhat right.

Someone needed to dive further into this mystery before it was too late, and Papa wouldn't do it. To that end, the potential of mortals in Alkarra was an assumption worth pursuing. Me pursuing this sort of goal had *Sisterhood leader* written all over it. Scarlett would either be proud or horrified. I couldn't decide which.

For several moments, I struggled with Leda's proposal. How could I rope Igor into a dance? Such a calculated move would be a blatant act against Papa's wish to be secretive and subtle. A mortal girl in the Central Network was his problem, the solution should be his decision.

Except . . . I *had* brought her here.

And he would have the reconnaissance done . . . when he could. Which, arguably, could also be too late.

"Listen," Leda said with a sigh. "You did the right thing calling me here to help. Now I'm here to stay, but I'm not enough. Someone needs to make sure the mortals aren't here to do worse than wave an amulet around."

Her gaze darted to Ava, who perused the book again but

seemed to keep half her attention on us. Based on what Ava had written on a piece of parchment, our alphabet was only slightly different. A few sounds off-kilter, and she had a few more letters, but not so far off base that everything would need to be learned again.

"I know," I said. "You're right."

Leda drew in a breath, then let it out. "I always love to hear that, but I *really* love it now. You can do more than Derek. Bianca, you may be the only witch that can. You need to be proactive in a way that he can't or won't be right now. There's more at stake than just your father's position as High Priest. All of us fought for this Network." Her chin lifted, and her throat bobbed imperiously. "And some of us gave our lives to our Network. I lost my brother and Camille, and I won't sit by now and wait until your father has a more advantageous position to pursue a result."

"I'll go to the ball and try to get more information from Igor, but that's all. Papa will do the right thing, Leda. We just need to let him have the chance."

She folded her arms across her chest. "I want to believe that too. Now, leave Ava to me, please. We have work to do and you have a ball gown to find."

The reminder almost made me groan again. A ball gown! Where in Alkarra was I going to find one the day before it had to be ready? I never looked for dresses that were up to date with the latest fashion trends. This was my fault. I should have paid attention to that detail weeks ago, but I hadn't because we'd been finalizing a new class of recruits. Frankly, I hadn't cared all that much.

I spun on my heels as Leda approached Ava, my thoughts twirling with exactly how I'd tackle a dance with Igor—and a subtle conversation about a subject that no witch *ever* brought up. The very word *mortal* sent a weird frisson through me. No one said that word anymore. I sighed. I'd have to accomplish this one step at a time. Papa would come up with a plan to keep me safe at the ball. I needed to find a dress.

Then I'd worry about conversations while dancing.

Once I approached a side table, I grabbed a piece of parchment and a quill, then scrawled across the top of the page.

Baxter,

I'm going to need a favor.

B

* * *

"Why do you smell like charcoal?"

The question came from just over my left shoulder an hour later. It jostled me out of my thoughts so hard I clutched my chest.

"A little warning?" I cried.

Baxter grinned and stepped up next to me. I stood out on Papa's balcony, my hands on the railing. Only when I noticed my white-knuckled grip did I release it and drop my arms back to my sides. Baxter would notice that I was unusually tense, and then he'd ask why. I didn't want to answer questions today. Particularly not after forcing Leda and Ava into the back room, and making them swear not to come out until summoned.

"But seriously," he said. "Are you burning something out here?"

The smell of ash had lingered in my nostrils all day. Could he smell it as well? As if the amulet had burned the magic out of me and it drifted out of my skin. The thought almost made me shudder.

"Ah, no?"

He grunted deep in his throat, but a curious gleam entered

his assessing gaze, which meant more questions. More questions meant he suspected something different about me, and Papa said he wasn't going to tell Baxter about my missing magic.

Time to change the subject.

"Thanks for coming," I said. "You got here fast. I just sent that message an hour ago."

He leaned one bent elbow on the railing in a lazy stance, eyeing me with a wary expression. Was it concern? It darkened his jade-colored eyes.

"I have a few minutes," he said. "Can't stay long. You all right? I've been worried about you. You might be a forest witch, but you're a punctual one. When you didn't show up for the Central Network dinner, I thought you must have died or something."

Close, I wanted to say when I remembered the fire ripping through my body after I touched the amulet.

"Not dead." I forced a smile and spread my arms. "Clearly still here. To that end—"

"You wish you weren't still here because you don't want to go to the ball tomorrow night?"

"Not true. I want to support Papa, I just—"

"Don't have a dress."

I sighed. "No. How did you know?"

"As always, the son of a god comes to the rescue with his extraordinary talents. Please, lay your eyes on these options."

Two elegant dresses sprang to life right in front of me, without a muttered word from him. Did he use silent magic to conjure *dresses*? Sure, he used silent magic more than most witches I'd ever met, but to use silent magic for a multiple-item summoning incantation? Odd. The thought sent a bolt of suspicion through me.

Just how was Baxter good at *everything*?

My thoughts whirled down that path while I stared at the dresses without seeing them. No doubt mistaking my attention,

Baxter quipped, "Are you rendered speechless by my choices? Because that's fair. I'm known for good taste."

I could *feel* the arrogant wink in his words.

"Ah, yes." I cleared my throat. "These are beautiful."

Two dresses that hovered a hands-breadth above the floor were, to Baxter's credit, not distasteful. Like him, they had a sense of modern, elegant fashion without being overbearing. By society's standards, particularly the extravagant culture of the East, they were probably boring. Each was a variation of gray. A sooty tone as deep as charcoal for the one on the left, and a bluish-gray that reminded me of a stormy sky for the dress on the right. The first dress dropped to the floor and had no sleeves. The second had a scandalous rise to the knee on the right side, with sleeves to the elbow.

Why society determined that women could expose their elbows, but not their knees, I would never understand.

"They'll match your eyes, at any rate."

The quality of the dress meant that they were no cast-offs. These had been prepared for elegance.

"You just found these now?" I asked in astonishment. "In the last hour?"

He tilted his head back and laughed, which ruffled his dark curls so they bounced a little. "No. Definitely not, but I'm flattered that you think so. I knew this very scenario would happen, so I had a Dressmaker's Assistant track these down weeks ago."

My mouth opened, then closed. Being anticipated felt like nails on a chalkboard, but I couldn't deny a refreshing sense of relief. At least I didn't have to worry about finding a dress, and they *were* lovely.

With a less astonished eye, I studied the dresses again. The first had a gentle shimmer, like rain on the ground. The hint of blue in the foggy-like material felt subdued. A low back would plunge halfway down my spine, but the neckline in front remained high. Papa would hate that, but Papa didn't have to know until it was too late. Chic simplicity was the best way to describe it.

"The one with the slit to the knee," I said. "That will do quite nicely."

Baxter smiled, his white teeth sparkling. "As expected," he replied jauntily. The first dress disappeared.

"It's borderline scandalous."

"Just why I thought you'd like it."

I had no response for that at first, but he spared me having to say anything when he continued speaking.

"We will attend the ball together." He grimaced. "Your father's orders, so you can't back out of a night with me even if you want to. I'm sorry for that."

A chuckle escaped me. "Nice try. You know I wouldn't try to escape you."

"Let's hope not. Your father seems to think there are witches that seek to harm you. He was very concerned about your safety and asked me to *be stuck on Bianca like sap on a tree, and if you interpret that like a hormonal teenage boy would, I'll have your head.*"

Despite the levity, questions lined his eyes. Ones I could tell he hadn't posed to Papa. Why else would he bring them to me? No doubt he wanted me to explain. But I wouldn't. Couldn't, in some regard. This was Papa's problem.

I turned back to view the grounds because it seemed easier to avoid his questions when I didn't have to stare down his curiosity.

"Papa has always been paranoid about my safety."

"Yes," Baxter drawled, "but the discussion he and I had this morning was . . . odd. A bit more intense than I would have expected, I guess, for a simple Celebration ball. I've heard nothing else amiss in the meantime. Nothing that would cause such dire concern for your safety. Is something wrong?"

My throat hurt when I swallowed hard and shook my head.

Did the smile that I forced out look as awkward as I felt? It must have because Baxter's gaze narrowed.

Before I could stumble into an awkward topic of conversation, Baxter straightened from his almost-slouch.

"Well, I may be reading into it. Feast your eyes on this."

Something else appeared next to the remaining dress. Startled, I could only stare for a moment before I realized what else he'd brought: two sets of male dress clothes for the ball.

I motioned to them with a lifted hand.

"Yours?" I confirmed.

"Mine." He nodded once.

Central Network fashion these days had men wearing coats with the jacket ends barely past their elbows. They used colorful scarves around their waists and coattails that trailed to their knees. The combination of open forearms and short waists lent an odd appearance to almost every formally-attired male I saw.

Thankfully, Baxter had maintained a classic feel instead of a more fashion-forward one.

The sets hovered above the ground. Each had similar tones of gray and blue, like mine, but altering color schemes. The pants and blazer on the left were black linen, light gray, and a gentle blue shirt. On the right, a sooty gray pair of pants and matching blazer—almost like leather, but not quite as heavy— and a deep sapphire shirt.

Baxter gestured to the sapphire pair.

"The one on the left is what I will wear to the ball tomorrow. The original color of the dress you chose was more of a green, but the Dressmaker's Assistant used magic to change it to gray so it matched your eyes. She then altered mine to have a matching theme. I thought we'd make more of a splash if we complemented each other. It looks better." His nose wrinkled in a move that made me think of a little boy. "*Conscientious fashion,* they're calling it?"

"Who are *they*?"

He shrugged, then laughed. "I don't know! The Dressmaker and her Assistant? They're the ones that dress Scarlett. Anyway, they insisted it makes a better impression. And if there's anything *you* need to do tomorrow, it's to make a good impression, talk to witches you don't want to, and dance with your father."

Another win for Leda's savvy, political mind. She'd already anticipated such a menu of requirements.

"Of course." I nodded with intentional zeal. "I'm ready. You'll look very nice in that ensemble."

He scoffed. Baxter had always been charming and handsome, gifted with that unknowable *something* that drew witches to him. As if one could resist the invisible pull of his personality, like a bright spot in the darkness. He didn't have a brawny torso like Merrick, but he appeared strong in a wiry way. His dark curls and the way they juxtaposed with his green eyes had always been attractive, but in those well-tailored and expensive dress clothes?

He'd be politically handsome. A quintessential, put-together Assistant and child of organization and diplomacy. The total opposite of me, in some regard, which could work in our favor. Besides, Papa had insisted that the two of us attend together, which was interesting itself.

The observation of Papa's paranoia, coming from Baxter, sent questions through my mind again. What had Papa told Baxter about my missing magic? Nothing, if Baxter's fishing questions meant anything, but I couldn't be sure. Baxter could be holding back to get me to talk even more. If I asked clarifying questions of Baxter, even thinly veiled, it would risk revealing too much.

But why did Papa trust Baxter with me at the ball, yet Papa didn't trust Baxter with Ava?

My heart raced at the thought that there was too much here I didn't know, and I made a mental note to write Papa a letter and demand some accounting. He'd done this before, with Merrick. Papa had known Merrick was a witch from the North and withheld that information. He'd do it again, if it were a matter of security or safety.

But was it?

I shook that off. I'd broach this *after* all his meetings, of course.

"Try it on tonight." Baxter tilted his head toward the dress and pulled me out of my spiraling thoughts. "If it needs alterations, you can use magic on it. The Assistant said the *linea* fabric holds up to spells just fine. We might be able to find her. She was going to finalize Scarlett's dress this afternoon."

Panic slipped through me at the thought of altering with magic, then calmed. Since I couldn't do magic, Leda would have to do the alterations. She'd spent half her childhood altering dresses for herself and her younger siblings so they'd all have something to wear.

"Of course. Thank you."

He eyed me again with that look that meant he knew something was off, but he asked no questions. Both my dress and his clothes disappeared.

"Thank you, Baxter." I infused extra meaning into it. "You really do have a talent for political coordination."

A rueful grin crossed his lips. "It's my pleasure, as always. Just try not to fall in love with me tomorrow night, although I recognize that's difficult. Son—"

"—of a god," I finished for him with a smirk. "Right."

"I anticipate a very unforgettable experience, Miss Monroe," he said with a little twinkle in his eye. "Please, do try to deliver something memorable."

His grin widened seconds before he disappeared off the balcony. The air felt empty in his wake. Before I could think too much about it, a tingly feeling lingered at the back of my neck. I gazed around with the feeling of being watched. Below, on the Wall, a familiar head of sandy hair strode away.

Merrick.

I sucked in a sharp breath.

Wasn't it? Or did I just want it to be?

The figure disappeared inside before I could know for sure.

Chapter Twelve

The first time I had set foot on the whirling floor of a ball, Mabel had tried to murder me. Creatures called Clavas, born of dark magic and determined to kill, swooped into the ballroom with murder in their eyes. I'd fought them off until I could make my way through broken glass and bleeding Guardians to Mabel. By the end of it, my grandmother gave her life to save me.

Which is why I paced back and forth across the apartment the next evening, ten minutes before Baxter would escort me to *this* ball. The two other Celebration balls had been perfectly safe and I'd been nervous then, too. But I'd had magic. With no immediate escape plan or magical safety, my heart wrung itself out like a lemon at the thought of all those witches surrounding me.

No magic, I thought in cadence with my feet hitting the floor. *No magic. No magic. No magic.* It sounded uncannily like my other internal refrain. *I'm sorry. I'm sorry. I'm sorry.*

Would other witches notice? Would they suspect? So far, Leda, Papa, and Reeves said they didn't notice anything, but would that be true of *everyone?*

The cavern inside me still felt like an empty space. Only the occasional flitter of heat surprised me, like dredges of fire. How desperately I missed the ease of magic. The ability to conjure what I needed, travel in an instant, and with so little effort.

The safety, my heart whispered.

Oh, the safety and privilege of magic.

"You're nervous," Leda said.

I rolled my eyes.

"Of course I'm nervous."

"Why? You've been to a ball before. Several, in fact."

"When I had magic," I hissed.

She paused, then tilted her head to one side. "Fair. I forgot that little detail."

The idea of all those eyes on me when Papa and I danced was enough to make my heart skip a beat again. I put my hand on my chest to calm the diabolical fluttering. How could I keep myself safe? My Volare didn't work. The small, handheld dagger that shrank to whatever size I needed didn't work now either. Were magical objects dependent on *us* for the magic? It appeared so, although I didn't understand why.

Though tempted, I couldn't very well stalk into the ball with a sword strapped around my waist. Nor on my thigh since the incantations didn't work with me now. Maybe my calf, though. That would hide it well enough. My thought flittered to the dagger that Ava had stolen from my house, which hadn't surfaced again.

"Calm down," Leda said. She lazily turned a page in her book. Her legs were tucked up on the couch, her toes hidden by slippers with a hole over one pinky toe. "You're not walking to your death. This time," she tacked on.

"Not funny."

She made no response. A day full of work with Ava, and then on her own when Ava took breaks, meant she retired to her room after a snack in the afternoon and had only just reappeared. When she'd returned, she mumbled something about Sanako and gods and goddesses. At Papa's explicit command, Reeves hid Ava away in her room after dinner, armed with several puzzles to keep her busy while she unknowingly avoided Baxter.

I grabbed a handful of the dress I'd picked out and rubbed it between my fingers, then released it. With that kind of torture, the dress would wrinkle, and I couldn't do a spell to straighten it back out.

Jikes, being a mortal forever would be awful.

The *linea* fabric of the dress, a magically woven material that felt as thin as linen, soft as silk, and prevented sweat stains during stuffy balls, was sturdy and smooth. The gentle gray shimmer, like rain on the ground with a hint of blue, matched my eyes almost perfectly. The low back plunged halfway down my spine.

When combined with the scandalous rise to the knee on the right side, witches would be sure to talk. The high neckline in front nearly touched my throat, however, which nicely negated the need for a necklace. The sleeves just passed my elbow, which would keep things cool. Silk slippers with an edging of lace completed the ensemble. They felt like I was barefoot, but without the audacity of breaking convention.

"It matches your eyes in a lovely way," Leda said. She had it right—my gray eyes had brightened like a thunderstorm in this dress. "The Dressmaker's Assistant has good taste."

Right after reappearing from her room, Leda worked a spell that made my hair glossy. While muttering under her breath, she'd used magic to create curls that draped elegantly down my back, then swept them onto the back of my head into a pile that left my neck blessedly free. The whole thing required less than ten minutes, and, as of yet, yielded no headache.

She had her uses as a best friend.

"Camille would have loved this dress," I murmured, not surprised by the longing in my voice. "And the ball. And the slippers. Don't you think she would have dragged Brecken with her?"

If I hadn't failed her, came the thought.

I shoved it away.

Leda pressed her lips together, then nodded. A pang of affection, but painful and sweet, slipped through me. Nights like these were when I missed Camille's bouncy chatter the most.

A gentle knock came on my door to distract us both.

"Coming," I called.

"You can do this," Leda said quietly, with a firm nod. "Talk to Igor, dance, come back. Easy. You were made for this sort of thing, anyway."

Scarlett's reminder about the Sisterhood whispered through my mind, but I sent it away. By instinct, I tried to issue a spell to open the apartment door for me, but it fell into dead space. With a frown, I crossed the room and pulled it open. Baxter looked up and a languid smile broke across his face.

"Bianca Monroe," he drawled as he stepped inside. "You lovely witch."

My cheeks warmed as I smiled.

"You're very handsome yourself, Baxter."

He wore the sapphire shirt beneath a dark gray jacket that cut sharply across his shoulders. The subtle blue in the depth of my dress was highlighted by the dark tones of his ensemble. His dark breeches were smudged leather. No cravat colored his neck, and he'd left a scandalous button open at the top of his throat, revealing a gentle pulse. The thumb at custom was as subtle as the slit up the side of my dress.

Now I knew exactly what he meant by complementary outfits.

He drew in a deep breath as he looked me over one last time. "You're going to draw every eye in the room tonight, Miss Monroe. Are you ready for it?"

Underneath the sincerity lay a warning to prepare myself for a social onslaught. I nodded. He held out a hand and I slipped my hand in his. It was warm and gentle. The tips of his fingers had hints of ink stains just scrubbed off.

"Follow my lead," he said. "If you need anything, just let me know. Or if you see someone you'd rather avoid, just point them out and we can escape somehow."

"Thank you, I will."

Of course, I should have anticipated that Baxter would foresee a very real fear: there were witches I didn't want to talk to tonight.

Merrick for one.

Niko for another.

Igor, for a third, even if talking to him *was* my goal. I had little choice there, on that count Leda was correct.

For half a moment, I was tempted to pull Baxter into this wild scheme. To reveal Ava, my lost magic, and to ask for his help with Igor tonight. Despite a full day to think a plan out, I still had none. Trap Igor somehow? Cut into a dance? I needed to be svelte *and* cunning without any magic at all to back me up. If I'd had magic, I would have transformed into someone else and approached him, maybe a Western Network diplomat or something.

Papa's firm admonition to keep Ava and my lack of magic as secret as possible stopped me from begging for Baxter's help. No, it wasn't my place to reveal Papa's secrets, no matter how much I trusted Baxter.

"We'll stay a few hours at most," Baxter said as he held out a bent elbow. "First thing we'll do is mingle. Say hello to witches, wave, be seen. That sort of thing. Second, we must find your father. Once witches see the two of you dance, you can speak to a few strategic others that may approach. Marten, for sure. Council Member Aldred, potentially."

My sharp gaze shot to his. Council Member Aldred? He was the witch leading the opposition against my father and the very last witch that would want to speak with me. Baxter laughed.

"Kidding!"

"Not funny."

Baxter sobered, but his eyes still danced. "Right, no more funny business here. I anticipate no problems. Protectors and Guardians abound tonight. But, of course, if you need anything, I promised Derek I'd be at your side all night."

The promise of protection sent an ominous shiver through me. How would I escape to find Igor? I'd have to figure it out. He seemed oblivious to my mental flailing as I accepted his offered arm.

"Ready to go?" he asked.

I drew in a deep breath.

Ready to stride into a ballroom where hundreds of witches with magical ability would be present, and I'd have no power to save them from an attack? Whether physical or something else. No. I'd never feel ready for this.

Still, I accepted his arm with a firm nod.

"Let's get this over with."

With Baxter by my side, I steeled myself for the most frightening night of my life.

* * *

My hand remained in the crook of Baxter's elbow as we slipped through the castle without speaking. By the time we made it to the ballroom, I felt grateful for his steady presence. My stomach wobbled around like a flopping fish.

In the ballroom, chaos abounded.

"Steady," he murmured when my arm clenched around his. "You're safe here."

We moved quietly into the ballroom and skirted along the edge of the black-and-white tiled floor. A mixed orchestra of

Central Network violins and Eastern Network flutes and drums thrummed out familiar songs. The dancing was already well underway. Couples swirled in dizzying lines around each other in the middle of the room. Dresses and cravats flashed with bright colors and styles from all of Alkarra.

Dance with Igor, get out of here. I reminded myself when the dazzle of it all threatened to overwhelm me. *Dance with Igor. Get out of here.*

The far left of the room hosted a lavish spread of early appetizers and light wine meant to keep energy high. Around midnight, an official dinner would be served in the banquet hall, which hid behind two massive doors currently closed. The Southern Network, with their love of traditional harp music, would provide interludes while witches ate and digested. The plucking, gentle strains would put half the witches here to sleep, I imagined.

On the right was an area with plush chairs for those who wanted to stand, sit, and mill in conversation. Open windows kept the room from getting too stuffy, while torches lent an acrid scent to the air. Candles dripped fat beads of wax from bright sconces along the walls. The ambiance buzzed with excitement.

"There's Scarlett." Baxter pointed toward two chairs near a fireplace with heat-less flames. A favorite incantation of Marten's, who loved the comfort of fire without the blaze.

Scarlett stood with two Council Members from the Central Network. One of them was a relatively new Council Member named Greyson that hailed from the Western Covens. He had wide hazel eyes, a neatly trimmed beard the color of pitch, and an unassuming face.

The Western Covens had fared the worst in the war because they bordered the Western Network, and Greyson had been cleaning up the mess left behind since the war ended. So far, in terms of political prowess, he proved sharp as a razor. Although the ideas he came up with were unconventional, they often worked. He was one of the two Council Members undecided on loyalty between Papa and the growing unrest around the Highest Witch paradigm.

Scarlett caught me regarding them and nodded to me, one eyebrow arched high. The look on her face suggested a question. Was she talking to Greyson about the Sisterhood? Rumors abounded that Scarlett had started to push a Sisterhood agenda far more frequently now, which meant if I didn't get on board, she might move forward without me.

I wasn't sure how I felt about that.

Tonight, she wore a red gown. Although the dress was lovely on her, the gentle twist of her mouth indicated she felt as awkward as a dressed-up board in an evening gown. Her curiosity was sincere enough when she gazed around with her quick, assessing stare. Greyson spoke rapidly, if the quick flash of his lips meant anything, and I wondered what they said to each other.

My nerves twitched as I eyed the windows where the Clavas had once broken through, their misty, contorted bodies still a dark memory in my mind.

Lana, the High Priestess of the Western Network, smiled at me as she passed by. She wore a dazzling dress of black sequins, emerald beads, and a rainbow of lace that changed color as it wound down her dress. A peacock feather splayed behind her auburn hair, which had been pulled back into a tight bun, then curled in giant loops around her head. I brought myself out of memories to return the smile.

She disappeared into the crowd with her maid towing just behind her, carrying the rest of her lacy train.

"Your father," Baxter said, "is on the other side of the room, near Igor. Let's speak with Derek first so you can get the dance done. Crossing the room around the edges will certainly help you be seen faster, even if it takes longer. Agreed?"

"A good plan."

The nervous surprise of an easy approach to Igor set me on edge. Would this be simpler than I expected? I sincerely hoped so. Two minutes in and no one had stopped me yet. No one had shouted, "Imposter! A witch without magic!" I took it as a good sign and gathered my courage. Maybe no one really paid that much attention to me.

A luxury, I thought.

Just as I spotted Papa through the crowd, a flash of dirty blonde hair appeared on my left. Merrick. My neck tightened when he whirled by with a woman from the North. His gaze caught mine for half a second before he disappeared back into the dance.

My heart slammed in my chest as I followed Baxter along the edge of the room, my thoughts swirling in tune to the dance. Seeing him tonight had always been a possibility, but I hadn't realized how disorienting it would feel. Like someone had tipped my world upside down, then righted it again. I didn't want to talk to Merrick. Not tonight. Not after two years. But that was a lie, wasn't it? I *did* want to talk to Merrick.

So much.

Oh, why did he have to come?

I sealed my lips together, as if that could prevent a confrontation, and focused on navigating through the piles of fabric worn by the Eastern Network females on this side of the room. They tittered at something a witch said in their language, *Ilese*, as we passed. Baxter broke the way ahead of me, but the task still wasn't simple.

To distract my mind from Merrick, and wandering into forbidden avenues of *what if*, I kept an eye on the ballroom. Waiters strolled around with trays of wine glasses held secure on their trays by spells. Silk banners gilded with gems from the Southern Network crawled from wall to wall in elegant patterns. Western Network hors d'oeuvres topped the silver platters that followed the wine. Papa cleverly designed every event as a gathering of Networks, so every Network contributed something.

True partnership, he'd said before the first Celebration. *No more posturing. Networks will either agree, or they won't. Either way, it doesn't have to divide us.*

The distraction only lasted a moment, because my mind soon turned back to my former sweetheart. This was the first time we'd been in the same room in two years. Our first opportunity to make sense of what happened between us.

My heart continued to pound, as if Merrick had never left my sight.

Had he?

To confirm my growing suspicion, I glanced over my shoulder. Amid a teeming crowd of witches, I caught a glimpse of him. Merrick followed us, gaze intent, face fixed in concentration as he tried to wade through the same crowd after me. His heart filled his eyes. He looked . . . desperate. Terrified. Hopeful.

Everything that I felt.

I whirled back around, my heart in my throat.

A nearby marble statue of a desert nymph holding a silver heart reflected the movement of the ballroom. Art from the West, no doubt, where some of the tribes worshipped nymphs in the depths of the sand. Something about the woman holding her heart in her hand, a broken, anguished expression on her face, stopped me.

I squeezed Baxter's arm.

"Baxter, wait."

He immediately glanced back. Seeing the expression on my face, he slipped off to the side. We stepped to an empty spot on the wall.

"What's wrong?" he asked.

My thoughts scattered like sand. Merrick would be on us in seconds. Knowing that, I could barely think of the words that I would say to him.

"Ah . . . nothing. Everything is fine. It's just . . . Merrick is following us. I think he wants to speak with me."

Understanding flooded his features.

"Oh."

Although he didn't look out on the crowd, I could feel his attention heighten. Baxter had been there when the disaster happened over two years ago. When Farah, the Northern Network High Priestess had died of a fever. Her sister Geralyn claimed the throne with her more diminutive, quieter sister Samantha's support. Geralyn called all Northern Network witches back, Merrick included. If he hadn't obeyed, he would have been exiled from his family for the rest of his life.

Then he never returned.

Baxter had been present several times when I'd cried in Papa's arms, mourning the withdrawal of my first love. A flicker of movement, then a pause, registered just out of sight to my left.

Merrick had found me.

Baxter's arm dropped to his side. "Is this the first you've seen him since Geralyn took power?" he asked.

"This close? Yes."

His nose wrinkled. His eyelashes were thick and dark, lightening his already startling eyes. "Two years ago? Has it seriously been that long?"

Longer. It had only been months after the war ended before we had to split. I swallowed hard.

"Yes."

"That's . . . awkward."

"Is it?"

"Might be for you. If he's trying to corner you, then we can dance all night."

With Baxter's smooth steps—he was as gifted with dancing as everything else—I couldn't deny I was tempted to avoid the confrontation I'd both dreamed of and dreaded at the same time. But the curling feeling of being a coward wouldn't go away. With it was a lingering breathlessness, an excitement I wouldn't let myself understand. I sighed.

"I need to talk to him, don't I?"

Baxter's voice was surprisingly gentle when he said, "If you want to be really done with him, then yes. Talk to him. Get your closure. Clear the air. Then, you can move on."

"Aren't you too busy with your job to have any personal experience with heartbreak?" I quipped, just to give myself a moment to breathe.

A frown smudged the smooth skin of his forehead. "All of us have experience with heartbreak." Then his roguish smile reappeared to smooth out the lines. "Even the son of a god." He sobered. "What would you like me to do?" he asked in a low rumble. "He's not far away, and he's watching. Of course, I'd be more than willing to dance all night, but I think you know that he'll probably cut in eventually."

I hesitated, torn in the decision. On one hand, I wanted to dance with Papa, talk to Igor, and get back to my room. On the other hand . . . Merrick and I had parted, then never spoken again. Would tonight offer final closure?

A gap between the past and now?

But . . .

"It's been over two years," I said. "So much has happened in that time. Wouldn't it be easier to act as if we don't know each other?"

Baxter laughed. "I've never known Bianca Monroe to be afraid of anything."

My spine straightened as if he'd just offered me an insult, but he hadn't. Conversely, it was a compliment. Perhaps a reminder. Whatever he meant to do, it worked. My courage found her legs again.

"You're right. Best to get this over with."

"I will step away," Baxter said, "but I won't leave you alone with him. I promised your father not to let you out of my sight.

However tempted, I also promise I won't listen in to your conversation."

His unintentional reminder of my lost magic wasn't necessary, but it made my stomach clench all over again anyway. A traitorous part of me feared absolutely nothing at the thought of being with Merrick again. That part of me was the one that felt so safe with him.

"Thank you. I will be safe with Merrick."

But maybe my heart won't be, I thought.

Before I lost my courage, I turned. Merrick stood there, hands folded behind his back. His hair was pulled away from his face into an elegant braid. A trimmed beard filled his jaw, a normal custom for the roguish Masters of the North. It was a dark brown, unlike his hair. Intense eyes, slightly bothered, regarded me.

A thousand memories rushed back with that stare.

Baxter released me, then nudged me toward him. "Go," he whispered quietly. "If you can survive a witch like Mabel, you can do this."

Chapter Thirteen

Alone, I stood before Merrick with one thought: *he's changed.*

Time had passed in his face alone. Worry lines on his forehead. Wrinkles around the eyes. Despite the signs of passing time, glimmers of the old Merrick still lived in the intensity of his gaze and a gentle warmth in his smile. It made me wonder what he saw on my face. How had I changed?

The weight of his stare slammed all the way to my soul. For a long time, neither of us said a word, then Merrick closed the space between us. My stomach did a somersault at the sound of his voice, murmuring so quietly.

"I hope it's okay that I interrupted you, little troublemaker."

My nickname off his lips sent a thrill through my bones. "No interruption," I croaked. "I'm happy to see you."

He smiled.

My heart dove.

My statement felt true: I was happy to see him, even if so many other emotions swamped it. Terror. Uncertainty. Frustration. Rage. Elation. Giddiness. My goal to dance with Igor faded away when he held out an arm, curiosity in his tone.

"May we talk somewhere else?"

"Of course."

I slipped my arm through his. A frenzy of butterflies resurrected in my stomach when I touched his arm. Merrick guided me away from the ballroom without a word and I followed, relieved he hadn't offered his hand. That kind of touch felt too . . . close. Too intimate. I wasn't ready to relive such power again. Already my heart ached. Memories from our time together whispered over me. They were reminders of what we'd had, and what had been taken from us.

Minutes later, we stood on a calm balcony attached to the ballroom. Only a few other couples stood there, and none of them seemed to notice us, which gave me considerable relief. I wanted a chance to catch my breath.

Cooling air touched the open part of my dress, across my bare back. The night still bore the weight of the day's heat, but it was not as scorching. It felt cooler out here than inside, and my flushed cheeks calmed. Darkness clouded the ground far below, where torchlights flickered and Guardians stood at attention.

Merrick stopped at the edge of the balcony. He set his hands down, gazed out for several moments, and finally drew in a deep breath through his nose. His eyes fluttered shut.

"I've missed the smell of Letum Wood."

I laughed softly. Complimenting the forest was surely the fastest path back into my graces. Not that he had reason to recover my graces. What had happened wasn't either of our faults.

"You certainly had enough time in the forest for all the runs we went on."

For several more moments, neither of us said anything. In the calmness, I thought I felt some healing. He turned to face me with the half smile that had always melted my knees. An undeniable affection filled his tone.

"It's good to see you, B."

"You too."

Merrick had been my best friend. My first kiss. My first relationship. The hidden delight behind eighteen-year-old Bianca's desperate attempts to save her Network, her father, and fight a war. I viewed that version of Bianca as entirely different from the witch I was now. Someone else, from far away, who had experienced so much.

But the very circumstances that pulled us together eventually ripped us apart.

"How are things in the North?"

The question felt loaded with unsaid things. *What do you do with your day now? Why didn't you ever come back? Do you regret leaving me behind? I've missed you.*

"My mother has handfasted again."

My eyebrows rose. Merrick lost his father as a teenager and held a deep reserve of affection for his mother, Kalli, and his younger sister Jacqueline.

"That *is* big news. Do you like him?"

He smiled gently. "I do. He'll be good to her. My little sister has started working as a seamstress for the High Priestess Samantha, and she's happy there for now. She loves the castle and all the witches in it."

A memory of his bright little sister surfaced in my mind. Yes, she would love something as social and changing as the castle. Her vivaciousness and youthful spirit reminded me of Camille.

"Did you come to help protect Geralyn?"

He nodded.

"But you didn't come last year."

"No, I asked to stay behind."

My brow came together. "Why?"

"For a lot of reasons," he said with an edge of hesitation in his tone—a reminder that we didn't know each other as well as we used to. "And you? What is keeping the great Bianca Monroe busy these days?"

He canted his body so he could lean back against the railing and fully face me. His palms sprawled on the top to brace him from behind, which gave me the full power of his stare. His shoulders spread far, a daunting prospect for anyone who wanted to fight him. Those arms once held me close, and I missed the safety of his smell.

I also wondered about the quick change in subject.

"Working with the new recruits as an instructor in sword work," I said. Blood rushed to my cheeks. Why did I feel embarrassed?

His brow rose. "Oh?"

"I enjoy it."

The sentence came out with too much force, like I defended something. But I couldn't take it back. His troubled expression returned. The one that was all heavy brows and a slight pout of his bottom lip. I knew that face too well. It had borne him out of here in our final goodbye. For months after he left, that expression had haunted my dreams. Even my waking hours. Yes, I had thoroughly mourned Merrick.

To have him stand before me again was . . . surreal.

"I see," he murmured.

Was that disappointment in his tone? Instantly on guard, I asked, "What does that mean?"

He peered at me for several assessing moments before he said, "I guess I thought you'd already have started the Sisterhood by now. I looked forward to hearing your progress with it. What you'd learned and accomplished."

Frustration coursed through me in frissons of heat that could have been rage. I drew in a breath to calm the annoyance that surfaced. The surge of defensiveness was telling, but I didn't want to look into it. Not tonight.

"No," I said stiffly. "No progress has been made on that front."

His gaze tapered. "Why not?"

"Maybe because I'm not interested anymore."

He scoffed. "You'll never convince me that's true."

"Why not?" I bristled. "Because I'm happy living in peace? Because I don't want more bloodshed or terror or . . ."

"That's an excuse," he immediately countered.

I gasped. "You have some courage to come here after almost three years and say that! I never sought bloodshed."

A bold smile slipped over his lips. "C'mon, B. You were made for the Sisterhood. You love adventure. You crave that path. You can put it off, but it's going to find you. You know that it will. Fate is a fickle mistress. Isn't that what you always said?"

Heat built inside me from frustration and annoyance and a hidden sense of him being right, but me not wanting to face it.

"I don't want to talk about this," I said through clenched teeth. "It was good to see you again, so let's leave on a positive note."

Merrick studied me. Unwilling to appear cowed, I met his gaze. Quiet voices murmured behind us. For a fleeting moment, I recalled the press of his lips against mine. The way our bodies had molded together whenever he held me. The dusty smell of his armor mixed with the forest. The memories swept me away in a breathless flurry that I forced myself to leave.

Practicality called. The North had just promised to close their borders. Any venture down a path lined with Merrick would invite a darkness I didn't want to grapple with again. I had already failed my lost friends.

I couldn't fail myself again.

"Niko has been asking about you," he said. "I thought you should know. Of course, I wanted to see you—I always want to see you—but I also wanted you to know about Niko."

An edge of protectiveness lingered in his tone. One that told me he hadn't given up all affection. My stomach turned to stone at his words. *I always want to see you.* It blockaded my thoughts so that the only reply I could manage was a single word.

"Oh?"

He frowned. "He didn't ask anything too detailed. Basic information, at first. I think he wanted to see if I'd reveal anything before he asked what he *really* wanted to ask. When I didn't tell him anything, he left. He's not very good at being subtle, if he was hoping to be. But I had the impression he didn't care either way. Like he wasn't really hiding something."

An odd move on Niko's part. What could Merrick possibly know about me now that would assist Niko at all? We had been apart for over two years.

"Did you tell him anything?"

He studied me out of the corner of his eyes. "Of course not. Besides . . . what is there to tell that I would know? Until right now, everything about you and your life for the last several years would have been based on assumption."

A fair response, if not a sad one.

"What did he ask?"

"About your interests as of late. Where you spend your time. Where you lived in Letum Wood. That sort of thing. He didn't seem to realize that we'd broken up. Or if he knew, he acted as if he didn't."

My heart raced. *Where you lived in Letum Wood.* My thoughts instantly drifted to Priscilla. No doubt he thought I was harboring her. Which, of course, I was. Maybe. Had she gone to Michelle's? If so, had she stayed? Priscilla didn't like being alone. I could see her bouncing between me and Michelle whenever she could be useful. A wash of guilt flooded me. I should have checked on her again.

But how would I have done that?

"You told him nothing?" I asked, breathless.

"Nothing true."

Relief made me weak. "Thank you, Merrick."

The whole thing puzzled me, because Priscilla had known that Merrick and I were broken up. Niko, if he knew as much as he claimed, should have known that as well through Priscilla. Or did she not tell him trivial things like that? He could have played dumb as a way to throw Merrick off.

"Interesting," I said for lack of anything else to say.

Merrick's voice dropped. "Not as interesting as a rumor I heard about a stowaway the East is searching for."

All my control kept my face nothing more than startled. "Stowaway?"

He shrugged. "Must be important if Niko is patrolling all of the Eastern seaboard for a young girl stowaway, and sending out word to the islands in the North. Some rumors say he's attempting to search Letum Wood too, but that seems too bizarre. Why would he go there? Unless . . ."

Merrick trailed away, his gaze intent on mine. The knowing in his eyes meant he'd already drawn a parallel between Niko asking *where* I lived in Letum Wood, and rumors of Niko searching the forest.

I kept his stare by sheer will.

He continued as if no odd pause had happened. "They're searching for a young girl, they said, with dark hair and braids. No explanation, of course. Couldn't help but wonder if you were somehow connected, considering he also asked about you."

I swallowed hard. "A stowaway could be anyone."

"I know."

"Why would he be interested in a stowaway?"

"That," he murmured, his eyes alight now, "is what I'm asking."

The possibility that Merrick came to alert me—but also to gather information for the North—sent a little pang through me. If Niko had inquired to the Northern Network islands, then the North would be suspicious to follow up on such a strange coincidence. Perhaps Merrick was simply making the best of an old friendship.

"I'll keep my eyes peeled for stowaways here," I said as I looked away.

He scoffed again. Although I couldn't confirm it, I had the feeling I didn't fool him at all. My lack of addressing his curiosity regarding a possible connection between me and the stowaway had been intentionally ignored. Merrick wouldn't have missed that, just as I hadn't missed several dropped conversational threads of his.

"I've missed you, B."

Unable to resist, I responded to his quick grin with a smile of my own.

"I've missed you, too."

The words wobbled. For a second, I thought he'd reach out and touch me again. His thumb on my cheek, the way he used to. At that moment, I wanted the warmth of his palm against my skin more than anything.

He straightened. "Thank you for letting me talk to you. I just . . . I wanted to speak with you. To see how you've been. If you recovered from . . . well, if you're all right. You seem to be."

His tone rang with supposition. *You seem to be.* What did he think of the fact that I'd showed up to the ball with Baxter? Maybe Merrick thought I was with Baxter.

Maybe I wanted him to think that.

"I'm glad we spoke."

Familiar notes of amusement, admiration, and a shared history warmed the flavor of his smile. For a moment, I let myself curl up in our past. Running through the forest. The challenges. The way he seemed to know what I needed when no one else did. What would my life have been like without him there to help me get over Mama?

"As always, you stand on your own two feet. I'm glad to see

it. If there is any witch that could make this Sisterhood happen, it's Bianca Monroe. I look forward to hearing how you do it."

With that, Merrick disappeared.

My heart beat a hollow rhythm in my chest as I stood there, staring out at the dark forest. The lack of magic made me feel hollow, but now I felt filled with fire. Thoughts shuffled through my brain slowly, and I let them march, surprised to find them foggier than ever. My legs itched to run the trails and experience the heady euphoria that came with letting my body turn loose.

Or maybe memories of Merrick beckoned.

For just a moment, I allowed myself to imagine that the trees reached out to me. That they felt my heart and, even from this distance, sent their quiet comfort.

You belong to us, they would say.

"I still do," I murmured, and swallowed the tears that burned at the back of my eyes. With great reluctance, I turned away from my quiet forest and put my attention back on the ballroom. This was the worst time to get distracted.

Igor and Papa. I reminded myself. *Then let's get out of here.*

* * *

As I approached the ballroom doors again, a body stepped up next to my side.

"Merry meet," came Baxter's low voice. "Did it go well?"

"It did."

"Are you glad you did it?"

"I think so."

"Then you're ready to dance with your father?"

"Yes, please. Let's get this over with. Is he still with Igor?"

"I don't believe so. Derek moves frequently."

A sense of relief followed the ability to set aside Merrick and the tangle of jumbled emotions he'd stirred up inside of my mind for the moment. With that behind me, I could focus on the real task: talking to Igor.

When we stepped back into the muggy ballroom, the reality of my predicament renewed with the feeling of a fist around my heart. A ballroom full of witches. My magic, gone. Mortal in the Network.

Ugly arithmetic.

Baxter tugged me back into the stuffy heat right as the violins flowed into a waltz. He pulled me into the next dance with an arm around my waist. Close enough to discourage anyone else from cutting in, yet not so close Papa would have something to say about it.

"Thank you," I said. "I needed to speak with him."

A quick, charming smile came and went as someone waved to me. I lifted an arm in a returning wave, but the witch had already disappeared. A couple from the Western Network flashed by with bright grins and nimble laughs. The easy fracas gave me a moment to restore myself.

"Did Merrick say something to upset you?" Baxter asked. His gaze ran from left to right as he studied the witches around us, no doubt searching for Papa.

"Yes. Well, no. He . . . startled me with some news, is all."

"Care to share?"

At first, I hesitated. Niko had spoken to Merrick about me to get information from me. Perhaps about Priscilla. I *was* guilty of harboring the "stowaway" he sought, but not of any crime. The question that lingered in my mind now was *why* Niko cared about Ava.

Did he know she was mortal?

Had he been expecting her?

The frustration of not being able to speak with her compounded inside me again, but I set it aside. Leda worked ceaselessly on Ava's language, so I'd have to trust her. At least we'd gotten to work and weren't waiting. Still, I loathed the day when Baxter found out we'd been hiding her from him. Would that break his trust?

"Niko asked Merrick about me." My stomach whirled with us as we slipped around the ballroom. "Merrick said that Niko was asking questions about where I lived and what I did these days."

Baxter's brow furrowed. "Why would Niko ask Merrick?"

"I'm not sure."

"What did Niko ask?"

Once I finished recounting what Merrick had shared, neither of us spoke as we digested our separate concerns. The movement of my feet helped me feel less stuck on the question, and the dance flowed easily between us.

"Oh, there's Derek," Baxter said.

On the other side of the room, Papa danced with the Southern Network Ambassador, Alina. A former shieldmaiden to the High Priestess, she'd been the first woman appointed to a position of any power in the South. It had been Igor's first move, and it was a wise one at that. Not only did it immediately prove that he'd be a different—and better—leader than Mikhail, but it already helped to calm the constant tension between the clans and the Network leadership.

Baxter nudged us onto a slightly different dance path that would take us directly to Papa. "I'm going to take you to your father so you can cut into their dance," he said.

"Where will you go?"

"To meet with the Coordinator of Celebration Events, of course," he said in a light tone that suggested he'd be doing anything *but* that. "I'll be back before you step out of your father's arms. You have reminded me of an important task."

Three steps later, Baxter spun me out of his arms with a grand flourish. I whirled to a stop exactly two paces away from Papa, who lit up with a relieved smile. Alina stepped away from Papa's arm to regard me through assessing eyes.

With a curtsy that would make Scarlett proud, I said, "Merry meet. May I cut in?"

Alina stepped out of Papa's arms and extended a hand. "You may," she said. "I would be honored to dance with you."

The last thing I saw before she whisked me away was the bemused expression on Papa's face.

* * *

Surprise kept me from speaking.

At first, I only comprehended the unexpected shock of her response before her obvious skill at dancing caught up with me. Alina led like a dream.

"From what I have heard of you," Alina said quietly next to my ear, "I believe you're not afraid to break a little Central Network convention and dance with another woman. In the South, men dance with men and women dance with women and no one cares. Up here? They are not so friendly."

"I don't mind."

"Certainly not with a dress like that."

"Papa always taught me that stale traditions should be broken," I barely managed to say. A hint of a smile came in response.

Her eyes had a deep slant, like most shieldmaidens in the South. Recruited from their families at a young age, these girls were forced through a rigorous lifestyle and regime to prepare them to protect the High Priestess with their lives. The same intensity that I often saw in Mildred and Scarlett lived in Alina. As if determination could be caught, fostered, and grown from woman to woman. And why not? In her world, she certainly needed it.

Alina had black hair cut short around her ears. It accented sculpted cheeks, sharp as razor edges. Her strong jaw gave way to a lithe neck. Despite her natural thinness, she had a tension that gave away her strength. Her lack of magic certainly didn't belie the sense of deadly power within her. Given the opportunity to choose, I'd fear Alina most of all witches here.

Was she still a *witch* now? The question swirled through many circles. If a witch couldn't do magic, what separated them from being a mortal? Before now, I'd ignored the question. Didn't matter. After the amulet, I feared it.

What am I? beat with the dull thud of my heart.

"Dancing with you is an honor," I said when my thoughts caught up with me. I hadn't expected her, and I scrambled to pull my plan back together. She may not be Igor, but she was second-best to knowing the affairs of her Network. "You and Igor have sparked my curiosity with what you're doing in the South."

She kept an eye on the crowd and ignored the compliment. With expert skill, she navigated her way through the song. Although I wouldn't call the quiet between us burdened, it wasn't easy. My mind scrounged for things to ask her, but they all seemed too much at first.

What was your greatest strength as a shieldmaiden?
How do you find your weaknesses before they find you?
Has your population size increased suddenly?
Noticed any dramatic changes in culture amongst witches in the South?

"How often do you run in the woods?" she asked, breaking apart my scurrying thoughts before I could decide on a path. The question was an odd one. Spoken in a bland voice, as if she searched for her own desperate topic, but still nuanced. Too blunt to be musing. The question revealed her at least a little. Anyone would have to know me well to ask such a pointed question. I doubted it was an accident.

Relieved for any start to the conversation, I said, "Almost every day."

"For how long?"

"Hours?" I shrugged. "Depends. I go where the trees need me, and as my body can take it. Sometimes only a little. Sometimes, it feels like I run all day."

When I have my magic, I silently added. No one would spend that much time in the darkest, beating heart of Letum Wood without it.

"Why not transport?" she asked.

"Sometimes I do, but there's something in the movement of my body across the earth that . . . brings the forest to me."

My reply was probably too candid, but she gave no outward response at first. Instead, her thoughts moved behind her eyes like smoke in a glass jar.

"And what weapons have you trained with?" she asked.

Her direct questioning made me want to squirm. Why so curious? I forced myself to endure it in the hope she'd reciprocate. Likely, I'd be able to respond just as straightforwardly as her.

"Most."

"Let me guess," she drawled. "A bow and arrow? It seems to be a favorite amongst women in the Central Network. So many *maidens.*"

Her observation almost made me wince, mostly for the truth of it. *Maidens* in the Southern Network was a shortened term for *shieldmaidens.* Only the women who endured the requirements and schooling of the shieldmaidens could hold the full title, so the derivative *maiden* was spoken as an insult to those who wanted the position but could never do it.

Many daughters of wealthy witches in the Central Network had skill shooting a bow and arrow . . . when the target was paced out and unmoving and their arrows easily accessible and sharpened. Competitions sprouted up here and there, awarding currency to the most accurate. Few of them could hit a moving target or sharpen their own arrows, so the skill was almost purposeless.

"I can shoot, but I'm not very interested," I said. "My sword, a blade from the swordmaker Andrei, was destroyed in the final battle of the war. I've struggled to find her replacement."

"Andrei, you say?" she murmured.

"You know him?"

"Hmmm." She swept me in almost a full circle to avoid colliding with another couple. "One could say that it takes a great deal of power to break one of his blades."

"I know."

My wrists still hummed with the memory of the force that slid through my body when Viveet shattered. It had nearly broken both my arms from the physical force, and my heart from the grief. For months I'd mourned the bright blue flame that had consumed Viveet when I touched her hilt.

Alina studied me with an open expression now. Since we started to dance, her gaze flitted around often. Tracking the room was likely an instinct after all her training, but also a necessity since the withdrawal of her magic. I felt that same drive keenly.

Which, I wondered, drove her more now?

Focus, I told myself. Alina had taken control of the conversation, and I hadn't yet figured out how I'd steer the topic to mortals. I hadn't seen Igor again yet either. If I lost the opportunity to talk with him tonight, I could at least learn something from her.

"You're very close to your father," she said before I could edge us to a different topic.

"Yes."

"And your grandfather?"

"Yes."

"You don't seem to have many friends."

"A few."

"And how long has your magic been gone?"

My hands turned to ice. If she hadn't been leading, we

would have come to a dead stop in the middle of the dance floor. Conversely, she couldn't have chosen a more private spot. Witches whirled in such dizzying circles, and the floor had become so crowded, that no one paid attention to us. She'd spoken the question as if it were a common subject.

"I'm sorry?" I whispered.

She laughed.

"Once you've been away from magic for long enough, you start to sense it in others. You can sense it in a way that never happens while it lives in you. The longer I go without it, the more I feel it in the air around me. Magic is a burden." She frowned. "Uncomfortable. Heavy in the air. Makes breathing difficult, sometimes. Around certain witches like your father, it's powerful to the point of pain."

Her critical gaze turned to me then, sharp and glittering.

"We haven't spent much time around each other, but enough for me to know that you used to feel the same way."

"Me?"

"And now you don't."

She deserved credit for observation, but I didn't like that it had been so easy. Then again, she wasn't truly an able witch anymore. All the other dangerous witches in the room wouldn't be able to sense my lack of power the same way.

Or would they?

When I realized she studied me, I gazed away with a noncommittal noise in my throat.

"You're wise not to give me any information," she said with a tone of approval. "I respect silence when it's given. Whatever has happened to you, Bianca Monroe, I'm not sure. But I know a witch without magic when I feel them."

She pulled me closer so that our chests touched and her breath was warm against the shell of my ear. Even so, I could barely hear her words.

"Know that you've been given a rare gift. The opportunity

to learn our world without the driving force that runs it. Use it. Take advantage of such a time. There are strategic advantages that come with your situation. This is an opportunity I wish every witch could have. And be careful. I won't be the only one to sense it and ask questions."

She pulled away. I barely had a chance to catch her sharp gaze before a man cleared his throat behind me. Alina's eyes lifted. Her lips tilted in a smile so unlike the interrogator she'd just been for me that I could only stare at her for a moment.

"May I cut in?" Papa asked.

"Thank you for first allowing me the pleasure," Alina murmured. She looked at me with a musing expression, stepped back, and faded into the ring of witches at the edge of the dance floor.

Before I could claw after her with desperation and ask her more about her Network, Papa whisked me back into the dance. The crescendo of violins had begun to fade, which meant the dance would end in minutes.

"How are you tonight?" he asked quietly.

He guided us toward the outer rim of couples, where women whispered and sighed as we drifted by. Some of them exclaimed over Papa—a handsome, rugged witch in his own right—or the sentimentality of our dance together. Whatever it was, I didn't care, so long as it gave them what they wanted.

My voice shook when I said, "I'm all right."

"Baxter has been—"

"Attentive."

He relaxed only slightly, his posture softening under my hands. "Good."

"And you?"

"I'll be better when you're back in the apartment." He grimaced and pulled his neck to the side. A black cravat wrapped around his throat, on top of a pristinely white shirt that I had little doubt Reeves handled.

Papa added as an afterthought, "I'll be even happier when this is over . . . for all of us. Igor just returned to his apartment, so that helps. One less thing for me to pay attention to. Although he doesn't expect me to keep him safe from potential dangers, I feel obligated to do so."

My heart dropped into my stomach. Igor was already gone? That couldn't be. I squeezed Papa's hand in reassurance so he didn't notice my distraction. The temptation to tell him about Alina's observation of my missing magic swept through me, but I stifled it. No, Papa had enough on his mind right now. He needed to focus on the Celebration so we could move on to more important matters, like getting my magic back and talking to Ava.

Besides, Alina hadn't revealed anything that put me in more danger. Although I couldn't explain why, I had the distinct feeling that she wasn't a threat to me. Perhaps it was for the best that I didn't meet Igor tonight. He may notice my lack of magic immediately.

The smiles Papa and I gave each other every few steps were real enough. He kept me amused with observational chatter. I bantered back about political savvy, and he dipped me to the happy sigh of several watching women. Scarlett nodded approvingly, and Greyson, who hadn't left her side, watched with a curious expression.

The dance ended quickly. Before I whirled to our final stop, Baxter appeared at my side.

Papa sent him a questioning look that I thought I understood, but then realized I didn't when Baxter simply shook his head.

"Where?" Papa asked.

"Nowhere."

Papa frowned. I glanced at Baxter in question. He mouthed, "Niko," and a knot formed in my stomach. Somehow I hadn't noticed his absence tonight, despite the fact he was a topic of conversation several times. Some Sisterhood member I'd be if I didn't even notice my greatest threat had been missing.

"Keep me apprised?" Papa asked Baxter.

"Always."

"Thank you. And thank you, B." He placed a gentle hand on my cheek for just a moment and I could see pride, and a twinge of sadness, shining in his eyes. "You look like Marie tonight."

Papa stepped off the ballroom floor while Baxter put his arm out for me to accept.

"Doing all right?" Baxter asked.

With Igor gone, I felt lost. Where would I find him to get answers? How could I protect my Network—maybe even my magic, by some extension—without talking to him?

"Yes," I said. "I'm fine."

"Let's get some refreshments, speak with your grandfather to kill some time," he said with a quick turn to the other side of the room. "And then we can both get out of here."

Chapter Fourteen

Hours later, I sat in the shadows of my bedroom window.

Torchlights winked in the distance. Every now and then, a distant laugh or shout floated up from the gardens. Couples escaping the stuffy air of the ball, no doubt. In the quiet, I felt the full extent of my fatigue.

Merrick.

Niko.

Alina.

Igor.

The four of them swirled around my mind like individual dancers in their own ball.

I felt lonely without the warm stir of magic and power that I usually felt all the time. Alina's words whispered back through my head. *Know that you've been given a rare gift. The opportunity to learn our world without the driving force that runs it. Use it. Take advantage of such a time.*

Take advantage of such a time. The words echoed through my head. Hidden in them was an implication that there *wouldn't* be a time like this. As if I'd get my magic back. But that might not even be possible.

This empty void could be the rest of my life.

I reached up to cover my heart with a hand, unable to contemplate such a devastating loss. A loss that Alina and countless others had been struggling through for years now. My compassion for the struggles of the witches in the Southern Network expanded. No wonder they'd been having trouble scraping their lives back together.

With almost rote machinations, I attempted to do several simple spells. Call the Volare. Summon another drink of water. Nothing happened. The hope that my magic had been simply paralyzed dwindled with every passing day. The hope had never been great to start with because of the emptiness inside. I felt absolutely hollow.

My face ached from smiling all night, and my throat grated like sandpaper when I swallowed back emotion again. I wanted nothing more than a hot bath to wash the scent of the ballroom off my skin. But I couldn't heat a tub full of water without magic, and I wouldn't wake up Reeves at four in the morning to do so. Luxury would have to wait.

Instead, I wrapped my arms around my knees and drew in deep breaths until the frustration subsided. My mind drifted to the exchange between Papa and Baxter over Niko. Clearly, Papa was having him watched. That reassured me. But the questions still bounded through my mind.

Why hadn't Niko attended? Did it have something to do with Priscilla? If he were searching in Letum Wood, the way Merrick had alluded, he could stumble on my place. Unlikely, but not impossible. I'd write Priscilla in the morning and ask Reeves to send it, but it bothered me that I couldn't write it and send it with a spell now.

My thoughts turned to Merrick then. The urge to touch the hollow of his cheek, where the stubble had been the lightest, swept through my fingers with a tingle. I curled my fingers into my palm, as if that would change anything.

The restlessness I'd felt for several days seemed stronger than ever.

This time, I wasn't sure if that was because I'd lost my magic . . .

. . . or Merrick.

* * *

A pair of golden eyes woke me the following morning.

I gasped and sat up. Ava reeled back seconds before our foreheads smacked together, her eyes wide. She scrambled off my bed, her hair in a halo of crimped strands that had clearly once been in braids. She clutched the bar at the end of the bed before my mind untangled itself from sleep and caught up with reality.

"What are you doing?" I cried.

Shafts of sunlight streamed into the room from the window, where the drapes had been pulled open. Dust motes danced in the air, not unlike my thoughts in my head and the vague dreams that had accompanied them.

Ava glanced at the bed. "Sl-leep?" she said. The *L* lingered restlessly on her tongue as she over-pronounced it.

With a groan, I fell back to my pillow. An arm flopped over my eyes to block out the sunlight. What time was it, anyway?

"Yes," I moaned. "I need more of it."

"Go," Ava said. "Go Ava."

My eyes blinked open. Jikes, but was she that far with the language already? Toddlerish or not, the girl could already put words together. I sat up again.

"Where?" I asked.

Ava's brow furrowed. She yanked the amulet out of her dress and waved it around. The middle of it remained cracked. Once, it had looked like a burning coal. Now, it seemed like a dark heart ripped from some evil being. I ducked away out of sheer instinct. With a fist over the chain just above the amulet, she shook it.

"*Monilay.*"

"Monilay?" I repeated.

She nodded and jabbed an impatient finger to the bedroom door. With a sigh, I shoved the blankets off of myself. What in the name of the good gods did she mean? Breakfast? No. Why would she hold the amulet if she wanted something to eat?

Seeing me get out of bed, Ava bounced to the door like an eager puppy. I slid into my day dress and padded into the hallway. She hurried to the front door of the apartment, but Reeves materialized there before she could reach for the handle. Ava growled at him, but he returned a bored stare.

"*Monilay!*" she cried. "*Monilay mal.*"

"What does it mean, Reeves?" I asked through a yawn.

"Mistress Leda isn't certain," Reeves said dully. "Mistress Ava has been repeating it all morning and attempting to leave the apartment each time. Twice she's almost gotten out through various forms of trickery."

He sniffed, clearly mortally offended by the attempt. *All morning*, combined with the bright light outside, meant it was likely somewhere near noon.

"And *mal*?" I asked.

"Also uncertain."

"Where's Leda?"

"Taking a break, I believe, before she, and I quote, 'Loses my scholarly mind and makes it so the mortal girl can't ever speak again.'"

Jikes, but it must be bad. Ava made a guttural noise of annoyance again and waved the amulet around. I held up a placating hand.

"*Monilay,*" I said to appease Ava's growing frustration. "*Monilay.* We're . . . trying."

With a scowl darker than midnight, she shoved the amulet back into her dress and stomped off, hair waving wildly around her shoulders with each step.

"Can she get out of her room?" I asked.

"I have secured her windows."

"How about mine?"

Reeves opened his mouth to reply, frowned, and then immediately stepped away with a brisk pace I'd never seen from him before. An enraged cry from Ava seconds later meant he'd intercepted her just in time.

"*Monilay*," I murmured.

Leda's voice came from behind.

"My best guess is *leader*."

I whirled around to find her emerging from the hallway, her face a mask of stone.

"Although, given what very little I know of the culture at the time of the splitting between mortals and witches, the word may also mean father, protector, or some powerful figure. The ending *lay* suggests male, but that's a hunch. Could be a god, even, as some texts suggest, but that's a little *too* undeserving to be recognized, based on historical precedence."

My mind scoured, somewhat dully, the events of the last ten minutes. Ava's desperation and rage were palpable. Why show me the amulet, then attempt to leave? How could we help her see it wasn't safe?

"You think she's trying to find someone?" I asked.

Leda hugged a book. "I think it's likely, but when it comes to her, I have no official opinion on anything."

In the light of day, Leda appeared haggard. Yesterday, their lessons had been long, intense, and quiet. Leda always thrived in that sort of demanding mental work, but whatever Ava had attempted today had pushed Leda to the end of her rope.

"The amulet must have some purpose," I said and shoved

hair out of my face. "She keeps holding it when she says the words. What you think *mal* means?"

She shrugged. "I don't know. My instinct says that it's some version of *bad* or *ill-mannered*. Maybe even annoying, like a young boy that's a nuisance or something. There's little historical proof, but some."

"So she's trying to find a young boy that's a nuisance?"

Leda glared at me. "Your conclusions are almost offensive."

"I'm only half awake!"

"I believe she's searching for someone, yes, and I believe it ties into the amulet somehow. But anything else beyond that is mere conjecture. She's making remarkable progress learning *our* language, but I'm having a much harder time understanding hers. All morning I've tried to figure out what *monilay* or *monilay mal* means but have only succeeded in frustrating us both. She keeps gesturing to the amulet, refusing to try new vocabulary, and then trying to break into your room to wake you up. Reeves, thankfully, has managed to keep her in the apartment, albeit barely."

"I'm sorry, Leda. I didn't know this would be so challenging."

She sighed. "Can we talk about something else while I have the opportunity? You need some food or tea to wake you up. It's time for you to make an accounting of what happened at the ball last night."

I fought an inward grimace. Leda wouldn't be happy about last night because I had nothing to report, but she didn't know that yet. I could attempt to stall, but my mind was too sluggish. Putting it off would never work, not with her at her sharpest.

With a sweep of her hand, she gestured to the nook where the table awaited with a silver dome at one end. Reeves had likely been keeping breakfast warm for me. The clock that I passed on my way over confirmed my lunchtime suspicion. At least I'd been able to make up for some lost sleep.

Over a warm breakfast of porridge with a side dish of berries, I told Leda everything. Reluctantly, I relayed the reunion with Merrick, which she glossed over with a wave of her hand and a promise to *analyze that whole mess later* in favor of discussing the issues of Niko and Baxter.

In the end, she stared at the breakfast table, as solidly confused as me.

"Whatever Niko is up to," she muttered darkly, hands in her lap and a fierce expression on her face, "it doesn't sound good. Is Priscilla at your place now?"

"Yes." I managed a sheepish smile. "I forgot to mention it before, sorry. She may be with Michelle, though. You know how she hates to be alone. Can you spell her a message?"

"Yes."

While I finished the last of the porridge, she stewed and glared at the tabletop. In the silence, my thoughts around Ava coalesced.

"Can we focus on *monilay* with Ava some more?" I asked, then hastened to add, "I know you've already been doing that, and it has been intense. Instead of pushing her to learn more of our words, we could focus on her language. Maybe I can find ways to track down Igor while you do that?"

Leda's eyebrow lifted in surprise. "Yes," she answered, adding plenty of tone to it so that I knew she wasn't happy.

"We need to find out who she's trying to find."

"You plan to help her find said witch or mortal or whoever she's trying to find?"

With great hesitation, I met Leda's incredulous gaze. "Yeees."

"But . . ."

She trailed away, and I didn't try to stop her. No doubt Leda's quick mind was rapidly detailing out all the reasons why this was the *worst* decision ever, and her conclusions wouldn't be far from my own. But I knew they had to happen.

Ava had clearly arrived in Alkarra here for some reason. I had my doubts that a mortal just *wandered* over an entire ocean. She seemed determined to do something. Whatever her motivation, Ava's quest was putting her in danger. I didn't like the idea of a mortal girl so young attempting to do anything on her own in a world of witches and magic, but the other side of that was captivity. Hold her hostage or help to clean up her mess?

Neither felt safe.

But if Ava wasn't helping me clear up this magic mess, then who would? She and I were tied together now. Perhaps we had to help her before she could help us. We had to be with Ava, or against Ava.

For my part, I hoped we were on the same team.

* * *

Later that afternoon, Leda and Ava had come to a sort of pointy-talky way of speaking. Leda put all her considerable brainpower and library access into discovering Ava's intent. Ava, seeing that Leda meant to help, had stopped her escape tactics. Now, they bent over two books at the table while Reeves ironed a tablecloth and I paced restlessly near the window.

Incantations ran through my head, a comforting pattern that still yielded no results. Frustration compounded by my seemingly magicless state.

What could I do?

While I silently ran through plans for ways to "run into" Igor, a note appeared in front of me. The edges of the scroll opened and slammed shut like an angry butterfly. The moment I touched the message, it calmed and rolled open.

Scarlett's office.

Immediately.

Scarlett sent all her messages with a crimson ribbon and a wax seal if it was supposed to be discreet. This note had neither, so I passed the parchment to Reeves with a furrowed brow.

"Look at this, please?"

He accepted the note, read it in a flash, and handed it back. "It appears you have a meeting to attend."

"But who do you think sent it?"

He raised an eyebrow.

My suspicions wondered if this could be a trick from Niko . . . but how? He would be at an Esbat with Papa, where they were discussing how the West could diffuse the burden of refugees placed on their already fragile ecosystem. Seconds later, a note and a quill appeared in front of Reeves. The scritch of feather on parchment followed. Within thirty seconds, the note folded itself and disappeared with a *pop*.

"I have summoned Baxter. Your father left early and has insisted you not leave the apartment alone."

The precaution annoyed me. The Celebration meant Baxter was almost as busy as Papa. Surely, the last thing he'd want to do is babysit me. But with Niko looming large in my mind and Ava's safety at risk, I didn't push Reeves on it. He clucked and pushed Leda and Ava into the back room to study while I sank into a chair and a quagmire of thought.

Who had summoned me?

My mind churned on the mystery until a rap came on the door. Before I could spring to my feet, Reeves appeared from the back, sent me a glare that said don't-you-dare-answer-it, and allowed Baxter inside.

Baxter's dark hair was wet and his eyes bright. He'd smoothed the wild curls down and scraped his usual dark stubble off. A white shirt with an unbuttoned gray vest led to a pair of brown pants.

"Merry meet. Everything all right?"

"Fine." I held the note out for him with a gentle warming of my cheeks. "I'm sorry to interrupt anything, but . . . do you have time to come with me and make sure this is . . . safe? I'm not sure who sent it. This was all I received."

After he glanced at the note, one brow rose. Curiosity glimmered in those lime green eyes as he held up the note. His hands propped on his hips and his brow had wrinkled, as if he was puzzling something out.

"Sure," he drawled. "Are you not safe going alone?"

My stomach clenched. "Not really?"

"Is that a question?"

I sighed. "It's all a question right now."

"Why do I get the feeling there's something you're not telling me?"

"Because it's true."

Surprise brightened his gaze. He blinked, clearly not anticipating me giving at least part of the truth. With feeling, I said, "I'm sorry, Baxter. I promised Papa I wouldn't say anything. I . . . I want to tell you everything. Suffice it to say, I'd like to see who sent this, but it may not be safe. Can you help me?"

If possible, his concern deepened. He seemed to set aside his concerns—and perhaps some hurt—for the practical issue at hand. Something I deeply appreciated.

"Do you think Niko may be behind this?" he asked as he toyed with the edge of the paper.

I shrugged. "I don't know."

"Niko returned this morning as if he never left last night, but we don't know what he was up to during the ball. Certainly *was* suspicious."

"Do you recognize the handwriting?"

"Not at all. I'll be right back."

He made a thoughtful noise in his throat, then strode to the doorway and out of the apartment. I sighed. Why didn't he just transport? Witches could transport out of Papa's apartments, just not into them.

Yet, as I thought about it, Baxter rarely transported. While I yanked a quick comb through my hair and braided it away from my face, Reeves fluttered around with a feather duster. Without the quiet murmur of Leda and Ava in the background, the apartment felt strangely silent.

Within minutes, Baxter let himself back in. "Scarlett's office is normal," he declared. "Only Scarlett's Assistant, the new one, is inside."

"Assistant?" I asked, my voice piqued with curiosity.

"Hiddle-something. Can't remember. Let's go see what he wants. I'm willing to bet he sent this."

With a shrug, I followed.

"Thank you."

Chapter Fifteen

Baxter walked close to me in the hall, and we both kept an attentive eye out. No witches passed by as we strolled past statues, chairs, and paintings the size of a door. The last thing I wanted was to run into Niko again, although I may not have minded a collision with Merrick. And that thought sent my mind tumbling until I forced myself to think of something else. What could Scarlett's Assistant possibly want?

And when had she hired him? I'd been avoiding Scarlett in case she spoke about the Sisterhood for the last several months, and rarely did I interact with her in an official capacity anyway—mostly stolen moments in Papa's office or a hallway. It wouldn't be unusual for her to have an Assistant I didn't know about. These days, she had several. Most likely, however, this Assistant was new.

Very new.

Apparently, Leda's timeline had expired.

We approached Scarlett's office only a few minutes later. Baxter remained back a step, his gaze down the hall on one side, then the other. He kept his arms at his side, but I sensed his stewing tension. Did he feel betrayed by Papa? By me?

Before I could knock on Scarlett's door, it whipped open.

A lean witch with a serious expression and eyes the color of moss stood there. He had full lips that gave him a striking mien and appeared to be in his early thirties. His hair was long, gathered into rope-like locks that hung halfway down his back. Ink stains covered the tips of his fingers.

The man looked at Baxter with sudden surprise.

"Didn't know you were coming," he said, his voice pitched with surprise.

"Merry meet," Baxter said stiffly.

The man narrowed his eyes. "Well," he murmured, "isn't that a plot twist?"

I couldn't peg his accent. Central Network, certainly, but from the lower Covens, perhaps. Baxter stared at him, his usual genial air replaced with something more calculating. The switch set me on edge.

"You summoned me?" I asked and held up the note. The awkward air broke between them, and the witch looked at me.

"Come inside."

With only a slight hesitation, Baxter lifted up an arm to indicate I should go inside first. "Do you know him?" I whispered as I walked by.

He shook his head.

Scarlett's office appeared as normal as ever as we advanced into the room. She'd be at the Esbat now. The witch took the spot behind her desk as if it were his own. After he settled in, he peered at me over the top of steepled hands. In the right light, he'd appear almost diabolical. Now, he just seemed strange.

A flicker of bemusement passed through Baxter's expression as we came to a stop on the other side of her desk.

"I'm Hiddleston." He waved us into two chairs that slipped over from near the fire. "Scarlett's newest appointment to her team. Head Assistant, if you will."

"Is that a real thing?" I asked.

"Soon."

Not wanting to feed into his apparent hunger for power and to keep the upper hand, I didn't respond. The intensity of the quiet that followed didn't seem to bother Hiddleston, who swiveled until he faced me fully.

"I called you here because of what happened at your little cottage in Letum Wood a few days ago. Would have called sooner, but I needed to see how events played out before I became involved."

My hands tensed on the arms of the chair at his easily spoken words. Baxter, despite not knowing what Hiddleston spoke of, showed no sign of concern or curiosity except for a little twitch of his hand.

"Excuse me?" I asked softly.

Hiddleston's smile showed all his teeth, which were shockingly white. He lounged back in Scarlett's chair with a forced laugh. I struggled not to squirm, discomfited by the strangeness of this entire situation.

"Silly little witch, touching an unknown amulet and losing her power. You make light of something that's been so . . . catastrophic."

My whole body tensed.

Baxter straightened. "Amulet?" he murmured.

Panic filled me, just like the crushing fire from the amulet, and I wrestled it out of my voice by sheer determination. "What are you talking about?" I asked Hiddleston coolly, in a desperate bid to buy myself some time.

How had he known those details?

Who was he?

Hiddleston rolled his eyes.

"You give yourself away, Bianca. Also, don't insult me. I can access everything that has ever been. Much of it, anyway. A few things aren't clear to me . . ." His gaze slipped to Baxter. ". . . yet."

Hiddleston leaned back and stared at the ceiling, his throat pulled tautly, fingertips still pressed together. For an obnoxiously long moment, he didn't say a word. Baxter met my questioning gaze with a calculating concern of his own. His eyes begged a silent question.

What happened?

Just as I almost told Baxter we should leave, Hiddleston dropped his head and looked right at Baxter. "Double interesting, you invisible mongrel," he muttered.

To me, he said, "I invited you here to talk about the amulet you touched." He leaned forward. "You can pretend that you didn't touch an amulet and lose your magic, but it would only waste precious time. You do want your magic back, correct?"

Baxter shot to his feet. "What amulet?" he barked. My heart raced. Papa would have his hands around Hiddleston's neck for this.

Hiddleston pointed to me.

"Ask her."

Incredulous, Baxter whirled on me. "Is he correct? Did you touch an . . . amulet?"

I swallowed hard.

"Yes."

Shock, confusion, then something like fear rotated through his eyes. "Please," he whispered, "explain exactly what happened. Now. As quickly as you can. Tell me everything about the amulet that you remember."

I glanced toward Hiddleston, who just lifted his eyebrows innocently, as if he hadn't engineered this situation. With a growl in his direction, I let out a long breath and said, "I . . . I touched an amulet that I sort of . . . found. My magic has been missing ever since. We've hoped it was paralyzed but . . ."

Baxter's whole attention focused on me with startling intensity. Such a fixed stare gave him an entirely new appearance. Why would he care about the amulet? Something lingered on the edge of my mind.

Hiddleston rolled his eyes. "That's it? That's all you have to say? I already *know* you found an amulet. The question I have, which *he*—" Hiddleston motioned to Baxter with a wave, "—may have just answered, is *how*."

"What color was it?" Baxter asked.

"Blood red," I whispered. "But it . . . sometimes it appeared orange or maybe even yellow. It changed color."

Baxter stiffened further. "Like fire?"

"Like fire."

"A reddish-orange-yellow amulet in Letum Wood that removes magic?" Hiddleston asked carefully, but his playful tone meant he already knew as much. "What happened after you touched it, other than losing your magic?"

"Tell me how you know first," I snapped.

"I already did. I know everything that has happened since the event. Well, almost everything. I—"

"You didn't explain. You were evasive. The only witches that know about the amulet have been put under blood oaths and would not have broken it already. Not without us being aware. Papa would not have forgotten to tell me *that* detail."

If possible, the grooves in Baxter's brow deepened.

Hiddleston's lip drew up in a mocking expression. "Oh, and that's the only way to know anything, is it?" he retorted. "There is magic you obviously have no comprehension of, daughter of the great Derek Black."

My mouth opened, then shut. Baxter straightened up and ran a hand through his hair, mussing the curls.

"Doesn't matter how I know." Hiddleston straightened up and tugged on his shirt sleeves. "I know a *lot* of things, and many of them would be useful to you, if you'd just listen."

"Give me one reason why I should tell you anything."

Hiddleston pushed to his feet and leaned over Scarlett's

desk. "You are Bianca Marie Monroe. Born in a small cottage in Letum Wood to Derek Black and Marie Monroe, two witches that should never have been together. There is a scar behind your left ear that indicates the mark of Almorran magic when Mabel possessed your mind. You love to run in the forest and used to see ghosts of your mother in the trees. When Merrick deserted you, you curled up in the roots until—"

"Stop."

I commanded him with my darkest voice. How I'd gotten to the edge of Scarlett's desk to glower at him from a breath away, I had no idea. A hand touched my shoulder as Baxter pulled me back.

"The past is a touchy subject." Hiddleston held up two hands. "I get it, trust me. But you asked."

"Fine, you've proven yourself. If you know so much, why don't *you* tell me the description of the amulet?"

"Reddish-orange-yellow, as you already so bluntly stated. It's an oval, set in what appears to be filigreed metal, but it's no metal I've seen here, in *Alkarra*." His gaze shot to Baxter, then back to me. "You touched it with the edge of your thumb, though I can't fathom how you found it in your house in the first place. The paths aren't . . . always clear on details."

I blinked.

What?

He knew about the amulet, but not about Ava?

Startled, I reeled back slightly. He must have mistaken my shock for something else because he continued with a coy curl in his tone. "After you touched it, you blacked out. Woke up, blacked out again. Finally, you came awake in the morning and stumbled your way to Michelle and Nicholas's house. But much of it doesn't make sense. Unless there was someone else there with you. Someone else I can't see."

The details he gave seemed like he had some sort of insight

into my world. Was he spying on me? Had he actually seen it happen?

If so . . . why did he see it?

How?

He turned away so I could only see his profile as he stared into the flames. Another obnoxious silence passed, but it gave me a chance to scramble my brain back together. Again came the same question—who *was* he?

Baxter hadn't let go of my shoulder and his firm hand had an oddly grounding presence. "Who do you see for?" he asked Hiddleston.

The question pulled Hiddleston out of his thoughts, and he turned with a slight smile that wasn't entirely kind.

"Look who knows so much."

"Who?" Baxter asked.

Hiddleston's locks swung around his ears when he replied, a suspicious gleam darkening his eyes. "I see for any witch that I'm in the same room with. Not *you*, certainly. Which only increases my questions."

Baxter paled slightly, but no change showed in his features. Such grave tension seemed misplaced on his usually bright face. I glanced between the two of them.

"What are you talking about?" I asked.

Hiddleston sighed. "Isadora clearly never told you about Defenders."

"Defenders? Isadora?"

"It would be very appreciated if witches stopped ignoring our talent. We're not hiding anymore!" he called to no one in particular. Then he turned to me with that knowing look again. "Magic is complete, is it not? With balance in all things? Such is true even of Watcher magic. Historically, Defenders have been known as the anti-Watchers. We are the counter to the glorious, thrilling, future-saving powerful Watcher magic." He smiled like a snake. "Defenders are the same as Watchers, except we see the past. We're their counter. Neither magicks are good nor evil. That designation is reserved for the witches that receive the magic. But still . . . Defenders have a dark reputation of being evil."

Stunned, I stared at him, unsure of how to respond. In theory, it made sense, but I didn't know enough of Watcher magic to understand how it happened, notwithstanding a viable counter. The thought had simply never occurred to me.

"Why have I never heard of Defenders before?"

"We like to hide. Some of us, anyway," he tacked on as he sat back down in Scarlett's chair and drummed his fingers on the armrest. "Like Watchers, we have been persecuted. Most witches only want to see what the future could bring. They want certainty in what *could* happen and they think Watchers offer that, so we have been largely ignored. We remained that way to save our own lives. Yet . . . Defenders have influenced history more than any other group of witches. I would know."

"Are you the Head Defender?"

His gaze flickered to Baxter, then to me. "No. I see for anyone that I'm in the same room with. Makes crowds a nightmare, so I avoid them. All things told, I'm relatively new to my Defender magic. Late receiver, you see."

Baxter began to pace. "We can discuss all of that later. Tell us more about the amulet, please. Bianca, from whom did you get it?"

His question made the hair on the back of my neck stand up. *From whom* was very different than asking *from where*. Which meant Baxter might know something—or several somethings— that Hiddleston didn't know about the amulet.

"Doesn't matter."

"Oh," Hiddleston murmured, "but it does."

"What are you going to do if I don't tell you?" I asked. "Beat me? Good luck. I may not have magic, but—"

"Calm down, kitty," Hiddleston muttered with an eye roll.

"Of course I'm not going to touch you. You're clearly my superior in such gruesome skills. I called you here to potentially warn you, believe it or not. I'm on your side."

I gritted my teeth. *Kitty* didn't sit well, but for the sake of getting through this, I let that pass.

"Potentially warn me?"

"The source of the amulet has a massive bearing on what I would tell you today, if you'd just give it up already."

"Why do you care?" I asked.

His eyes rolled so hard I thought they'd fall out of his head. He groaned, clearly annoyed, but I stood my ground. Seeing I wouldn't be swayed, he said, "Because I want to influence history for the better, as my predecessors have often done. And . . . maybe other things."

"Then tell me why you brought me here and I'll gauge whether I want to tell you the source of the amulet."

Hiddleston spread his hands. "It would be my pleasure. But first, an agreement."

"What?"

"I'll help you, you help me?"

"How?"

The first flicker of uncertainty appeared in his eyes, but it faded as quickly as it had appeared. "I'll help you with your magical problem if you introduce me to Leda."

The unexpected request threw me off kilter and it took me several moments to process her name off of his lips. My surprise came too quickly to hide.

"Leda?"

"You are the weakest part of her considerable emotional armor, to be sure. History proves that time and again. An introduction from you would be . . . powerful."

"That's the whole reason you brought me here?"

"Aside from a desire to positively impact history, yes."

"What do you want with her?"

"A discussion, that's all."

I hesitated. Leda would rightfully destroy me, even with these sorts of circumstances, if I made an agreement on her behalf. Besides, it didn't seem entirely safe.

"Why should I take the chance? You might not have anything important to say. You might try to hurt her."

He rolled his eyes. "Were you born this suspicious?"

"No." I smiled gratingly at him. "The great Derek Black taught me."

"I could hold the answer to getting your magic back. You aren't going to agree to introduce me to your friend just because of what I might say to her?"

"Or what you might do to her." I leaned forward. "I always protect those I love."

To my surprise, he didn't seem annoyed. "Fine. I'm impressed with Leda. I want to speak with her about her impressive intellectual confidence and her love of history."

For several moments, I debated. It seemed innocuous enough, but almost too innocuous.

"That's it?"

He shrugged.

I frowned. With the fate of my magic—and my life—hanging in the balance, an introduction was a small price to pay. She'd hate me for a week or two before she forgave me, if this was truly what he wanted.

"I'll introduce you," I said, "but only in a safe place with other witches, and that's the most I will promise. The agreement allows her to take the choice from there."

"Not good enough. I could introduce myself and have, in fact, attempted to do so several times. She's stubborn."

"I'll do it in a way that will provoke her curiosity. If you know Leda at all, that's as good as you'll get. I won't force her into anything."

He scowled. "Fine."

"Then we have an agreement. You reveal whatever you know that could help me get my magic back. I will introduce you to Leda in a way that makes her curious."

"We are agreed."

My stomach twisted with fear when he leaned forward, a smile of delicious enjoyment highlighting his features.

"Then let me tell you what you have done, Bianca Monroe. You have ushered god magic back into Alkarra."

* * *

My heart seized.

You have ushered god magic back into Alkarra.

What was he talking about?

Hiddleston stood with his hands planted on the desk again. He loomed close to me, his voice terrible and dark. Baxter felt like an overwrought harp string behind me, ready to snap at any moment.

"Through that amulet you touched, god magic is now present again in Alkarra," Hiddleston continued, "and could destroy every witch that's here if the amulet you touched falls into the wrong hands. History is clear on that one point."

"But the amulet is broken."

"Is it?" Hiddleston asked, but he looked to Baxter.

Baxter just frowned.

My heart beat so hard that I felt sick to my stomach. I lowered into the chair behind me, my thoughts as shaky as my limbs. Hiddleston tipped his head toward Baxter, but he kept his gaze on me.

"Until you brought him with you today," he clarified, "I wasn't sure how you'd found the amulet. But now I realize that maybe I just needed to meet *him* to find the answer to my question."

What he said didn't make sense, and I didn't have the brainpower to work it out anyway. My mind kept tripping over the same words over and over again.

God magic.

God magic.

God magic.

Impossible.

"You can't be serious," I whispered, then whirled to look at Baxter. He crossed his arms across his chest, fingertips white from gripping his upper arms so hard. Light illuminated him in a vague halo from the fire. Baxter tore his gaze from me to look at Hiddleston, his face hard-lined now.

"You're certain of this?" he asked.

"I've seen the amulet before." Hiddleston tapped the side of his head. "Took me days of searching through the paths of the past. I almost starved to death and very nearly didn't make it *back* out of the magic, but I was able to go back that far. Long, long ago, when gods and mortals still destroyed witches in Alkarra. Back in the days of Esmelda, when Letum Wood was little more than a grove. It's an old amulet."

"Baxter?" I murmured.

Baxter didn't say another word. He just stared at Hiddleston, his entire body thrumming with tension.

"Son of a god," Hiddleston said, his grin thick with irony. "And *that* is not just a saying."

"I've sent a message to Derek. Not another word," Baxter muttered, "until he gets here."

I melted against the chair, my entire body suddenly weak. A joke. That's all this was. Some expansive prank meant to frighten me, perhaps? When my mind skittered back to *god magic,* my thoughts stalled. A witch like me that was born into Alkarra would be unable to comprehend what *god magic* meant. No one spoke of them. They were almost a non-entity. Legend, not fact. So forgotten that most witches scoffed or mocked their supposed existence.

Gods were . . . not real.

Or were they?

Just because we didn't believe in or talk about something didn't negate the possibility of its existence. At least, I didn't think so. Conversely, believing in something didn't make it real. Except . . . the gods might be real if the amulet was real *and* my magic was gone.

Right?

Or this was just a bizarre explanation of what happened with the amulet? I couldn't deny that *something* had taken my magic. The hissing voice in my mind that said *you're not welcome here, witch* hadn't been my imagination, nor had the fire that took my power. The gravity in both Hiddleston's and Baxter's tones told me this was no wayward thought.

No joke.

If Hiddleston spoke the truth, then somehow Baxter was tied into amulets and gods. Somehow, he knew about this strange topic. I realized too late that Baxter had mentioned Papa, and my heart sank further.

The last thing Papa needed was the pressure of the Celebration in addition to this news. Now, everything would be even more unstable. If god magic was really loose in Alkarra, with myself tied to it in various ways, I'd brought an even larger disaster here than I thought. In fact, I *had* brought god magic here, by bringing Ava, who carried the amulet.

And why did Ava have it?

What piece was she in all this?

The timing of such a catastrophe couldn't be worse.

Sometime in my shocked mental spiraling, Baxter must have sent a note to Papa because no one spoke. We sat there and waited. I tried to remember what part of Papa's schedule we'd be interrupting. A luncheon? No. Esbat? Hopefully not. It could be ages before Papa arrived.

Baxter turned to me with great hesitation. "I'll explain everything, Bianca, but I need to know who gave you that amulet."

"Now that I think about it, I believe I can answer part of that question," Hiddleston said to Baxter before I could summon up the ability to speak. "Since I can't see you in the paths of my Defender magic, Baxter, that means I likely can't see who gave Bianca the amulet. That tells me there are other god-like troublemakers afoot in the Central Network. Aren't there, Bianca?"

Baxter's gaze darkened further.

Hiddleston's interference gave me a moment to gather the fragmented parts of my mind back together, but what I could grasp wasn't much. All I knew is that I'd fallen farther into this disaster than I ever thought possible, so I did the only thing that felt safe.

"I'll tell you when my father arrives," I said.

Baxter accepted that with a reluctant nod.

An interminable silence followed while we waited. What felt like hours was only minutes before a sharp rap came on the door and Papa entered. I couldn't imagine what Baxter said in his message to get Papa so quickly, or for Marten to follow close behind him. We had minutes, at most, to break Papa's entire world.

Concern lined his features until he saw me. He relaxed only marginally. Marten strode over until he stood next to me, and I felt comfort in his familiar presence. He eyed Hiddleston with curiosity. The moment he saw Papa, Hiddleston shifted, as if a new personality had slipped over his old one. With a humble bow of his head, he acknowledged my father, who nodded distractedly but otherwise ignored him.

"What is it?" Papa asked Baxter.

"New developments just came to light regarding . . ." he hesitated for a beat, ". . . an amulet and god magic."

The lines between Papa's eyebrows thickened. His gaze darted to me. "Did you tell him?"

I gestured to Hiddleston. "Not really. Hiddleston called me here to ask how I found the amulet. Baxter came with me to keep me safe and he heard what Hiddleston said. I haven't told either what happened, but they know I lost my magic and touched an amulet."

During my rushed explanation of all that occurred so far today, Papa studied Hiddleston until I thought he'd drive a hole through him. Hiddleston dropped his gaze immediately and stared at the desk. The moment my explanation ended, Papa said to Hiddleston, "How long has your Defender power been present?"

Hiddleston risked a quick glance up. "Since I was seventeen, Your Highness."

"How powerful are you?"

His head tipped back slightly. "Close to the most powerful I've met."

"Who do you see for?"

"There hasn't been much I can't see, except those not in a room with me. And, apparently, Baxter. What that means yet, I haven't figured out."

Papa's jaw tightened. His voice grated when he turned to Baxter and said, "I kept secrets from you about Bianca and recent developments for which I will explain my full reasoning later. Please, trust my instincts. You have five minutes to explain everything to Bianca."

Baxter's expression dropped into one of shock, then cleared. He nodded, swallowed hard, and turned to me. His voice held a rushed tone, but the cadence remained confident and strong.

"As you already know, I'm not from the Central Network. In fact, I'm not from . . . not from Alkarra. I'm from a land called Alaysia, which, translated from ancient Declan, means the Land of the Gods."

Next to me, Marten shifted his weight. Papa's expression gave no sign of surprise. Not even Hiddleston appeared shocked, just thoughtful.

"Land of the Gods?" I repeated dumbly.

Baxter nodded warily. "Yes."

"So you're . . . a god?"

"Not a god. Son of a god. Technically, I'm a witch . . . sort of. By one standard, a witch is a person with the ability to do magic. That's what I am . . . except I'm not." His shoulders slumped a little. "As you've seen over the last three years, I can do magic effortlessly. But I use god magic, not goddess magic. Mine is not incantation-based. And I am not a witch by *other* standards, namely heritage. I am . . ." he pulled in a sharp breath, "a demigod. Born of a mortal and a god."

Had Baxter lost his mind?

At first, I looked to Papa, at a loss for words. Papa returned my stare, but his eyes revealed nothing. His utter lack of surprise —and his direction to Baxter—meant he already knew all of this.

"You knew?" I asked.

Papa nodded. "Scarlett, Marten, myself, the head of Guardians, and the head of Protectors. We all know. Or, should I say, we have all believed him when he told us."

"I didn't hide it," Baxter said. "I've never hidden it. The truth just has never been well received."

This revelation had to be a fit of lunacy. Before I could question it, Baxter pressed on.

"I'm a son of Ventis, god of wind. A good god, because there are . . . manipulative, lazy gods. Father sent me here three years ago because other demigods outside of his control have been rising up against their fathers, the other gods. When word reached Alaysia that there were mortals in Alkarra again, some of those demigods wanted to come back."

"Why?" I asked, my voice hoarse.

Baxter met my gaze, as serious as I'd ever seen him. "To give themselves more power. Demigods are only considered as powerful as the number of mortals that have given their allegiance to them."

"Jikes."

He pressed his lips together. "Exactly."

I swallowed and looked at Papa, who still didn't seem surprised by any of this. How long had he known about it? Since he met Baxter, probably. For that matter, Marten still seemed unsurprised as well.

Baxter continued.

"Some gods force mortal women to have their children, and some gods genuinely care for their mortal child-bearers. Either way, they create demigods. But not all gods rule their demigod children, which means the demigods exploit the mortals they are meant to care for. There have been murmurs of a demigod uprising for decades now. With mortals in Alkarra, my father was concerned the uncontrolled demigods would come over, claim the mortals, and rise to greater power. And, ultimately, wage war."

Papa shifted, his arms folded across his chest and brow heavy over dark eyes. Marten's forehead had creased, but he said nothing.

"War?" I asked Baxter. "With who?"

"The goddesses."

Only sheer surprise kept me from laughing. "Goddesses."

Baxter nodded solemnly.

My heart stuttered with an uneven *thunk*. The goddess paradigm, like the gods, had been mostly dead for centuries. In my minimal perusal of history, and from what Leda tried to force on me, there weren't even shadows of it in the last one hundred years. Except for Samako, of course. Magic had taken over. We'd stopped asking about origins and looked, instead, toward what came next.

"You're serious?" I asked.

"Very."

"But . . ."

My words faltered. *Gods* were hard enough to comprehend, but *goddesses*? Now we talked more along insanity than reality. Except, no one else laughed. The solemnity felt as real as anything I'd ever known.

"My father sent me to Alkarra to see if any other demigods had come here. When I arrived three years ago, it was the start of my mission." He ran a hand through his hair. "The goddesses have been stirring for the first time in a while and my father is . . . concerned."

"That the goddesses will be angry?" I asked, my voice pitching a little too high.

"Well, yes. The goddesses banished gods and mortals thousands of years ago. To come back to Alkarra would break that command. The goddess sisters wouldn't take that lightly, and they have tended to rule and be more powerful and united than the gods. My father and the goddess of the forest, whom witches call Deasylva, are . . . not exactly friends, but they are amicable. As long as the gods keep the demigods under control, all has been well."

"Oh."

"I didn't actively hide being a demigod," he added. The slight frown on his face spoke to something uncertain in his bearing. Was Baxter afraid of what I'd say? Of how I'd react? "I *have* told witches, many of them. I say all the time that I'm the son of a god and ask for clarification on local customs or what-have-you. But witches' responses have been . . . not as I expected."

My heart sank a little lower in my chest. The thought of Baxter very seriously telling a witch that he was the *son of a god* almost brought a deranged laugh out of me. They probably thought him mad. *I* hadn't taken him seriously.

But Papa had, apparently.

"What happened when you told them?" I asked, absurdly invested in knowing if other witches responded the way I wanted to. Namely, with hoarse screaming and terrified disbelief.

"One witch ran away when I suggested it," Baxter said with a chuckle. "Another tried to bind me and take me to an apothecary. Another witch with dark curly hair asked me about gods for hours. We talked on the beach until night came, and then she thanked me for entertaining her with made-up stories."

He shrugged, hands held out in front of him, as if to ask *what do you do?*

"You've known for how long?" I asked Papa.

"Since he told me he was the son of a god," Papa replied with a similar shrug. "I asked him more about it. He told me everything. I told Scarlett, she interviewed him, and the same with Marten."

"Why didn't you say something to me?"

"Would you have believed me?"

My mouth popped open with a bristling reply, then closed again. Baxter had told me that he was the *son of a god* for years, but I hadn't considered it to be anything more than a joke. Not once.

"Besides," Papa added quietly. "It seemed prudent to keep it outside of common knowledge while we dealt with bigger issues."

"And you believed him right away?" I asked.

Papa hesitated. His eyes darted to Baxter, then back to me. "Eventually," he drawled. "I proved him out as truthful and honest the best I could, the way I would anyone. Yes."

What *proved him out* meant, I couldn't even fathom. Memories wavered on the edge of my mind, fuzzy from being tucked in forgotten corners. The days after Almorran magic had been banished were a physical relief as the dark magic lifted from our world and Mabel died, but then a new yoke of bondage had fallen upon us.

Survival.

Crops, cattle, witches. So much failed. The South grappled with their loss of magic. The East from their loss of leadership and Guardians. The West and North from new normals, leaders, and different interactions between borders.

Months passed before Papa truly recovered from fighting Mabel, and in that time, the Central Network had needed him more than ever. He'd lost the High Priestess, Stella, when she died in the battle over Chatham Castle. Every day back then felt swamped in shadows and desperation.

Although the memories were hazy, I reached farther back in my mind. Baxter appeared after what seemed like days after Almorran magic had been destroyed. In a world of broken hearts and grieving witches that could barely face the next day of hunger, Baxter had been a light. He'd been efficient with the tasks my father needed, practiced in magic, and capable. He didn't carry the same grief as everyone else.

"I mourn for all of you," he'd once said after I first met him. The lack of *us* had startled me then, but I'd ignored it. It seemed oddly clear now. He had never claimed this as home or us as his witches. Hadn't he always joked about being the *son of a god*? Of how strange things were in the Central Network?

My scattered mind sank into the haphazard memories. Looking back made it so clear. Baxter's natural talent for most things. That charming quality I could never peg down. With a sharp intake of breath, I shoved all that aside for the looming question that resurrected in my mind.

"The amulet that took my magic." I leaned closer to Baxter. "Was it god magic? Is Hiddleston correct?"

Relief flooded his features. "The amulet, yes. I'd have to see it to know for sure, but I think it could be. Who gave it to you?"

My gaze shot to Papa. He waved a hand as if to say, *spill it.*

"What does *monilay* mean?" I asked Baxter.

Baxter frowned. "*Monilay* means demigod in our language."

"And *mal*?"

"Bad. Evil." Baxter straightened, immediately on edge. "Who said that? Did someone say those words to you?"

"Her name is Ava."

Baxter blinked. "Ava," he whispered, gaunt. "Ava is here? She . . . she gave you the amulet?"

"You know her?"

"Dark hair? Braids? Young?"

"All of that."

Panic filled his expression. "Where is she?" He stepped toward me. "She's alive?"

"Yes, she's fine. I found her on the beach in the Eastern Network, when I went to have lunch with Priscilla."

"It cannot be," he whispered.

"Who is she?"

Baxter frowned, oblivious to my question. "She . . . no, she's too young. Too . . . mortal. To wield an amulet? It could only mean . . ." Anguish filled his expression. "Please, I beg of you. Take me to her right now."

Unable to deny the desperation in his voice, I nodded. "Of course. She's at the apartment."

Papa's voice grew weary. "We'll finish this conversation later. Marten, come. We need to return to the Esbat. B, expect to give me a full recounting tonight. Hiddleston, meet me at my office the moment the Esbat ends. I have some work for you to do. And all of you? Not a single word about any of this. Not to a living soul."

Chapter Sixteen

Minutes later, the door to Papa's apartment opened ahead of me. Baxter rushed inside in two steps. His gaze darted around for a moment before he paused. I slipped behind him just as a breathless cry of, "Ava?" wrenched from his throat.

Across the room, Ava sat at the table in the nook with Leda. Her head snapped up. I held my breath in the three seconds it took her to process what she saw.

Ava let out a cry.

She shoved away from the chair, tripped over her own feet, and darted across the room. Baxter dropped to one knee and caught her as she threw herself into his arms. My heart caught in my throat at Baxter's shocked whisper.

"Ava."

Leda looked to me in question, but I waved a hand. "Later," I mouthed. Leda rose until she stood next to the chair where Ava had been sitting.

Baxter crushed Ava to him. He murmured something quietly, a soothing sound, as she sobbed in his arms. Silently, the door closed. Leda and I moved to stand together. Baxter's eyes screwed shut as Ava sobbed something to him, pressed tight against his chest.

"I guess we missed a few details," Leda murmured.

"A few."

What felt like an eternity later, Baxter pulled away. His hands framed Ava's face as he wiped off her tears and spoke quickly in their language. Ava responded. She put her hands on his shoulders and tripped over her words. Leda's face became a mask of concentration as she listened to the back-and-forth exchange. Relief filled Baxter's eyes. Ava spoke so quickly she seemed to stumble over her words, although I couldn't tell between her hiccuping sobs of relief.

Gently, Baxter seemed to ask a few questions. Torment showed in his expression as Ava responded. Every now and then, tears would well up in her eyes. She'd catch a sob and press on. Eventually, she turned and gestured to me. Her hands waved back and forth until she finally plucked the amulet from her dress and held it out.

Baxter sucked in a sharp breath.

I jerked back a step.

The darkened amulet twirled on the chain as Ava held it toward him. The crack remained down the middle, a gaping fissure that sent an ebony color throughout the facets. Crimson still stained the delicately-filigreed edges, like the fading remains of a once-beating heart.

With a frown, Baxter took it from her. Ava's expression was bright now, almost hopeful, as if she sought approval. Baxter ran a thumb over the face of the amulet, then smiled gently at her with a little nod. Then she frowned and gestured to me again with a murmured reply. He glanced at me, then the amulet, and I felt a pit deep in my stomach.

The trouble in his eyes didn't reassure me.

For a brief moment, I thought I heard the voice in my head

again. A quiet snap, like fire. Leda broke it when she leaned closer and asked, "Is that what you touched?"

I nodded.

"Jikes," she muttered. "It's the size of my fist."

Ava's words flowed like a river now. She drew in a deep breath, let it out, and then threw herself back into Baxter's arms with another cry. He wrapped his arms around her, but this time he looked at us.

For a moment, I had the thought that this could be his daughter, but then I banished that idea. No, that didn't make any sense at all. Why would he be here if he had a daughter *there*? Wherever that was.

A relative of some sort, perhaps? The emotion in his eyes meant they were somehow connected, perhaps deeply. Baxter pulled Ava away, she said something in a throaty way, and he nodded. With the back of her wrists, she wiped her cheeks off and turned to us with a wide smile that I couldn't help but return, even though mine was weak.

When Baxter stood, he kept her hand in his. She took his hand and didn't leave his side. The dark amulet sparkled on her chest, a massive thing against her lean frame.

"Ava is my niece," he said.

Hearing him speak our language again sent a shock through me at first. The intensity of his expression had deepened since he saw her. I couldn't tell if there was any malice against us, considering we'd kept her a secret for days. Leda edged closer to me. While I knew Baxter wouldn't harm us, something big lived in him now.

"Niece?" I asked.

His nostrils flared and he swallowed, as if it were an effort to hold something out of his voice.

"My sister, Christa, was her mother."

My heart fell into my stomach. *Was*. The word rang through my mind, as apparent as the gentle wobble in his voice. Now I knew what it was. That big, unknown, sharp something I could sense in him.

Grief.

Pain.

How well I knew that agony of expression.

"Was?" I asked quietly.

He struggled to compose himself. "Christa and I weren't very close, but we did care for each other. She lived on and off with one of her allegiant mortals, and their daughter, on a collection of islands. Ava is a favorite of mine, if I'm allowed to have one. Ava is my *tamaiti.* My . . ." He frowned. "There's no word in your language that equates it. For better or worse, I'm her teacher. Her *tagata.* Assigned to her from birth to be a special guide. A safety. Protector, if you will."

Dread pooled in my stomach at his lowering tone.

"She's your student?"

He shook his head. "It's deeper than that, more emotional. Familial, if you will. As *familial* as a mortal could be with a demigod. Ava just told me that Christa was killed. A demigod named Bram came and argued with Christa. They fought over Ava, and Bram killed Christa. Christa managed to pull the amulet off him when they fought. With her dying breath, she gave Ava a . . . a mission, for lack of a better word in your language. She told Ava to take the amulet, find me, and not rest until she and I together could return the amulet and Bram to our father, Ventis."

While Baxter struggled to compose himself, Leda and I shared a silent, questioning gaze. Leda's face was a puzzle without the previous conversation in Scarlett's office to help her.

"Demigod?" she asked under her breath.

With a little shake of my head, I said, "I'll explain in a little bit."

She frowned, but fell quiet to give him a moment to grapple with the news. Sometimes, death had to be softened into facts in order to get through the initial shock, like right now. He seemed to pull himself back together for Ava's sake, but it couldn't have been easy. My heart ached for him. He'd been reunited with a beloved niece he probably hadn't seen in a long time, only to find that his sister had been murdered.

"Why would Christa send Ava to you?" I asked. "She must have known what she was sending Ava into to find you."

"I don't know."

"Could Ava go back to your father now?"

"Mortals approaching a god . . . it isn't done. Especially not at Ava's age."

Next to me, Leda made a choking sound. No doubt the words *demigod* and *mortal* and *god* made her mind trip over itself. Mine certainly still did. *Monilay mal* and the frantic tone Ava had said it with suddenly made a *lot* more sense.

A thousand things swirled through my head, but only one grew big enough to truly focus on.

"Are you going to take her home?"

The question I most wanted to ask remained locked up inside me. *And what will happen to my magic if you do?*

His grip on Ava's hand tightened. She had been staring out a window, but she looked up at him. He said a few things in their language, likely to let her know what we said. Concern instantly crossed her young face and she shook her head.

A brief exchange followed.

"I can't take her back yet," Baxter eventually said. "She's the only mortal that knows which demigod killed Christa *and* she has a mission to complete. She's bound to it. It's a coming-of-age ritual sometimes given to mortal children of a demigod parent. Or sometimes not of a demigod parent. Regardless, Ava *must* complete her task."

"But didn't she do that? She's found you now."

"She must find Bram so he and the amulet can return to Alaysia together. To return the amulet without Bram would be pointless. He could disappear for the rest of his life and never face what he's done. Besides," his voice dropped, "a broken amulet is no small matter. This amulet belongs to Ignis, god of fire, and was one of his most beloved ones. He will not be pleased."

Any attempt to comprehend all of this rocked me, and a new level of weariness followed. This had been too much for one day, so the next steps would need to come later. With a deep breath, I gestured between me and Leda.

"How can we help, Bax?"

He glanced at us, then to Ava, and back to us. His mouth opened, then closed again. The large emotion returned to his gaze, and he seemed as if he'd aged ten years in a moment. Understanding what he didn't say, I held out an arm and gestured for Ava with my hand. He needed time. Space. A moment to gather himself back together. Ava hesitated only a moment, then stepped to my side until she stood between me and Leda.

"Take a night, Baxter, to process all of this. We can talk about the rest tomorrow. Ava will stay with us, of course."

Relief flooded his face.

"Thank you."

Baxter crouched down in front of Ava. She listened as he calmly spoke, then threw her arms around his neck, clenched her eyes tight, and let out another little cry. When he pulled away, she smiled bravely, then shuffled back to my side with sparkling eyes. Baxter straightened.

"Thank you," he said to me, then to Leda. "I'm forever indebted to you."

"We'll be here when you get back," I said.

Baxter nodded, and with a whisper like the wind, disappeared.

* * *

Sleep eluded me.

That night, I tossed on my bumpy, straw-stuffed mattress and tried to deal with the fact that I couldn't use magic to shift the lumps around and make myself more comfortable. Alina had been right. Removal of the magic changed everything. It would change *me* forever. Particularly if I couldn't get it back, which was an option I refused to entertain.

Baxter's words whirled through my mind well past midnight.

Demigods.
Ignis, god of fire.
Mission.
Christa.
Ava.

My thoughts shuttered to Ava. Only an hour ago, she'd tiptoed down the hallway and to my room. My door had creaked open a sliver before she slipped inside, then crept to my bedside and climbed in. I pretended to be asleep as she lay on top of the bed, curled into a ball, and proceeded to fall asleep. Once her breathing evened out, I covered her with a heavy blanket and stared at the ceiling.

Why had she come in here? Why not with Leda? She seemed to prefer burrowing in because the covers hid her face. Her hair fanned out on the pillow beneath her head. Every now and then, she'd give a little murmur. After Baxter had left, she'd been brighter than I'd seen before. A weight of burden had clearly lifted off, and she smiled more.

Leda and I hadn't said a word since Baxter left the apartment. She'd disappeared into her room and hadn't come back out. Meanwhile, Ava and I looked through several books together, even if she couldn't understand me, for an hour. My mind had been far away as I pointed to pictures and said their names. Reeves had thoughtfully supplied books with single words that I could point out and she'd repeat. Eventually, Ava had fallen asleep on the couch, and Reeves had carried her to bed with a levitation spell.

When the quiet, distant chime from a clock tower in nearby Chatham City announced two in the morning, I slipped out of bed. Ava didn't stir as I pulled a blanket around me and stepped into the hallway. A fire crackled in the hearth as I slipped out, but seemed to issue no heat. For light, then? A white-blonde head of hair shone at the table near the fire. Scattered books, parchments, and moving quills littered the top. Leda had always been a late busybody when she had something on her mind, so I wasn't entirely shocked to see her there. And, maybe, just a bit relieved.

"Hard time sleeping?" I asked as I sat across from her, and reflexively sent out a spell for a warm cup of tea. When nothing returned, I stood to get it myself near the fire. Leda waved me back into the seat, then used silent magic to issue the spell for me. A teapot zipped over from where it hung near the fire, then poured itself into a cup that manifested just before the water would have spilled across the table.

"Thanks," I murmured, irritated that I couldn't do it myself. Leda glanced at me, sighed, and dropped her gaze back to her book.

"I'm trying to make notes on what I observed of their language when Baxter and Ava spoke to each other," she said, but her voice had a high-pitched edge to it. "Like stepping back in time."

"Jikes," I rubbed a hand over my bleary eyes, "but this is a mess."

"A very big mess."

"Do you need me to tel—"

"I think I figured it out," she cut in before I could ask. "The pieces aren't too difficult to puzzle together, given what Baxter said and the running commentary of Sanako in the back of my mind. Baxter is a demigod, son of a god that he didn't mention in front of me, I presume. Ava, obviously his niece, brought an amulet she shouldn't have, I'm also assuming, to here."

A thousand other sentences lay behind that narrowed view, but I was too tired to say them tonight.

"That . . . sums it up."

Her brow grew heavy. "Sanako will have a field day over this when it gets out. She's spoken of demigods before, but I can't remember all the details of what she said."

The mention of the Librarian at the Great Library of Burke that ardently believed in the god and goddess paradigm came back to me with a cold little rush. Sweet Sanako, who so many witches had regarded as strange and bizarre, had been correct all this time. Good for her.

Not good for us.

"I heard back from Priscilla," she said.

"Oh?"

"She's with Michelle for now. Apparently, Niko's Guardians found your house in Letum Wood."

I froze.

"What?"

Leda held up a staying hand. "Calm down. Priscilla wasn't in the house when they came. She was outside and thought she heard witches coming, so she hid. Said they knocked, then went inside. She left it unlocked so it didn't appear suspicious or paranoid. When they didn't find her, they left, but someone remained behind, hiding. She waited. Eventually, a dragon came over with Nicholas, whom Michelle sent to check on her. Nicholas stayed out of sight, but the dragon fought with the witch, and they barely escaped with their life. She said the East Guards are terrified of Letum Wood and she doesn't think they'll be back. She's staying with Michelle, for now, to help with the baby. The dragons don't seem to mind her, but they're wary."

I sank back in my seat.

"Good."

Relief whispered through me. She was safe, at least. My house hadn't been broken or destroyed. I gently blew on the top of the tea as steam roiled off of it. The billowing heat smelled like lemongrass and felt like silk against my skin. Leda regarded me with an assessing gaze.

"I'm assuming your father knows about Baxter and his demigod status?"

I nodded.

"Interesting, because I'd wager the Council doesn't?"

"I believe not."

Her white-blonde eyebrows narrowed further. "That has some big implications," she said in a low voice. "When the Council finds out your father has been harboring a demigod without telling them. They will not be happy."

The thought hadn't occurred to me, and it sent a shiver through my spine. Technically, there had been no *harboring*. If the Council chose not to believe Baxter when he claimed his heritage as the *son of a god* every day, wasn't that on them? But, no. That would never work as an excuse. Even I hadn't liked it, because it still implied Papa hid Baxter, even if that was not entirely true.

"I hadn't thought of that," I said.

"Of course you haven't," she muttered. "It only gives the witches who are against the Highest Witch paradigm the power they need to sow distrust amongst the populace. With time, that could potentially overthrow our entire government structure. That's all."

Leda's quick thoughts on these subjects and uncanny observations—despite not knowing all that much about this situation—turned my mind back to Hiddleston. I regarded her in a new light.

Leda had always been lovely, albeit rough around the edges. She kept herself subdued to stay out of the spotlight, but her thin frame, light hair, milk-pale skin, and differently-colored eyes were attractive. Quietly stated, but elegant when her scowl didn't try to set a room on fire. It was easy to see why Hiddleston would be, presumably, attracted to her. Or, at least, desire her company even if he didn't care for her romantically. Her brilliant mind was a power that helped her understand things that most witches would never, magic or not.

"I met a Defender yesterday," I said. "That's where this whole mess started."

Leda cast me a sidelong glance at the change in subject, but she didn't stop her gentle riffle through more pages of her book. The words were illegible to me.

"Congratulations."

My lips twitched off a smile. I'd almost hoped she'd ask what a Defender was, but of course, Leda knew about them already. She probably knew more about me than I knew about myself. She was insufferably correct about most things.

"His name is Hiddleston."

Her entire body tightened so fast I thought her spine would break. *Interesting*, I thought, but kept going as if I hadn't noticed.

"I believe that Papa has, or will, ask Hiddleston to look through history for . . . something. Perhaps an establishment of the goddess paradigm. I'm hoping Papa has him looking for a way to get my magic back, but Papa and I haven't spoken since all of this broke. Interesting, isn't it?"

Her nostrils flared so wide she reminded me of a horse.

"That's . . . nice," she ground out.

Ah, so there had to be some history here. Leda wouldn't have responded like this unless she already had a reason to find Hiddleston contemptible. Ever since the disaster that was Rupert—an interested male witch that had annoyed her more than anything else—Leda's general irritation with eligible men happened often.

I had a long sip of cooled tea while she gathered her thoughts together. The crackle of the fire in the silence had a calming effect, and I enjoyed the heat that spread through my belly.

"I . . ." she said, then stopped. "That is . . ."

She frowned.

Perhaps I could save her.

"Hiddleston has expressed some interest in you," I said. "He wanted me to arrange a way for you to meet directly. I told him I'd present the opportunity, but wouldn't force you to do anything."

She closed her eyes and pinched the bridge of her nose. "You can tell him to eat with the dogs the next time he says my name."

Her voice turned shrill as she slammed her book shut, then commanded them together with a spell. Every scroll rolled itself back up, quill zoomed away from the page, and book shuffled to her arms. All of them lifted into the air around her like a flock of deranged library supplies.

"And tell him to stop looking so hard for the establishment of the goddess paradigm in history," she snapped. "He only needs to go back as far as Isadora and Sanna. The precedent is there."

With that, she disappeared into her room with the slam of a door. I blinked, looked at the near-empty table, and sighed. What precedent of the goddess paradigm with Isadora and Sanna was she *talking* about?

I sank further into the chair and watched the flames curl around a charred log in flashes of orange and crimson. Their buttery, long arms were a mesmerizing force until the blessed reprieve of sleep stole over me, and I slipped into a quiet, easy doze.

I dreamed of gods and goddesses.

* * *

Hours later, the touch of something on my face woke me with a quick start.

Darkness had settled on the apartment, and with it came cooler air. Outside the windows, stars popped out of a velvet sky with white-hot tenacity. The fire had banked to a low bed of coals that glimmered. Their subtle light gave vague definition to shadows as I blinked awake and straightened, my neck stiff from sleeping at a kink.

Only when I felt a brush of something against my cheek again did I notice a small scroll hovering near my head. There was no ribbon or twine around it, which ruled out Scarlett or Priscilla or Michelle. Nothing but a spot of wax the size of my pinky nail, the color of slate gray. My stomach jumped.

Papa.

Late headlines in the *Chatterer* yesterday had proclaimed a stasis between negotiations in the Networks. The twenty-year plan to provide safety for the Southern Network had been submitted to the delegation by Papa and Igor last night. It called on all Networks to create a collective draw of resources for the South to use. Rotational Guardian assignments. Training. Greater weapons resources. The Southern Network couldn't create standard magical swords without their magic, so now they had to figure out non-magical swords. The transition would take time and the plan remained under heavy scrutiny.

With that thought on my mind, I touched the scroll and it unfurled.

My office, please. You should be safe to walk yourself.

With a yawn, I stood up and pulled the blanket farther around me. It must be close to four in the morning. No one would be out, so I'd risk walking there wrapped in a blanket. My thin summer nightgown barely reached my calves. My sleep had been fast, but deep, and the cobwebs of my mind had cleared.

Reeves had left several windows cracked open, allowing ribbons of air to whisper inside. Barefoot, I shuffled to the door and stepped into the hall of the castle.

Torches illuminated by magic led my way down the hall. Before now, I hadn't ever considered who issued the spell that kept the magical torches bright. The maids, likely? What I'd give for even that small ability.

Papa's office wasn't far from his apartment or the throne room, but I felt tension all the same. Any witch could come along, cast a spell to harm me, and I could do nothing about it.

In the distance, I thought I heard the hum, clang, and hubbub of the kitchen rise from several floors below. The crash of pots and pans often wound its way through the turrets and up to the higher floors in a comforting sort of clatter.

I turned a corner and skidded to a stop.

Outside Papa's office, three large chairs were available for witches to sit in. There, filling the far chair with his short body and tight eyes, sat Igor. He held a pipe in his hand and stared at the distant wall. When I appeared, his gaze flickered to mine, held it, then skittered away again.

Quickly, I recovered my surprise, approached the remaining two seats, and sat in the farthest one. An open chair remained between us.

Uncertainty streamed through my mind, along with a few curses. Of course, I wear my nightgown and a *blanket* the morning I encounter the Southern Network High Priest.

Should I make small talk? Ask why he would be here at such an hour? Bright light issued into the hallway from beneath Papa's office door, a sure indication that he hadn't gone to bed yet. He probably called for me now because he'd been too busy before. I—

"You are up very early for a voman of your young age."

Igor's voice had the deep, tonal quality that I remembered from the former High Priest of the Southern Network, Mikhail.

They all spoke with a sort of rasp, as if they collected their words before sending them out. I pulled in a breath and let it out before I turned to face him.

"My father summoned me."

He stared at me with an appraising expression. His dark eyes angled more sharply than most, which indicated some tribal heritage. His dark hair lay thick and full on his head, giving way to a well-maintained, full beard. The decorative gems that Southern Network males often braided into their beards were missing this early in the morning. He seemed smaller without the oversized topaz he usually wore.

Igor was likely in his late forties, but I wasn't sure. He had the stocky stature of most of the Southern Network, but he wasn't fat like Mikhail had once been. Igor had a leanness about him that spoke more to muscle than brawn. I hadn't witnessed him do much more than discuss things with other witches, but I had a feeling he could move fast if he needed to. The pipe had been replaced with an unlit cheroot, but the air still had the earthy smell of pipe tobacco.

"You alvays obey your father?" he asked.

The word *yes* sprang to my lips in response, but I pressed it back. That would not be any form of the truth. My beat of hesitation lasted only for a moment before Igor laughed, a fulsome sound that made his shoulders shake up and down.

"Very good daughter," he said. "Very good. You only listen vhen you vant, yes? A true daughter of Derek Black."

"Are you waiting to speak with my father?"

"Yes. Alvays," he tacked on, then chuckled to himself.

Do it, said a voice in my head. *Talk to him about the mortals. About his Network. About anything!*

A thousand questions filtered through my mind, but they all spun away. In the silence, I could hear my chance ticking away. I had wanted to talk to Igor *before* I knew everything else about gods and witches and demigods. Now, all my questions seemed elementary at best.

Any demigods in your Network? I could ask, then shuddered at the implications. That's all Papa needed—word to get out that another enemy could be on our shores.

Not could be . . . *was.*

"Losing magic is hard on a personal level," I finally said, then hastily tacked on, "I would imagine. Dealing with it as a whole Network has likely been very challenging for you. You walked into a big mess when you became High Priest."

Igor appraised me again, this time from the corner of his eye. I hadn't noticed the fur-lined cloak on his shoulders at first, beneath which lay a linen shirt that stretched across a wide plane of chest. Dark chest hair sprouted at the top beneath his beard.

"Very hard," he intoned. "But life is not vithout challenges, no? The important thing for the Southern Netvork is that ve pull together. Ve must be loyal to each other now, because other Netvorks . . . they have their problems too. Vould you agree?"

"Yes, for the most part."

"There is something vith vhich you do not?"

I hesitated, recalling a few very short visits to the Southern Network before the war. Pulling together and teamwork had never been a strength for the Southern Network. Was now really the time to start creating that?

But then if not now, when?

"It's . . . it's a big challenge," I managed to say, "in a Network that has always been divided between the clans and the rest of the witches. The South has never been known for its ability to pull together."

Igor waved a hand and a gaudy ring with an emerald gem on his thumb sparkled. "That sort of movement starts with the leader. They need to be loyal to me, then I can help them be loyal to each other. Once I can make them safe, they vill do so. You vill see."

He slumped to the side of the wooden chair where he sat, propped his chin on one hand, and stared hard at a carving across the hallway. It was a representation of a tree from Letum Wood. It stretched overhead in a flat, marble version of the forest. Branches and leaves sprawled along the edges of door frames and snaked down the hall in white, chiseled beauty.

"Has the Southern Network lost many witches since the magic was taken?" I asked.

"Not very."

"Your population has increased then?"

My voice pitched a bit too high—the question didn't really make sense. But he didn't seem to notice.

"No. Ve are fine."

"Oh."

"It's all in the leader," he said with a wrinkled brow, as if he responded to something in his own mind instead of what I asked. "They have no loyalty to each other now, vhich is part of the problem. Mikhail, he failed them. Us, I mean. He failed all of Alkarra. He cared about himself before the rest of the Netvork, and now," he shrugged. "Now, ve are here, and ve need a leader."

"He was one in a long line of leaders like that," I said with a brief recall of Southern Network history. The South had had some worthy, gallant leaders, but the latest run of High Priests had been a force of terror.

"Yes."

"How will you do it?" I asked. "How do you create loyalty to a Network with hundreds of years of dissension between themselves? The clans—"

"Have not had representation." He lifted a finger. "For a vitch to be loyal, they must feel they have a say."

"Which is why you instituted Alina?"

He tapped his thumb on the top of his other hand, a gesture of approval in the South. I mulled that over for a moment, recalling the stomach-whirling dance with Alina that happened only a few days before. After all that had happened in the mean-time, it might as well have been lifetimes ago.

"One of the reasons." He shifted in the seat. "She has her own potential, and she is voman."

"So you're turning your nose up at the common Southern Network convention?" I drawled. "Don't you also have a harem?"

Igor's lips twitched. Mikhail had done little more than use women as concubines during his reign. Mikhail's harem had been twenty women strong, the largest that history had ever seen. The harem was a common tradition in the South, which is where the shieldmaidens came into play.

When there had been a High Priestess, who would have been the married partner of the High Priest, the shieldmaidens protected her. Mikhail had done away with the shieldmaidens, except for the harem of women he kept for his pleasure. The shieldmaidens had turned their power to protecting the harem.

"You do not like my harem?" he asked.

I shrugged. "It's not my place to judge."

His eyes glittered with amusement. "No, but you are. I understand. My three vomen are vell cared for. Happy. They give me children, and they don't hate each other. They chose each other, did you know?"

"No."

He shrugged. "The vorld is filled with different ideas and places. So many, you could never even know."

I wanted to ask how *he* knew so much, but I held my question back. He'd spent his whole life in the South, just like I'd spent it in the Central Network. His magic-less status had limited his travel since the closing of borders. But I'd already trespassed enough on his society that insult could have been given long ago. Better to play it safe and say nothing more.

Igor's lips twitched.

"I like to say ve are creating new customs, not feeling sad

about the old ones. For all vitches to give their loyalty to the South, they must all feel seen. Vomen are part of the vitches there. They vill be seen and heard and their loyalty svorn to their leader. It is our only vay into the future."

Such conviction startled me, but at least he moved in a better direction than Mikhail. His plan for better in the South sent a little shot of hope through me, particularly when I didn't have to be on the bureaucratic side of making it happen. At least Igor was doing something, at any rate, even if progress was historically slow.

"You still call your witches, witches?" I asked gently.

He eyed me again. "Are they not? They have had something taken from them, yes. They have no magic now, but are they fundamentally that different? No. They are vitches. Not . . . not . . ."

"Mortals?"

His nose wrinkled in obvious displeasure. "Please," he muttered with a roll of his eyes. "Ve do not use that vord in the South."

I bit back a deranged laugh. For a moment, I wanted to tell him about the amulet and the fire and the void inside me. To ask him how it felt for *him* when his magic left. Did he feel rage toward Mikhail like I felt toward the amulet? Did he miss magical ability as deeply as I did? Did he attempt to do spells every day, even by accident? Finding someone else that could understand a hint of my position gave me a little thrill.

Again, I bit the words back, knowing that he'd have too many natural questions about it. Besides, Igor didn't strike me as the friendly type.

"Good luck," I said when a shuffle of movement sounded from Papa's office door. "I think your endeavors in the South are worthy and I look forward to seeing what comes of your work."

He sighed wearily. "Thank you. I am alvays hoping for the best."

The door creaked as the latch released and drew open. Light illuminated the mostly dark corridor, and two silhouettes shuffled forward. Marten and Scarlett, both bleary-eyed. Igor stood, bowed his head to Scarlett, nodded to Marten, and slipped past them into Papa's office without another word. The rustle of his cape remained the only sound until the door shut, sealing me into the hallway.

"Bianca," Marten said and hooked an arm around my shoulders. His quick, warm embrace gave me courage in the dark night.

"You're both up late," I said.

Marten squeezed my shoulder. "And ready for bed. Forgive me, but I believe I'll retire to get a few hours' rest before a new day begins. Scarlett, always a pleasure. B, I'll see you later."

I wanted to call him back. Both he and Papa had answers to give about Baxter. They had plenty of opportunities to tell me more about him, so why didn't they? Doubts assailed me after that question, however. Because was it my place to know all the Network secrets? No. I never made an effort to involve myself in everything at the castle. I remained in my position with the recruits, whom I deeply missed now, and my trees.

On one hand, why *would* Papa and Marten tell me about Baxter's hidden birthplace? I'd never shown any desire to be part of the bureaucratic process. On another, why *wouldn't* they?

"Merry part, Marten," I said. "Sleep well."

He departed, hands folded behind him. Concern lived in his eyes now, and it haunted me as he left. Likely, he had heavy thoughts after meeting with Papa. If there was so much I already didn't know about what the Network faced these days, what else remained?

"Good to see you again," I said to Scarlett with an attempt at a lighthearted smile. "Productive meeting with Papa?"

Scarlett's brow rose as she glanced at the door behind her. A brilliant display of carved wood showed all the High Priests and

High Priestesses from years past, each represented by a symbol and their name. When a new Highest Witch came to power, the carvings shrank to make room for more. Where the magic for this door came from, I had no idea. It must have been powerful to endure for so long, however.

"Business as usual during the Celebration," she said. "The Central Network has much on its plate these days."

I almost laughed. Business as usual? *Mortals come all the time, do they?* I wanted to ask. Before I could respond, she said, "I hear you've gotten yourself into some trouble. In several ways," she added drily. "Your father has updated me fully."

I shrugged.

She sobered quickly. Her voice dropped, even though I doubted anyone would hear us here. "At this point, I imagine your world has been rocked. Mine was when we questioned Baxter more deeply several years ago."

Understatement of the year. I swallowed hard and nodded.

Earnestness filled her gaze, perhaps a bit of pleading too. "I have not given up on the Sisterhood, Bianca. Even this development around your magic can be used to our advantage . . . if it's reversed. Your father has some hope that it can be, which is why he's summoned you tonight."

My heart pattered in my chest like a wild thing.

"Really?" I whispered. "He knows something about my magic?"

"He *hopes* something about it. Use this time to your advantage, Bianca," she replied. Her dark hair shone in the light, highlighting a wrinkled expression and tired eyes. "There is much you can learn that could be helpful to our plans later."

"To the Sisterhood?" I asked, shocked. "But how?"

The Sisterhood hadn't even occurred to me in all this, but of course, she hadn't let her plans go. If I truly had lost my magic, it seemed impossible that the Sisterhood would be an option for me anymore. The sinking feeling in my stomach took me by surprise, and so did the panicked breath that followed. A few weeks ago, I would have said I didn't care about the Sisterhood, even though I'd helped Scarlett start to plan it.

But the pang in my chest told me otherwise.

She put a hand on my arm, and her fingers were warm and soft. "I mean to yourself. There are lessons to learn which can help you later. The Sisterhood will soon be more needed than ever. Get your magic back, Bianca, however you can. Your Network is going to need you."

The sound of Papa's door opening again took me by surprise. Igor had only been in there for mere moments. Scarlett stepped back, her chocolate-brown dress swaying around her legs.

"Good luck," she whispered, then transported away as Igor stepped back outside. Papa's broad shoulders filled the doorway behind him as he sent me a glance, then turned to stride down the hallway. Once he left, Papa turned to me.

"B."

Exhaustion tugged at all his features. Papa was often tired, but he was usually tattered and filthy to go with it. To see him in clean clothes with his hair only slightly askew, and not a bit of blood to be seen, almost made me giggle. Political exhaustion was, apparently, a force to be reckoned with.

The windows in his office revealed a murky blue sky with disappearing stars. Papa straightened, then gestured down the hall. "Morning is coming. Let's walk together in the gardens."

Chapter Seventeen

Several witches from the Western Network, Council Members from the South, and a few of Niko's butlers from the East passed us as we stepped down the turret. Seeing them made me think of Niko, and then Priscilla. I wondered if either of them woke up early.

The time must have been closer to five in the morning. By the time we set foot on the lush grass of the distant gardens—far enough away for privacy, but close enough for us to be seen—we had encountered almost fifteen witches. The tickle of grass on my bare feet, and fresh air in my lungs, felt like freedom after days in the apartments.

Anything that took me closer to the forest made my heart trill, but I also suspected that Papa suggested this walk so we could be seen together. Witches would see me in my natural state near the forest, but I wouldn't have to go in and be unsafe. With him at my side, he could transport me away should danger arise. He'd given me a glimpse of the forest to settle my heart, no doubt, and we could speak without interruption or surprise.

The fading night felt cool on my skin as we stepped through the dewy grass. Ahead of us, the black band of shadows that was

Letum Wood seemed to stretch eternally overhead. Papa strolled with a thoughtful expression, his brow creased, and I wondered if he also wanted the cool, outside air to wake him back up.

He nudged us into an expanse of grass far enough from the castle to avoid listening incantations and near open gardens where no one could hide. There, he stopped. He folded his hands behind his back and stared at Letum Wood for a long minute.

At his side, I drank the forest in. It looked like a dark, angry thing from this vantage point, soaring to an intimidating height overhead. Dawn brightened the sky right behind it. My heart pattered at being close to it again. I instinctively sought the voices of the trees, and I felt the resounding emptiness of their silence in my soul.

Were they reaching for me?

Did they see me now?

I always come back, I silently told them, but feared they couldn't hear me.

"First," Papa said, startling me out of my thoughts with a little jump, "the Council Member Luncheon is today. Will you please attend with me?"

"Me?"

"Yes." His lips pressed together for a moment. "I think it would make up for the missing dinner. It will be far safer than the ball, and you can come in and leave as quickly as possible, so you don't get caught talking to a lot of witches."

"Sure."

He eyed me. "Thank you."

I gave him a smile. He continued to walk, but it was slow and methodical. His head bent down slightly, brow burdened with a frown.

"Second, I want you to know that I trust Baxter as much as I trust anyone. But I have had to trust his, and only his, explanations of Alaysia and the world of the gods. When Ava arrived, she provided an opportunity for me to prove Baxter's story. I wanted to speak with her first. To verify what Baxter said and ensure that *he* wasn't someone we should fear. Yesterday, Hiddleston forced my hand. Thankfully, I believe all has worked out, but it could have been ugly."

A dark feeling grew within me that I hadn't considered before. Baxter could have been someone we shouldn't have trusted. In his own way, Papa had been trying to protect Ava. Yes, he would have pushed off communicating with her for too long, but he had thought of her safety. For some reason, that settled me.

"I hadn't fully considered that," I admitted quietly.

"Why should you?"

Because Scarlett wants me to start the Sisterhood, I thought, *and that's the kind of thing I would need to be aware of.*

But I sent that thought away.

"You know what happened at the apartment when Ava saw him?" I asked.

"Reeves has informed me, and so has Baxter."

Despair tripled through me. "All of this is my fault, Papa," I whispered. "I'm sorry. If I had never brought Ava here then—"

"No." He reached over, put a hand on my shoulder. "While I wished you hadn't accidentally touched that amulet, you did the right thing bringing Ava here. Imagine if all of this unfolded unbeknownst to us? What if she had fallen into Niko's hands?"

The thought made me sicker, if possible. What if a witch in the East found her? What if they knew about the god magic and wanted to use it for whatever nefarious purposes for which it could be used? We knew nothing about this form of magic. All of this would be unfolding without us knowing, and that seemed far more daunting.

"Still, I wish . . ."

His voice dragged with fatigue. "Me too," he murmured, and

I had the feeling he knew my thought even though I couldn't complete it

"What now?" I asked, overwhelmed with thoughts. Everything had been flipped upside down with Baxter's revelation last night. I felt, more than knew, that a new world existed somewhere beyond the void of the ocean. Somewhere in the vague unknown that suddenly seemed to press on us.

"Baxter returned home," he said.

"Did he learn anything?"

Papa chewed on his bottom lip, as if he sorted through his own thoughts now.

"Once he returns, he'll have more information, I hope. Should be soon."

"Whoever it is, they're probably in the Southern Network, don't you think?"

"Probably," Papa murmured. "Which makes it more imperative that our protective plan for the South goes through. The votes will likely tie at the first pass today. Two for, two against. With one tiebreaker."

I could already guess how Networks would vote. Details of the Esbats were released in the *Chatterer*, so I'd loosely followed most of the meetings and their agenda items. But the real meat of the Esbat wouldn't truly be released until after the Celebration to protect the decision-making process. Particularly on such vast topics as protecting an entire, magicless Network.

"The South and the Central will vote for the plan," Papa said. "And the East and the North against."

Hardly surprising, considering Geralyn's announcement that the Northern Network would withdraw from the Networks yet again. The entire Esbat regarding whether the North should vote during the Celebration had resulted in a positive return: the North could still weigh in, despite their plan to close borders. The plan they'd set forth to isolate could require up to a year of border preparation and trade negotiation issues. New supply lines had been set up from the North in the past three years. To cut those off without time to find others could be seen as an act of war.

"Lana in the West is the tie-breaker?" I asked.

"I believe so. The issue of the Southern Network's safety should have been resolved in a single Esbat," he muttered in a carefully controlled tone, packed with frustration. "But members of my Council have blocked our every step by talking to and frustrating the other Networks."

My jaw dropped open.

"What? How?"

"Council Member Aldred has gone behind my back to other Networks, with attempts to prove to delegation leaders that I don't have control of the Network."

"No!"

"We're working on finding physical proof, but it's a difficult process. The Protectors are obviously loyal to me, so I need more than their word to the Council. Aldred has clearly already reached Niko. Lana appears to be undecided. She gave me the courtesy of letting me know that someone had approached her. Based on rumors from a source that she didn't disclose, she questions whether I'll be in power to see the Southern Network plan through."

My jaw dropped. "She thinks the Council will have removed you by then?"

"That is all I can presume."

"But your idea is to initiate the Southern Network's protective plan in a month."

"And if I am out of power before that month has started, then all previous agreements would be null and void until renegotiation."

"Papa!" I gasped.

He continued toward the forest again, but slowly, as if he couldn't bear to stand still. "We stand at the edge of a precipice, B. One wrong move in either direction and we fall off."

"Get rid of the Council already!" I hissed.

"And confirm what they've been saying?" he snapped. "If I act like a tyrant, even a new Council would vote to move me out immediately. It could be part of Aldred's plan, in fact."

"Can they move you out of Highest Witch?"

"Yes. There's a distant, vague clause that is rarely enacted, supposedly, where the Council can, by majority vote, remove a Highest Witch from power. We're trying to prove that it exists so I'm not removed on a rumor. The Esmelda scrolls say nothing. Hiddleston is looking into it for me," he added as an aside, and I remembered Papa's charge to Hiddleston yesterday. "The opposition on the Council may be trying to push me so I act rashly, so we must be careful. Any retaliation to them has to be done diplomatically."

"Then what is your option?"

"Greyson said the opposition on the Council, led by Aldred, would be willing to work *with* me if I agree to their rules on a new government structure. One where the Council receives the right to approve all orders given by the Highest Witch."

"Greyson," I muttered, thinking of the new Council Member that had been talking to Scarlett at the ball. He was young, but perceptive and well-liked enough. "I thought he was one of the neutral parties?"

"He is," Papa murmured. "That's why he came to me. They don't want individual retaliation against those who want to close the Highest Witch paradigm and get rid of me and Scarlett. He's acting as a go-between."

My head spun in circles just thinking about it. I scoffed. "So you'd be their puppet? Have to pass every measure through them, I assume?"

"Essentially."

"It's not worth it."

Weariness showed in Papa's gaze as he shook his head. "I don't see the path out just yet, B. I'm sorry to say that. I'll figure it out, I'm just not sure how. For the time being, I'm going to do nothing. I'm going to get through the Celebration and then deal with Ava and all of this."

My heart ached for him. No wonder he hadn't slept last night, and now he had to step into a volley of new diplomatic meetings. If my magic worked, I would have sent him a new mug of coffee on the hour, every hour.

"No matter what you do," I said after a dark thought occurred to me, "things are going to be ugly if the other Networks find out about Ava."

He gritted his teeth. "I'm aware."

"Still . . . there are things that can't be put off, Papa. What if the Council isn't the greatest threat? For all we know, the demigod could be *on* our Council and running this agenda against you."

He laughed. "Aldred is no demigod."

"Baxter has been here three years, why not Bram?"

"The Protectors have their orders, B. I have this handled."

Shock stalled my next response, and I was grateful for the grounding effect of soft grass beneath my feet. Of course, Papa had thought out every angle—even the ones I hadn't. The forest distracted me, allowing my thoughts to calm. The wavering, humid air. The caws and cracks of sound that drifted out of the forest. It soothed my ragged spirit.

"I need time," Papa said. "That's it. Time to get through the Celebration and focus wholly on Baxter, Ava, and the mortal situation. Handled correctly, this could re-engage the Council's trust in my leadership."

Or shatter it, but I didn't say that.

Time was the one thing we couldn't control. The wheels of time had never been in our power. Not even magic could truly take us backward or forward in time. Some more powerful magic systems might give us a glimpse of it, like Watchers and Defenders, but not truly move it.

"I'm sorry this is happening, Papa."

"Me too."

Together, we stood and stared at Letum Wood, our backs to the castle. The steady rise of the sun left the grassy knoll more illuminated now. Anyone watching would see what they wanted to see—a High Priest and his daughter. Something so ordinary it would reassure witches that regular routines remained intact. They had no idea of the danger that simmered under the surface. The turmoil of my lost magic, or mortals in Alkarra. My mind drifted to Niko, then to Priscilla.

"Do you think Niko knows about Ava? That he's pursuing it as a means to bring you down before the end of the Celebration?"

"I do."

My stomach felt like a heavy weight inside of me at the thought. What would Niko gain by getting Papa off the throne? Who would replace him? There was an enemy on the Council now.

Or were there several?

"Tell me how I can help, Papa. What should I do?"

"For now, we focus on Baxter finding the demigod before the Celebration is over. We need to remove the threat first. Then we'll deal with the fallout later. He should return soon with more information."

The sound of someone approaching came behind us, followed by an unceremonious throat clearing. I glanced back, startled to see Merrick striding our way.

"Oh," I whispered.

Papa turned and an expression of surprise—then concern—followed. Before I could speak, Papa held out an arm. Merrick clasped it in his with a warm smile. "Merry meet, Your Highness."

Papa rolled his eyes and not-so-subtly put his body between me and Merrick. "Please. Once a brother, always a brother. None of that formal stuff. It's good to see you again, Merrick. How can I help you?"

Annoyed, I shot Papa a glare and stepped out from behind him. Merrick looked at me, nodded in greeting, and said to Papa, "Actually, I came to speak with Bianca."

Papa's brow truly rose then. He'd never been excited about Merrick having a romantic relationship with me, and although he'd been patient and kind after Merrick returned to the North, I sensed relief in Papa once Merrick had been out of the picture.

Merrick's chosen path as a Master was significantly dangerous, lonely, and all-too-similar to Papa's life as a Protector. Papa wanted a better marriage for me than Mama had with him, even though for her Papa was enough. She'd never have chosen anything different, but he never seemed able to accept that.

Now, Papa just seemed puzzled.

"Good to see you again, Merrick," I said. "I was just on my way back to the castle."

"Can I walk you back?"

"Of course." I jabbed an elbow in Papa's ribs. "Papa and I just finished up here."

Papa opened his mouth to say something as I swept by, but a firm glare stopped him. I could feel him watch us go with the same sense of confusion.

I knew the feeling.

* * *

Merrick kept his arms at his side and appeared easygoing, even if I sensed the tension in the set of his jaw. We sauntered forward for several paces, separating us out of hearing distance from Papa, before I spoke first.

"Everything all right?" I asked.

"Yes."

I sorted around for something to say, annoyed that conversation didn't come more easily. My mind flitted to the events of the day.

"Is the North looking forward to the combined luncheon hosted by the East today? Rumor has it that chefs from the East have taken over the kitchen. Doubt that's gone well. They were up quite early working."

"Yes. Should be delicious."

"I imagine a room full of all delegation leaders and all the Council Members in Alkarra will be hot and stuffy. Also, imagine cooking for that many people?"

"A nightmare," he agreed blandly.

The conversation paused as we walked. Several quiet moments passed before I realized he'd fallen into thought, and he didn't seem likely to come back out on his own. I suppressed the instinct to touch his arm to draw his attention. Instead, I stopped walking.

"Merrick?"

He blinked out of his thoughts and hastily stopped at my side. "Sorry, I . . . I just had some news I felt I should pass along, although I'm not sure why. Instinct, I guess. Have you heard that Hector, Niko's Assistant, has been injured?"

"No, I hadn't."

He chewed on the inside of his lip and gazed past me, to the Wall.

"Oh."

The event was nothing spectacular. Hector, a bulldog-like man, could have been hurt in several different ways. But heard in light of Priscilla's more recent letter to Leda, it became a lot more interesting.

"Where?" I asked.

"Nothing confirmed, but some saw him exiting Letum Wood with a bloody leg, farther north of here. He's disappeared from the delegation, but no official word has been issued anywhere."

"When?"

"A day ago, I think."

My heart began to patter, but I calmed it. Leda had just heard from Priscilla last night, so the events must be the same. Hector searching for Priscilla in Letum Wood when the Celebration happened here was the only thing that made sense. As Niko's Assistant, why wasn't Hector here with his High Priest? I couldn't fathom Papa being parted from Baxter at a time like this.

Not for anything less than an emergency.

The news was nothing I could act on for now. Merrick delivering the news seemed more of a thinly-veiled excuse to talk than an actual issue. Something altogether too small to be important, at least against the grand scheme of things. Merrick may have *other* stakes in telling me. Was he attempting to get information for his High Priestesses as well?

His tone seemed to die as he spoke, as if he knew how weak the information sounded. So why did he come to say it? A written message would have been just as effective.

"I just . . . wanted you to know," he said quickly, as if he read my mind. "Just in case it might mean something."

"Thank you."

We paused like a pair of awkward school kids while I scoured my mind for what to say next, and he seemed to do the same. Such strangeness between someone that had been such a large part of my world felt like a cruel joke. Merrick had often gone on missions, even after the war. *Especially* after the war. There had been nothing about our relationship we could have considered normal.

Still, it had been something special.

What could we even say to each other now? Questions about his job to protect Geralyn felt too intrusive. Although I had no official political title, I bore enough influence in my Network that any probing question that I asked of Merrick could have other ramifications. Geralyn might assume I was attempting to extract information and spy, the way I'd wondered about him. He'd already told me about his mother and his sister, so any other topic would venture into personal territory, like if he dated someone or how he dealt with our breakup after it happened.

And perhaps I didn't want to know those details.

"How are you?" he finally asked.

At the same moment, I said, "I better go."

He laughed, and his quick, genuine smile broke the tension. I let out a long breath to ease the transition out of the awkwardness.

The roguish burr in his voice made my stomach flip. "I guess we're not as smooth now as we were then, eh?"

I smiled. "Perhaps not."

"Comes back with time, I hear."

We turned and began to walk again. There was so much I wanted to tell him. Years worth of life that we could catch up on. For months I'd dreamed of him swooping back to the Central Network. We'd talk all night about what had happened during the dark times apart, and he'd stay. He'd stay and my heart would knit back together and the world would make sense again.

Now, all the words that I'd carried around for years stuck in my throat.

By sheer willpower, I didn't allow myself to watch his teeth worry his bottom lip as he slowly sauntered across the grass. His gaze slid away to look into something beyond us again.

By the good gods, was Merrick nervous?

Around *me*?

"Actually, I also wanted to speak with you about something else," he said, a bit sheepishly. "That's why I came."

I waited, but he said nothing more. The sound of a distant call drew my head around, and I looked toward the castle to see

Leda standing at the top of the grass, only a few paces away from the Wall. She waved one arm, then disappeared. A wink later, she stood ten steps away. With a startled blink of her eyes at Merrick, she turned to me, breathless.

"Baxter needs you for something at your father's apartment."

My stomach flipped. Baxter was already back? Hopefully with good news. I nodded. "Thank you. I'll come right now."

"Good to see you, Merrick," she said with a little smile. Merrick returned it before she disappeared again. The urge to transport after her followed me uselessly. I'd have to settle for the long trek back on foot. Maybe it would give me time to analyze this side of Merrick, and then stuff it away to never think about again.

"You needed to speak with me?" I asked.

Merrick smiled again, but it didn't quite reach his eyes. Instead, he took a step back. "Not important. We can discuss it later. Good to see you, B."

With that, he whirled around and strode off, disappearing into a transportation spell seconds later. I stared at the spot where he'd left with a hearty sigh, then headed up the hill with the feeling of grass in between my toes and a heavy burden on my heart.

* * *

When I returned to Papa's apartment, Baxter stood near the fire. Two chairs were pushed close together with their backs to the room. One arm was folded across his chest, and one fist against his mouth. He stared at the flames with a troubled, heavy gaze. Bags lingered under his eyes.

What had the last day been like for him? Clearly, it hadn't been restful. He grappled with a new reality now. He scrubbed a weary hand over equally bleary eyes. I doubted he'd slept at all last night, like Papa. Like me. Maybe countless others. I couldn't help but wonder what it was like for him to return home to Alaysia. How did he use god magic? He had transported before, although not often. Did he do that last night?

My questions about his world continued to populate in my mind, but I sent them back.

Later.

Ava sat at the table in the nook near the patio. Burgeoning sunlight grew in the windows behind her, casting her in silhouette. Outside, the sun had just crested Letum Wood and shot yellowed rays of sunshine into the fluffy treetops. The rest of the sky filled with a watery palette of pink, interrupted only by clouds rimmed with orange, like lines of fire.

As I stepped closer, it became apparent that her cheeks were reddened, as if she'd been crying. She rubbed the tips of her fingers against the multifaceted amulet in her lap in an unconscious motion. Reeves had supplied breakfast, but she didn't seem to have touched it. Did she miss home? Her family, perhaps? If Baxter and Ava held such affection for each other, I couldn't imagine what the rest of her family must think of her absence. The real question of her arrival in Alkarra still hung in the balance.

How had she even gotten here?

Leda stood near the buffet table, saw me, nodded, then crept up to Ava's side. She put a hand on Ava's arm and gestured to some books. A quiet murmur that seemed to be a question followed, and I assumed it was in Ava's language. With a weary sigh, Ava nodded and said, "Yes, please," in a clear tone.

"Very good," Leda murmured, then pointed down the hall, and to her chest. "We'll go to my room. It's quieter."

They shuffled out, and I sent Leda a grateful look. She acknowledged it with a nod and disappeared into the hallway.

Baxter blinked out of his thoughts and looked at me as I entered.

"Ava do all right last night?" he asked. "She said she slept with you because it made her feel safe."

A shot of guilt followed such a statement. How could others see beyond the truth? My protection was as fallible as anyone else. Many had died without me being able to save them. Although the daughter of the great Derek Black, I was not Derek himself. Not even Scarlett's belief in me starting a Sisterhood could erase the fact that, when it came right down to it, I couldn't trust myself to save other witches.

"Of course," I said to Baxter and banished those thoughts. "From what I observed, she slept well."

He nodded, clearly relieved. A yawn overtook his face for a moment. Not only had he lost sleep, but this hadn't been a fun welcome home. I lowered into the chair on the right. Echoes of my grief with Mama, Camille, Stella, Grandmother, all the others that I'd lost stirred in my chest. Baxter carried hints of that pain now in his gaze and the remembered grief caused me a moment of weakness.

"Well?" I asked quietly. "How are you after returning home?"

"Tired."

"You look it," I said gently.

His jaw tightened, as if he didn't want to go any further into that. "I spoke with my sisters and my father. They found Christa a month ago."

"A month?"

He nodded, seeming a bit lost with the deep lines in his head and downturned lips. A puzzling timeline. If Christa had been dead for a month, what had Ava been doing for all that time? Why hadn't his family told him before now? It indicated a likelihood that Baxter didn't return home all that much.

Or perhaps they didn't want him to know.

His voice remained steady, but now it held more of an edge. Perhaps the shock had begun to fade. Now that he'd been back to his family and they had actual facts, he seemed harder than ever, like the edges of a diamond. Anger simmered through him.

"I'm sorry, Bax."

"Me too."

In the quiet that followed, I wondered if this was his first chance to really think about what had happened. To consider that his sister was dead and he'd never see her in this life again. The weight of that kind of grief sank in with surprising speed.

"My father is relieved to hear that Ava kept the amulet safe from Bram," Baxter said with a little shake of his head, as if to clear his thoughts. "He's eager to have this closed without a problem. All of my other sisters feel betrayed by Bram and what he did to Christa."

"Are they worried about Ava?"

His gaze became more troubled. "Not exactly," he said slowly. "*I* am Ava's *tagata* and have grown very fond of her, which isn't surprising. She's intelligent and curious. But my sisters don't know her well. Christa rarely spoke about her. Considering that Ava is a mortal and most demigods follow the lines we have, anyway."

"What lines?" I asked.

"Between mortal, demigod, and god. It's a carefully maintained system, even for demigods that partner with mortals. We stay separate and distinct. Children born to a demigod and a mortal will be mortal, which makes it difficult. Sometimes a mixed child like that will display magical tolerance, but rarely."

So many questions came to mind, but I forced them away to keep the conversation centralized. Still, one snuck out. "Can demigods partner together?" I asked.

He nodded, said, "Sure," and left it at that. Before I could ask more, he continued. "At any rate, my sisters agree that Ava must complete her mission."

A sense of shock rippled through me at his statement. Unknowingly, I'd spent most of the night assuming Ava would return to Alaysia. That Baxter had been hasty in his assessment that she was needed—and safe—here. He'd return, take her back, and . . .

And what?

The return of my magic would be more in question than ever without Ava here. She held the amulet, which was somehow my biggest hope that my magic could return, and probably a false reassurance at that. Because I didn't even know how that would work. The amulet had broken, so could the magic be reversed? Obtained?

I forced those thoughts away.

"Your father can't protect her?" I asked.

"He can." Baxter scoffed, but it had little energy. "But he can't protect the mortals, Alaysia, or Alkarra if we don't find Bram. Ava's the only one that can positively identify him. I've never met Bram, and neither have my sisters. They're trying to find another demigod or mortals they trust to describe him. Bram is a lesser demigod with little talent, no allegiant mortals, and few prospects to get an amulet from his father. He's power hungry, but he hasn't proven himself worthy of an amulet yet. Which means he must have stolen the amulet Ava has. There must be other demigods trying to find him. Makes him unpredictable here, if you ask me."

"At least we know we're looking for a male," I murmured, but it still sounded bleak.

Baxter began to pace. "Male, but not distinct in any way."

Unlike mortals, Baxter had no definable characteristics to set him apart from witches, like amber eyes. The other demigods, I presumed, would be the same. They could appear to be anyone.

"So we find Bram," Baxter said, "and go from there."

"And you think that's the end of it? That we'll be safe once the demigod is gone?"

"That would be ideal."

"But not likely?"

He just shrugged, and I had the feeling he didn't want me to know everything. "My father has five children. Four daughters and me, the youngest. Gelas, god of ice, has seven. Ignis and Tontes, the two bad gods? Hundreds of children and all of them hungry for more of their father's magic."

"Sounds grim."

He ran a hand over his head. "Two of my sisters are going to sneak into Ignis's domain and listen for rumors of a missing amulet or Bram. It seems unusual that a demigod returning to Alkarra would be unnoticed. Someone must know what he's doing. Besides, a wayward amulet is no small thing."

"Sneak in?" I asked, startled. "They can't just go to find Bram?"

He shook his head. "Demigods are territorial, and so are the gods. A child of my father, Ventis, venturing into Ignis' domain is immediately suspicious."

"Just how big is Alaysia?"

A little smile illuminated his face. "Alaysia is a place of waters and islands. Most islands move around as they float on wide, circular currents. Some remain stable, but the demigods tend to claim those. Most mortals, Ava and her father included, live on a floating island. Those are more isolated, connected only by special ropes traded from merpeople to prevent them from breaking in the water."

I stuffed aside the casual mention of *merpeople* for now. Thoughts ran through my head. Bram. Islands. Ignis. Merpeople. The fire that had once consumed me after I touched the amulet seemed to rush back through in a flash, then disappear. The grating voice still echoed in my head like a living memory.

You are not welcome here, witch.

"Ignis, God of fire," I said.

Baxter finally lowered into a chair with a sigh. For a moment, he looked like a lost little boy.

"The amulet?" I asked to give him firmer ground. "Any information on the amulet?"

"Father wasn't that surprised that it had broken when you touched it, and believes it was one of Ignis's. Ignis is flashy that way. Bold. The amulet is too large."

"Do you have an amulet?" I asked, and a dozen more questions populated in my mind. New magical systems popped up in Alkarra all the time. A grimoire would be discovered somewhere, someone practiced it, and copies were made and distributed. It allowed witches to live their whole lives learning something new. Or old grimoires of ancient magic were rediscovered, and the system renewed.

But a new *magic* was something else altogether.

With his right hand, Baxter slipped his left arm sleeve back. A familiar, leather arm guard was clasped against the skin. I'd seen it before. *Gift from my father*, he'd once said. *Gives me extra power.*

I'd thought it was a joke, and had even laughed and dismissed it as a temporary charm, or something. Now, the puzzled expression on his face that had followed my amusement made far more sense.

The arm guard stretched from his wrist to halfway to his elbow. The leather was a supple black color, inlaid with dozens of smaller, gray gems. They glimmered in gentle, winding swirls, like tails of summer wind.

"Several small amulets." He ran his fingers over their bumpy tops. "All of these are amulets that allow me to use god magic. The amulets are forged by the gods and distributed to demigods. My father is Ventis, god of wind."

The subdued nature of the amulets, which appeared to be distinctly colored diamonds, was a stark contrast to Ignis's massive amulet around Ava's neck. A reflection of the gods' personalities, if it meant anything, I assumed.

Baxter tugged his sleeve back down. "He issued these

amulets to me so I could live amongst you with whatever magic I'd need to survive. We don't use magic as much in Alaysia."

My voice rose. "Really?"

A flicker of amusement passed through his gaze. "God magic is different. There are no spells or incantations. We think it, and it happens. Call it thought-magic, if you will. Much easier, faster. But we have to be gifted it through the amulets. It isn't inherent in us."

"Jikes."

So many questions about gods and demigods and mortals moved through my mind. Did the use of magic tire Baxter? How did he travel? Was it similar to transportation? It *appeared* like he had transported, the few times I'd ever seen him do so. Silent magic made spells and incantations fairly similar to god magic, but it still wasn't the same. We had to practice, find grimoires, and mold ourselves to the magic. God magic, apparently, molded itself to the witch.

"Powerful in comparison," I said.

"Very. Witches have no limit in the fact that any witch can do magic, but it's slow and cumbersome and requires time in comparison to thought-magic. Only demigods with amulets receive this ability, though, which is limiting itself."

My thoughts multiplied out over the implications of thought magic here in Alkarra.

"Interesting," I murmured, but my tone darkened. "And daunting, considering the fact that this demigod, Bram, may not have pleasant things planned for Alkarra. How could we fight against such a fast magic?"

"You *can* fight it," he countered. "Just . . . at a great disadvantage. But I believe that Bram doesn't have another amulet. To have one is hard enough, but a second? Extremely unlikely."

"Then how did he get back here to Alkarra?" I asked.

"That is a wonderful question. However he did it, I think he's here and acting as a mortal with basic demigod strength.

Heightened abilities, if you will. If Bram was smart, he'd lay low. But I'm willing to guess he's not entirely hidden. He's power hungry."

My mind spun out ahead of him. "You think he's trying to get into a position of power, then. Somewhere to gain some allegiance."

"I've wondered. A Southern Network Council Member, maybe? A leader of a village in the South? If he accrues mortals here, maybe he could figure out a way to prove his power to Ignis."

"A Central Network Council Member, perhaps?" I asked, and my mind floated to Aldred. "One that wants to stir the Networks to war, perhaps? One that would influence Niko and help to destroy my father."

His gaze darkened. "It could be. Your father appointed new Council Members years ago. If Bram has been here the whole time, just like me? Perhaps."

The accusation against Council Member Aldred remained on the tip of my tongue. I wouldn't release it yet, but I wanted to. It would levy a powerful force, *and* we'd need to prove it.

"Bram *could* have another amulet though, right?"

Baxter shrugged.

"That," I muttered darkly, "would make it decidedly complicated to figure out."

The effort of comprehending all these different angles made my head start to hurt. I pressed my fingertips to my temple and closed my eyes for a moment, my head a whirl of new ideas.

He tilted his head to one side with an amused little smirk. "It's nice, you know? Being the one to explain custom instead of attempting to figure yours out."

He grinned wearily, and I smiled back. His fingers slipped to his arm guard again, and the tips ran over the tops of the various amulets.

"In Alaysia, amulets are treated like demigods or mortals,"

he explained. "They have personalities and names and are known for their power. Some mortals even track amulets. They monitor their owners, colors, responses, and attitudes. Anyway, the amulet you broke has a name but we're not sure what it is yet. My sisters are seeking a mortal that keeps records of the different amulets. They should be able to find out."

"Then that amulet," I muttered, "was a grumpy old cur."

Baxter chuckled. "Which makes sense for Ignis."

"He's cranky?"

"He's . . . complicated."

The burning question I'd held all this time slipped out next. "Can your father do anything to help restore my magic?"

Baxter drew in a deep breath, held it, then let it out all at once. "No. At least, not yet," he added hastily. "He said that the god and goddess magicks interact unexpectedly when brought together in such a way."

"But you use god magic around us."

"Only when I have to, and the magic never interacts. What you touch with your magic, I try to avoid."

The truth, for sure. All the times he'd walked instead of transported whispered through my mind. The hand-written notes instead of an enchanted quill. He reached over and touched my shoulder in a comforting way.

"He said he'd try to learn more. Historically, the magicks tended to distort or disable the other, and he hasn't seen a way to restore it that didn't involve the goddess doing it herself."

Fat chance, I thought. Because there was a small part of me that still didn't believe any of this was actually true. But was that in doubt anymore?

How did one speak to a goddess, anyway?

"What's the plan now that you've spoken with your sisters and your father?" I asked. "What can we do to find Bram and get my magic back?"

"My sisters are going to search for Bram, which is not an easy task. So many of those demigods vying for power . . . for mortals . . ." He shook his head, hands fisted. "It's . . . sickening."

The thought that maybe fire had been the better choice made me shudder. If fire had such an effect, what would thunder have done? Rent my body in half? Shook my teeth until they chattered like old bones? I understood almost nothing of the relationship between god and mortal, but I knew enough to sense that Baxter must be a rare demigod. A kind one. One that actually cared.

Knowing him, it made sense.

"And Ava?" I asked.

"Ava has to look for Bram while she's here. I can't return with her until she does. The sooner, the better. The first opportunity I find to get her in front of all the Central and Southern Network Council Members, I'm going to take it."

My heart skipped a beat with a brief moment of both fear and hope. We needed to put Ava in front of Council Member Aldred, too. And search for a potential amulet on his chest while we were at it.

What if *he* had been Bram all along?

"Could there be any correlation between my magic and the demigod?" I asked quietly. "If we find him, can I restore my magic?"

"I don't know."

The hope was a long one. A vague one. One extremely unlikely to make a difference, but I held onto it all the same. Baxter glanced behind him, as if to find Ava. When she wasn't there, he rubbed his eyes with the heels of his hand.

"I need to go," he said. "The Council Member Luncheon preparation is underway and I need to make sure the food will be ready in time. You're coming, correct?"

I sighed. "Yes. Papa has asked me to come to make up for the dinner I missed."

"Ha!" He slapped a knee as he stood. "Serves you right."

"This is one of the biggest events of the Celebration," I said drily. "Don't mess it up."

He flashed me a smile reminiscent of all the simpler times together, and it seemed to give both of us courage.

"Every Council Member and leader in the same room, while Niko gives a big long speech about how right he is?" Baxter's teeth flashed with his grin. "Just a normal day in my life, thank you very much."

Chapter Eighteen

Later that day, I breezed through the castle toward a room packed full of witches with a smile fixed on my face. While I casually strolled past the banquet hall—annoyingly *not* protected by transformative magic so I had a different appearance—I glanced inside.

The Council Member Luncheon, hosted by the Eastern Network, was minutes away from beginning. Sunlight streamed into the sprawling banquet hall, where ten long, wooden tables filled the middle of the room.

White tablecloths ironed to perfection stretched across each tabletop, where crystal wine goblets and silver forks sparkled against the backdrop of crimson, emerald, purple, and sapphire silk napkins. Five elegant chairs with whittled woodwork marched along each side of the table. There would be over a hundred witches eating lunch here today, and the cacophony of chattering voices rose uproariously now.

Across the room, Papa stood by Marten near a window. His bright laugh rolled over the tables and comforted me, even if I could hear the strain in his mirth. Not far from Papa lingered Igor, who spoke quietly with Alina. Scarlett spoke with the

Western Network High Priestess Lana. Niko, who would lead this luncheon, was nowhere in sight. The thought sent a dark cloud over my mind.

I ducked behind a large bookcase, closed my eyes, and drew in a deep breath. How Papa mentally prepared himself for all these social events, I would never understand. I wouldn't even interact with all these witches in an official capacity, just a visible one, and I felt the strain.

Or perhaps I just felt uneasy.

Like the calm before a storm. Something didn't feel right, and it may just be the fact that anyone could be Bram. It didn't seem to be just me, though. A hidden strain of tension rippled through the room, obvious from too-bright smiles and darting gazes. Everyone seemed to feel it, even Marten. He stood alone now, half-frowning at the tiled floor.

To make sure I didn't embarrass the Network, Leda helped me pick out a simple blue dress with sleeves to my elbows and a lace back that hid easy-to-loop buttons. My raven-black hair gleamed on my shoulders, freshly washed, and I'd donned new sandals. Not extensively formal, but enough to satisfy general convention.

For all intents and purposes, the Council Member Luncheon should be an easy event. Little more than a way for Council Members and their Assistants and other formal dignitaries to be acknowledged in this diplomatic process. They'd mingle together, talk about peace and troubles and solutions, and pretend we didn't feel this stifling politeness.

Still, I wished I didn't have to be here.

Arrive as soon as it begins, Papa said in a letter after Baxter had left. *Sit by me, then leave as it ends. That way, you won't have time to talk to witches. Recent developments with your new friend will eventually come to light after the Celebration, and the Council will be hostile to me as a result. Your presence today will be helpful to my cause and show our mutual loyalty to the Network.*

Now, I just had to get myself into the room at the exact right moment.

Although we had no reason for witches to suspect that I'd lost my ability to do magic, Niko loomed large in my mind. Particularly with his motivated approach to finding the stowaway, and Hector's injury—probably from a dragon. Niko knew *something*. Until we knew what that something was, the last thing I wanted to do was surround myself with powerful witches.

The bookshelf I'd ducked behind hid me from the main flow of witches coming out of a turret nearby and exposed me only to the servants' entrance at the end of the hall. Witches slipped into the banquet hall at my back in a gentle ebb. A conversation between three female witches caught my ear, so I turned my attention to them.

"Surprised we haven't seen her here before now," said the first.

"He normally parades her around," replied another. "Maybe there's some troubled water brewing in Magnolia castle."

I leaned closer to the bookcase, as if that would help me hear better. Magnolia castle indicated they spoke about the Eastern Network. *He* must be Niko.

But who was *she*?

What I'd give for a listening incantation right now!

"They're not even engaged," said a scandalized third voice. "Can't imagine how their Council Members can show their faces here when their High Priest is flaunting his mistress so blatantly. How do you think her parents feel? She's from here, you know!"

"I hear they don't speak with her anymore."

I gaped. Priscilla. They had to be speaking about Priscilla.

Was she here now? No, that would be impossible. She'd been staying with Michelle and Nicholas.

A drawl came from my left.

"A new form of spying?" I whirled around to find Merrick standing there, an amused half-smile on his face. He wore half armor that stretched across his shoulders in a mixture of leather and metal. A tendril of hair escaped his braid to tumble down his face. My heart whirled in my chest as it calmed from my initial shock.

"I didn't hear you," I muttered.

He laughed. "I could tell. It's a rare moment when I can catch you so unsuspecting. The gossip must be good."

"Not really."

"You look . . . lovely today."

Although my stomach flipped at the compliment, I brushed it aside for more important business. "Thank you. Can you tell me . . . is Priscilla in there?" I pointed to the banquet hall. "Can you see her?"

My expression must have betrayed fear because he sobered. "I haven't noticed her there yet."

"She must be with Niko," I said breathlessly. "Please, can you try to see?"

Merrick disappeared, likely under an invisibility spell. Several heart-wrenching moments later, he returned.

"She's inside."

I let out a long, stabilizing breath, but my stomach still tied itself into knots. Priscilla was inside the Council Member luncheon, which meant so many things. Niko had found her, first of all. But how? Was Michelle all right? Nicholas? Why hadn't we heard anything? My thoughts whirled for a few moments.

"How does she look?" I asked.

"Pale. A bit thin. But otherwise all right."

"Is she near Niko?"

"Yes."

"Any bruises?"

He frowned. "What is going on?"

"Tell me, Merrick." I snapped impatiently.

"Of course not. Not visible, anyway."

"Is he holding onto her, or is she holding onto him?"

Whether it was Merrick's experience in the Masters, or all the time we'd spent together over the years, the strange question didn't seem to faze him. "He has an arm around her waist. She was smiling, but she looked tired. At least from what I saw."

"Thank you."

"Everything all right?"

My mind raced. "No," I whispered and chewed on my bottom lip. My first impulse was to skip the luncheon and save Priscilla. But no. That would only draw suspicion and attention and Papa needed me. I had to go to that luncheon, catch her eye, and then try to talk to her afterward. But Niko wouldn't be an idiot. He'd keep her right at his side.

But *why*?

The *tap tap tap* of a spoon on glass cut through the air and pierced through the bustle of voices. Sound in the hall stilled immediately, and Papa's booming voice replaced it. His words were too muffled to make out individually from where we hunkered outside. I swore under my breath when I uselessly attempted an invisibility spell.

"Jikes," I muttered. "Not now!"

"B?"

"Can you do me a favor?" I grabbed his arm. "Conjure a small note and a quill, please?"

They appeared seconds later. I scribbled a quick question mark, followed by a B, blew on it until the ink dried, and hoped Papa kept talking for a few more minutes. At this point, I'd have to enter the luncheon late no matter what, so I might as well have information when I arrived.

When I held the note out to Merrick, he accepted it, but his gaze had narrowed considerably.

"Transport this to Priscilla, please. Make it appear next to her plate, on the opposite side from where Niko could see it."

"Why can't you do it yourself?" he asked, his voice low with uncertainty, maybe even concern.

"Please?"

He hesitated, then the note disappeared a breath later. Within seconds, I motioned to the door with a tilt of my head.

"See if she got it?" I appealed quietly.

With only a moment of pause, he disappeared again. When he returned, he nodded. "As far as I can tell, it's there. Whether she's seen it or not, I can't be sure."

Papa's voice rang in the background, indecipherable. My hands balled into fists as I waited, my heart slamming against my ribcage. The questions spun through my head in a mad tangle.

What happened with Niko and Priscilla?

What did Niko know?

Was Ava safe?

"What's going on, B?" Merrick asked quietly.

Before I could answer, a small, square handkerchief with a sprigged flower design appeared in front of me. The wrinkled fabric looked as if it had been clutched in a hand or tucked into a pocket.

As we stared at it, the bright yellow buds in the middle of the handkerchief altered to a duller hue, only subtly different. Words spelled out in the low-toned flowers.

Do nothing.

"The good gods," I muttered. What could this mean? Nothing good. Was Niko flaunting her for my benefit? Why bring her to *this* luncheon? There could be so many reasons. Concern instantly marred Merrick's brow.

"Is Priscilla in danger?"

"I can't imagine a scenario where she's not," I murmured as I studied the hallway. With the onset of Papa's speech, it lay empty now. I needed to get inside the banquet hall or Papa would be alone again with an empty seat and the Council would wonder about my loyalty to him. That would look so much worse.

Could Merrick cast an invisibility incantation on me so I could sneak inside, then appear in the chair to draw fewer stares? Yes, but the impracticality made it a bad idea. What if I needed to pull the spell off? Besides, transportation had hurt when Marten brought me back from Letum Wood. Perhaps other spells would feel just as unpleasant.

Merrick cleared his throat. "Listen, I don't want to interrupt what is going on right now, but I came to warn you about something else."

The concern in his voice pulled my mind from the already-forming plans to break Priscilla away from Niko.

Startled, I blinked and turned to face him.

"You what?"

He leaned a little closer. "I shouldn't be here, B. And if anyone ever asks, you didn't hear this from me, right?"

"Right."

With a glance over my shoulder, he hesitated, then nudged me away from the bookcase and down the hallway. A thin door that housed a storage closet opened up and he motioned me inside.

A candle on the wall sprang to life as he shut the door behind him. Shelves lined the wall on the left and the right. Buckets. Brooms. Old mops that smelled sour. The air was close here, as if it hadn't been accessed in years. Shadows from the candle cast him in a new light, and his body seemed to swallow all the space.

"Geralyn told us to prepare for a potentially explosive luncheon," he said.

"Explosive?"

"Niko warned her last night that he plans to announce

something very . . . troubling, was the word she used. But I don't know what the announcement is. I can't stay here long. I'm supposed to be supervising our Guardians, who she told to be ready to leave at any time. She doubled the Guard too, just in case. Geralyn has been in meetings about it all morning with Regina."

My mind raced with possibilities, but they all started and ended with Ava. None of this strange day pieced together quite yet. Even Merrick telling me about what his High Priestess said was far outside normal bounds. Was this a setup? I dismissed that.

No, this was Niko posturing, likely.

With *what* information though?

Now that Niko found Priscilla, had he forced information about Ava out of her? My stomach clenched at the thought, and my rage soon followed. I forced it to cool. I'd be of no use to Ava or Priscilla if I went into a tizzy. Besides, Priscilla instructed me to do nothing. Surely she had a reason for it, and I'd have to trust her.

"What do you think the explosive thing is?" I asked.

Merrick shrugged. "I don't know. Niko has been hard to read this entire time. But I'm sure it's something against your father, which is why I wanted to warn you."

Although I had no facts to base this conclusion on, something deep in my gut told me this was about Ava. Maybe Papa *and* Ava. What a perfect weapon to use to utterly destroy him.

Before I could summon up the words to reply, Papa's voice slipped through the seam of the wall and the floor, where light peeked through in the dark closet. It was easier to make out his voice now.

"And now, I turn your attention to Niko Aldana."

A cold feeling crawled all the way up my back. The scraping of a chair indicated Papa had sat down, and footsteps not far away sounded next. My entire body felt as if it had turned to stone when Niko's voice filtered through the wall with its silky, smooth words.

"Thank you for your attention, Council Members, Assistants, and Delegation leaders. Today, we celebrate and honor you for all the work you do daily. To my deepest regret, however, my Council and I have a grave concern to present. We are grateful to do it in a united fashion."

My eyes closed. Merrick shifted his weight, causing a floorboard to emit a groan. I held my breath, but no one threw the door open to us. The quiet shuffle of uncertain whispers followed next. I could just imagine what Papa looked like now.

"Oh no," I whispered.

"Witches of Alkarra," Niko declared in a loud, booming voice that no one in the near vicinity could tune out. "There is a demigod and a mortal girl loose in Alkarra. The esteemed leaders of the Central and Southern Networks are harboring them in a bid to control all of the rest of us."

My stomach lurched so hard, I nearly vomited. The quiet that followed Niko's announcement crashed like a thousand drums. I put a hand on the wall next to me and willed my knees to remain steady.

What in the name of the good gods was he talking about?

"Bianca?" Merrick asked, his voice a steely question.

"There is *no* time to explain," I whispered. "Please, if you have any hope for Alkarra in your heart, help me?"

He hesitated, brow drawn low, then nodded.

In the banquet hall, an uproar finally sounded. Upraised voices. Shouted questions. General chaos and strangeness. For several moments, I had to straighten out my thoughts and cobble together a hasty plan. It wasn't a great plan, but it would have to work.

"First, another parchment and quill?" I asked.

They appeared in front of me while Merrick turned his attention to peering outside the closet. A thin line of light dropped across his face as he checked outside. Concentration lined his brow. I dashed off a quick note, then blew on it and waved it around to dry.

"Transport this to Alina, please. She can't miss it. It has to be seen right away and needs to be discreet. Her plate should be sufficient."

If anyone else saw it, we'd be doomed for sure.

"Alina, the Ambassador of the Southern Network?" he asked as he took it from my awaiting fingers.

"Yes."

Although questions filled his eyes in earnest now, he didn't ask them. Once he folded the letter in half, he sent it away with a silent spell.

"Now's the hard part," I said.

While I explained what I wanted him to do, the resistance built in his gaze until I felt certain my plan had already crumbled into pieces. Chaos raged in the banquet hall as Merrick stared at me. His jaw flexed beneath his trimmed beard.

"Doing this could be seen as treason against my Network," he said quietly. "You do realize that? To help you, I'll have to abandon my post without first explaining my actions to my High Priestess."

I swallowed hard. "I would understand if you told me no. If you do, I'll figure this out. But it may be our only chance to stop the Networks from going to war, and a demigod from rising to power."

"Demigod?" he whispered hoarsely.

I nodded.

For an interminable time, Merrick considered me. Although we were pressed close together—I could reach out and touch his chest if I wanted to—he never felt so far away.

"Answer my questions first," he said.

"Yes?"

"Is your magic gone?"

"Yes."

"Is it because of this mortal and demigod?"

Reluctantly, I nodded.

His eyebrows rose. "And did your father know about the mortal and demigod before right now?"

The damning truth sounded so bleak in such simple terms. Nuance layered this more than anything I'd ever experienced before. But still, it *was* correct. Papa knew of mortals and demigods and had for some time. The depths of his knowledge weren't clear, though. All the details that Merrick's questions left out mattered, yet there was no time. I forced myself to nod.

Merrick's gaze clouded.

"For you," he whispered. "I do this for *you*."

A thousand replies surfaced, and then disappeared. "Thank you."

He clamped a hand on my shoulder. Within a breath, a transportation spell painfully whisked me back to Papa's apartments. I couldn't stop what Niko had just done, nor could I save Papa from what was about to occur.

But I wouldn't let Ava be taken. This time, I wouldn't fail another person that looked to me for safety.

No matter what.

* * *

"You are *insane*, Bianca."

The declaration dropped from Leda's lips without a second of hesitation. While I shoved clothes into a bag, Leda stalked around my room with judgment and wrath in her differently-colored eyes.

"We have to get Ava out of here," I said. "Now *everyone* knows about her and they are hopping mad."

"Mad enough you think they're going to storm your father's apartment?"

"I think they could!"

"Hardly," she scoffed. "Your father has a hoard of very loyal Protectors at his disposal. There's nowhere else in Alkarra that you can go and be as safe as you are here."

"You're wrong."

Leda darted in front of me when she thought I headed to the bedroom door. "It's not your call." She folded her arms over her chest. "It's Ava's mission, remember? She has to find the demigod."

"You think it's wise to push an eleven-year-old girl in front of that livid delegation?"

She sighed. "No. You know I don't."

"What is the alternative here, Leda?"

"We wait for Baxter."

"To do what?"

"Make the decision *with* Ava."

"It'll be too late. What if they get her? They'll kill her. It's going to be a mob. Niko's accusation . . . the words . . ."

She rolled her eyes. "They're not going to pull their swords out and run her through." The confidence in her tone slowly died with every word she spoke. At the end, she cleared her throat. "Fine, maybe *someone* would. They're bound to be scared and angry. I know that I was at first."

Nicholas's reaction when he first saw Ava ran through my mind. Priscilla's. Even Marten's. Leda had been far more subdued, but I'd given her some advanced warning that something crazy had happened, and nothing I did anymore seemed to really surprise her. The Council Members for every Network were already going to be frothing at the mouth with rage at Papa.

My rage was directed right at Niko.

The liar.

"She's eleven," I said. "She can't go before that hostile crowd because she'll never make it out. Papa's going to be lucky to make it out of his web of secrets alive at this point. All we can do is protect her. Papa would want it."

Leda's voice had a gentle tone amidst her annoyance.

"She's not Camille, Bianca."

The hackles on the back of my neck lifted. My teeth gritted together because her words pierced deep. For several moments, I wasn't sure what I'd say next. This wasn't about saving Camille. Maybe I hadn't been able to keep Camille safe. Or my grandmother. Or all the other witches we lost in the war.

But this was about *Ava*.

"You don't know what you're talking about," I snapped. "I know that she's not Camille, she's Ava. She's under my protection now and I won't fail her. Not this time."

Unwilling to let it go, Leda just shook her head. "Listen, Bianca. Saving Ava won't bring Camille back. You didn't fail Camille, just as you didn't fail Mildred. Both of them made choices that were theirs to make. Ava has her own. You can't save her from everything. It's her mission to do this. She's the *only* one that can. Maybe Baxter will want her to stand before the delegation to see if the demigod is there. You said yourself that he thinks the demigod could be anyone."

"Two days!" I cried. "I just need two days. If Niko has kidnapped Priscilla, probably for leverage against *me*, what do you think he'd do to a young mortal girl? Priscilla would not have gone willingly, Leda."

Leda opened her mouth to reply, but closed it again.

"Exactly," I hissed. "Niko is not going to let Ava go out of the warmth of his heart if he gets his hands on her, and you know it. Neither would Lana or Geralyn for that matter. We either let Ava get herself killed, or we take her somewhere safe until we can come up with a better plan. Either way, we still have a better chance to find the demigod and . . . deal with everything else after that."

Like fixing my magic, reminded a wild echo in my heart, but I forced it to quiet for now. This wasn't about my magic anymore. This was about Papa, Ava, and the Network. My magic would have to follow.

I yanked the bag off my bed and threw it over my shoulder. Leda followed with a frustrated growl as I headed down the hallway, toward the main apartment area. No doubt Papa would retreat from the banquet hall eventually. Maybe even soon. We had to be out of there before he saw us.

Besides, witches could mob the hallway, the entire castle. Word of Niko's declaration would spread to the *Chatterer* at any moment now because the luncheon had been an open one. Most likely, they already knew.

The clock ticked down the minutes we had left. Merrick would be here any moment if he hadn't already left me to deal with this mess on my own. Which, if he didn't show back up, I wasn't sure I would blame him.

"What are you going to tell Baxter?" Leda followed at my heels like a furious puppy. "Ava is his niece, and she's her own person. She should be able to make her own decisions."

"She will as soon as she's somewhere safe."

Leda scoffed. "You're not going to tell her everything, are you?"

"I don't speak her language, so no. I'll figure out a way to tell her what she needs to know. An eleven-year-old couldn't possibly understand the danger she's in and there's no reason to frighten her unnecessarily."

"What's your plan, Bianca, once you get out of here?" Leda asked with a heavy sigh. "How are you going to protect her? How are you going to get her anywhere? You're like a puppy in a lion's den."

"I already have a plan," I muttered.

Down the hallway, a door opened and Ava peered her head out. I gave her an encouraging smile and she skipped to my side, fresh braids decorating the sides of her face and bundled in the back to hold her hair out of her eyes. Leda eyed the two of us with some annoyance, then said a few more things to Ava, who shook her head.

"Can you explain to her that we're taking her away because the other witches found out about her?" I asked. "That I'm trying to keep her safe."

"I'm not a dictionary, Bianca. I don't have all these words in my head yet."

"Try?"

Leda shot me her signature glare and proceeded to stutter through a few words with Ava. Hand gestures accompanied it. While Ava focused on what Leda said, I gathered up the scrolls and books that Baxter had brought Leda from his personal quarters and shoved them under my arm.

"Fine." Leda's thin fingers twirled the ends of her hair around, her expression troubled. "I think she understands that it's not safe and you're taking her somewhere safer, but I didn't tell her that her uncle approved."

"That's fine."

I pushed the scrolls into a different shoulder bag when Reeves appeared out of the back just as a knock came on the door. Relief rippled through me as the door opened up and admitted two cloaked figures. They stepped into the room on my command. As soon as the door shut, Merrick ripped the fabric off his head.

Alina stepped forward, peering from the depths of her hood. "We're ready."

I smiled with relief. "So are we."

With an exasperated sigh, Leda stepped forward. "Fine," she muttered, hands on her hips, "I'm going with you."

Chapter Nineteen

Five minutes later, I opened my eyes.

Merrick held onto my right arm with his hand, but he released me once the transportation spell ended. The lingering effect of his touch buzzed on top of my skin long after he let me go. Thankfully, Merrick had far more precision with transportation than I had. Transporting somewhere unknown was inherently dangerous, but Alina must have described this place with sufficient detail when he first brought her here. We arrived safely.

He stepped away, a storm in his gaze, as I caught my breath and my bearings. The prickles in my skin and blood began to fade, painful effects from the transportation spell. It had never hurt this much before. Merrick sent me a concerned glance, then transported away to bring Ava back.

Next to me, Alina sat on the edge of a narrow chair, her face ashen in a similar state of unrest. Apparently, transportation magic didn't sit well with either of us, which didn't make me feel any better about getting my magic back.

I stood in the middle of a small room built from stone, with thick timbers across the ceiling. To my right was a square wall with a thin wooden door I'd have to turn sideways to walk through. The room tapered to a sharp point behind me in the shape of a triangle, with one window off to the right. A stuffed mattress, thick with dust, lay on the floor. Two rolled pillows perched on top, as if waiting for someone to return.

"Where are we?" I asked.

"The *bezopasnost* is a safe house," Alina said. "You may call it the *bezo* for short. The word is tribal."

Color returned to her face when she stood. She yanked on a thin leather loop that hooked into the door. It swung toward her and led to an open space shaped like a decagon. Eight additional closed doors ringed the interior.

Only a single, stone table waited in the middle of the place, with chairs and stools ringing it in equal distances apart. An ornate rug lay beneath, woven from what appeared to be coarse strands of a fibrous braid. A glass chandelier shone dully overhead with different colored gems, ones not unlike the enormous gems that Southern males wore in their beards. Old candle stubs were unlit and thick with dust in their holders. Only one wall didn't have a door in it, and it housed a modest hearth.

The entire place felt forgotten.

"A safe house for whom?" I asked quietly.

"The shieldmaidens."

Alina's accented voice felt like a distant gong in the strange silence. Some emotion thickened her reply, but I couldn't tell what it meant. Her expression gave nothing away. Had she lived here as a young shieldmaiden? The common area, collection of rooms, and general air reminded me of a school.

Could this have been where the shieldmaidens trained?

My thoughts still felt blunted from the transportation, but I forced them to clear. From what I could see through the thin, high windows in the bedrooms, the trees outside looked like Letum Wood, even if they weren't so old. They stacked together in a tight tangle, with rows that seemed oddly intentional. When

I opened a few other doors, those rooms also had triangular shapes, like the one we landed in. Together, they gave the *bezo* the shape of a ten-pointed star.

Merrick reappeared with Ava at his side. Seconds later, Leda followed on her own. She blinked, shaking off the transportation more gracefully than I had, and dumped a load of books onto the table. Her eyes were wide as she took it all in. Ava rushed over to stand next to me, her uncertain gaze darting around. She tilted to the side a little, as if transportation made her dizzy.

"A *bezopasnost,*" Leda murmured reverently as she ran a hand over the back of a chair. "Never thought I'd see one of these."

Alina smiled wryly. "You were never meant to, but Bianca needed a place to hide without question. This is the place."

"What exactly is it?" I asked.

Leda shot me an annoyed glare. "Only one of the most sacred places in the Southern Network."

"It's where the shieldmaidens train," Alina said as she stepped away from the table. "This is where the girls are taken when they commit their lives to the safety of their High Priestess. Because of their sacrifice, it's regarded as a holy place. At least, it used to be. Mikhail changed many things in his . . . difficult reign. Igor, thankfully, has proven more amenable to such things. Most tribes consider this equivalent to a place where they worship their giving god. Igor is willing to tolerate open beliefs as long as we pull together as a Network."

The words *giving god* rang through my head with reverberating tones. Such easily spoken things came with more context now that Baxter had revealed himself as a demigod. Did they know how close their beliefs were to the truth?

Was there a *giving* god?

For a moment, my mind drifted back to the Central Network, where all lay in chaos. In the utter stillness of this place, that seemed a far cry away.

Only then did I notice empty leather hooks, loops, and nails dotting the far wall. I felt a little thrill. The *bezo* had an old weapons cache. What sort of weapons did a shieldmaiden get to train with? Many, if the wall mounts were any indication. My fingers itched to discover more.

"Give me one moment," Alina said, "while I check on something."

She pressed her fingertips to the wall, then slipped through another thin door that blended so seamlessly into the wood near the hearth that it was nearly unrecognizable. Leda's fingertips trailed along the table as she strolled around it, taking the oddly-shaped house in. Wooden stools were tucked underneath except for the ends, many of them twisted with age near the bottom.

Merrick's gaze darted around the room, encompassing the loop of leather below warped, stained glass windows that led to, I assumed, the main door. When Merrick's eyes landed on mine, he softened just enough to let me know I hadn't lost *all* favor. How he wasn't furious with me after all I had asked of him, I'd never know.

"Thank you," I said.

He nodded. "I need to go."

"Of course."

"When do you want me to return?"

My eyebrows rose. "You're willing to return?"

"I'm already this far in," he said wryly, "might as well see it through. Besides, I've never been on an adventure with Bianca Monroe that I regretted."

The casual words still struck a deep tone in my chest, and I wanted to swim through the feeling it left inside me.

"Come when you can," I said. "Leda can bring us what we need for food since she decided to come, but . . . updates would be most appreciated." I glanced at my hands, clasped tightly together in front of me, and back to him with a sense of deep guilt. "I'm most worried about my father. Baxter will be with him but . . . "

But I'm not and he needs me.

"Of course."

Alina reappeared right then with a cryptic look on her face. "There's a little kindling in the back." She gestured to the now half-open door that led into a room equally as large as this one, like a trail to a shooting star. "Some flint if you want to start a fire. You'll have to get some firewood. It will be safe, just . . . don't venture too far away?"

"Of course."

She studied me, then nodded.

"Thank you, Alina."

"Don't make me regret this." Her eyes moved to Ava, and then back. "But . . . perhaps you've done the right thing. She's safest in the South, and no safer anywhere else in the South than here."

She stepped back and motioned to Merrick with a preparatory grimace. With a respectful hand, he took her arm, looked at me with an unreadable expression one last time, and they both disappeared.

* * *

That evening, Leda and I sat at the stone table together.

I perused a dusty, enchanted book I'd found in one of the rooms. The paper curled at the edges, and a braid of twine bound them together at the seam. The words were incomprehensible, but when Leda touched each sentence, the ink would reform into words I could read. The title was scrawled across the front in an unusual simplicity for a book in the South, where they often had full titles for books.

Chants of the Shieldmaiden.

Not all the words would translate. Most of them edged together near the right side of the page in jagged lines, like a poem. I murmured the words under my breath, something I would have never done if I held magic. My lips formed around them like forgotten friends. I recognized the cadence of incantations, even if I couldn't do magic. For some reason, it comforted my fitful heart.

Leda poured over parchments Baxter had given her that held the scribbled-down basics of their language. Word lists, grammatical rules, structural hints, and more. Leda hadn't looked this giddy in years. Probably since she'd last eaten one of Miss Celia's heavenly cinnamon rolls while we were in our first year at Miss Mabel's School for Girls.

Meanwhile, Ava sat next to me, slumped back in her chair, frowning over a needle, thread, and a piece of fabric she found in one of the rooms. Intricate, tiny stitches already formed a rudimentary picture in the cloth. Like always, she made grunting noises. Sometimes she threw it down and glared at the fire, only to pick it back up again later. She twitched, muttered, and paced often. Her gaze flitted to the door every other minute.

The day came and went, finally passing into darkness. Cooler air filled the *bezo* from under the door frames as the light faded from the high windows.

Sometime around dinner, a knock came on the door to the room that Merrick had transported me and himself into, which startled Leda. She glowered at it, then at me, and turned back to her books.

"Well," drawled a languid voice. "If it isn't my two favorite witches."

Hiddleston.

Leda's head slowly lifted. A feeling of dread pooled deep in my stomach when she glared at me with the force of a thousand suns. He stood in the doorway of the room we'd transported into, and my breath left me in a long whoosh. Leda's pale face turned stiff and brittle.

"Bianca," she hissed.

"I didn't invite him!" I cried. "I don't know why he's here either."

My heart pounded as I whirled around to glare at him. "What are you doing here?" I snapped.

He ignored me.

"Merry meet, Underlibrarian Leda."

He sauntered into the room, wearing a black shirt with a gray vest, the loop of a pocket watch draped lazily over his left breast pocket. His dark locks were tied out of his face in a wide knot behind his head.

Leda shot to her feet. "Get out of here."

He held up his arms with a cat-like smile. "Bianca is my friend too, didn't you hear? I'm as welcome as anyone else. Just checking in, anyway, to see how you are. I'm not here to cause trouble. Consider me a concerned citizen of the Central Network."

"I've told you before and I'll say it again—I am *not* your friend," she snapped. "I won't stay in this room with you for another moment."

The back of Leda's neck had grown so red it would start on fire soon. Hiddleston, on the other hand, appeared to be . . . delighted. He ignored her anger, dismissing her comment with a wave.

"You will stay because you don't have a choice," he said calmly. "Where else will you go? You left the library entirely, and I'd wager you'd rather talk to me than return to *all* of your siblings and their special chaos. Your best friend is here and you wouldn't abandon her for a moment, even though you might act like you would."

She snorted.

He pressed on, undaunted by her pretty rage. "Since you're not otherwise engaged, you and I can have a lovely chat."

She snarled.

Hiddleston grinned.

The delight in his expression made him attractive enough, with his slim nose and broad cheeks, but there was something in his eyes that woke up my instincts. Predatory wasn't the right word, but it wasn't far off.

"What is going on?" I demanded.

Leda straightened, arms folded tightly over her middle. "This . . . *witch* . . . has been trying to corner me into a debate for the last year. He showed up at the library one day and now I can't get him to leave me alone."

Several thoughts dawned on me all at once. First, Leda's aversion to Scarlett's offer as Assistant made a lot more sense in light of Hiddleston being employed by Scarlett. Had Leda known Hiddleston worked for her?

Second, Hiddleston's motivation to talk to Leda became a great deal more clear now that I saw him with her. Hiddleston was taut as a violin bow beneath what appeared to be a calm veneer. Whatever easygoing facade he wanted to give, I wasn't buying it. Something else was at play here.

Did Hiddleston *like* Leda?

Also, a debate?

For several moments, I was too astonished to speak. The signs all added up, but the tension in the room felt at odds with someone that would want to court Leda.

"I won't force this on you, Leda," Hiddleston said easily. "You have a choice whether or not we debate the point. But I do urge you to try since you have nowhere else to be tonight. You may end up enjoying yourself."

His entire focus seemed to be on Leda. Seeing that he hadn't come to mess up our plans or anything else, I began to relax. My shoulders dropped back when I pulled in a deep breath. "What's the point you want to debate?" I asked.

Hiddleston lifted a lazy eyebrow. "Whether the advancement of language in a stable society is a reflection of normal, cultural evolution. I posit that language is stable, and she opposes."

Leda turned away, her jaw tight. Beneath her hauteur, I could see her mind spinning. The twitch in her jaw meant she wanted to discuss a clearly well-sculpted debate point. A topic, I could tell, he'd created *just* to snag her attention. Odd, but clearly effective and precisely on point for Leda.

Oh, Hiddleston knew *exactly* what he was doing.

As if to emphasize that he wouldn't force her into the debate, Hiddleston settled into the chair farthest away from her. Leda smoothed her dress and returned to her seat, clearly determined to ignore him. Seconds later, her quill scratched at the parchment.

Silence returned with a crash like a waterfall.

Hiddleston closed his eyes and leaned his head back against the chair. Had he gone back to the paths again? Isadora had done it on occasion, but not as often or as blatantly as this. She seemed far more subtle than him. Though I had no idea what it actually meant, anyway. He seemed content, at any rate. As if he'd just wanted to doze for a bit. I bit back the urge to interrogate him on how he found us. The Defender magic, of course. No doubt he wanted to take advantage of Leda being "stuck" here with me and Ava.

Several minutes later, Hiddleston blinked himself back to the room and looked right at me.

"Sanna was goddess-touched," he declared.

Leda's neck stiffened further, if possible. He ignored her entirely. Instead, he leaned forward, fingers curled around the end of the armrests, where snarling wolf heads glowered from chiseled wood.

"The goddess of the forest, Deasylva, personally visited Sanna at one point," Hiddleston continued. "Which clearly means that she was goddess-touched. This is an assumption I've made because even a magic created by Deasylva will not reveal her appearance in the magic. Historically, Deasylva has liked to remain . . . anonymous. But the blinding light and expression of awe on the sisterwitches' faces indicates they had seen a goddess. Besides, they'd just won a war for her. One would hope she'd repay them."

War. Goddess. Blinding light. The words swirled in my brain for a bit because I had no idea what he spoke of.

"Fine, but what does it mean to be goddess-touched?" I asked.

"Nothing," he said blandly, then leaned back in his chair again. The tops of his fingers drummed the wood while he regarded the flames. "It means absolutely nothing that Sanna was goddess-touched."

He paused, as if waiting.

"It doesn't mean *nothing*," Leda snapped, so annoyed her consonants crackled with force. "It creates an implication that may have some bearing on Bianca's life right now, thank you very much."

He lifted a falsely startled eyebrow. "Such as?"

"Sanna being goddess-touched—and visited by said being, *if* it happened at all—likely means that the origin of the magic within Letum Wood came from a goddess. Otherwise, and according to Sanako, Deasylva could not have revealed herself there. Sanako says the goddess' stay out of each other's domains."

"And?" he dismissed, seeming as if he didn't care. "How does that have any effect on Bianca?"

"The implication is already clear that opposing magic, such as from a god, has a suppressive or deleterious effect on goddess magic. God magic, when combined with goddess magic—or someone that is arguably *goddess-touched*—can destroy goddess magic. It's practically science at work!"

"Disagree."

Her neck flamed. "Disagree?" she muttered, then gestured to me with a sharp jab of her finger. "We have proof. Bianca may not be as clearly goddess-touched as Sanna, but she does work for the goddess of the forest, and, when exposed to god magic, lost all her power."

I blinked.

I was *what*?

"Have you defined the line between suppressive and deleterious?" he asked.

"We can neither confirm nor deny either yet," she replied shrilly. "We don't *know* what happened to Bianca's magic. Could still be suppressed or entirely gone." Her chin tilted. "Your point requires more time."

He shrugged. "Still, the implications aren't clear for Bianca."

"Support your point!" she squeaked with fury.

"Sanna being goddess-touched doesn't imply anything in *Bianca's* case because Sanna was never exposed to god magic." He moved a finger from side to side. "You make assumptions. No, no. In Bianca, we have a witch that touched an uncontrolled amulet created by a god that, supposedly, robbed her of goddess magic. That's not proof. We don't even know if Bianca is goddess-touched, like Sanna, although strong assumptions can be made. Nevertheless, the factors are different. God magic may have the same effect on any witch that has magical ability given by a goddess, not just those who are goddess-touched."

Leda's mouth opened to counter, then stopped. I held my breath, realizing that Hiddleston had her there. Now, she blinked several times, then leaned back in her chair, eyes slit. The scowl on her face would have burned through stone. Hiddleston met her glare without fear. I suppressed a giggle.

Finally! Leda had met her match.

As if to drive his power in the conversation home, Hiddleston raised his brow. "Does that startled expression mean you're part of the scientific proof paradigm?"

"No," Leda snapped.

"Nothing wrong with it." He lifted two hands. "Just asking."

"I don't know what I think," she muttered, squirming. "Isadora told me about the goddess years ago, before she died." Leda glanced at me with the weight of a guilty expression, as if to anticipate my silent question of *when*? "She was giving me some tips on things that could help control the Foresight curse. She mentioned that the curse was an offshoot of the Defender and Watcher magic, which was created by and originated in Deasylva, goddess of the forest, whom she met."

My mind spun. Leda *knew* the goddess paradigm was real? Or, at least, she had been exposed to it before now. As if she read my mind, she quickly added, "But that doesn't make it *true*. It means two witches believe they saw a goddess. That's it."

"Disagree!" Hiddleston said brightly, his back straight now.

Leda snarled again.

"Besides," he continued, "it's been fascinating to see Sanna in history, particularly when one pits Sanna and Bianca against each other. One could almost say the goddess has a . . . favorite sort of witch. Can goddesses be archetypal?"

Unable to deny the new bait, Leda glared at him from under pale eyelashes. But she didn't blink away, and that seemed to embolden him. Hiddleston leaned toward me. Although his gaze found mine, I could feel all his attention centered on Leda.

"There are some marked similarities in personality between Sanna and you," he said to me. "Ranging from a strange affiliation for Letum Wood to an inherent wildness that is far outside normal bounds, such as not wearing shoes or adherence to social conventions."

"What?" I cried. "No way! Sanna is the cranky one. I am *way* more like Isadora. Leda is the cranky one."

Leda's are-you-kidding-me? glare sent a shot of annoyance through me.

What did she know anyway?

Hiddleston pretended like I hadn't even spoken. "That means you are likely goddess-touched, Bianca. Perhaps not so blatantly as the sisterwitches, but goddess-touched nonetheless. The trees communicate with you? You are considered the caretaker of the forest?"

"Yes."

"Goddess-touched," he declared, as if that explained everything.

"Counter!" Leda screeched. "*You* have now given conjecture built on assumptions. Two instances do not make a pattern. We have no proof of Bianca being goddess-touched as she's had no definable experience with a goddess."

"Supposition creates a strong enough argument in favor."

"You wish," she muttered. "Besides, you've drawn no parallel to Bianca's current dilemma, except to flaunt your Defender magic."

Hiddleston smiled coyly until I thought Leda would scratch his eyes out.

"So if I am goddess-touched, or whatever, why isn't the goddess saving my magic so I can keep taking care of Letum Wood?" I asked.

He shrugged. "From what I have seen, Deasylva rarely saves anyone. She appears to have a general fondness for her witches, but she rarely offers direct intervention. I can't be sure because, although I've sifted through a lot of history, it's still a mere fraction of all that's occurred. From what I've managed to see, Deasylva is . . . curious, but not overly visible."

I threw my hands in the air.

"This is no help at all!"

He peered at me with peevish annoyance. "Isn't it?"

Leda rolled her eyes again. "Let me spell it out for you, Bianca. This is Hiddleston trying to impress me—this isn't about you. He's simply trying to goad me into a different debate because I've refused his official one."

He winked at her, eyes twinkling. "Well, can you blame me? It worked," he sang as he stood up. "And I, for one, have never had more fun. Thank you both, ladies. I believe I'm all finished here. Hopefully, we shall see each other again soon."

Hiddleston let himself out by disappearing in a transportation spell. For several long moments, Leda glared at me. She pointed a quill in my direction.

"This has you *aaaaaaall* over it," she cried. "What did you promise him?"

"Just that I'd talk to you about talking to him! There was no invitation, I swear."

She growled at me, then turned back to her parchment with a huff. "Never again," she hissed. "Never *ever* again. Insufferable toadstool of a man. His debate was poorly structured, nothing was resolved, and he brought in too many outside factors. He's *trying* to infuriate me, that's what he's doing. It wasn't even linear!"

Her mutterings continued for another ten minutes before she fell into silence and stared at the parchment, her eyes half glazed and fingers limp. I turned my attention back to the book with a sigh.

* * *

Two hours later, I threw a bundle of sticks against the wall and muttered a curse. Darkness had long since descended, but I was too wound up to sleep. The cold came with it, so I'd set aside the book in favor of building up a fire and doing something other than worrying over Papa, what was happening back at home, and whether I'd done the right thing. At least building a fire felt useful.

"Trouble in paradise?" Leda drawled.

She remained at the massive table in the middle of the room, books sprawled around her. After Hiddleston's departure, she'd grown slowly less annoyed, but still crackled around the edges every time she sent me a sharp look. I glared at her from over my shoulder and straightened. A crick had formed in my back from being bent over so long.

"No," I said. "I'll get it started without magic if it kills me."

"At this rate, it just might."

A scroll popped into the air, tied with a crimson ribbon. Scarlett. Leda glanced at it, but she said nothing as I tucked it into my dress pocket.

"Like it or not," Leda murmured as I struggled with another pile of kindling, "we are all but addicted to magic. Sobering thought, when you really think about it."

Oh, I thought about it all right.

The ease of having fire burst to life at my fingertips was something I missed, along with other simple things. Drapes closing from across the room. My teapot refilling my teacup before it cooled. Magic seemed most abundant in the little things.

"Scary thought," I said.

Leda humphed. With a resigned sigh, I turned back to my task. What felt like eternities later, a small spark gave a little smoke. Face nearly pressed to the ground, I blew on it. It snuffed out a moment later. With a growl, I shoved away to draw in a breath of cleaner air.

Across the room, Ava slept in a little bundle on the floor. Two blankets lay across her curled-up body, and her chest moved up and down rhythmically. I didn't stare at her too long, for fear of being almost consumed by the doubts and worries that would surely follow.

Had I done the right thing?

Should I take her back?

Somewhere in the bowels of Chatham Castle, Papa faced a pack of wolves without me. All of Alkarra would be distrustful of him after this. The peace he'd worked to carefully build for so long now threatened to topple, as if it were no more than a house of cards

My gaze darted to the wall, where two enchanted sticks rotated around carved marks in a wooden beam. A very unique clock that, unfortunately, revealed too many hours passing far too slowly. Merrick and Alina had returned to the Central Network hours ago. Now it was late evening, and my pacing had nearly driven Leda crazy.

"For you to read," Leda said crisply as she used a summoning spell. A *Chatham Chatterer* appeared on the ground in front of me. "It will keep you at least a little informed, although most of it will be speculation."

I swallowed in dread as I stared at it. The visible headline at the top of the scroll screamed at me.

Mortal in Alkarra!

The three words still sent a shudder through me.

"The news scroll already knows, of course," she muttered with dark annoyance. "I've been reading every article as they appear, but nothing is actually correct. The rumors are still wild and uncontrolled, which may be to our benefit. Your father is making an official statement to the Network tonight."

"He's still alive," I said. "That's something."

All day I'd braced myself for an angry letter from him, or a letter from Marten that reported something terrible happening to Papa, but nothing had come. Several reasons could be behind that. Papa may be too upset with me to write, too busy to have the time, or he agreed with what I've done and trusted me with it.

For my part, I assumed the first.

Nicholas and Priscilla's reactions filtered back through my mind and made my stomach queasy.

Was that happening all over the Network now? Fear? Panic? My chest burned when I thought of the underhanded, public way that Niko had handled this disaster. He'd come out with the information at that luncheon to publicly humiliate Papa, and I wouldn't forget that soon. It would only be a matter of time before my name was tied into this whole mess, anyway.

I rubbed a hand over my face. Leda's eyes darted over the page as she read through her own copy of the *Chatterer*, then snorted.

"One article poses the idea that *you* have been a mortal all along," she said with a scoff. "Nevermind that everyone has seen you do magic. Another says that your father has created a secret alliance with mortals across the ocean and plans to bring them back to Alkarra to build up his Guardian force."

"As a means to protect the South?"

She rolled her eyes. "Ridiculous."

The outrageousness of the speculation gave me no comfort because hints of truth lingered in each one. I hadn't been mortal all along, but I was as good as one now. And Papa had no secret alliance, but he had Baxter, didn't he? Bram certainly wanted the mortals here to form a more powerful position for themselves.

The only comfort in the madness was the fact that no one knew about my missing magic yet. Not that the *Chatterer* identified, anyway. Right now, only the swirling rumors, interposed with basic assumptions and fears about demigods and mortals, circulated.

I returned to my fire with a mumble, more deeply annoyed. Starting a fire without magic could take me days to master, despite being in a stable environment, at that. How did mortals do it?

Ava probably knew.

The challenge gave me something else to focus on, so I fell back into the task. Time passed quietly. Slowly. Like the plod of similar days that never seemed to end. Finally, a second spark flared to life and leapt onto a small pile of dried kindling I'd prepared. I let out a cry, gently blew on it to make it grow, and promptly snuffed it out again with too much breath. With a snarl, I smacked it all into the hearth and turned to Leda.

"Would you—"

She didn't even look up as flames sprang to life behind me with a rush of warmth. I sighed.

"Thank you."

With the fire crackling in the hearth, I settled next to Ava on the floor. We'd dragged mattresses out of the individual rooms—that had all been decorated with the same vague mattress, chair, and little else—and into the main living area. The air was much colder in the South, despite the usually warm time of year, and I felt better with Ava in my sight. Leda snorted at another article while I lay back and studied the ceiling. It was unusually high. If I stood on Leda's shoulders, my fingertips would just graze the top. The windows in the bedrooms were over my head, allowing a glimpse out at the top, but no glimpse in.

I couldn't help but wonder why.

The *bezopasnost* was a strange building filled with secrets and questions I'd been asking myself all day. Why the odd shape? If this were a school, there were only a few books. What did they learn? What were the tattoo-like drawings on the walls below the windows? Small and intricate, with lines so thin they must have been painted on with a pine needle tip. Not for the first time, I wished I had more reliable access to Alina. Perhaps she'd explain what all this meant to me.

Or maybe no one else was allowed to know.

The *bezopasnost* settled around us with the quiet shuffle of Leda dictating something to her quill. Ava's gentle sighs filled the room, so much more content than I imagined my sleep had ever been at her age. She seemed too young, too fragile, to be put through this. Still, in her beating heart, I could sense a familiar current of steel. There were monsters in our world, but I had a feeling she wasn't afraid of them.

A low candle flickered on the floor at my side when I pulled the scroll out of my pocket and peeled it open. Scarlett's signature filled the bottom, as expected. With a sigh, I lay on my stomach to read it. She'd included no greeting or salutation, which meant she didn't want my name on the paper.

Allow me to admit I harbor no surprise that you have disappeared as the news of a mortal girl in Alkarra has finally broken out, as we knew it eventually would. This early, of course, is not pleasant.

I wanted to let you know that the presence of the mortal has spurred chaos the likes of which I've never seen. Central to the discussions in the Council is protection.

The Council will be more interested in witches that can protect the Network than ever, and I believe that may supersede gender. Our ideal opportunity to present the idea of training worthy female witches to be Protectors may shortly manifest itself.

I'm not sure whether or not you are amenable to such a thing again, but if you have any inkling that this could be a path for you, I urge you to be careful.

To put it bluntly, do nothing stupid, rash, or do anything that has the slightest chance of breaking trust with the Council and hindering our opportunity. As I write this, and with my knowledge of you already, I am aware that my caution is likely too late, but I felt I must issue it all the same.

A Sisterhood could be a monumental move for your life, and our entire Network.

Please, keep hold of yourself.

S

The not-so-subtle censure in her words rubbed like sand in a wound. I balled the message up and lobbed it into the fire. Then I turned my face away from the light, put my chin on my hands, and closed my eyes.

Camille flashed into my mind so quickly my eyes popped back open. Brecken followed. The slain blue forest dragon came next. Haunting memories of the war came on their heels, when everything was bloody chaos and nothing certain. So many lives were lost, yet somehow I'd survived. After all the Clavas that could have killed me and all the witches that died instead of me, somehow I had made it through.

I'm sorry, I thought automatically. *I'm sorry I survived and you didn't.*

The flash of Tiberius falling off the wall followed. Stella's quiet, peaceful repose as we laid her to rest next to the grave of her young son who died as a small child.

My heart hammered in my chest, while my mind continued with the familiar, almost unconscious refrain. *I'm sorry. I'm sorry it was you. I'm sorry Mabel orchestrated such evil, and I survived. I'm sorry. I'm sorry.*

With a shudder, I flipped onto my side, my back to Leda. Ava lay with her hair splayed across the pillow next to me while another ghost haunted my already frazzled mind. *Spurred chaos the likes of which I've never seen,* Scarlett said in her letter. Would the chaos be so great if I'd left Ava there? Worse, likely. Worse if the mortal was apparent in front of their eyes.

Or would it be?

Was rumor more frightening than fact?

The uncertainty over what stood before them?

These thoughts lay heavy on my mind, accompanied by the grim reality that I may have made a big mistake *and* dragged my best friend into it. *Ava has a mission,* Baxter's voice whispered through my mind. *It's the way things are done.*

I studied Ava, so quiet in sleep. For a moment, I could only see Camille. Even when I blinked, the image didn't seem to clear. The bright expression, youthful features, and future full of optimism. Ava clearly *wasn't* my best friend. She was a mortal girl stuck in Alkarra.

Memories of Camille's burial popped back into my mind, even though I hadn't invited them in. The way her aunt Bettina stood stoically, her skin gray as a statue. Her face had been utterly immobile. Angie sobbed into a limp handkerchief, her wails winding through the woods like the lament of an invocation. Brecken's parents had clung to each other while they quietly wept over the grave that held both Camille and her husband. The gaping hole seemed so deep, the earth so dark, and it would forever contain Camille and Brecken in their double casket.

For long moments, the burial memories were all I could see. Could I create more of that pain by starting a Sisterhood?

Yes.

The last thing I wanted was more loss. That path wasn't mine—not anymore. With a firm mental shake, I forced myself out of that spiral of thought. No, my life was happy. Stable. Non-violent . . . sort of. Working with the recruits brought a sense of stagnation that was . . . desirable to most witches.

Sort of.

I thought of all the routine days. The warmth of the recruits, whom I now deeply missed the way I would my little brothers, if I had any. Who taught them now? Maybe they'd moved ahead to phase two, and I'd reintroduce swords after all this had died down. Or maybe they'd simply paused their sword training. I didn't know, and I missed that connection with them.

Yes, there was stability in working with the recruits. But there was also . . . a sense of something lost.

Without Letum Wood to guide me while I cared for it, where would I find my adventure?

There was no obligation for me to form a Sisterhood. Plenty of other witches could do it, despite what Scarlett thought. Besides, The Highest Witch and the Council technically held the job of protecting the Network, not me. Papa would protect the Network . . . somehow. A scoff bubbled out of me. No. The whole Network would be different after what Niko had done.

Yet . . . I couldn't clear the picture of Camille that seemed to lay over Ava, nor remove thoughts of Viveet. Fighting with Merrick. The power of my body protecting myself and those I loved.

Well, I had protected Ava tonight at least. The Networks hadn't gotten their murderous hands on her yet, and that was something. Only when my jaw began to ache did I realize I'd been clenching my teeth until they threatened to crack.

Too late, I wanted to say to Scarlett. *The Council is already going to hate me after they find out what I've done and what I'm still willing to do.*

An uneasy feeling escorted me into a restless sleep.

Chapter Twenty

A gentle hand on my shoulder shook me awake.

"B?"

Merrick's husky voice, lined with fatigue, brought me out of my dreams. I blinked a few times to see his figure hovering over me, a blur against the smudge of darkness in the room. For a moment, I could only stare at him. Dreams from when he first left tangled in my mind. Was this real? Or one of those heartless imaginings that brought itself back to life every now and then? The dream of Merrick returning. Of Merrick at my side, waking me up.

I blinked those thoughts away as I struggled to take my location in. The *bezo* lay quiet in the still-night air. Leda had retreated to a room by herself, the table swept clean of her books. The fire had banked in the hearth, leaving a cool edge in the air. Next to me, Ava sighed gently.

"Can we talk?" Merrick asked.

I nodded and pushed off the ground with bleary strength. A restless night of half-awake dreams and mental ramblings I couldn't control lay behind me. Now, through the high windows in the decagon, slivers of gray light began to appear. I tied on my sandals and followed him out the back door, into the forest.

My breath fogged in front of me as we stood shoulder-to-shoulder and stared into the thick, verdant woods, still gummy black with night. I waited to hear the trees until the forest returned with its own whisper, unintelligible. Was this part of Letum Wood? Perhaps. Letum Wood trailed into the southern portion of the Central Network, but the South had their own strange forests not connected with mine. My heart ached with their loss, then calmed. A breeze drifted by and a nearby branch rattled.

"It's colder here than I expected," I said to break the unnerving calm.

He chuckled, and his breath steamed in front of him.

"This part of the South is almost always cold at night, even at the end of summer. The days aren't as long here anymore. They're starting to fade now."

Which indicated we were much farther south than the border, and this forest wasn't Letum Wood.

For several seconds, the prickling, chilly air filled my lungs and tied me back to reality. The half-sleep I'd suffered all night slipped away. My eyes felt hot. Every time I blinked, it felt as if sand moved under my eyelids. But my body felt wired. Ready to run. To move. To defeat . . . *something*. It was the kind of feeling that led me to believe that maybe Scarlett was right.

Maybe I was made for a different kind of non-routine life.

"How are things?" I asked.

"Chaos," he muttered with a little shake of his head. The fatigue in his expression and the lines around his eyes likely meant he'd slept as little as me. "Derek was almost taken by Guardians at the command of Aldred on the Council, except the Guardians wouldn't do it."

My upper lip curled.

"Of course," I muttered.

Aldred was a portly man with time-reddened cheeks and an attitude of having been slighted his whole life. He'd led the opposition against Papa ever since he'd become Council Member when Papa appointed him at the beginning of the peace.

Merrick shrugged. "Protectors surrounded Derek while all the delegations fell into absolute mayhem. Eventually, Marten got a hold of the place and every Network separated until delegation leaders could meet on their own to discuss next steps."

I grimaced with a heavy drop of fear in my stomach. Papa stood all alone now. Not for the first time, I regretted my hasty decision. The terrible reality of what I'd done had started to descend. Now that I heard what was happening, there was no stopping it.

"The delegations have agreed to focus on *the mortal issue* in an emergency Esbat controlled by Lana in the West. Geralyn will be a second moderator, considering that Niko has shown open hostility to your father."

The name *Niko* ground like glass under my skin.

"The Central Network Council is going to meet this morning to decide what will be done with the Central Network leadership. Five Council Members are now ready to throw Derek out of power and halt the Highest Witch paradigm. They want to call for an immediate cessation of the Celebration while the vote is cast."

My eyes closed. "No," I whispered.

Merrick said nothing.

While all that happened at home, what was I doing here? The truth seemed so blatant in the morning light, when no shadows cluttered my mind. I'd run away. Stopped Ava from fulfilling *her* mission. And why? Why had I abandoned Papa so that I could save a girl that, for all I knew, didn't need me to save her? If anything, we needed her to fight *with* us, not hide.

A long silence followed. In it, my thoughts churned and whirled like a storm.

"I miss her," I whispered.

My voice was thick and choking. Tears filled my eyes with a wet heat, but I didn't force them away. Merrick didn't ask who I meant. Somehow he seemed to know, even though I hadn't said Camille's name.

He let out a long breath, tall and lithe and strong at my side. Just the way we had always been, back when things made more sense. When this ache in my heart that I'd tried to cover up all this time wasn't so deep.

"I know," he murmured. "I think you'll always miss Camille."

Desperate, I turned to him. "You were the only one there with me that night at the final battle," I said quickly. "Could we have saved Camille? What if we had done something differently? We lost so many. Stella. Tiberius. Brecken. Leda's brother. The blue dragon. Maybe we should have approached the battle from a different vantage or had Camille—"

He reached out and put a hand on my shoulder. The warmth calmed me. My hollow heart knocked against my ribs and my knees almost gave way.

"B, you did everything you could. We did everything we were supposed to do." He paused and stared into my eyes, and I saw that the memories haunted him as well. Then he cleared them with a quick shake of his head. "There was nothing we could have done to save Camille. She made her choice. It wasn't yours to control."

"After you left," I said quietly, "I began to wonder if I have always lived a lie. Papa struggled so much to recover and . . . and so did I. The questions hounded me so mercilessly. What if I'd done something differently? What if I'm the problem? I can't save witches! And I . . . I didn't want more of them to die. When the moment came to prove myself, I failed. What if I've always thought myself strong and powerful and able to protect myself and others, but really it wasn't true."

"We all wonder that, B," he whispered.

His smooth voice and the way he spoke as if the years apart hadn't happened, brought a sob out of me. A second later, he pulled me into his arms. I tucked myself into the hollow of his neck with another cry.

"All the witches in my life have something terrible happen to them. Mama. Grandmother. Camille. Stella. Mildred. The ones I care about . . . it's like they're not safe with me. What if I bring death? The Sisterhood would just make that worse. I'd be a capable, walking curse to Alkarra. It's why I let you go without fighting more. I didn't want to bring this to you."

The words sounded ridiculous as they crossed my lips, but I couldn't help the way they came from the deepest, darkest parts of me. As if this is what I'd been running from all this time. The thing I'd wanted to hide since the war ended and reality began.

That, at the bottom of it all, I felt like a failure.

His grip tightened on me. "Has Leda died?"

"No."

"Your father?"

With a sniffle, I murmured, "No."

"Neither has Marten. Or Ava. Or Michelle, Priscilla, Nicholas. You, which is a bloody miracle, if you ask me. Do you see them too, or are you just seeing what your fear is showing you?"

The feeling of a string being pulled through my heart made me breathless. *Are you just seeing what your fear is showing you?* At that moment, I had no ability to deny that he was right. I saw whatever evidence conveniently proved my fears correct, and enabled me to hide.

But the truth was far more forgiving.

Fear had a stranglehold on me, choking out all reason. All

facts. Pure emotion stirred in my heart now, and it was terrifying in its power.

"I don't want to lose anyone else," I said. "That path I was on toward the Sisterhood, it . . . it seemed so bad for everyone that I loved. I couldn't bear the thought of losing again. Of having something taken away. When we fought Mabel, we fought Clava's and evil magic. But a Sisterhood? I'd have to fight witches. There would be more death. The deaths of all those witches and creatures have been a burden that I can't carry anymore, Merrick. I can't. And if Ava dies so young and innocent because of something I did or didn't do, how would I live with it? That's why I brought her here. That's why she's not with Baxter because I couldn't bear another death on my conscience."

"It's not up to you, B."

"But—"

"No, it's not." His voice held a firm, commanding edge now. "You don't control fate or inevitability or anyone's path. I get it. It's hard not to feel like it's your job to save all these witches. But it's not. You're here to help them on their path, not stop them."

He pulled away, then hooked a finger under my chin and tilted my head back. His murky eyes swam when a fresh batch of tears welled up in my eyes, as if all time had been erased between us. His touch burned, burned, burned.

"You saved your Network and you saved your friends. You survived Mabel. Helped your father ascend to the most powerful throne in Alkarra after a war with dark magic we would not have won without his power. You *are* saving witches, you just have to let yourself see it. Bianca, you are a success."

He tucked a piece of hair behind my ear. His touch lingered like fire on my skin, and it felt like no time existed between us at all.

"If you started the Sisterhood, there would be more of the same. Maybe it would be hard for the witches in your life, but the good you did would counter all of that. And those witches would stay."

Papa letting me go to school, face Mabel at the ballroom, be captured and kidnapped—I understood his fearful position so much more clearly now. He allowed fate to step in for me, too. If he hadn't, I would never have become the Bianca of today.

Both my parents had let go of control and protection to see me grow and mature. I had to do the same for Ava. For others— even those that had already passed on. Camille's death wasn't my fault, and neither was Mildred's. They had stepped into their own lives and the roles they were meant to play in the grand scheme of things. Now, it was time for me to do the same.

But I wasn't about to stand by and do nothing.

"The Sisterhood," I whispered. "I'm afraid of it. That's why I haven't listened to Scarlett when she wanted me to get it going."

His hand dropped back to his side. A gaze full of emotion followed.

"Why? You think you could fail them, the way you think you did Camille and Mildred and Marie?"

Tears returned, hot and stinging. I cleared my throat and blinked them back. One leaked out at the corner, and I quickly swiped it with the back of my hand.

"Yes."

The whisper wobbled, nearly taking all my control with it. For several moments, I could only breathe. The tears built in my throat as I recalled the look in Mama's eyes when Mabel struck her with a killing curse. The boneless way her body crumbled to the floor. Papa's guttural agony that followed.

"Love will never be safe, Bianca. If anyone knows that, it's us."

The pain of his voice sent a hot lance through my stomach. I pressed a hand to quell the feeling, breathless.

"But living *safe* is no life at all," he continued. "There's a time to rest, and a time to stand. If we don't take what fate is willing to give us, she moves onto someone else and we become shells. Half-witches. We become a witch we never wanted to be."

Something lined his voice. Regret, was it? Pain. Despair. Experience. I couldn't help but wonder if he regretted the day we parted. If he blamed himself for taking the wrong path. If he destroyed himself over it now.

Because I did that.

Merrick shifted his weight and pulled in a deep breath. Stability returned to his voice when he said, "You can choose to look at the situation however you want. You can see those who made their choices, and then fell. Or you can see those you saved. Me. Your father. The Network. Leda. Yourself. Without you, Bianca, would the Network have survived?"

The moment that I slipped back into Mabel's mind, when I understood the war of agony in her soul, had provided Papa the moment of distraction he needed to stop her. To defeat the Almorran magic that would have consumed our entire Network.

"I hadn't thought of it like that," I whispered.

"There are others who will need you. Are you willing to let them down?"

His words rang in my mind for what felt like eternities.

"No."

"Then your season of rest is over." His fists clenched at his sides, fingers grinding together. "Maybe for all of us," he added quietly. "The time to fight has returned, and I'll be damned if the Central Network could survive it without Bianca Monroe."

My second-greatest fear resurrected itself as I said, "I shouldn't have taken Ava away."

He sighed. "Probably not, but you can still make it right."

Dew glittered like diamonds on the foliage around us as I shuffled back a step. The movement took me out of his mesmerizing presence. I wiped tears off my face with the back of my hands. Everything was clear now. So clear I couldn't believe I hadn't seen it before. Hadn't seen *this* path before.

I had to let Camille go, let Ava stand up for herself, and fight *with* my friends. None of us could do this alone. If they chose their path, I'd be with them on it. But it wouldn't be my responsibility to bear.

My Network needed me.

Merrick lifted one eyebrow. "Uh oh," he sang quietly. "I've seen that face before."

Determination filled my voice as I said, "It's time to go back, Merrick. Papa is not going to face that Council alone. Not this time. Besides, Ava has a mission to complete, and I have a friend to help escape the Eastern Network. No one else is going to get this done without us, are they?"

He grinned, a slow, lazy smile that made my breath catch.

"Those are the words I've been hoping to hear. Let's go, little troublemaker. It's time to save the Network again."

* * *

A guttural shout filled my ears the moment I stepped back inside Papa's apartment. I braced myself, prepared for a blow to the stomach or a slap to the face. Neither came. Instead, a head of curly hair and burnished skin crossed the room in two strides and had me by the arm.

"What have you done?" Baxter hissed. "Where is she?"

Merrick stepped between us and shoved Baxter away with a glare of warning. Baxter dropped my arm and backed off. He stepped to the side to see around Merrick and pointed a livid scowl right at me.

"Wait!" I held up two hands. "Your anger is justified. I shouldn't have left with Ava. I will explain everything, but Merrick won't leave to get Ava until he knows I'm safe here."

Baxter's nostrils flared as he looked to Merrick, who nodded once. Baxter took another stride back.

"Fine," he muttered. "I won't touch you."

Merrick eyed Baxter warily until I quietly said, "You can go get her, Merrick. Thank you."

He stepped back into the hallway to transport to the *bezo*. Baxter glowered at me from several steps away.

"You have every right to be furious with me," I said quickly, hands still in the air. "I was presumptuous and wrong, and I shouldn't have taken Ava. I'm sorry, Baxter. I meant well and wanted her to be safe, but didn't think she'd be safe here. I was afraid you'd have her stand before the Council or something. And I didn't want another person to die on my watch. Merrick helped me come to terms with what I needed to deal with, and I apologize you were the person that had to suffer while I worked it out."

Slowly, the ire in Baxter began to ebb. By the time I finished my apology, a shuffle at the door followed. Ava stepped inside with Merrick behind her. Leda followed, arms full of books. Merrick eyed Baxter, but seeing him nowhere near me, relaxed.

Baxter let out a relieved breath, swept Ava into his arms, and said something to her in their language. She beamed at him, chattered back, and he gradually let her go. They spoke for a few moments while Leda stepped farther into the room, surrendering her armful of books to Reeves. Her curious gaze kept a close eye on Baxter.

When Baxter turned back to me, I forced myself to be ready for more deserved censure. No doubt, he'd suffered mightily while worrying about where I'd taken her amidst an almost all-out war between Networks.

"I understand why you did it," Baxter muttered. He ran a hand through his hair, making it stand on end. "That doesn't mean I like it, but I understand it. Most importantly, you brought her back so she can complete her mission. Thank you."

I nodded.

He studied me, then let out a long breath. "The Council is about to meet to discuss your father. They have ninety minutes to talk before the Esbat begins."

A wince found me. "Was he furious when he found out what I did?"

"He was glad you got to somewhere safe, just in case word goes out about your magic. I think he would have taken you somewhere else himself. He's been up all night with Marten, attempting to make all of this right from Niko's . . . ah . . ."

"Betrayal?" Leda offered.

Baxter conceded with a wary nod.

"Do you think the Council will move against Papa?" I asked.

He nodded. "Yes, but only because Derek has asked for us to finish the Celebration before he reveals everything."

My thoughts instantly clouded. Papa didn't spend the night explaining himself to the Council? Stubborn witch!

"Because of me?"

Baxter hesitated before he said, "He refuses to tell the Council what he knows and what happened with Ava because he doesn't want to reveal that you've lost your magic. Not until the Celebration has ended. He tried to bargain to reveal all then, for your safety. He also wants to test the trust of the Council."

"That's insane."

Baxter shrugged. "He is adamant, Bianca. Aldred is foaming at the mouth, saying Derek has betrayed them all and is continuing to lie to them. Aldred believes that Niko is correct and the government must be changed. It's in the *Chatterer* and everywhere else."

My stomach twisted. This mess was even worse than I thought. Baxter ran a hand through his hair.

"If Derek doesn't reveal everything now, he may be able to bargain to keep his position, but cede his power."

"Then what's the point of him staying as High Priest?"

"Salvage his pride? Gradual transition?"

I rolled my eyes.

"Jikes, Papa," I muttered, "I can take care of myself."

Except, without magic, could I? Had Papa always allowed me such freedom and uninhibited freedom because he'd trusted my magic and my power? My ability to do the things I needed to do to keep myself safe?

So why didn't I trust myself?

My mind spun away from that thought when Merrick stepped forward. "The North will take you should you need somewhere to go."

"Let's hope it doesn't come to that," I quietly replied, then turned to Baxter. "When is the Council meeting?"

"They're discussing it now. Derek, Marten, and Scarlett have not been invited."

"Where?"

"The Council Hall."

"Is anyone sympathetic to Papa?"

"Four remain loyal, we think. We're not sure if their trust is shaken enough that they'd take massive action, though. Greyson, for sure, is still undecided. If the four remain loyal, Greyson will be the deciding factor. If he votes in favor of giving Derek time, then we can proceed to the Esbat with your father in power. If he votes against it, Derek is stripped of power for the rest of the Celebration and the Council will take over—likely with Aldred in Derek's place."

Grim, I nodded.

A plan had started to cobble itself together in my mind.

"Papa shouldn't face the Delegation Esbat alone, nor should the Council make the decision without understanding everything. I came back so we could find Bram and figure all of this out." I looked to Ava and back to him. "Both of us."

Ava brightened. "I go?" She reached for the amulet. "Witches? Bram."

Her *r* rolled in an adorable way.

"Time for you to avenge your Mama, Ava," I said.

Baxter murmured a translation, and she beamed. A calculating gleam entered her eyes, one filled with wrath, pain, and hope. Likely the same way I appeared when I had faced Mabel at the ball. "*Manulele*," Ava said.

I put a hand on her shoulder. "We will help you."

She smiled. "*Monilay mal.*"

With a determined nod to her, I whipped around to face Merrick. The edges of my plan cobbled together. "Are you certain of her promise? Would Geralyn allow us in the North if we were to be exiled?"

"Yes."

"We may need to take her up on it after what I have in mind," I said gravely. "I have a new plan, but it's a bit wild and I'm not sure whether it will work. We need a few minutes to prepare it, especially since I can't do magic. Can you help me with it? I need you."

The words almost tripped over themselves. I'd said those three words before, through a quivering sob when he told me the news of Geralyn's command for him to return to the North almost three years ago.

Merrick's expression softened with pain, as if he remembered it too.

"Always," he whispered.

The burr in his voice sent heat down my spine. Would there ever be a time when his gentle smile, witty retorts, and quick loyalty didn't have the same effect on me? As if the years between us existed as nothing more than a blank chasm, and now we stood together again. I shoved the heat off. Time for romantic recollection would have to come later.

For now, we needed to save Alkarra.

When I turned to Leda, she met my gaze with relief, as if she'd also been waiting for me to come to my senses.

"The Council isn't going to just trust your story, Bianca," she said. "You're an incarnation of your father. Wild. Unpredictable. That's what they don't like about Derek. They're never sure what he's going to do or what he hasn't told them."

"I know."

Her pale eyebrows rose. "You know?"

"That's why I have a job for you."

"Oh."

"Are you with us?" I asked.

"Of course."

I stepped back to see the ragged band of witches, a mortal, and a demigod that we'd gathered.

"Together," I said with an edge of promise, "we'll save Alkarra again."

Chapter Twenty-One

Baxter flanked me on the left as I strode down the hallway, toward Papa's office. Merrick lingered at my right under an invisibility spell. I could feel him there and his presence comforted me.

Good luck, Leda, I thought.

She had her own mission now, and the good gods help me if she never spoke to me again afterward.

"Expect Greyson to be the leader of the Council meeting," Baxter said quickly. We only had a few seconds before we'd turn a corner and find the Council Hall. "He's the only neutral party that remains, so focus on him. It will be easier than trying to persuade all of them. They're too emotional."

"What do you think he will do?"

"I don't know."

I nodded, my throat filled with cotton. Bright sunshine spilled through windows as we passed them, revealing hints of Letum Wood outside. I let my heart reach out to them for a moment of courage.

Even in their silence, I found some power.

"Any last advice?" I asked as we approached the final corner.

"Don't be stupid."

With that, Baxter peeled away before anyone noticed him. Papa's office wasn't far from the Council Hall, so I wasn't sure what to expect. I turned down the hallway that led to the Council Hall, where the emergency meeting had convened for security purposes, and skidded to a stop. Six scowling faces fanned around Papa's office door in a half dome. All of them were varying shades of height, hair color, skin color, and eye color. The only thing they had in common was a mutinous expression and a position in the Brotherhood of Protectors.

So Papa *wasn't* alone.

Tears filled my eyes at the sight of their ferocity on Papa's behalf. Never had I seen them this angry. Not collectively.

Not as one.

They already stared at me—I hadn't been quiet on my approach. Likely, they guarded Papa's door and the Council Hall to make sure neither was disturbed, but they showed their loyalty by standing near Papa's door.

Despite knowing every one of these men like second fathers, even *I* felt a shot of uncertainty from their fierce expressions.

Still on my right, Merrick removed his spell.

Matthais, the current Head of Protectors, stepped forward. He had jet-black eyes and matching skin, like a person born of shadow and strength. His steely gaze and strong jawline cut an imposing figure, something at odds with a jovial personality. No mirth hid in his gaze today.

"Bianca," he murmured.

One hand rested on the hilt of his sword. He eyed Merrick with curiosity and a hint of relief. Merrick had been in the Brotherhood with Matthais for several years before Merrick's loyalty to the North forced him to leave. The two clasped arms, and relief trickled through me. Until that moment, I didn't know if Merrick would be well-received by them or not.

"Matthais," Merrick said.

"Good to see you again, brother."

"I need to get into the Council Hall," I said.

Matthais opened his mouth to protest, but I stopped him.

"I brought the mortal into Alkarra and started this whole disaster. You know Papa will protect me until he dies, and the Network cannot lose him now. Not with a demigod on the loose. You have to let me in so I can tell the Council what has really happened."

He hesitated. His gaze flickered to Merrick, who nodded.

"Your father," Matthais purred, his voice a low rumble like a jungle panther, "will have my head for letting you by."

"Not if I snuck by you and you couldn't catch me."

Matthais raised one doubtful eyebrow. "You snuck by six Protectors without magic?"

I smiled. "If you say so."

He chuckled, but stepped aside. "Be wise."

"Thank you, Matthais. I appreciate your trust. There will be two other witches coming. You'll know them. Let them by, too?"

"As you say. There are two Protectors inside." He looked at Merrick. "But I'd recommend some extra assurance."

With a nod, Merrick disappeared back into an invisibility spell.

The weight of their stares lay heavy on my back as I headed to the Council Hall door, then faced it with a little tremor in my bones.

A *very* hostile Council waited inside. Not only did most of them want to see Papa removed from the throne for their own agenda, but they also wouldn't welcome unexpected interruptions. Nor would they appreciate what I'd unknowingly done.

Plus, if Aldred *were* the demigod, I may reveal too much. Would he run after I told my story? Would he stay and fight?

Was *he* even the demigod?

The chance had to be taken. I had to trust the Central

Network Council in the same way Papa wanted them to trust him. At least the Council would know everything, see it from all angles, and be able to decide for themselves. Some of them, mostly Papa's opposition, already saw me as wild and unpredictable, a blight on the beauty of the castle. This attempt might not buy any credibility, but I did need their cooperation. Plus, I didn't need all of them to believe me enough to give me a little more time.

I just needed one.

Greyson.

The admonition from Scarlett's letter rang through my mind. *A Sisterhood could be a monumental move for your life and our entire Network. Please, keep hold of yourself.*

She'd been right all along. The Sisterhood *was* my calling, but I'd just been afraid. I'd let ghosts bog me down. Now that I squared myself to my inevitable future and let fate have her reign again, I wanted the Sisterhood.

Except, after this, I'd probably lose it.

I reached out, grasped the cool metal handle, and let myself inside.

* * *

The grind of the hinges, and the creak of the door as it opened, drew every astonished eye right to me.

I stepped inside the Council Hall without fear, my shoulders back and chin high as I gave space for Merrick to invisibly follow. The door thudded to a close behind us. I skimmed the room with one quick gaze.

Several stunned faces stared right at me.

Six Council Members sat in chairs that formed a ring around a weighty wooden table with lions roaring out of the bottom of the legs. Aldred, two newer Council Members I didn't know well, and Greyson stood together on the other side of the table.

Aldred stood with his hands on his hips and agitation apparent in his low-lidded expressions. Greyson wore a crisp vest, a pair of brown slacks, and a stare that not even magic could have read into. The somber air in the room reflected in his eyes. A few premature streaks of white ran through his thick hair, giving him a paternal feel despite his young age.

Aldred snarled, yellowed teeth bared as he stepped forward.

"What," he hissed, "are you doing here?"

I ignored him.

"Council Members," I called into the ringing quiet. "I request an audience. I have come unbidden to explain the circumstances behind the mortal girl and the demigod. My father is not aware that I am here."

A murmur traveled through the room. When no one spoke directly to me, I continued to walk further inside. My gaze remained on Greyson.

"I am Bianca Monroe," I said to him, an arm outstretched. "Forgive me if we've never formally met. I understand you're the leader of this meeting?"

He nodded once, wary as I approached. He clasped my forearm, then immediately dropped it. The other Council Members shuffled, murmuring to each other.

"Allow me to speak to the Council?" I asked Greyson. "I will explain what my father will not, as well as why he won't."

"You believe that's wise?" he murmured.

"I hope so."

He hesitated, then gestured to the table with a wave of his hand. When he backed up a few steps, I turned my back to Aldred and faced the rest of them. Hostile Council, indeed. All of them glared at me through varying levels of trust. Even the Council Members that were supportive of Papa looked uncertain. Through the depths of their collective rage, however, burned a bright, morbid curiosity.

"The mortal girl is named Ava," I began, "and she's eleven

years old. I found her in the Eastern Network, and I'm here to tell you everything."

For the next twenty minutes, no one else said a word. The sun climbed higher in the sky and fell in ribbons on the ground near the far wall. Shadows shifted in the room with the burgeoning light. Council Members squirmed when I revealed my lost magic, then proved it with verbal incantations. I discussed Priscilla and Niko. Baxter's revelation of his family history, and his warm affection for Ava. My throat ached by the time I finished my story.

"I returned Ava this morning so she could complete her mission and rid us of the demigod, Bram, that came with ill intent." I let out a long breath. "Papa didn't want you to know all of this because it would have revealed my lost magic. I believe he thought that the danger to me, while Niko was still in the Central Network, was too great to risk it. And," I added, unable to help myself, "perhaps as a test of loyalty to his Council. Are there any questions?"

"You're trying to tell us," Greyson said with a concerned gaze, "that there are *two* demigods running around Alkarra? Not just one. After what Niko said, we thought . . ."

He trailed away.

I sighed. "Very likely there are more, but we aren't certain."

Silence replied.

Finally, Aldred cleared his throat. He stepped forward, a bloodshot eye on me. Behind all his blustering ire, I saw a tired, frightened man. Could this be Bram? Maybe, but something in his face made me doubt it.

"It's noble of you to try to help your father," he said, "but how can we know if any of this is true? Your loyalty to Derek rivals only his loyalty to you. This could all be a setup. You could be lying and have your own agenda."

I scoffed. "You think my father would have let me anywhere near you?"

His face turned to stone.

"I didn't expect you to believe me. For that reason, I've brought someone to verify exactly what has happened."

Unseen by the Council—but perhaps detected by Greyson, because he had eyed the spot where Merrick hid several times—Merrick swung the door to the hallway open. Hiddleston stood out there. Once the door opened, he advanced inside wearing his usual gray shirt, black vest, and long, gathered locks.

"Thank you for coming, Hiddleston," I called.

Leda walked at his side as they entered the room, her white-blonde hair pulled away from her face in a graceful bun, her expression surprisingly serene considering what she'd just done. She'd hang the fact that she'd gone to Hiddleston and asked him for help over my head forever. His rampant confidence, dark locks, and expressive gaze posed a stark contrast to her calmer features.

The Council turned to glance that way. Surprise registered only momentarily on Aldred's face when he saw the two of them. Leda and Hiddleston stopped halfway across the room. The distant expression returned to Hiddleston's face that indicated he'd mentally moved into his Defender magic. I hurried to give him a few moments to *read the paths,* or whatever that meant.

"As proof," I gestured to Hiddleston, "I've brought the Central Network's strongest Defender." I paused to let that sink in. "He can use Defender magic to go into the past of any person that is in the same room as him and see what has happened."

Shocked, wide eyes followed. I kept a wary gaze on Aldred, but he didn't seem any more reactive than anyone else. Perhaps startled, but not frightened. Watcher magic was a commonly-known magic, but Defender magic, its counter, was less known. The Council Members, however, didn't seem *that* surprised by it.

"Hiddleston's power is one of the greatest the Central

Network has seen in many years," I said with a quick glance to him. He remained in his distant expression, which meant I had to buy more time. If he only saw the past for witches in the same room as him, he'd need a chance once he stepped inside to read those here. But I could only bluster my way through this for—

Aldred snarled. "You provide your own witness!" he cried. "The two of you may have been working together, for all we know. Why should we trust him? He could be making it all up just the same. Until we see the mortal girl and question her ourselves, this is all conjecture. We can't trust Derek or his wild daughter. That's the bottom line. There is no trust."

Hiddleston blinked back to himself and lifted a lazy eyebrow. "Council Member Aldred," he murmured. "Lovely to see you so bright and fresh today. You had a difficult time sleeping last night. Around three o'clock this morning, a request was sent for a young maid nam—"

"That's enough," Aldred cried. Heat flooded his cheeks as he waved toward the Council Members around the table. He turned his back to Hiddleston. A tinge of red turned the top of his cheeks a bright color. "You may cross-question him and prove what that wild girl has said."

Greyson's jaw tightened when he glared at Aldred, then turned back to Hiddleston. No one said a word until Greyson said, "Thank you for coming, Mr . . . ?"

"Hiddleston."

"Hiddleston. You are Scarlett's newest Assistant, I believe?"

"Lead Assistant, yes."

"May we ask you a few questions about recent events concerning Bianca Monroe, her father, and the mortal girl?"

Hiddleston hesitated, then nodded. "I can't see the mortal girl in my paths, but I can see Bianca now, and I have seen for Derek previously. I'll answer as best I can."

Seeming pleased by Hiddleston's honesty, Greyson extended an arm. "Will you take an oath of truth on it?"

Hiddleston extended his hand, and Greyson clasped it. Light swirled around their wrists in a quick burst of color while Greyson murmured a powerful incantation that, for the next hour, would bind Hiddleston's tongue if he attempted to lie. Once it ended, they dropped the grip.

Greyson turned to the Council with an outstretched hand toward Hiddleston.

"Please ask your questions, but do so swiftly. We don't have much time before the delegation Esbat."

A chorus of mutterings followed until a Council Member at the back piped up with their first question.

"Tell us what you see of Bianca on the day the mortal girl arrived."

My stomach twisted as Hiddleston disappeared into deep thought for a moment, and then returned. With ease, he related what he saw in the paths of his mind, and the details aligned with my memory and my accounting.

Further questions shot at Hiddleston across the room, simple verifications of details, the way I'd expected. They ventured from my story to Papa's. My fingernails dug into my palms at their rapid-fire interrogation. Clearly, their agitation had grown on receiving the truth. They all had something they wanted to say and the truth to seek.

While Hiddleston responded to their questions, I kept an eye on Greyson out of the corner of my eye. He was the only one that mattered here—unless a Council Member in support of Papa chose to switch sides. Then all would be lost, and my plan would fall to pieces.

My tension didn't ease as the interrogation continued for another ten minutes. Time wasn't on our side, and they seemed determined to take as much of it as they wanted. Finally, the questions seemed to calm until someone asked the one thing I needed them to ask.

Prim, a Council Member from the Ashleigh Covens, piped

up from the other side of the room.

"When did Derek know about Baxter being a demigod? Can you see that?"

Hiddleston shook his head. "When I was last with Derek and in his paths, I could see only Derek. I cannot see Baxter, nor can I hear what is said."

"Baxter has never hidden his heritage," I couldn't stop myself from saying. "According to Papa, Baxter has told everyone about being the son of a god."

Several murmurs followed, and by the creased frowns, they didn't like the insinuation that they, also, had culpability here. Aldred shifted forward and into my line of sight, and my stomach twisted. This is where I pressed into the rest of my plan and things became more complicated.

"What now?" Aldred asked.

He eyed me, as if he already knew I must have some other reason for telling them. I shifted my body to see him better, while still keeping myself squared to the majority of the Council Members. The shock had started to fade from their expressions, replaced with a sort of numb weariness. I sensed Merrick shifting across the room and closer to me. He also knew that this is where things could go drastically wrong.

"I have a plan," I said with as much confidence as I could muster. "As I mentioned, Baxter has reason to believe that the demigod, Bram, is amongst the Council Members in the Southern Network. We want to sneak Ava inside the delegation Esbat so she can see all of them."

Aldred growled. "You want to bring the mortal girl amongst us?" he hissed.

"Yes."

A flutter of protests rose from various bodies around the table. Only one or two stared at me with a steady curiosity, as if they considered it. Greyson was amongst them. If anything, I'd only deepened his wariness of me with all that I'd revealed.

"All I need," I called over the flurry of activity, "is for you to do what you do best, Aldred. When you stand up to announce the decision of the Council regarding Papa's position, buy us time. Time for Ava to look through the crowd, then get away. Once she sees him, we'll take it from there."

My stomach twisted at the blithe sentence I tacked on at the end. As if we knew exactly what we were going to do at that point. This cobbled-together plan felt less certain with every word that came out of my mouth. Greyson's wariness had only grown, and I felt the same uncertainty from the rest of them.

Aldred scoffed, hands folded behind his back. "Insane," he muttered. "You want to parade a mortal girl around an Esbat packed with powerful witches? Why should we go along with you? You would do anything to prove your father is right."

"Correct. I would."

Aldred glared at me.

I stared back.

He tipped his head to the side, regarded me through lidded eyes, and finally said, "If we go along with this, we risk angering the other Networks. We'd be acting against this very situation without informing them or involving them."

"Yes."

"Why should we take the risk?"

"Because it's the only way to stop the demigod before all the information is out there. It's the only way to attack them before they attack us. I took a risk," I pointed out, "that *you* are not the demigod. I chose to trust. Now you must also."

Aldred recoiled and scowled at me. But in the depths of his response, I detected some sincerity. Horror even. No, Aldred was *not* Bram.

He muttered something that sounded like, "As if any of this is even true," but I couldn't be sure. Still, I couldn't help but appreciate his shock. I'd felt the same way at one point. Empty-handed and unable to prove or disprove any of this. Baxter was with Ava now, preparing her, so he couldn't tell his portion more convincingly.

They'd have to do the impossible and trust me.

But they wouldn't, I already knew that. So I had to force Aldred's hand. Because where he went, others would follow.

"To make this safer, I'll make a deal with all of you," I said into the ringing silence. Aldred turned to me, one eyebrow canted. Only a few paces away, Greyson shifted, hands folded in front of him and a look of deep concentration on his face.

"Go on," Aldred drawled.

"If the Council will support my plan, I will guarantee one of two outcomes. We find the demigod today, or you may exile me and Papa to the North."

Aldred straightened. A gleam of interest overtook his gaze. Meanwhile, a shocked murmur slipped through the room. I could feel Merrick's hot glare from across the table because I hadn't mentioned this bargaining chip. Neither Baxter, Marten, nor Papa would be any happier about this.

Too late now.

"If I'm wrong, Aldred, I'm giving you exactly what you want," I pointed out. "A way to get rid of Papa."

"You cannot speak on his behalf this way," Greyson said. "Bianca, you play a very dangerous game."

"She's already said it!" Aldred cried. He stepped forward hastily. "It cannot be taken back. Vow with me."

Aldred thrust a hand out. I stared at it for a moment, and wondered if I'd finally gotten myself in over my head. His eyes had brightened with the opportunity to get rid of me and Papa.

"I will stall for no more than five minutes so Ava can search for the demigod in the delegation Esbat," Aldred said. "If no demigod is brought forth before the proceedings begin, you and your father will leave the Central Network in exile."

My fingers twitched at my side as I considered his words.

"You guarantee an honest attempt to stall for those five minutes?"

"I do."

"And if I can prove that Papa didn't know about the dangerous demigod Bram, you'll remove consideration of Papa's future on the throne for the weeks following the Celebration? This will allow Papa to make the decisions on what happens next during the Celebration."

"Agreed."

I looked at Greyson. "Does he have the power to speak for the Council at the Esbat?"

Greyson pulled in a breath, then passed a hand over his eyes. "As leader of the majority, yes."

Aldred's face shone with excitement. He thought I'd fail. He thought this plan was utter madness, totally hopeless, and unlikely to go well.

There were a thousand ways this could go wrong and I felt silent screams of *caution, Bianca!* running through my head. But we had no other choice. The clock on the wall ticked away the time, and the delegation Esbat would begin in less than ten minutes. I reached out and clasped Aldred's hand in mine.

"I accept."

Magic prickled like heat around my hand as he issued a binding that sealed us to the agreement. Pain shot through my body from it, like lightning at my palm. The moment it ended, I jerked away with a hiss. He studied me, shocked. I stuffed my hand behind my back.

"Then we have an agreement," I said. "I will see you in the banquet hall."

Chapter Twenty-Two

The milling crowd felt as friendly as a pack of forest lions.

Council Members from all across Alkarra lingered in the banquet hall, which had been turned into a meeting room. Instead of tables, chairs made up four sections in perfect rows. Each Network had a portion of the room, leading to a circular dais in the middle where a witch could pivot on one foot and speak to everyone. The expansiveness of the soaring ceiling made all the voices bounce around overhead, creating a chaotic nest of sound.

I pretended to glance over my shoulder, toward the door. Baxter remained behind me, a few paces away. He kept his intense gaze on the crowd, arms at his side. He looked as cagey as I felt, the way his fingers twitched against his pants leg.

"Everything all right?" I asked without meeting his gaze.

"Fine."

A gap of space where Ava walked lingered between us. She was hidden by Baxter's god magic. Her hand brushed up against my back every now and then as she struggled to remain hidden from, and not jostled by, the crowd. It took all my willpower not to reach back and protect her as she struggled to remain unseen, while still scanning the crowd for signs of Bram.

A tug came on the back of my dress.

I paused, as if to decide where I wanted to go. We had advanced only a few paces into the room, and the bodies remained cluttered and thick around us. From this vantage point, there was a clear view of this side of the room. Ava's hand remained on the small of my back, a firm, warm presence. Then it slipped away. She murmured something, and Baxter said, "Continue."

I shuffled forward again, disappointed.

Glimpses of familiar faces appeared here and there in the crowd as I advanced, attempting a slow, but casual, pace. A glimpse of Scarlett's dark hair and a thin-lipped smile. Lana's eccentric dress from the West. A few maids righted chairs that had been skewed by the crowd before Council Members sat down, and some of the kitchen staff laid out hors d'oeuvres that were largely ignored.

The presence of Guardians from individual Networks made everything more cluttered. No one would trust the Central Network for their protection now, so they all provided their own.

On the other side of the room, Regina stood near Geralyn, who spoke with several of her Council Members. A purple sash and robe hung from Geralyn's left shoulder and matched the elegant turban, tucked with an opal, that swathed her dark hair. The Council Members wore the same sash, perhaps to make them more easily identifiable to their Guardians in a chaotic moment. Regina's face was an intense mask of concentration where she stood near the wall. The Northern Council Members appeared agitated. Next to Geralyn, Merrick watched me with a careful stare. I sent him a reassuring glance, but his face deepened into a frown.

My stomach felt like a knotted stone as I stepped further

into the crowd. The stench of too many bodies pressed into one room lingered in the air. The presence of so much magic pressed on my shoulders, feeling as if it had physical force. Ava felt it too, I'd bet, if her heavy, faster breaths meant anything.

Did we bear magic as a burden every day? Was it possible to carry a weight of which we weren't aware for all of our lives? Perhaps living without magic was the better existence. Harder, certainly. But, on some level, maybe simpler and freer. These thoughts swirled with me as I sidestepped a pair of East Guards.

Somewhere in the crowd, Marten waited. Papa hadn't appeared yet, although I felt certain he was here. Invisible, but watching. Central Guards stood at intervals, and all of them nodded or sent their gaze my way as we strode by. With a tight nod, I kept moving. The tension remained palpable.

There was a blessed sense of anonymity that came with a distracted crowd of this size, but my fingers still twitched to have a weapon in hand again. An old knife of Reeves' was strapped to my arm—a sharp little thing, with a thin hilt that made it either slippery or nimble, depending on how it was handled. Easily concealable, under my sleeve. I wanted to pull it out, but might accidentally stab someone and create a new ruckus.

Safety was an illusion anyway.

The cool marble floor radiated through my thin leather sandals as we walked. We just needed to get to the middle, find Papa, and settle near a chair so Ava could stand on top.

"Papa," I murmured. "Where are you?"

The bargain I'd just made with Aldred hung over my head as we navigated the simplest route from the edge of the banquet hall into the middle. Put simply: If we found no demigod, Papa and I were forever exiled. We would walk out of this meeting as castaways, or as winners, and there was no in-between.

Twenty more paces into the melee and no second tug.

Frustration made me grit my teeth. I kept going, attempting to find pockets of space where we could pause for a moment and give Ava a better chance to see. None came. The packed crowd grew in number every minute. A gentle murmur whispered from between us as Ava said something, then Baxter translated.

"No one yet," he replied gently.

This risk we took in having her with us in this crowd felt like razors under my skin. If the god magic wavered at all and someone caught sight of Ava's amber eyes, they'd know her right away. Panic would ensue. If Ava *did* see the demigod here, we'd have the problem of subduing him. Baxter could protect Ava better with god magic than I could with Reeves' deft little knife, but I still didn't like our odds.

Across the way, two witches huddled together caught my attention. Quills scratched quickly against curled parchment. They wore a brown shirt with their name embroidered near the right shoulder and the letters CC underneath. The *Chatham Chatterer* journalists.

We spilled into an open spot near the Central Network section of chairs. I stopped, startled to see Papa standing there already. The chairs funneled from several rows of ten at the back, to four at the front. Matthais stood with Papa, not far from Scarlett and Marten, who said nothing as they gazed around.

Papa looked haggard, but not hopeless. The strain in his gaze was apparent to me, but others would not notice it hidden behind layers of what appeared to be concentration. While Matthais spoke, Papa stared at the floor and listened. Reeves must have helped Papa clean up. He wore a freshly laundered shirt buttoned all the way to the throat, a fresh pair of leather pants, and his favorite boots. While he didn't have the political elegance of Niko Aldana, he posed a formidable presence.

Despite the opposition piled on his shoulders, Papa was clearly ready to present himself to the Networks and see these troubled waters through to the end. My heart swelled with pride for him. I slipped the rest of the way across the space to stand at his side. When I stopped, I remained a few paces in front of a chair and hoped Ava climbed on top.

Matthais gave me a nod, then Baxter, before he disappeared. Papa gazed over to me, then behind me to Baxter. He studied us, clearly suspicious.

"B," he murmured wryly. "Baxter."

"Papa."

"Another lovely day, isn't it?"

My lips twitched. "So I hear. How was your breakfast?"

"Bland. And yours?"

"Forgotten."

"Yes," he drawled. "When one is sneaking into the Council Hall and attempting to take matters into her own hands, one does work up an appetite. And, at the same time, one removes the opportunity to eat."

It took all my control to keep my expression straight.

"So I hear."

"Your Highness," Baxter said. "A word?"

I forced myself not to look at him—or the space around him—in an attempt to find Ava. She should be standing exactly in front of him or on the chairs behind us, but it was impossible to tell. God magic was surprisingly thorough.

C'mon, Ava, I thought. *You have to see someone.*

While Baxter blithely discussed something related to the events of the day with Papa, I kept my attention riveted on the chairs behind us. One nudged just a little, as if someone had squirmed on top of it. By sheer willpower, I didn't look over.

I waited, my future in Ava's young, capable hands.

With every passing moment, it felt as if my heart died a little more. The crowd Ava had to study remained thick, like the clustered, evergreen forests of the Southern Network. Witches moved here and there, practically in a synchronized dance. It made it impossible to really study a face or an expression. Once the meeting started, she'd only have five more minutes.

An impossibly few minutes.

The gentle blow of a horn from the Western Network reverberated through the banquet hall and made the windows shudder lightly from the force of the sound. Conversation ebbed as witches turned to regard the Western Network High Priestess standing in the middle of the room, on top of a raised dais in the circle.

Lana stood in a stunning dress of deepest mauve silk. It puddled on the floor, calling attention to the edges of black leather boots. Slivers of glimmering red highlighted her auburn hair and sparkled against her emerald-green eyes. Her hair dropped, straight as a razor, all the way to her waist in glistening, burnished red banners. Her expression was somber against an elegant backdrop of fashion. Her shoulders seemed more slender than ever without piles of hair wound all over her head in wild ways.

With a spell, she projected her voice.

"Witches of Alkarra," she called, and the last snuffles of sound ebbed away. "Let us begin the Esbat today. Central Network, send your Council Member representative forward to declare the results of your meeting. From there, the Esbat will commence."

* * *

The shuffle of Aldred heading toward the circular platform was the only sound in the banquet hall.

Lana slipped away as Aldred stopped in the middle of the dais, lifted his head, and gazed around the room until he'd encompassed every witch present. An immense number of eyes stared at him, waiting for Papa's death knell from the Council. It bought at least fifteen seconds of time for Ava to search.

My heart slammed in my chest. This moment decided everything. There was a solid chance that Aldred would risk the physical torment that came as punishment for a broken binding of that nature. In exchange for a day or two of pain, he could betray our agreement, declare Papa unfit for duty by popular vote of the Council, and push the power to the Council. If that happened, there would be protests, of course, then more delays. But Papa would have to be removed from power and pressure from the other delegations would empower the Council to act in his stead until later.

It all came down to the calculating mind behind Aldred's machinations. Would he risk his reputation to get Papa off the throne? Was two days of agony worth it to him to have Derek Black off his agenda?

Probably.

Aldred shot me a quick little glare, as if he sensed the darkening direction of my thoughts.

He cleared his throat.

"Networks of Alkarra," he began, his voice rippling over the crowd with a spell. "It is my pleasure to speak with you."

Do what you do best, I'd told Aldred before I left, with a cheeky little wave as I departed. *Say more than you need to without saying anything at all. Keep them busy. Buy Ava five minutes to locate the demigod. I'll take it from there.*

And I would.

I just didn't know how yet.

In fact, I hadn't even been sure we'd get this far. Now that we had, I wracked my brain for the next step. First, Ava had to identify the demigod—if they were here at all, which I fervently hoped—and then let us know that she'd found them. She had less than five minutes left to figure it out before Aldred would be forced to cede the power back to Papa and lose face on the Council, or take the Council for himself.

Aldred's voice droned into the background as I switched my thoughts.

"Anything?" I murmured to Baxter.

"Not yet."

"What," Papa whispered, "are you up to, Bianca?"

The hardness in his tone gave me no courage. I drew in a deep breath, my chest expanding, and said, "Nothing, Papa."

"The Council of the Central Network gathered together this morning," Aldred continued. He shuffled every few moments to spin and face another facet of the crowd. Most of the delegation leaders sat in the four chairs at the front of their Network, except Geralyn, who had been positioned behind Regina. In the interest of maintaining some facet of normalcy, Merrick remained near his High Priestess, but his gaze lingered on me.

It felt like an eternity passed before Baxter said something in his language, likely speaking to Ava. Aldred had only been talking for four minutes. It felt like forever and an instant at the same time. Which left only one minute left.

Silence answered Baxter's tentative question to Ava. "Where is she?" Baxter whispered, suddenly frantic.

"What?"

"Ava. I can't . . ."

My blood turned to slush. Had he lost her? Had her silence meant she wasn't *here* this whole time? A thousand regrets spilled through me. We shouldn't have done this. We risked too much. Papa and I would be exiled to the North and—

I forced the wild thoughts to slow, then shifted my right foot forward to search for her. My foot collided with nothing but air.

Baxter moved his left foot forward, nudging the space in front of him as well. Next to me, Papa tensed as Aldred wound toward the end of his long-winded declaration of a decision.

"And so," Aldred's gaze darted to me. Sweat had broken out on his forehead, and he mopped at it with his wrist. Frantic, I searched the air for any sign of Ava. For any sign of . . . *something*. "It is with great—"

"*Monilay mal!*"

A screech rent the air seconds before Ava appeared.

She stood only a few paces away from the dais, the amulet in her hands. It dangled from the chain in a gentle twirl, like a falling snowflake. The ugly, black gash remained in the middle, but it seemed to have grown like a stolid, festering wound. A dying glow crept around the edges. Crimson, with an edge of burnt orange. It rotated to an opaque yellow, like melted butter, before morphing back to red with the pulse of a quick heart.

Baxter sucked in a sharp breath.

On instinct, I reached for my sword, but Viveet was no longer there.

Before any witch could so much as move, Ava advanced. Fury filled her gaze as she stalked across the circle, headed right for Niko. My heart leapt into my throat. Niko? No. That would be utterly impossible. It made no sense.

Just when I thought she must have it wrong, she rushed beyond the stunned witches of the Eastern Network and stood before an astonished Igor. She skidded a stop, rage bright in her bared teeth.

"*Monilay mal!*" she cried.

Her knuckles turned white from gripping the amulet chain so hard. A ripple of gasps spread through the banquet hall. Igor's heavy brow narrowed into a glare. His gaze darted from the amulet, then back to her in astonishment. His lips moved wordlessly.

"Mortal," whispered someone nearby.

"The mortal girl."

"What is happening?" asked another.

The startled exclamations faded into the background when Baxter whispered in an astonished voice, "Of course. Igor."

My heart almost stopped.

Igor?

My mind spun to catch up. How could the demigod be Igor? Then, how could it not be? He was in the South, in a position of power as Baxter suspected, and incapable of magic. Supposedly, anyway.

It's all in the leader, Igor had said outside of Papa's office days before. *For all vitches to give their loyalty to the South, they must all feel seen . . .they vill be seen and heard and their loyalty svorn to their leader. It is our only vay into the future.*

Sworn to their leader.

Igor's plans to have witches swear loyalty to their Network had really been them swearing loyalty to *him*. Allegiance. Baxter had said as much. *Some of those demigods wanted to come back. To give themselves more power. Demigods are only as powerful as the number of mortals devoted to them.*

Sneaky cur.

Igor's lips twitched in a snarl directed at Ava. I comprehended that he could reach out, grab Ava's neck, and Ava would be dead in seconds. Baxter must have realized the exact same thing because we sprang into motion together.

I rushed away from Papa and toward Ava. Reeves' knife felt cool in my palm as I ripped it off the sheath on my forearm, tearing my dress in the process. Baxter must have used god magic to place himself on the other side of the room because he appeared in front of Ava less than a second later.

Ripples of shock spread through the room.

Baxter stood with his body braced, one leg in front of him. He held a hand up by his hips and a wary expression.

"Bram?" he ventured, his tone tentative.

The gray gems from Baxter's amulet glittered in the daylight. Igor's gaze darted from Ava, to the amulet in her hands, and then back to Baxter. His gaze lingered on the slowly twirling amulet once more. I felt a moment of utter disbelief swamp me.

Igor.

No. The betrayal . . . the sheer audacity . . . Papa had been *helping* Igor for so long. But really, he'd been helping a demigod that wanted more mortals to take for himself. All this time, we'd been played for fools.

Papa appeared to my left. He stepped forward, flanking Igor on the left. I slipped to the right. Baxter, Papa, and I formed a sort of semicircle around Igor—no, Bram—with Ava in the middle near her uncle. In the back of my mind, I registered Protectors moving into place near the back of the room, blocking exits.

The entire place seemed to hold its breath.

"Igor," Papa said, his voice hard. "You have an opportunity to explain yourself before you make any rash decisions that you can't make right again. What is going on?"

The multiplying silence jarred Igor back to himself. Instead of his bewildered expression as he regarded the amulet, Igor's cheeks relaxed. His chest heaved when he looked around the banquet hall, and seemed to make a decision. His reply was a low snarl, and he spoke it right to Ava's stormy eyes.

"What happened?"

Ava smiled, then spoke in tones that once sounded lyrical and gentle. He screamed something back. She brought the amulet closer to her chest and began to chant.

"*Charamant. Charamant.*"

He hissed something.

Ava shouted. "*Charamant! Charamant!*"

"You know nothing, mortal girl!" he shrieked. "Nothing of what you've done. Ignis will rip every strand of hair from your head until you die! You will pay for what you have broken by the god of fire!"

Igor lunged. Ava ducked. Baxter threw himself at Igor's meaty frame at the same moment. The two crashed together, like beings made of stone. The force of Baxter's weight knocked Igor off balance and he crashed into the chairs behind them. Witches scattered with startled shouts, headed for the exits. Papa sent me a warning look. I smiled and held up my hands to indicate that I wouldn't join the fight.

But oh, how I wanted to.

Ava skittered to my side, deftly avoiding being crushed beneath Igor's weight. I grabbed her shoulders and pulled her close. The amulet bounced around her chest like a wild thing. Baxter held up an arm when Merrick peeled away from Regina and advanced toward Igor. Geralyn slipped outside a side door, gone in a heartbeat.

Merrick completed our circle around Igor as he shoved chairs away. Witches scuttled out of reach of the dueling demigods.

"Stop!" Baxter shouted to Merrick, then to Papa. "You'll never be able to fight him. He'll kill you in a blow."

Igor rolled back to his feet, then charged Baxter. Witches from the East shouted, scrambling to get out of the way when Baxter and Igor collided again with guttural shouts. The sound of their crash to the floor echoed with the crack of splintered wood. I gritted my teeth. That had to hurt, but they continued anyway.

Igor disappeared, then reappeared a second later behind Baxter. At the same moment, the glittering gem on Igor's thumb caught my eye.

He *did* have another amulet.

Ava winced as Baxter attempted to extricate from Igor's grip. Igor's hands burst into flames. He cried out and disappeared again, but reappeared on Baxter's back. His hands lightly smoked, the flames extinguished.

Papa rocked on his feet, as if he held himself back from joining the ruckus. The sound of grunting and grappling continued as Ava peered up at me, a question written in her gaze.

I crouched next to her.

"*Monilay mal,*" she whispered as she clutched the obnoxiously large amulet. "*Manulele.*"

"Your . . . Mama?" I guessed.

What little remained of her childhood must have lived in her eyes right then, bright with fear. Tears welled up in her eyes. Whatever *manulele* meant, it seemed to hold a lot of space in her heart.

With a little breath, she pulled the amulet off her neck. The gem glittered in her small hand, the fingers cupped around the backside of it, where it shone with blunted light. Tendrils of red escaped around the facets of the gem, like a dying ember. Even the metal filigree looked burned on the edges.

Ava looked at me, ferocity in her gaze. Although I didn't know for sure, I had a feeling we shared a similar history. That same desperate determination had once lived in my heart when I yearned to face Mabel and make her pay. I had lived for that exact revenge against my mother's murderer.

This was Ava's battle now, and I wouldn't stand in her way. I squeezed her shoulder. "*Monilay mal,*" I murmured.

She clumsily pulled the small sword she'd taken from my wall from a pocket in her dress. I nodded to the fighting demigods and she nodded back.

Ava turned, wrapped her fingers around the amulet, and focused her concentration on Igor. Blood dripped from Baxter's nose as he dodged a flying fist. A torch appeared in Baxter's hand, and he swung it. Igor bent backward to dodge it, then shot upright with unimaginable speed, as if propelled by god magic.

Papa stood back, legs braced, arms folded across his chest as he waited for Baxter to need him. Merrick edged around the other side to offer support if needed there.

The two demigods clashed like breaking stones. The floor cracked beneath Baxter's feet as Igor rammed into him. Chairs shattered when Igor crashed on top. Behind the fighting demigods, witches scrambled to get out of the room. Chairs, scattered pell-mell, littered the floor with their legs upturned. Panic filled the air.

Amidst it, Papa watched Igor and Baxter with a calculating stare. His thoughts moved too fast to comprehend, but I could see a hearty amount of rage in him. Next to me, Ava crouched, balanced on the balls of her feet. The amulet dangled in her right hand, the chain dragging the ground, with the small sword in her left. I couldn't be sure of her plan, but I had a good idea. I nudged her forward a few steps, then nodded once.

Baxter crashed to the ground beneath Igor's next drive. The wooden dais splintered at their back and Baxter let out a shout. Igor leapt on top of him, yelling something in their language. The guttural tones had no trace of the Southern Network. No distinguishable accent. No sign of Igor.

Igor, the High Priest was gone.

We faced Bram the demigod now.

Baxter yelled something and Igor paused. He leaned all the weight from his knees into Baxter's chest, making it impossible for him to breathe. Papa shuffled forward a step, a sword appearing in his right hand.

"Igor," Papa barked. "Make no mistake that you will be thoroughly condemned for this, but if you kill him, I will make sure you survive long enough to suffer for the rest of your life."

A moment of confusion flashed through Igor's eyes and caused him to pause. Then he started to laugh. A grating, rolling, low sound.

At that moment, a flash of black-and-crimson appeared from just behind him. Ava leapt onto Igor's back, threw the amulet around his neck, looped it onto the knife, and twisted it around twice.

Then she leaned back, and she pulled.

Igor toppled backward. His arms flew through the air before he tried to grab at the chain that dug into his fleshy neck, but she'd created too much tension. The minuscule chains on the necklace dug into his skin too far for his fingers to reach. His arms wheeled as he toppled backward.

Ava fell back with him and slammed into the ground with an *oomph*. The breath seemed to leave her, and her grip slackened. I darted over and skidded to the ground. Igor's meaty hands clutched at his neck. I grabbed a flying wrist, wrenched his hand back, and yanked the amulet ring off. It clattered on the ground as I tossed it toward Papa.

Bram gurgled an enraged shout.

I hurried next to Ava and grabbed the chain. Bram's face reddened with color. Together, Ava and I pulled. Bram's demigod strength began to fade as he struggled to breathe. An errant hand smacked me in the cheek. I shouted and kicked him in the left rib with my foot, and then again in the back when he tried to wave me off like a pest. Ava let out a guttural scream, tears in her eyes.

She gasped for breath.

We pulled harder.

The color leeched from Bram's face as Papa and Baxter stumbled over, the ring on Baxter's thumb. Bram's frenetic movements had begun to fade, easing slightly. Papa conjured a rope with a spell and extended it to Baxter, who muttered something indistinguishable, then grabbed Bram's weakening arms and tied them together.

"You can do it, Ava!" I cried.

Bram choked, tongue out as his arms flailed for purchase. His hands scrambled to reach us, his long, yellowed nails desperate to pierce our skin. I braced my feet on his shoulders as Ava screamed next to me.

"*Manulele!*"

Bram's scrambling hands calmed. My fingers began to bleed with the force of the chain in my skin. Ava sobbed.

"Let him go," Baxter said.

Ava hesitated only a second, then released the amulet with a cry. The chain went limp in my hands as Baxter grabbed Bram and slammed him into the ground. Papa held his other shoulder. Too weak to fight, Bram was bound within seconds. A line of crimson blood trickled off his neck and onto the floor.

Ava scrambled away as fast as she could, legs flailing. Tears jarred out of her eyes when she slammed into a fallen chair, then went still.

I stood and followed her until she stopped moving, then I knelt on one knee at her side. She bent over, retching. Bram rolled onto his side with a groan, coughing and sputtering and only half-conscious. Baxter stood next to him, talking low. He nudged Bram's face to the side with one of his feet and growled. Papa crouched next to Bram and said something, but Bram gave no response.

A moment later, Papa straightened.

Matthais materialized right next to Papa. Three other Protectors appeared behind him. Scarlett and Marten stepped away from a crowd of witches that ringed the far perimeter of the wall. Leda came away with them. Next to her, Hiddleston. Without a word, Leda rushed over.

"You're all right?" she whispered as she grabbed my arm.

"Fine."

She eyed me with uncertainty, but she must have seen something in my face that reassured her. She dropped to her knees, wrapped an arm around Ava, and pulled her close. Ava turned to her with a cry, limp in Leda's arms. Leda made a low, crooning sound as she rubbed Ava's back and Ava sobbed into her shoulder.

"Get a chair for Igor," Papa called. His command rang through the room. "Marten, the Veritas potion, please. Our prisoner has questions to answer—in front of the entire delegation."

Chapter Twenty-Three

Minutes later, my chest heaved and my head spun.

I leaned back against a wall in the hallway, eager to feel the press of the chilly stones against my heated body. My face felt flush, my heart thready and fast. Flashes of Igor—no, Bram's—face floated through my mind. I sent them away and opened my eyes again.

Now was not the time to lose it.

I still had enemies to face.

I hid behind the bookshelf again, out in the hallway. The exact spot where this whole disaster had first begun. Despite chaos within the banquet hall, this hallway felt quiet and calm. Only a few witches walked by, but none came into this little corner. Everyone was too focused on the interrogation inside.

My racing heart slowly calmed as I listened to the murmur of voices that came from just down the hallway. The two *Chatham Chatterer* journalists ran to get back into the room. Council Members from all Networks regrouped and entered again.

Rumors zipped around, along with messages that cluttered the air. Apothecaries hustled by as they dealt with a few minor wounds from a stampeding crowd. Witches bustled here and there, speaking low as they attempted to make sense of the circulating gossip. New Guardians rushed into position, barking low commands.

Minutes had passed since everything unfolded, yet it felt like days.

Bram's voice rang out every now and then, occasionally distinguishable against the background of the rest of the castle. He'd clearly come out of his almost-choked delirium, and sounded fighting mad.

Another five minutes passed. My racing heart slowed. The banquet hall quieted, and Bram's voice returned. This time calm and monotone. Clearly, the Veritas potion had been administered.

"I came with the power of god magic three years ago," he intoned dully, a result of the forced truth from the potion. Not even demigods were immune to potions, apparently. "When word of witches becoming magicless first entered our region, from the goddess Prana."

I tuned him out.

As Papa had always trained me to do, my mind reviewed the last twenty-four hours. All the commands I'd given myself. The choices I'd made. The things I'd thought. All the events that happened. I let them all slide through my mind in a steady blur of thought that organized my body again.

Memories of a Factios attack on Chatham City over three years ago flashed like bright lights within my recollections. The Factios had set fire to Chatham City and created pandemonium. Merrick had been there while I attempted to save my friend and her brothers. Afterward, when I realized exactly what risk I'd taken, he held my hair while I retched over the side of the castle wall. The sheer shock of the smell of burnt skin still lingered with me today.

He'd reassured me then that it was normal for my body to

feel weak and tired after such a traumatic event. And I had. I'd felt spent at the end of it.

But none of that happened tonight.

My mind slid through the events as easily as smoke. The facts slipped by, one at a time, distinguishable and distinct and not at all frightening. I drew in a deep breath and let it back out. My heart had calmed to a dull thud and an easy bounce against my ribs. I recalled Ava, Baxter, the blood, the shock, the uncertainty. My movements had been confident and certain. I'd known what to do.

I'd trusted what to do.

This is what I was *made* to do.

The certainty filled me with new determination. The Sisterhood was only one path for me now—had only *ever* been one path. But I'd been hiding from it long enough. No more. Tonight, I would find Scarlett and I'd tell her the truth.

The Network needed me, and it was time for our Sisterhood.

Although the problem of my magic resurrected in my mind, I shoved it aside. If we couldn't fix this, I'd learn to live with it. Alina couldn't do magic, but that didn't make her any less formidable, or any less intelligent. Even if I didn't act as a member or leader of the Sisterhood, I could help bring it to pass.

This *was* my path.

I shoved away from the wall ready to find Scarlett, throw myself at her mercy, and beg forgiveness for my tardy arrival to the Sisterhood plan. Everything had changed.

When I turned to head down the hall, I stopped almost as soon as I started. My breath caught in my throat. Niko stood there, his cravat was pulled askew, eyes lined with shock. He blinked several times. I sucked in a sharp breath through my nose.

We stared at each other without saying a word for several long moments. In the background, Bram's words echoed.

"Many demigods know of the mortals. They have already come to Alkarra."

A murmur of Papa's voice. Bram answered.

"I don't know how many. It has begun. The demigods are already here."

With the echo of Bram's words ringing through the air, Niko's hands trembled at his sides. Niko had seen and experienced plenty of violence in the war. So why would he be trembling now?

Why was he out here in the hallway while Bram gave a full confession inside?

There was only one answer.

Niko was scared.

Of me.

Bram's steady confession gonged a death knoll for Niko's sentence against Papa and discredited Niko in front of all Alkarran delegations. Niko had stood up in front of every Network and accused Papa of treason without giving Papa a chance to defend himself. He'd created distrust, rumors, and unnecessary political drama. Now, Bram exonerated Papa.

In a word, Niko had been wrong.

Very wrong.

And now he knew it.

The realization lived in his eyes now, and I could almost assign the expression on his face to one of terror. My fingers curled into my fist until the nails dug into my palm. *Yes*, I wanted to say. *Magic or no, you have reason to fear me.*

Instead, I waited. The silence seemed to unnerve him even more. When he finally spoke, the words were rushed. "I was coming to . . ." He trailed away, blinking. Then he cleared his throat. "I have come to apologize."

I held up a hand.

"Please, spare yourself the agony. It's not to me you need to apologize, Niko. First, Priscilla. Second, my father."

He reared back. "Priscilla?"

My lips pressed together. "Yes, Priscilla. Did you force her here?"

"No." He recoiled. He frowned and ran a hand through his hair. "I . . . I *found* her here. She came . . . willingly . . . once we discovered her in the forest."

His definition of *willingly* was under scrutiny based on the way his voice wobbled, but I'd have to let that pass for the moment. Priscilla and her child's safety was paramount in my mind.

"Where is she now?"

"Safe." Stubbornness clouded his features, removing some of the uncertainty. "That is all you need to know."

Power welled up inside me, and I recognized it as the way I felt when I did magic. I'd always thought it *was* the magic. But it wasn't magic at all. It was my power. My ferocity. My ability.

My strength.

The power came from within me, not the magic. Is that what Alina had meant when she counseled me to learn all I could?

To see my real power?

I didn't need magic to be powerful, and I didn't need magic to get my point across. Like Alina, my ability came from myself. Niko's expression darkened as I stepped toward him, thrumming with power.

"Release Priscilla," I said evenly, "or you will deal with me *before* you have a chance to apologize to my father. My friends are under *my* protection. Magic or not, I will see their safety through to the end of my life. I invite you to try me."

The words vibrated with force.

"Bianca Monroe," he stated, "do not make an enemy of my Network."

"You have already done so," I hissed.

He paused.

"Shall I lay it out for you?" I continued. "You gathered Central Network witches and forced them to return. You led one of our most beloved witches to believe that you'd handfast her, and then accused her of spying. You created rumors, distrust, and falsehoods about my father and my Network. Without proof, you attempted to throw him off his throne because of your own insecurities."

Niko's jaw tightened, but he didn't look away. "There have been mistakes," he whispered. "You are correct."

"Whatever assumptions you made about my father, and then publicized with reckless disregard for the truth, have taken something from us that we can't get back. Trust. Peace. The witches that have always been safe with him will now feel otherwise. In some instances, there is no fixing the damage you have caused. You have spread gossip in my Network and broken the heart of one of my closest friends. You have made several grave mistakes, Niko, and made an enemy of me. It's not my Network you should fear. It's *me*."

He hesitated, mouth opened to speak. Flint appeared in his eyes before he nodded once, then shuffled back a step.

"I see."

"You may address me as Miss Monroe," I snapped in a final removal of any friendly ties that once existed between us. "Priscilla is to be released immediately and escorted to my father's apartment. I invite you to leave Chatham Castle as soon as Priscilla is on the castle grounds. I advise you: do not come back unless you have been invited."

Niko opened his mouth to say something, then closed it again. He swallowed hard, bowed slightly at the waist, and turned on his heels. He walked away from the banquet hall and didn't look back.

The fire building inside me blazed to an inferno. I set myself back on the path to Scarlett's office.

My time had come.

* * *

Darkness crept across the sky later that night, drawing a dark blue cape behind itself. Stars sparkled in the velvet landscape, bright spots of white against the darkness. I slouched in a chair in Papa's office. My brain ached. My hair spilled out of a hasty braid and I missed the magic that took care of it for me.

Scrolls cluttered Papa's desk, and mayhem abounded outside. Journalists from all Networks had gathered in the hallway to gather what information they could whenever someone walked out of Papa's office. They chattered like hens the moment the door opened, clucking their questions.

Delegation leaders, Council Members, Protectors, Masters, all clogged the hallways in an attempt to restore order to the pandemonium of the day.

Meanwhile, Papa, Marten, Baxter, and I took refuge in the High Priest's office. Marten sat on the chair next to me, a thoughtful expression on his face as he regarded the dancing flames in the fireplace. Fatigue tugged at his expression.

"Well," he said. "It's been quite a day."

Greyson hovered near the door as he spoke with Papa. Words like, "Discuss this at a later time," and "Aldred revokes the exile for the moment," popped up in intervals during their conversation. For now, I didn't fear Aldred or the Council.

That was a fear for another day.

Moments later, a thin door hidden in the back wall opened with a slight *thud.* Several stones against the far wall gave way, folding back into the pitch darkness of a secret passage. Scarlett slipped into the office from the back way to avoid the mayhem in the halls.

Neither Marten nor I glanced up as she entered and joined us near the fire. She settled next to me with a little rustle of her skirt. Despite the hot day ending outside and the cool breeze that trickled in from the windows, the low crackle of Marten's favorite heatless fire gave some comfort.

Scarlett's hands folded loosely in her lap, her back straight. She regarded me with an unreadable expression every so often. I ignored it for now—no doubt she'd have something to say about my conduct in the banquet hall later. And who could blame her? I'd taken a blatant and heavy risk. If Ava hadn't recognized Bram, Papa and I would be brooding over this mess in the Northern Network.

Besides, I hadn't had a chance to talk to her about the Sister-hood yet, so we'd have a very in-depth conversation later.

After Greyson left, Papa stood behind his desk, arms at his side. He rubbed a hand over his face and turned.

"What?" I asked, exasperated by the long way he glared at me without saying a word. He'd used it as a get-Bianca-to-talk tactic when I was five, and I'd hated it then, too.

"What?" he repeated, so clearly that the *t* crinkled like onion skin. "Were. You. Thinking?"

I straightened. Having anticipated this conversation all day, I was ready. "I was thinking that I had to do something at a time when you couldn't."

He opened his mouth to speak, then closed it again.

"I'm sorry," I continued. "It's the only plan that I could come up with at the spur of the moment. Was it probably stupid? Yes. But at least it was effective. We had to get Ava in front of all the delegation leaders just in case she spotted Bram, and the only way Aldred would let that happen was a steep bargain. I hedged my bets."

"The Network would have paid the price for such foolish-ness," Scarlett snapped. "Have you considered that?"

"Yes! But the Network would eventually have repaired itself, especially with you here. The Network has survived far worse things than an exiled High Priest, even if it would take a while to repair." I gestured to Papa and myself. "We would have paid the greatest burden. And would it have been worse than what you will face next, Papa?"

Papa's expression became grim, and fleeting shadows crossed his face. He relaxed until his whole body slumped, then he collapsed back into his chair and rested his head on his stacked hands.

"Not likely."

An uphill battle against the Council would follow in the weeks after this died down. Just because Aldred had given way, for now, didn't mean he'd finished his battle yet. Tonight, however, Papa had been saved. The Central Network could rally, and we'd form a plan to find the rest of the demigods, whatever that would take.

"I fear," Marten said, "that we don't fully appreciate the depth of our situation. We've never faced anything like this before—not in the thousands of years that separate witches and mortals."

Papa's voice was grim.

"I agree."

Marten stood and carried himself closer to Papa. He sounded distant. His voice, thick with age, was burdened.

"From what I hear, the Council fears you, Derek. You are too used to the Protector way of life. You take matters into your hands without receiving advice from them. You keep information they would rather have, and they don't like that."

Papa accepted that with little change in expression. Gears churned behind his eyes as the room absorbed it.

"Then we must approach the Council in a new way," Papa said. His lips thinned. "After we deal with these demigods."

Epilogue

Letum Wood seemed to wrap itself around me.

A week had passed since the discovery of Bram's betrayal of Alkarra and I had finally worked up the courage to step into my forest.

As I stood beneath the sprawling canopy, my heart gave a thrill and a lurch. The mossy, damp smell of forest lifted from the ground. My soul had missed the trees. Even if they no longer spoke to me, I felt comfort beneath their canopy. Warmth. The feeling of returning home.

Celebration business would wrap up this evening, and all delegations would transport home in the morning, after a final breakfast. The end of this nightmarish season had come to a close, and everyone was ready for it to finish.

A new normal awaited somewhere in the uncertainty of the future.

The Northern Network agreed to halt their period of isolationism for one more year, until the extent of the demigod invasion could be determined. Their work in reducing supply lines and enforcing borders would continue, however, as they prepared for their still-desired isolation.

Niko would shortly return to a tempestuous reunion with his own Council. His pre-emptive calling out of my father had percussive ramifications through their entire political structure. A weakening of relationships and ties would sift out over the next month or so. The Aldana family legacy wobbled on a precarious perch. In the midst of it, Niko Aldana would return home to an empty house.

Priscilla returned to Papa's apartment as I had demanded, and she now lived in my cottage with Ava. Baxter, Ava, and Bram had returned to Alaysia with the broken amulet and the stolen ring amulet. Little was reported of what occurred in Alaysia, but Baxter had returned, grim-faced, and asked if Ava could remain with us. "It's not safe for her there anymore, and she doesn't want to leave Alkarra."

I had quickly agreed.

Leda visited daily for their language lessons. Ava's ability to speak our language expanded every day under Priscilla and Leda's tutelage, and we learned more about her love for birds, water, and food. For now, Ava remained safe where other Networks dared not venture.

The Western Network would return to their desert home to await the unfolding of the demigod problem, with heightened patrols of West Guards along all their beaches—just in case. Lana seemed to tuck her ambitious nature back for now, but it always felt like she had a desirous eye on the Southern Network.

Finally, the Southern Network faced a bleaker prospect than before. Papa was the only leader who agreed to help protect their witches. Guardians would cross the border with Alina, who had taken over command. She would be blessed as the High Priestess by the next evening and start her reign in the most impossible of circumstances. They had no magic, no faith in their leadership, had been infiltrated by demigods, and had little outside support to get them through.

Somehow, I had a feeling Alina would figure it out.

These thoughts played through my mind as I stepped farther into the woods, my fingertips skimming along the tops of leaves. Ferns tickled my palm. A gentle sough of wind whispered through the treetops. It stirred my hair, a friendly presence. In the breeze, I thought of Baxter's father, Ventis. God of wind. My mind trailed to Hiddleston, who had changed jobs. He would work directly under Papa while they tried to sort this mess out.

Leda, having accepted a second and final offer as Head Assistant for Scarlett, would be around far more often. Hiddleston's quick response to our time of need had, I dared to say, softened Leda enough to tolerate his presence every now and then. She stopped rolling her eyes every time his name came up.

The crack of a twig from behind gave my thoughts pause.

Chatham Castle was still within sight behind me, but if a witch stumbled across me here, I'd have no ability to fight their magic. There were spells that could very simply snuff my life out, as Mabel had done to Mama. Plenty of witches wished for my demise as their revenge against Papa. Now, with full transparency before the delegation, everyone knew of my magicless state.

I tightened my grip on a borrowed sword hilt and spun. The metal raced out of the scabbard, hissing. Merrick stood back there, regarding me through carefully neutral eyes. My racing heart settled.

"Oh." I shoved the sword back. "It's you."

While I wanted to connect with my forest—had yearned for any sign of our previous relationship to manifest itself—having him there settled a quiet fear of Letum Wood. Without the trees as my protection, and without magic, I had no place here. It broke my heart.

"You came through yet again," he said with a little smile. "Despite impossible odds, Bianca Monroe prevails."

I laughed. "The accolades belong to Ava, and, very luckily, thanks to the help of many others, yourself included."

His amusement turned to soberness in the space of a breath. "So . . . your magic. We haven't really spoken about that, have we? Any sign of it returning?"

"No."

The word stuck in my throat and left a rock there. I had to swallow past it. All the fear and emotions surrounding my magic had been balled up for weeks. Only in the past few days had I started to think about it. To comprehend what this could possibly mean for the rest of my life.

To understand that it might never come back, and I couldn't change that.

"At least, I think it's gone," I continued because my thoughts had become too heavy, too fast. "We had hoped it was paralyzed but . . . I think it's not coming back."

"I'm so sorry."

Until I said the words, I hadn't acknowledged it with my lips. The old Bianca had been utterly safe with the old Merrick, so tears filled my eyes. As if years of separation and heartbreak hadn't occurred. It seemed so easy to forget that we were different witches. That time had passed and would again. With the Celebration winding down, came the gruesome reality that Merrick would return back to his life in the North.

I blinked my emotions back as I turned and swept my arms in an arc around me, indicating all of Letum Wood.

"I came to . . . to test it. I can't hear the trees anymore and haven't been able to. It's been about two weeks now."

His voice was low. "They were your best friends."

I bit back a sob.

"They were," I whispered.

The breeze ruffled my hair. I kept my body canted away from him while I gathered myself back together. Tears filled my eyes, blurring the verdant canopy I so deeply cared for. No doubt to save me, Merrick spoke next.

"I came to talk to you."

"Right." I sniffled the emotion back. Between the battle with Igor and now, Merrick and I had seen each other only a few moments in passing. A wave here, a nod there. But I'd still looked for him every day. I forced myself to face him, the tears banished for another time.

When I met his gaze again, he held his soul in his eyes.

"You leave in the morning, I assume?" I asked.

"Geralyn leaves in the morning."

"Geralyn?"

"With the delegation, but not with me."

His voice had a trailing aspect to it. My stomach flipped.

"I don't understand."

Merrick scraped at the top of an exposed root with the toe of his boot. "Geralyn asked me to be an Ambassador during the demigod crisis. She wants me here, at all times, to observe what's happening and receive reports from Baxter as he acts as a go-between for Alaysia and Alkarra."

"Oh. So you're the new Ambassador to the North?"

"Sort of."

My brain tried to wrap itself around what this would mean, but I struggled to keep up. The only thought that whirled through my head was *Merrick will live here. Merrick will live here.*

Merrick will live here.

"Your father has offered me a room at Chatham Castle, and I've accepted it. It's a shoddy little thing, but still better than I had as a Protector."

He smiled and I found myself returning it, still dazed.

"Well, that's . . . good news?"

The corner of his lip twitched. "Yes, it's something that makes me happy. I . . . I've been a bit lost for a while, so to speak. This assignment will be a refreshing change of pace. And I'm always happy to be back in the Central Network."

"I'm happy for you."

His gaze burned as he studied me, and I didn't let myself read into the fire. The heat. The *hope.* There were so many things that could be said, but most of them didn't seem wise. The ground between me and Merrick felt as stable as quicksand. One wrong step, and I'd be lost to him forever.

Again.

Unable to bear the quiet between us, I cleared my throat.

"I am on my way to visit with Scarlett after this," I said. "She and I are having our first official planning meeting."

"Oh?"

"For the Sisterhood."

His lips spread in the biggest grin I'd seen in three years. "Really?"

I couldn't help but smile back. "Really. We have to figure out how I can contribute to it if I don't have magic. It's unlikely I'll be a key member, but . . . we'll see."

Scarlett aside, of all the witches I could have told first, I had wanted it to be him. Papa still didn't know—and may not for some time. Not with everything he had to figure out. Now that Merrick knew, I couldn't wait to mention it to Marten.

He shifted his weight, his face a mask of concentration now. "What changed your mind between then and now?"

"A lot of little things. I guess I realized, when we talked in the Southern Network, that I had been holding myself back. I was scared. And after dealing with Ava and Bram, I . . . felt like I'd done exactly what I was meant to do."

His teeth flashed in quite a show of white. "Congratulations," he said. "I'm so happy for you. You know if you need any training help—"

"—I'll call on you."

A moment of shared levity passed between us. Merrick drew in a deep breath, hands held up. "Well, little troublemaker. You've saved the Network once again, and will in the near future, I have little doubt."

"Thank you for your help. Without you, I couldn't have done it."

"My pleasure."

He took a step back, and I wanted to ask him to stay. But I let him go because the implications of Merrick being back in our Network were too massive to comprehend. I needed some space and time to lay it out in my head.

"Merry part, for now, B."

I smiled.

"Merry part, Merrick."

He disappeared in a transportation spell, and I nearly called him back. Instead, I sealed my lips together, then turned around. The forest rolled ahead of me in a tangled mess of emerald. Vines swooped from the branches. Flowers bobbed gently from chains that wrapped around trunks like ivy.

And a stream burbled at my feet.

I frowned.

That stream hadn't been there before.

Water rippled near my toes with an odd, silver quality. It gathered in a puddle that stretched across the trail and wound into the forest, crystal clear all the way through. The wind had stopped its gentle dance, and the birds ceased twittering. The hair on the back of my neck stood up as the water crept toward me. Instead of pooling at my feet, it skirted me in a wide arc, then crawled along the trail.

I half-turned to find it moving toward Chatham Castle.

With a tilt of my head, I followed.

The water remained on the left side of the trail, slipping through the grass and undergrowth, a few paces ahead of me. When I glanced back, the stream sparkled in a winding ribbon. Unable to help myself, I withdrew my sword again, but I kept pace as it hurried ahead.

The growing stream swept along at a rapid pace, forcing me to jog to keep up. It led me back toward the gardens, but before it spilled onto the grass, it took a sharp right. Through the edge of the forest, it crawled along the littered remnants of summer leaves. Another minute or so passed before it paused.

I glanced up, startled to see the hedge that marked the boundary of one of Chatham Castle's quietest gardens. Several water fountains cluttered the inside, with an enchanted stream of water that circulated endlessly. Plants of every variety grew around the stream, draping the square space in exotic scents, wild colors, and mats of different types of ivy. Hedges formed the walls, at least as tall as two witches, then formed a gentle dome of fragile skeins over the top. Sunlight slipped between their leaves and tumbled to the ground.

The water crept under the hedge and moved inside.

Unable to follow that way, I dodged around the outside of the hedge, found a slim entrance, and scooted inside.

I skidded to a stop.

A short, squat woman stood there. She peered at me through thin eyes, upturned at the edges like Alina's. She had a distrustful expression. Her upper lip was curled, as if she found something distasteful. Her skin appeared wet. The water shimmered at her feet, around which a skirt that appeared to be made of seaweed gathered. Dark, curly hair hung around her shoulders in lines of ebony. An otherworldly aura surrounded her in a strange kind of bluish-green glow.

I stumbled back a step.

The hedge grew into place behind me, locking me in.

"Daughter of Deasylva," she hissed. "How long I have waited to meet you."

I said nothing, utterly at a loss. Water droplets on the ground at her feet climbed into the air until it touched her, then dropped back down and did it all over again. The stream that circled eternally in this garden had moved out of its path and now flooded the grass at her feet. Water clung to her ankles, sliding up and down her legs.

Something about this witch wasn't . . . right.

"I wish I could say the same," I finally managed to say.

She glared at me.

"Ungrateful wretches," she muttered. One thin eyebrow, sharp as a pencil line, rose. "None of you know a goddess when you see one?"

I suppressed a sharp intake of breath.

"No."

She snorted. "Truthful, at least. My time is short. Any moment now, Deasylva will sense me here. Then we'll all be in trouble. We're not supposed to trespass, you know."

I had enough presence of mind to remember that Deasylva was, allegedly, the goddess of the forest. This . . . *goddess* . . . could only belong to the sea if all the water was some indication. If this wasn't some extraordinary joke, that meant a goddess had revealed herself to me. A not-so-nice-appearing goddess. I wracked my mind to remember what Sanako had said about the goddess of the sea.

Parma?

Patty?

The name came to me in an instant.

Prana.

Hiddleston's conversation about being goddess-touched rippled through my mind. *Daughter of Deasylva* she'd called me. Which meant I probably had to be *very* careful.

"May I help you with something?" I asked.

"I will deign to let you call me Prana, goddess of the sea."

"Prana."

Her nostrils flared. "Spoken with some reverence would be preferred, thank you."

"I have only questions at this point."

She rolled her eyes. "You're wasting time. Let me put this simply: you and I both want the same thing."

"What's that?"

"The demigods and mortals *out* of Alkarra."

The thought of Ava and Baxter leaving Alkarra didn't sit well with me. The more Ava's language inched along, the more I started to understand that what she left behind hadn't been great. Baxter had shown inexplicable loyalty to me and Papa through all of this, and he'd been my friend for years now.

"I didn't say that."

She hissed, and I shivered when it reminded me of a sea serpent. I'd heard them a few times when I visited Sanako's family on the Western Network shore to buy new sandals. They writhed in the water and caterwauled at the full moon.

"Of course you want them out," Prana snapped.

"Why would you care?" I asked.

Her broad forehead pulled low, which nearly made her eyes disappear into her head. Her skin had a strange quality, so pale it could almost be translucent, with a hint of yellow to it like she rarely saw sunshine. Did the goddess of the sea live *in* the sea?

"My motivations are not your business," Prana said imperiously. "You, for some reason, have my sister's trust."

"Sister?"

"Deasylva." The look of utter loathing that followed the word gave me the distinct feeling that Prana wanted to drown me. "The goddess of the forest you seem to love so deeply? The last witch, the one called Sanna, held the same position of honor. She was the exact witch that destroyed my favorite magic." Darkness slipped through Prana's face, accompanied by a little shiver. "If she was able to do such a heinous act and survive, and you are similar to her, then you are potentially the only witch alive that's worth meeting."

Shock rendered me speechless again. Prana shuffled forward. The water came with her. A chill seemed to emanate from her as she closed the distance between us until she stood only a few paces away. Cool water swamped my toes. I ignored it by sheer willpower. I just wanted her to go away.

"What do you want from me?"

"Finally," she muttered, "a question worth answering. I want to make a deal where I give you your magic back."

My heart seized.

"What?"

She smiled, but it had no warmth in it. Flashes of eternal oceans and vast depths of water flashed through my mind. Cold came with it, as if she'd just submerged me into the heady darkness of her watery desert.

"Let's just say that I've run into an issue with the demigods being in Alkarra, and I want it taken care of. You have an issue of lost magic. I restore your magic, you get rid of the demigods. Agreed?"

Prana held out a piece of seaweed, cut to the size of half my hand. I eyed it, then looked at her. Memories of Mabel and her unknown deal flashed through my mind. She'd controlled my life—and the lives of those I loved—for far too long. Would I take such a risk again?

No.

Not even for magic.

"Tell me why," I said.

"No."

"Then no deal."

She grinned icily. "Nice try. I can *hear* your heart pounding. Can feel your desperate need to get the magic back. You can bargain all you want, but the terms of this deal are mine. Agree to get rid of the demigods and I will restore your magic."

"The same magic?"

"Goddess magic is the same regardless of the sister of origin." She gave me a bored look. "Maybe you should read up on your history more."

I licked my lips as my mind raced. There had to be an angle. At the moment, I couldn't see it. Until I could get my hands on some more information about goddesses, I wasn't likely to see it.

Also unlikely I'd get a second chance at this.

"No. I've made deals like this before. I'd rather not have magic than be at the whim of a goddess."

Prana snarled. "You're a fool!"

So are you, I thought, but kept my lips sealed. Prana studied me with the deepest loathing. I could feel her hatred all the way to my bones. My answer had been the steepest kind of bargain. If she so desperately needed me to solve her problem, she'd have to be more honest.

Or find someone else.

"Fortunately," she murmured with contempt, "I am in a mood to explain myself. Word of witches with lost magic in Alkarra may or may not have originated from something I said to the demigods in Alaysia." Her chin tilted back so she had to peer at me through almost-closed eyes. "If a war breaks out between demigods and witches, my sisters will hold me accountable. It is not a tribunal I wish to face."

"I see."

She snarled. "Let me assure you—you don't."

What could another goddess do to her? Whatever the answer, it sounded bleak. Still, I couldn't bring myself to feel compassion.

"If what you say is true, then you are the real reason I lost my magic," I said, arms folded across my chest. "Why should I help you prevent punishment for something you did? The rest of us are certainly suffering from it now."

"Because I will restore it and prevent worse from happening. We prevent the rise of the demigods, or war between gods and goddesses will follow. Don't you see that? All of you would die. The gods and my sisters will gladly destroy each other and simply start over with new mortals or new witches again. It has been done before."

My knees trembled at the thought, even though I couldn't comprehend what it honestly meant.

Total annihilation.

Scarlett and Marten's premonitions about our upcoming battles were certainly proving out.

"I will not guarantee anything."

Prana hissed again. "Then you must agree to banish the demigods from Alkarra in exchange for your magic. If the demigods are not banished again—and before a war between gods and goddesses—your ability to do magic dies within you for the last time. Unless you have another method for communicating with a goddess?"

Five seconds passed while I hesitated. Could I get in touch with Deasylva on my own? Unlikely. Hiddleston had reported that she was rarely inclined to bother directly with witches. But she had communicated with Sanna and Isadora.

"You will deny me?" she screeched.

Water splashed around her waist, flying in droplets that landed back in the puddle below her with a strange frenzy. Prana's eyes, unmistakably queer but I couldn't figure out why, pierced mine.

Prana slipped back. Rage bubbled under the surface, revealing the depths of her desperation. For her to agree to something so vastly different than what she wanted meant that her hope must be very bleak, indeed.

"Fool. Just like Sanna!"

I stuck out my hand.

"I will agree to *try* to stop the rise of the demigods in exchange for my magic, and that is all that I can do."

The building fury in her gaze calmed. She paused, studied me with continued disgust, and eased back. "I am also in the mood to accept your worthless sacrifice. We have a deal," she hissed. "I will be in touch."

The piece of seaweed she held crossed the distance and fell into my hand. It touched my palm. On instinct, I wrapped my fingers around it. A percussive explosion of light rippled through my body. Muscles. Bones. They filled with something slippery, cold, and writhing.

Darkness overcame me.

I awoke to a gentle song over my head, and the strange feeling of something bent over me. The song grew to a whisper, then an explosion of hundreds of voices. My eyes opened to see trees gathered over me and a whisper in my mind.

She always comes back.

The Lamplighter's Daughter

CHAPTER ONE

It takes no skill to be a lamplighter.

That's why Tama has been doing it for decades. His whole life, in fact. At forty-eight years old, he's lived to an age most mortals never see. Some call him *ancient*.

I call him cantankerous.

He moves from lamp post to lamp post with a fire stick that smells like sulfur and illuminates them every evening. The wind sighs off the ocean and stirs his salt-and-pepper hair while he shuffles through the watery, sandy roads. There aren't a lot of lamps in our collection of islands but they're all spread out. It takes him a few hours every day to row the dinghy from spot to spot, brightening the torches.

Christa and Shara, demigod sisters, rule our collection of islands. Shara, pays Tama in food. He returns home without saying a word because Tama has never loved to speak words. He just snuffles out the stick by shoving it in the sea, hands me some of the food, and goes to bed.

Tama never misses a night.

As a six-year-old girl, when I was afraid of the darkness and the water beneath our stilted home, I'd go with him. While he'd light the end of the lamp, I'd tilt my head back and think about magic. My fingers would curl into a fist as I imagined magical fireflies drifting out of my fingertips. They'd swirl to the lamp and fill it with a flare of bright orange light. Then it would settle into a calm flame.

They were just dreams.

Mortals can't do magic.

So, I'd hum to myself as we walked, because the music seemed to keep the darkness at bay.

"Stop," Tama would snap. "Or I'll feed you to the mermaids."

As if a mermaid would tolerate even that little of him. They have always sensed mortals better than most, and he'd scowl a mermaid back into the sea if they approached him. Of course, they wouldn't.

Not even Shara approaches Tama unless she has to. Only Daemon, a fishermen, endures Tama. He's a man as thick as the trees that drop rind-grains. He has a wide face and a hairy chin, but clean cheeks. He used to frighten me as a little girl, the way he could sling around his scaling knives with impressive dexterity. Sometimes he still scares me when I see the burning light in his eyes. The light that craves revenge and wants to see the blood of the demigods spilled in the water.

But why kill demigods?

The gods would simply have more of them.

Instead of talking to Tama when I accompanied him, I learned to keep my lips sealed. Once we returned to our home, I'd retreat to the bird sanctuary made of hedges and whisper to my beloved manulele birds in the hedges. They'd coo and flutter their tiny wings, then settle in for a long night of restless sleep. They had always been my only friends.

Tama even lights the islands in the farthest reaches of our collection, where no demigod is watching. Not Shara, not Christa. Even though no one of importance lives there, Tama insists on lighting them anyway. He gets into his dinghy, rows along the ropes that keep our floating islands connected, and illuminates the lamps. For a mortal man that eats so little, it's a great deal of effort. Yet, he does it anyway. Without the lamps, Tama has no true work. No purpose.

Nothing to keep his mind alive.

One night, when I asked why he did it, he scowled and kept going. Tama never answered my questions. He's irascible. Brooding. I avoid him as much as possible, except for when he sings.

Lu Cantaray, the other mortals in our collection call him. *The Singer.* He hums as he works, even though he doesn't like for me to make noise. Sometimes, he sings a bolstering melody on certain islands—the shallowest ones. The ones where mortals hide in the shadows and don't make a single splash because they don't want to be seen by the demigods. No mortal wants to be seen in Alaysia, except my Tama, apparently.

Tama's clothes are usually rumpled and plain, patched with mismatched fabric that Christa occasionally provides. Even with a demigod as my mother, we are so poor, we don't even have scrap fabric. Christa may have birthed me, but any association stops there. Because, technically speaking, I shouldn't be here.

Shouldn't be *alive.*

There are Testers in Alaysia again. "Testers haven't been around for decades," Tama once said. Before *he* was born. But the gods are saying that the goddesses are stirring again, and the Testers returned the year of my birth. Unrest amongst the demigods is leading to uncertainty in Alaysia. So, the gods sent the Testers back out.

Because magic *must* be controlled.

Testers are lesser demigods who, with heartless regard, perform a series of tests on infants the hour they arrive. If the Tester can sense magical tolerance in the newborn that just came from the womb, it is given to the demigods to keep under control. If no magical tolerance is readily apparent, the mortal child is given back to the parents.

The Testers are not only the most hated demigods amongst mortals, but also other demigods. They are considered too weak to merit their own amulet, so demigods hold them as a lesser class. Tester work is busywork, and the demigods that fulfill it are usually bitter and churlish.

Although most mortals understand that being a Tester is a job assigned them by their fathers, or by more powerful demigods, their very art is a betrayal. First, the gods and demigods rape many of our women, then they take our children. We do not welcome the Testers, especially the most heartless of them all.

Bram.

He's a stoic, quiet demigod. Young—he's only 75—but beyond the lifespan of any mortal we've heard of in our collection. Bram rarely speaks. I've seen him once, during the Festival of Markedius, the biggest celebration in all of Alaysia. He'd been cold and unfeeling.

Tama doesn't want us to associate with Bram, even though Christa is a demigod and she still lives on our tiny island. Sometimes, demigods come to our manulele sanctuary to visit Christa, so Tama and I know more of them than most mortals.

Still, Bram betrayed Christa, in a way. When I was born, Bram did the most unexpected thing of all.

He lied.

Bram studied me, lifted me by an ankle, listened to me scream, and poked at my ribs. He said I had no magic, that I was the least gifted baby he had ever seen, and he never returned. It had been a lie. Christa had already known that I had enough magic that I could tolerate god magic near me, because she could feel it in me herself.

Most mortal children born of a demigod parent and a mortal parent didn't get the ability to tolerate magic, but *some* did.

"You ruined all our lives that day," Tama said often, then dismissed me with a wave. "You're probably the reason the Testers returned. Now leave me alone."

The question haunted me all my life.

Why did Bram lie?

According to Tama, after Bram gave me back and disappeared with a puff of magic, Christa had turned pale, fallen into a minutes-long silence, then handed me back to Tama. She disappeared and didn't return for a year. When she came back, I was already walking, babbling, and Tama acted as if she'd never left. Christa created a place for her to live in our house, and we remained that way ten years later.

As a mortal, I don't carry magic with me, just the potential for it, no matter how *little* that might be. Mortals and demigods need amulets to do any magic. Even if I got my hands on an amulet, which is unlikely, I wouldn't know what to do with it. Nor do I want magic. Not in theory, because what good is borrowed magic?

No, I want my *own* power.

There are demigods who have so much magic it lingers around them, almost like a smell. The kind that makes your toes curl because the stench is so disgusting. Those demigods never hide their potency. Why would they? Magic is a gift.

A sign of superiority.

Because of that fateful day when Bram lied about my magical tolerance, we've lived on our collection, floating around Alaysia on an island that was more swamp than firm ground. I've cradled the feeling that would one day, everything would change.

Then it did.

When Bram came back.

* * *

Ready to dive into the world of Alaysia? Because I think you're going to love Ava.

Visit www.katiecrossbooks.com to buy your paperback copy today. My independent bookstore is the only place these stories are available to purchase.

Acknowledgments

First of all, we all need to thank Mike Thompson.

Sometime in 2020 (in the days of COVID), Mike sent me a Bianca fan fiction story that he had been writing. Seeing the characters on the page again got my brain spinning. The question of: *What if I went back to Bianca?* spun around my head for days.

No, weeks.

I couldn't get the idea out of my brain, even though I'd written the possibility off years ago. It plagued me until I finally gave into it.

Mike, this is all your fault!

So a huge thank you. :)

To the countless fans that have written in asking for more— also a big hug for you. Without your hope and emails, I may not have picked this back up when Mike inspired me. It's your desire to see more of your favorite characters that have made this so compelling and exciting.

Now, I can't imagine my life if I hadn't.

Second, thank you to my team at KC Writing. McKenna, Samantha, Kristen, Gemma, Mike, Darcee, Evan, Jenny, and everyone that helps me produce these books. What would I do without you? You all pick up the pieces while I'm busy clacking away at the keys, and you give me hope when I'm convinced the manuscript is an abject failure.

Kate, Kirsten, and Sarah: every week day. 9:00. You are my anchor. Thank you.

To my family, who endured me while I juggled a new

manuscript, running a business, selling a house, trying to buy another house, raising kids, silencing dogs, talking to mortgage lenders, dealing with storage units, and attempting to pull my life back together. I adore you all. Thank you for your love and support.

And finally: to all my fans. You are the reason I am here. May your escape be long and courageous.

MUAH.

About the Author

Katie Cross is ALL ABOUT writing epic magic and wild places. Creating new fantasy worlds is her jam.

When she's not hiking or chasing her two littles through the Montana mountains, you can find her curled up reading a book or arguing with her husband over the best kind of sushi.

Visit her at www.katiecrossbooks.com for free short stories, extra savings on all her books (and some you can't buy on the retailers), and so much more.

www.ingramcontent.com/pod-product-compliance
Lightning Source LLC
Chambersburg PA
CBHW031305210726
48287CB00005B/1421